She wished they could go back in time, back to those two kids who had fallen in love, and try again.

Tell her younger self to be wise and give Carter another chance. But it was too late now because she could never ask him to leave their tribe and she was too ashamed to stay.

giddy _____ and her skin flushed.

Focus. You're in real trouble and this man doesn't want a woman who walked away from her family.

Carter had loved her. But he loved his people and his place among them more. He was not leaving and she was not staying. There was no future for them. Only more pain.

"Thank you for saving us back there," she said.

"I didn't get us out. I'd have been cuffed to the handgrip in a smoldering wreck if not for you."

He'd been the reason they had a chance to get out of that SUV and they both knew it.

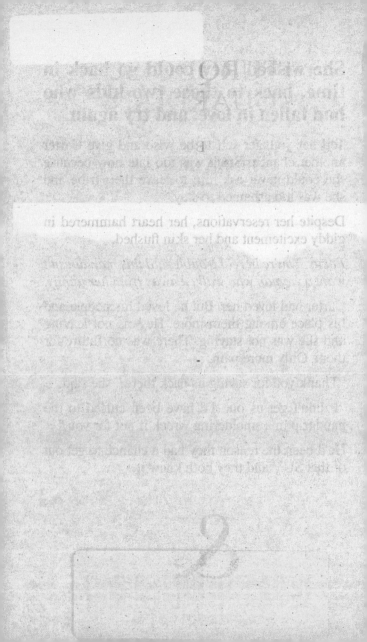

TURQUOISE GUARDIAN

BY
JENNA KERNAN

MILLS
BOON

First Published in Great Britain 2016
By Mills & Boon, an imprint of HarperCollins*Publishers*
1 London Bridge Street, London, SE1 9GF

© 2016 Jeannette H. Monaco

ISBN: 978-0-263-92852-5

46-0117

Our policy is to use papers that are natural, renewable and recyclable products and made from wood grown in sustainable forests. The logging and manufacturing processes conform to the legal environmental regulations of the country of origin.

Printed and bound in Spain
by CPI, Barcelona

Jenna Kernan has penned over two dozen novels and has received two RITA® Award nominations. Jenna is every bit as adventurous as her heroines. Her hobbies include recreational gold prospecting, scuba diving and gem hunting. Jenna grew up in the Catskills and currently lives in the Hudson Valley of New York State with her husband. Follow Jenna on Twitter, @jennakernan, on Facebook or at www.jennakernan.com.

For Ann Leslie Tuttle with many thanks for
sharing her expertise, invaluable critical eye
and friendship for more than a decade.

And for Jim, always.

Prologue

The idea of murdering seven innocent people should have sickened Ovidio Natal Sanchez. Instead he felt a grim anticipation. These people were responsible for causing that festering wound on the earth. He only wished he had been given free rein to kill as many as possible. But he was a loyal member of BEAR, and he would carry out his mission, with pleasure. He sat in a nondescript van before the loading dock of the Lilac Copper Mine, holding an automatic weapon with the safety switched off.

His driver's phone chimed, signaling a text.

"They're all in," he said.

"Give them twenty minutes to get to their desks," said Ovidio.

His driver cast him a look.

"I don't want to miss one who went for coffee."

His driver's sigh was audible, but he said no more, granting Ovidio a few more seconds to savor the moment.

His organization had supplied everything he needed: maps, head shots of each target, transportation and the automatic weapon he would use to kill every living soul in the procurement office of the Lilac Copper Mine. He didn't know why. He didn't care why. He just knew when and how.

Today. By his hand.

The twenty minutes ticked by.

A smile curled his lips. The next hole that went in the earth would be for their caskets.

"I'm signaling our man," said his driver and began texting.

The van was parked at the receiving bays.

Ovidio had worked protection for his boss for years. Even had to kill a few people. But nothing like this. He licked the salt from his upper lip.

In life, he believed, people mostly got what they deserved. Today was the exception. These people deserved worse. If it were up to him, he'd tie the owners of this monstrous mile-deep pit with their own blasting cord and toss them in with the next load of explosives. But his leader said they had bigger fish to fry. This time they'd make a statement that would not be buried on page six. One that the whole world would feel, and know that the earth mattered. That people couldn't keep assaulting the earth with impunity and that...

"You ready?" asked his driver.

The loading door was opening. He needed to focus.

"There he is," said his driver and looked expectantly at Ovidio. "Hurry up."

He wondered if his driver would really be here when he came out or would just leave him. But leaving him was dangerous. He might tell what he knew. He never would, of course. He believed too deeply in their cause. Still, they might kill him. Shoot him the instant he came out that door. He didn't care. At least his death would matter and they'd never forget him here in this miserable mining town.

Ovidio checked his weapon and slipped from the van. His body tingled as he mounted the five cement stairs that took him from the bright sunlight to the shadows of the loading bay, the sensation reminding him of sexual arousal. Oh, yeah. He was getting off on it because he knew he was on surveillance now. And what would they do with only their rent-a-cops and crappy wire fences for protection?

How long until they spotted him? In the hall? After the first shots?

His conspirator stood holding the door and, as he passed through, relayed a message.

"Ibsen called in sick."

"Address?"

The man passed him a sheet of paper. Now Ovidio had to get out of here alive to get Ibsen.

Somehow Ovidio thought after he told his commander at BEAR about the discovery made by the new purchasing clerk, Ibsen would know what was coming. Unfortunately it was too late to abort. Besides there was no way of knowing who in the office the clerk had spoken to about her discovery.

Ovidio stalked into the corridor. Today he would write his convictions in blood.

Ovidio continued toward his goal, inhaling the scent of machine oil coming from the automatic rifle heavy in his hands. He thought of the memorials and the anniversaries of the legacy he was about to leave behind. But this wasn't his legacy. The removal of men who violated the earth—that was his legacy.

Chapter One

"I'll be back soon." Amber Kitcheyan stowed the last of the receiving slips she needed signed by her boss in her satchel as she spoke to their receptionist. Then she headed out from the receiving department in the Lilac Copper Mine's administration building where she was a receiving clerk.

Their squat building sat at ground level perched over the thousand-foot cavity, which was the active open-pit copper mine. Below them, a constant stream of enormous mining dump trucks wove up the precarious roads, hauling ore to the stamp mills in Cherub. The pit covered two-hundred acres and the tailing piles covered even more ground. To Amber, it looked like a crater left by some absent meteor.

Amber always left by the loading dock as it was closer to the parking area. She stopped in the restroom for just a moment. Too much coffee, she thought as she left the stall. She glanced at her reflection in the mirror as she washed her hands, checking that her long black hair was all tucked neatly up in a tight coil. She wore nothing in particular that marked her Apache lineage because her face structure and skin tone did that adequately. The human resources had been happy to tick the box indicating they had hired a minority. She didn't care. A job was a job and this one paid better than the last.

But she missed her tribe and her sisters. And wished… no, she wasn't going there. Not today.

Amber tugged at the ill-fitting blazer she'd purchased used with the white blouse she wore twice a week. She slung the stylish satchel on her shoulder and headed out into the hall.

On the loading dock she paused to slip her sunglasses out of her bag and swept a hand over her hair. February in Lilac was a good twenty degrees warmer than the Turquoise Canyon Apache Indian Reservation where she had grown up. She longed for a cool breeze off the river but now wasn't the time to be feeling homesick. She stopped to find her keys. Amber didn't like to bother her boss, Mr. Ibsen, at home, especially when he was sick. But as a clerk she couldn't sign for a delivery this big. So she'd just slip out there, get his signature on the receiving slips and be back before the truck was unloaded.

She had called from the office and got his voice mail and followed up with an email. It worried her that he had not replied to either and that, on the day after she mentioned the problem she'd spotted on the receipts to her boss, he was absent. And he knew they expected another delivery truck today.

She could have them signed by Joseph Minden in finance, but the one time her boss had been absent for a delivery, she'd done just that and her boss had lost it. She'd never seen veins stick out of a man's neck like that before.

Minden was their CPO, Chief Procurement Officer, and Mr. Ibsen's supervisor. Later in the day, Mr. Ibsen had explained to her about chain of command and threatened to fire her if she did something like that again.

Then yesterday he had also shouted at her to get back to work. Amber was on shaky ground here, and she needed this job, what with the seemingly endless debt she was trying to pay down.

She couldn't afford to screw this up.

She'd only been here a month and was still getting used

to the copper mine's policies. But she would not make that mistake twice because she needed this job for at least the next six months. Then the loan would be finished, and she could go home, if she wanted. The pit of her stomach knotted at the thought as mixed emotions flooded in.

"Not now," she whispered to herself and strode across the loading dock. The Arizona sky glowed a crystal blue, and the sun warmed the concrete pad beneath her feet. The temperature would rise rapidly, she knew, and then drop with the sun.

She glanced at the deep navy van illegally parked before the receiving bay, then back at the sign that indicated parking there was prohibited. The driver had shaggy blond hair poking out from beneath his ball cap like straw. She cast him a disapproving look, and he leaned forward over the wheel to glare right back.

Amber descended the steps in a rapid gait, making a beeline for her vehicle, which was small, ugly, used and paid for. She didn't do leases. She paid cash or did without.

As she drove out of the lot, Amber glanced back at the van still illegally parked, and then turned onto the road that would lead her through the high chain-link fencing and off the copper mine's property.

CARTER BEAR DEN'S first sign of trouble at the mine came in the form of a yelp from the security guard seated at the lobby reception desk. The guard's eyes were glued to the monitor on his desk, showing a series of images from various security cameras. Carter leaned in to see what had made the man blanch.

Carter had a message to deliver. He didn't like it, but he was duty bound to see that Amber Kitcheyan received the letter. It had been given to him by Kenshaw Little Falcon, the head of the Turquoise Guardians, his medicine society and a tribal shaman.

Now, standing beside the security desk and the uniformed boy they had hired to check in visitors, Carter looked at the monitor that showed a masked gunman making steady progress along an empty corridor, and he stopped thinking and wondering. This time he saw the face of danger before it was too late.

Amber was in this building.

The security officer stood now, one hand on his pistol grip and the other reaching for the phone seeming uncertain as to which to use.

Carter had no such trouble. As a former US Marine with three tours of duty, he knew what he needed to do. Protect Amber.

The digital feed displayed a view of an office where the masked gunman proceeded past a fallen woman toward the cubbies tucked directly behind the receptionist's station.

"Where is that?"

"Purchasing," rasped the guard.

From the security guard's radio came a call to lock down. On the other monitors people scurried about, fleeing the halls for the closest cover.

Carter retrieved his Tribal ID from the high counter and tucked it in his open wallet as the shooting started, the burring sound of an automatic rifle blast unmistakable and close.

For just an instant, Carter was back there in Iraq with his brother and Ray and Dylan and Hatch. The next instant he was drenched with sweat and running.

Suddenly delivering his message came second to keeping Amber alive. Had Little Falcon known what was about to transpire?

The stabbing fear over Amber's safety took him by surprise. He'd been so sure he was over her. So why was he running into gunfire?

Although he now moved forward with the stealth of his

ancestry bolstered by the training of the US Marines, the stillness in the corridor was unnerving. It had the eerie quiet of a deadly game of hide-and-seek. Everyone was hiding except for him and the killer.

From down the corridor he heard a bang, like the sound of a heavy door slamming shut. He ran toward the sound, the light tread of his cowboy boots a whisper on the carpeted hallway.

He saw the blood trail as soon as he rounded the corner. It led from an office that read *Purchasing* upon the door. The gunman's boot prints were there in blood leaving the scene, dark stains on the industrial carpeting.

Amber's office, he realized. For an instant he was too terrified of what he might find to go inside. Was it the same as Iraq? Was it already too late?

He held his breath and stepped across the threshold. The calm sending his flesh crawling. He moved from one body to the next, checking for signs of life and the face that still visited his dreams.

Everyone in the outer office was dead. He moved to the two private offices. The man in the first was gone, shot cleanly through the forehead. In the next office he was greeted by the sight of dark legs, sprawled at an unnatural angle. One moved.

Carter was at her side in an instant, sweeping away the dark hair that covered her face. She was breathing, but she was not Amber. Her eyes fluttered open and flashed to his.

"Rest. Help is coming," he said, feeling his gut twist in sympathy.

He could tell by her sadness and the tears in her eyes that she saw death coming.

"Amber?" he whispered.

"She left. When the shooter spotted her empty cubicle, he said he would find her."

His heart gave a leap and hammered now, hitting his ribs so hard and fast it hurt.

"Where is she?"

"Left. Harvey Ibsen's home. Paperwork. Oh, it hurts. My kids. Tell them I'm sorry. That I love them." Her eyes fluttered shut.

Someone entered the office.

"Security!"

"In here," Carter called.

A moment later a man in a gray uniform shirt and black pants appeared in the doorway. His gun drawn.

Carter lifted his hands. "Unarmed."

The man aimed his weapon. Carter didn't have time to get shot.

"EMTs on the way?" he asked.

The man nodded, his face ashen.

"Come put pressure on this."

He did, tucking away his weapon and kneeling beside Carter before placing a large hand on the folded fabric over the woman's abdomen.

"You know a guy called Harvey Ibsen?" Carter asked.

"Yeah. He works here."

"Where does he live?"

"I don't know. In town, I guess. Who are you?"

"Friend of Amber Kitcheyan." Friend? Once he had planned to make her his wife.

"Yeah?"

Carter was already on his feet. He pointed at the woman. "She wants her kids to know she's sorry to leave them and that she loves them."

The security officer blanched. Carter stepped away.

"Hey, you can't leave."

Carter ignored him. If the shooter was after Amber, he had to go. Now.

"She also said that the shooter was looking for Amber. Send police to Ibsen's home. I think he's heading there."

The man's eyes widened and he lifted his radio.

"Call Amber's cell. Warn her," said Carter.

"She doesn't own a mobile. Or at least that's what she told me." The security officer's eyes slid away.

Carter groaned. Of course she didn't. That would have made the necessity of him delivering this message superfluous. He headed out, following the ghastly bloody footprints. His phone supplied an address for a Harvey Ibsen, and his maps program gave him the route.

Ibsen didn't live in Lilac. According to Carter's search engine, he lived in Epitaph, the tourist town fifteen miles north of here. The name, once a joke for the number of murders committed during the mining town's heyday, now seemed a grim omen.

Carter swung up behind the wheel of his F-150 pickup. Amber's boss was out the very day this happened. A coincidence that was just too perfect in timing. Luck. Fate. Or something else?

He didn't know, but he had a sour taste in his mouth.

Chapter Two

Carter headed out, turning away from the town of Lilac, named not for the color of the rock, but the name of the man who decided to crush the poor-quality copper ore in a stamp mill and make the low-grade ore profitable.

En route to Epitaph, he phoned his twin brother, Jack, a detective with the tribal police back home on Turquoise Canyon Reservation, and filled him in.

"We have no jurisdiction outside of the tribe," said Jack. "You're practically in Mexico."

Actually he was thirty miles from there and heading north.

"See what you can find out. Tell them that Amber is a member of our tribe."

"She left the tribe, Carter."

"They don't know that." Carter reined himself in. He wouldn't lose his temper or shout at his brother.

There was a pause.

"Ibsen lives in a small housing development in Epitaph. You need the address?"

"Got it."

"Okay. I'll call border patrol. They might have a check-point set up along that stretch. What is the shooter driving?"

"Don't know."

"Do you want me to call the others?"

He meant the members of Tribal Thunder, the warriors of the Turquoise Guardian medicine society. The ones charged with protecting their ancestral land and people from all enemies.

"Call Little Falcon."

"I'll call Tommy, as well. He's down there somewhere. Maybe he can help," said Jack.

Tommy was their brother. At twenty-six he had scored a spot on the elite all–Native American trackers under Immigration and Customs Enforcement, known as the Shadow Wolves, and had been down there on and off for two years. Carter supposed not all the Bear Dens could be Hot Shots. A Hot Shot was a member of an elite team of firefighters flown into battle forest fires, and the Turquoise Canyon Hot Shot team was one of the most respected and sought after in the nation, a reputation they had earned with hard, dangerous work. He and the other members of his former US Marine outfit all missed the buzz of adrenaline, and so had joined the most dangerous job they could find as a substitute.

"Great. Gotta go."

"Be careful," said Jack.

Carter hung up and slipped the phone into his front pocket. Amber still didn't have a cellular phone. She hadn't owned one the last time he'd seen her either.

"Please, don't let that be the last time," he whispered and pressed the accelerator.

AMBER HUMMED A tune about being happy as she rolled along. The fifteen mile drive out to Harvey Ibsen's was uneventful, and the scenery was lovely, so different than Turquoise Canyon. The roads were well maintained and flat as Kansas. She whizzed past dry yellow grass dotted with silver-green yucca and woolly cholla cacti with spines that looked like fur.

There were no cacti up on Turquoise Canyon. Here the planes stretched out wide-open to the snowcapped Huachuca Mountains to her right and the rockier Dragoon Mountains to her left where Apache warrior, Cochise, once kept a stronghold. The mountain ranges here did not look like those near Black Mountain, but at least the Huachucas got snow.

She missed home, still, after all this time. The Turquoise Canyon Apache Indian Reservation gleaned its name from the exposed vein of blue stone on Turquoise Ridge. Her tribe was a conglomeration of many Tonto Apache people, the losers in the wars against the Anglos, relocated twice until finally reclaiming a small portion of their lands. And the Turquoise Canyon Apache tribe had timber, turquoise and decorative red sandstone. They also had the best Hot Shots in the world. She supposed the warrior spirit lived on in the men of her tribe who now flew all over the West to battle forest fires.

Carter was a Hot Shot. Her smile faded, and her heart ached at the thought of the man she'd once loved.

She caught movement behind her and saw a dark vehicle closing fast. She held her steady pace and frowned as she recognized the van a moment before it swerved to the opposite lane and zoomed past her. It was the same illegally parked van at the loading dock, or so she thought. Her brow wrinkled as the vehicle vanished in the distance. How fast had that van been going to make her look like she was driving backward?

Amber continued on but now with a sense of disquiet that niggled at her. She signaled her turn, though there was no one behind her.

She checked the numbers on the houses she passed. She had been here once on a similar mission, but the houses were very alike; her boss's home had solar panels, so she studied the roofs as she passed. When she arrived at number nineteen, she slowed before the house. Harvey's hybrid vehicle was parked in the drive. That's when she saw the familiar blue van was already on the corner. She slipped the car into Park, instead of electing to turn into Harvey's ample drive. Something felt wrong, and she leaned forward to stare out the passenger window. Something about that van gave her the creeps.

Amber had to be back soon because the shipment was being unloaded as she sat there dithering. As she turned off the engine, she resisted the urge to start the engine back up again. The last of the air-conditioning dissipated, forcing a decision. She was being ridiculous.

She grabbed her satchel and then the car's door handle, stepping out into the street. She took a moment to tug down her cream-colored jacket and smooth her dark slacks. Then she closed the door.

She'd just made it up the drive when she heard a male voice speaking from inside the house. The tone was so strained that she did not at first recognize it, but then the strangled timbre became familiar, a version of Harvey Ibsen's speech that she recognized but had never before heard.

"I told you everything. I reported it, for God's sake. I told you we had a problem."

There was a pause and then Ibsen again, whimpering, begging now.

"Oh, but I'm one of you. I'm the one who—"

The sound of a gunshot brought Amber up straight. Her eyes widened, her jaw clamped, and her grip on the shoulder strap of her satchel tightened. Her mind struggled to catch up with her body as her heart rate leaped and a sheen of sweat covered her skin.

The second shot set her in motion. She spun and ran back to the curb. She dropped her satchel in the street beside her car as she crouched.

Her breath now came so fast she choked on the dry air. Heat from the pavement radiated up through the soles of her shoes, and her image reflected off the metal of her door panel before her. She could see herself in the white paint—all wide eyes and cowering form.

She glanced toward the van, perpendicular to her hiding place, and inched back out of sight, dragging her leather bag along the road as she moved away from the house. She ended up behind her rear bumper as she heard the sound of footfalls crunching on the ornamental stone. She peeked up over the trunk.

He held a long black rifle in his hand, and his head was turned toward her car, the one that he likely knew had not been there when he entered Ibsen's home. He looked directly at her and she at him. They made eye contact for one endless second and then another. His step faltered as he changed direction, raising the rifle stock to his shoulder as he headed for her at a quick march.

Chapter Three

Carter took the turn too fast, the wheels of his truck screeching in protest. This was the street. Where was Amber? And then he saw her. The car. The shooter. All at once.

Amber cowered beside the rear bumper of a rust bucket of a car that looked as substantial as an aluminum can. The dark blue van parked on the adjoining cross street looked right as a getaway vehicle. Before the house stood a single male, forties to fifties, dressed in jeans and an olive green windbreaker, an assault rifle lifted to his shoulder. His jaw was large and dark with stubble. Carter saw brown hair, a broad nose, a down-turned mouth and square forehead. Was this the man who had killed all those people at the copper mine? The gunman swung the rifle in Carter's direction as Carter's truck screeched to a halt beside Amber. He had expected her to open the door, but she didn't. Didn't wait for him to shout directions either.

Instead, Amber vaulted into the bed of his pickup and rolled as Carter accelerated. The spray of bullets peppered his tailgate as he turned away from the van. Behind him, the gunman stood in the road for a moment, then lowered his rifle and ran toward the van.

It wasn't over. He felt it in the pit of his stomach.

Amber pounded on the small sliding glass window that separated the cab from the truck bed. He swiped the window open and glanced back at her. She stared at him with wide eyes.

"You," she said.

He cast her a half smile and returned his focus to the road which was complicated by the distraction of Amber slithering through the narrow opening with the undulating ability of a belly dancer.

"You hurt?" he asked.

"No." Amber looked over her shoulder out the back. "He killed him."

"Ibsen?"

"Yes. I think so. I heard my boss…I heard shots. Maybe we should go back."

"No. Call 911."

"No phone."

"I'm buying you a phone."

"No, you are not."

He didn't have time to argue with her now. So he drew out his phone and passed it to her. She called the emergency number and gave them the address and situation. Her voice hardly wavered at all, but she kept her opposite hand pressed to her forehead as she spoke.

When she finished, she relaxed her hand, and his phone dropped limply into her lap. Suddenly she stiffened.

"My satchel!" She half turned in her seat. "I left it in the road."

"Forget it."

She pivoted back to place. "The packing slips. I'm responsible. They're gone," she said.

She settled in the seat beside him, her brow furrowed.

"Did you get a look at the one with the rifle?" asked Carter.

"What? Oh, yes. A good one."

"Driver?"

"Yeah."

"Think about them. Every detail."

"Are they coming?" Amber glanced back through the rear window at the road behind them.

"Not sure."

She gripped his forearm with both hands tight. The scar tissue tugged, and he winced. Who would have thought such a small woman would be so strong?

He scanned her worried face, taking in the changes, looking past the Anglo clothing and prim bun to the loose tendril of black silk caressing her jaw and falling away before her pointed chin. Her cheeks held a flush, and her dark eyes glimmered from beneath thick lashes, her eyes so black he could not see the pupils of her eyes. Her mouth, oh that mouth, pink and alluring with the small crescent scar cutting through the upper lip. That threadlike blemish had appeared while he was away on his first tour.

He turned back to the road. Beautiful, he decided, still and always the most beautiful woman in the world.

"How did you know where I was?" she asked.

"I was at the mine."

"But why are you here?"

There was no time for that now.

"There's been a shooting at the copper mine," he said. He made another turn.

"What?"

He debated only an instant and then told her everything.

"Everyone in my office?" she whispered. "Are you sure?"

"Looked like it."

Amber covered her face and wept. The urge to shield her from the pain surged inside him. But driving at top speeds he could not even loop an arm around her shoulders as she cried.

Suddenly, she lifted her head and stared at him with deep dark eyes glimmering with pain. Her pointed chin trembled, and her tempting pink lips were parted in surprise. He felt a familiar tug at his heart. They'd been so good together.

He forced his gaze away.

"That's why you wanted me to remember what I saw," she said. "You think it's the same man."

"I do."

He wondered if, instead of asking her to remember, he should tell her to forget. But it was too late. They'd seen the shooter. She'd seen the driver. They were involved.

She righted herself in the seat and closed her eyes. Then she lifted his phone, and dictated every detail she could remember into a text. The sound of her voice still stirred him.

When she finished sending the text she returned his phone.

"Who did you text that to?"

"Your brother Jack."

His phone chimed as Jack sent back a question mark.

"That way, he has it, in case anything happens…"

"Nothing is going to happen. I got you."

She stared with a solemn expression that made her seem world-weary. He summoned a quick smile he hoped looked reassuring.

"Why are you in Lilac, Carter? Why today?"

He had that creepy sensation again. The one he felt when he learned that her boss was out today of all days. "I have a letter for you from Kenshaw Little Falcon."

"What?"

She shook her head, not understanding. "My uncle? Why would he send you?"

"He heads my medicine society now."

Did she ask why he had been chosen or why the message needed to be hand delivered?

"It's not from my father," she said, the statement really a question. He knew from her mother, Natalie Kitcheyan, that Amber had been back to visit, but she timed her appearances carefully so as not to encounter her dad, Manny Kitcheyan. She also never visited Carter again. After that last time, he couldn't blame her. But the truth that she'd moved on tugged at his heart.

Carter's phone rang. He fished it from his front pocket and passed it to her again.

"It's Jack," she said.

"Put him on speaker."

She did.

"Carter? Where are you?"

"I got her. But the guy was there at her boss's house. He's there, Jack, or he was. Two men. Dark blue Chevy van. Unmarked. Arizona plates."

"I'll call Arizona Highway Patrol. You safe?"

"For now. We're heading north."

"You guys clear?"

"Not sure. Any chance you can send Kurt down here for us?"

Carter was referring to their youngest brother, who was one of the pilots for the air ambulance transport team out of Darabee. In other words, Kurt might be able to get his hands on a helicopter.

"Either of you injured?"

He glanced at Amber, who was ashy and bleeding from the knees.

"If you need us to be, then, yes," said Carter.

"There's a hospital in Benson. Head there."

"En route," Carter said.

She disconnected and dropped the phone in his front breast pocket. She leaned in, wrapping her arms about his neck.

"You saved my life."

She stared at him in a look that made his stomach tug. Those big, beautiful eyes open and grateful to him. How he'd missed her. Nine years since she'd broken it off. Seven since he'd laid eyes on Amber, but his heart remembered. He knew because it banged against his rib cage. He was thirsty for her, as thirsty as the desert longing for the yearly floods. He forced his gaze back to the road. He couldn't do this again. The longing receded, replaced by the betrayal. Why did she leave her people?

Why did she leave him?

They could have worked it out. He'd been so stupid, and she'd been so stubborn. Blown to hell like that Humvee back in the Sandbox. No way to put back the pieces.

He glanced at her. Was there?

He looked in the rearview, spotted the van and stiffened. Amber followed the direction of his gaze, turning to stare through the rear window as Carter uttered a curse.

"It's them!" she cried.

Carter accelerated toward the highway. His truck was tough, eight cylinders, but the van was gaining on them. That didn't make any sense.

Amber spun in the seat, kneeling to look out the back.

"He's got that rifle out the window."

Carter pressed her head down. Then he brushed her off the seat so that she sprawled into the wheel well.

"Hold on." His truck might not be as fast as whatever engine they had in that van, but it had higher clearance and tires especially made for riding over rock and through soft sand. Carter braked and swerved from the highway into the shoulder and then veered off toward the cover of the trees that lined the San Pedro River. He braced as more bullets punctured a line of holes across his truck's rear gate. The rooster tail of dust and sand obscured the view of the van and hopefully them as a target from the shooter.

He needed both hands on the wheel to hold his course as they bumped across uneven ground and plowed through cacti; as the tall dry grass lashed against his bumper, sounding like heavy rain. He kept going, making for the river that he knew was dry in certain stretches for much of the year. Amber sat on the floorboards with one hand thrown across the seat and one on the glove box as she braced herself for the jolting ride through the thick chaparral to the flat stretch of the thirsty San Pedro. He had to get her out of here.

"Are they following us?" she called to be heard against the thudding of brush against the fender.

"Can't see," he said and lowered his chin as bursts of another desperate flight flashed through his mind like a thunderstorm.

Chapter Four

Carter made it to Benson and found the hospital. Jack had called in some chips, and Carter found Kurt waiting beside the air ambulance to transport him, Amber and a cooler full of blood to Darabee.

"Lucky you, there was a wreck on Route 88, and Darabee needs blood."

"Fatalities?"

"Not if we hurry. Hop in."

Kurt began his check as Carter helped Amber up and onto the gurney where the single paramedic waited. Carter wouldn't feel safe until the chopper was airborne. He hadn't felt this afraid since Iraq. But this time it wasn't his own survival he contemplated, but Amber's.

She lay on the cot beside the paramedic who had already cleaned up the abrasions on her knees and palms. She was wrapped in a blanket and still shivering. Carter scowled and adjusted the headset that allowed him to fill Kurt in on the details.

When they touched down, both the sheriff and his twin brother, Tribal Detective Jack Bear Den, were waiting. Behind them stood a member of Carter's tribal council, Wallace Tinnin, the chief of tribal police, and Jefferson Rowe, the police chief from Darabee. Rowe was an Anglo, with dark curly hair that was receding and was clipped short at the sides. The deep parallel lines that flanked his mouth and the broad hooked nose did not quite balance his eyes, that were too widely set. Carter glanced to the parking lot beside the landing pad. He'd never seen so many police cars all in one place. Though he imagined the Lilac Copper Mine looked much the same about now.

"We have a welcoming party."

"Looks like a welcoming party from Grey Wolf," said Carter, referring to General George Crook by the name his people used. Crook had defeated the Tonto Apache with the help of Apache scouts, who were from a different tribe, back in 1883.

The slowing rotor blades kept back the welcoming committee temporarily, but Carter knew they needed to get onto sovereign land if he was to protect Amber.

The sheriff approached first. His brother was at the man's heels.

The sheriff shouted louder than necessary to be heard over the helicopter.

"Mr. Bear Den, I'm Sheriff Bill Taylor. I need you and Ms. Kitcheyan to come with us."

"Why?"

"She is a person of interest in an open investigation in Lilac," said the sheriff.

"Is she being charged with a crime?"

The sheriff shook his head, his hand going to his fleshy neck and then up to the bristle of hair that was all that remained after someone had taken clippers to his head.

"No. A witness."

"She's a member of our tribe and as such will be returning to Turquoise Canyon."

It was a lie. She wasn't a tribe member anymore and had no rights to protection from their people. But none of his tribe members corrected him. In fact, Jack had already opened the door to his tribal police unit and retrieved

Amber, who was now flanked by tribal police officers and tribal officials.

Chief Rowe and his men watched as the sheriff took a step to move past Carter, but he shifted to intercept.

"I'll go with you," he said.

"I was told Ms. Kitcheyan was in need of medical attention."

"Delivered en route," said Carter.

Amber was now in the backseat of Jack's police car. Possession was now theirs. Carter placed two fingers above his brow and gave the sheriff a mock salute.

Then he trotted to his brother's unmarked car and slipped into the passenger seat, dragging the door shut with a satisfying snap.

"I hope Kurt isn't fired over this," said Jack.

"Me, too."

Police Chief Rowe stood beside Sheriff Taylor, who watched them with hands on hips as their chief of police, Wallace Tinnin, and tribal council member, Zach Gill, ran interference.

"They get the two in the van?" asked Carter, hoping like hell they caught the man responsible.

"Disappeared," said Jack Bear Den to Carter as he pulled out. "Arizona State Police and local law enforcement are still searching."

Carter glanced back at Amber, whose color had improved, but her blank expression and vacant stare worried him.

"She's going to have to talk to them," said Jack.

"They had video surveillance all over that building. They don't need her."

"Only witness, they said."

"I saw him, too," said Carter.

Jack lifted his brows. "But you I can protect."

"You can protect us both."

He gave a slow apologetic shake of his head. "It's just a matter of time, you know. They'll figure out that she's not one of us, and when they do, I can't stop them from taking her."

Carter's gut churned like a washing machine on agitate. Why had she done that—abandon her people and her poor parents? It was so stupid, pointless. He didn't understand, didn't think he could ever understand her actions. She had thrown them all away like a spoiled child.

"FBI is en route with requests to interview Amber." Jack glanced back at his passenger.

"No," said Carter.

"Carter, they're the Feds. I might be able to hold them off for twenty-four hours, but eventually they're coming to speak with her." Jack had correctly guessed that his brother did not want to speak to the FBI.

Carter glanced in the rearview at Amber. "You okay back there?"

She nodded, her eyes still unfocused. The one-thou-sand-yard stare, the marines called it. Shell shock, PTSD and usually a domain reserved to soldiers. She hadn't signed up for this.

"I'm taking you to the station. I can arrange to have one of my guys there when the FBI interviews you."

"Just get us home."

He drove them to the station and into the squad room where all nine of the officers from their tribe had desks. The chief's office was in the corner with windows look-ing out at the room. Jack's desk sat by the window with a view of the parking area and the road beyond.

Jack motioned to the chair beside his desk, the one re-served for witnesses and suspects. Which was Amber? Carter wondered.

"I need to use the bathroom," she said.

Jack gave her directions, and the brothers watched her exit to the hallway. Carter's brother gave him a once-over.

"You all right?" asked Jack.

Carter shook his head. "I used to think so."

His brother had served with him in Iraq. But after one tour, Jack had left the service. Now a detective, Jack was also a member of the Turquoise Guardians medicine society. Recently, Jack and Carter had also been inducted into Tribal Thunder. Their elite warrior band defending their people and their sacred land. Today Carter glimpsed the seriousness of their duty. How had Little Falcon known?

"Did you deliver the message?" asked Jack.

Carter patted his pocket. "Not yet."

"What do you think it is?" asked Jack.

"A warning, maybe." Carter met his brother's troubled gaze with one of his own. They didn't have to speak. Carter knew what Jack was thinking. He was also wondering if Kenshaw Little Falcon had prior knowledge of the mass shooting. The implications were staggering.

Jack pressed his mouth tight, clearly disagreeing. They were twins but did not resemble each other. Carter had features he thought were classic for the Tonto Apache people while Jack was built like a brick house. Carter wore his hair long and loose, but Jack clipped his dark brown hair short to avoid others seeing the natural curl, and had eyes that were closer to gray than brown. The differences didn't end there; he was three inches taller and had thick eyebrows that peaked in a way that made Jack look dangerous even when he was just hanging out. There had been questions when they were growing up. They didn't look like twins. They didn't even look like brothers, and Jack didn't look full-blood Apache. His skin was too light and his features too Anglo.

"The FBI has agents en route," said Jack.

"Don't let them take her, Jack," said Carter. If she left

their land, Carter couldn't protect her. He knew it and Jack knew it.

Jack's scowl made him look even more intimidating than usual.

"Anything on Ibsen?" asked Carter.

"Head shot. Dead. My buddy on highway patrol says it looks like the same shooter as at the mine. Can't believe they missed the shooter twice. They've got helicopters, dogs, state and local cops, all searching and border patrol stopping everything heading south."

"Think they made it before the roadblocks?" asked Carter.

"Impossible."

"How do you think they got away?"

"Changed vehicles, split up. Likely they are within ten miles of where you saw them. They're doing a house-to-house in Ibsen's neighborhood."

"That will take some time," said Carter.

"I'm going to stick with Amber for a while," he said, and Jack's eyes narrowed, clearly not liking that plan.

"We should turn her over to the Feds."

Now Carter was scowling because that was not going to happen.

"It's my duty to protect her," said Carter.

He referred to his duty as a Turquoise Guardian, to protect their people and their sacred land.

"Guardians protect the people. She's no longer one of us."

Carter glared at his brother. "She's Apache. That's enough."

"Is it?"

"Yes."

Jack grimaced but said no more. He'd been there to pick up the pieces after Amber had left. Carter wasn't surprised that Jack was less than thrilled to have Amber back.

"Not again," said Jack.

Carter met his brother's warning with a glare of his own.

"She left. She didn't write. She didn't visit, not even after you were injured."

"I saw her after I came home from the hospital."

He hadn't told Jack. A rare omission that clearly surprised his twin.

"But she left again."

He couldn't deny that. But he knew he'd shown her the door. He'd been so hurt and angry. Yeager had still been MIA, and his days were filled with horror and hope. She'd asked about Hatch Yeager.

What do you care, Amber? Really. You disappear for two years, and then you think I owe you answers. I don't owe you a thing.

Carter met the disapproval in Jack's words with a steady stare. "Yeah, she left again after I threw her out."

Jack made a face. Carter couldn't tell what his brother thought about that.

"Maybe she's ready to come home," said Carter.

And maybe he was ready to let her. After today that was at least a possibility.

Jack shook his head. "Maybe she had no other choice."

Carter returned his attention to his brother, who raked a hand through his short brown hair. "What does that mean exactly?"

"She is a witness. They want her in federal custody."

"We both saw him. He was at her boss's house."

"And her boss is dead, too. Everyone is dead but Amber."

Carter didn't like the way Jack said that, as if this were all somehow her fault.

"Can't you just give her the message and forget about her?" Jack asked.

He'd never been able to forget about her. And oh, how he had tried. But even after all this time he wondered about what she was doing, thinking and if she missed him at all.

Could he?

He'd stayed away from her, but this was different. Because whether she would admit it or not, she needed him. He hated how much he needed that excuse to keep her close. He slipped both hands into his pockets, wishing he could give his brother the answer he wanted to hear and knowing he could not.

"I can't," said Carter.

Jack's mouth went tight.

"Carter, I'm telling you this as my brother. Let her go."

"Why?"

"Because Amber Kitcheyan isn't just a witness. She's also a suspect."

"How do you know that?"

"They told my boss. She should never have left the office with those papers. Makes her look guilty as hell."

"If she'd stayed, she'd be dead."

Jack glanced toward the window and swore.

Carter followed the direction of his brother's fixed attention. Amber was standing in the parking lot before the station alone.

Jack quirked a brow. "Still think she's innocent?"

Chapter Five

Amber stepped from the concrete building that included tribal headquarters and the tribal police station and breathed deep.

The air smelled so different here. She'd almost forgotten the crisp clean taste and the moisture. There was water here. Back in Lilac the earth was scorched and parched and thirsty. The dust was everywhere on everything and everyone. She didn't think she'd ever be clean again. Now she was. Standing here where she belonged.

Or had belonged.

Relinquished, they called it. Carter said it was irrevocable. She'd checked, of course, called the tribal council offices and asked if a tribe member who had relinquished their membership could reapply. The woman on the phone had been blunt. *No*, she had said. *The decision is not like a reversible blanket. Relinquishment is permanent and irrevocable.*

Amber added one more item to the list of things her father had stolen from her. And still he was her father and, as such, deserved to be honored. But not loved. He'd lost that along the way.

She thought of Carter, there when she needed him most, and found herself shaking her head in astonishment. He had a message from her uncle, his shaman. She wondered if the message he carried was from her mother or her father.

She set her jaw and breathed, the cool air calming her. What would she do now? She could not go home to her family or stay here on tribal land. She could not bear to go back to Lilac, knowing what had happened. She shivered, afraid of the ghosts of all the ones she knew, torn from this world in such a brutal and cruel way.

Carter would know what to do. He was always so sure of himself. So sure he did not need to ask her what was true, he just moved forward. Omnipotent. But that wasn't love. It was some kind of possession. He had been too much like her father, and she would not have one more man controlling her. So she'd ended it. The decision had been hard but right. So why did it still hurt so much?

But oh, he was more handsome now than ever.

He had grown out his hair since his military service, and now he wore it loose and long, so it reached midway down his biceps, the strands shining blueblack in the sunlight as they'd flown in the chopper from Lilac. From her place lying on the gurney she could see him sitting beside his brother Kurt. Carter was a Hot Shot now, according to her sister Kay who sent her letters of the happenings on the Rez. Carter no longer wore his uniform, as he had the last time she had seen him. After three tours in the Middle East, he had been honorably discharged and relinquished the US Marine's uniform for a pair of snug jeans. He wore them cinched about his trim hips with an ornate red coral and turquoise buckle and a soft chambray shirt that showed his muscular form. She wondered if Carter had made the ornament himself because he was a talented silversmith.

A Subaru SUV pulled into the station. She noticed it because such foreign cars were uncommon up here on the Rez.

The black vehicle circled the lot and came to a stop at the curb before her. The driver put the car in Park but didn't shut down the engine. His passenger met Amber's gaze, and a smile quirked his lips as he exited the vehicle.

He wore a gray blazer and dark slacks. His ashy brown hair was trimmed and a shade lighter than the closely cut beard. He looked vaguely familiar, but she did not remember where or when she had seen him before.

"Ms. Kitcheyan? Will you please come with us, ma'am?" He had a strong Texas twang in his speech.

Amber stepped back. He reached in his blazer, and she saw his shoulder holster and the black butt of a pistol. He drew out a leather cover and opened the case, revealing an FBI shield.

"I'm Field Agent Muir with the FBI. My driver is Field Agent Leopold. We'll be taking you to the police station in Darabee to record your statements," said the agent.

Amber slipped back as her eyes shifted from the agents and then over her shoulder to the station door. It seemed impossibly far. She did not want to go with this man but thought running would be embarrassing.

She glanced at Muir, trying to understand the deep dread congealing in her stomach.

"If you'll step into the vehicle, ma'am." Muir extended a hand, indicating the rear seat that lay behind dark tinted windows. She shivered.

"I can't. They're waiting for me inside." She thumbed over her shoulder.

His smile looked more predatory than reassuring. And then it clicked. He wore a sports coat and pants. Not a suit. A sports jacket. She quirked a brow at that; it didn't seem right.

"Ma'am," he said again, his tone carrying a warning.

She didn't hear Carter arrive, but heard him a moment later and turned as he spoke.

"What's going on here?" Carter asked.

Muir showed his shield and repeated his request for

Amber to step into the vehicle. His partner exited the driver's side and rounded the fender, his hand on the pistol clipped to his hip. He looked remarkably like Muir, with dark brown hair and aviator glasses that covered his eyes. He wore an ill-fitting black suit that puddled at his loafers.

Carter faced off with Muir.

"You're on tribal land," said Carter. "Sovereign land. You can't take her."

Muir and Leopold shared a silent look, and Carter spoke to her in Apache.

"These two aren't FBI."

Her eyes widened.

"You're not taking her," said Carter to Muir.

"Wanna bet?" said the driver, Leopold, drawing his weapon.

Horror immobilized Amber as the driver flicked off the safety and pointed the weapon at Carter. She moved to step before him, but he tugged her behind him.

"What's your name?" asked Muir.

"Carter Bear Den."

The men exchanged a second look. Leopold gave a lazy grin.

"Get in," said Muir. "Both of you."

They headed for the black Subaru SUV. Her eyes narrowed at the vehicle. Federal agents drove American-made vehicles. Impala, Taurus, Dodge Charger. She knew that from working a summer internship in Benson with Public Safety. What they didn't drive was foreign cars.

Carter was right. These two were not FBI.

She glanced to Carter, but he had his eyes on Muir who had now drawn his weapon.

"Get in," he said, motioning with his pistol.

Amber stepped up and into the SUV. Carter followed a moment later, and the door clicked shut behind them.

Carter spoke to Amber in Apache before either man got in the vehicle.

"Jack's watching from inside. He's seen them take us. We just have to stay alive until he can get to us."

Muir, or whatever his name was, got in first. He sat facing them, pistol pointed at Carter until the driver returned to the adjoining seat. Then they ordered Carter to lift his hands. The driver snapped a handcuff on one of Carter's wrists, threaded the chain through the handgrip fixed above his door before clipping the other cuff on his opposite wrist.

Amber swallowed and sank back in her seat trying to slow her heartbeat and think. Carter's face was grim, and she found no reassurance there.

Was there a tire iron or something? She glanced about and found a car so spotless it belonged on a showroom floor.

They left the small lot and turned away from Darabee. That was bad, she thought, because to the south was only Red Rock Dam and the resort community of Turquoise Lake. Beyond that, down the highway which many called the Apache Trail, lay Phoenix.

The Subaru accelerated. Amber glanced at the digital speedometer, seeing that they had reached sixty, and the speed was still increasing. Outside her window the town of Pinyon Forks quickly gave way to pastureland dotted with the tribe's cattle. Past the open stretch, the mountains rose, thick with lush green Douglas fir and ponderosa pine that grew in abundance on their land. The tribe's land, she corrected. Not hers. Not anymore.

"What will they do to us?" she asked in Apache.

Carter's jaw set, and she had her answer. They were dead unless Jack found them first or she or Carter did something. Muir still sat with his back toward the windshield. Gun pointed at Carter.

"Attach your harness," Carter said in Apache.

"English," said the driver.

Amber drew a breath at the implication and reached for her safety belt. Whatever Carter planned, it involved a quick stop, maybe worse.

She fastened her seat belt that included a shoulder restraint. Carter, of course, could not do the same. She grabbed the armrest tight and waited. They were going so fast now, the seconds taking them farther and farther from Pinyon Forks.

Amber cleared her throat. Whatever Carter planned, it needed to be soon. But Muir kept his weapon raised and his attention on Carter.

"I'm going to be sick," she said.

Muir didn't bite. "Go ahead."

"Pull over, right now!" she shouted.

His eyes flicked to her, but the gun stayed pointed at Carter. Leopold did not even flinch but kept both hands on the wheel as Muir gave her a ferocious glare. In that moment of inattention, Carter clamped both hands around the handgrip, lifted one booted foot and kicked the driver with such force the man's head impacted the side window, cracking the glass.

Muir looked to his partner as Carter swung the pointed toe of his boot in his direction, the tip impacting Muir's eye socket. The man yelped and slapped his free hand over his eye, his pistol dipping out of Amber's line of vision.

Amber gasped at the violence of the attack and because the car was swerving now, leaving the highway at dizzying speeds.

The SUV veered across the center line as the driver's head lolled back in the seat, his hands dropping from the wheel. Muir lifted the pistol, and Amber lunged, leaving the shoulder restraint behind as she grabbed his arm with both hands and yanked up as the first shot went into the roof. Carter was now wrapping his legs around both the seat and passenger, trapping Muir's arm beside his head.

The SUV careened off the opposite shoulder and slid down the short embankment of grass. The jolting ride pressed Amber back into her seat. She grabbed at the door handle, but the door did not open. They bounced and jerked as the SUV thrashed through the long grass and weeds before breaking through the barbed wire fence. Her shoulder harness engaged, pinning her back in her seat and giving her an excellent view of the looming drop-off to the stream she knew ran cold and deep all year.

Amber screamed as the earth fell from beneath the front fender. The vehicle tipped to a right angle, and she glimpsed the rocky creek bed visible only because the snowpack had not yet melted with the spring runoff. An instant later, they hit the rocky bank. Her shoulder harness bit into her chest and squeezed her hips as the vehicle came to an abrupt halt at the same moment the front air bags inflated, throwing the unconscious driver and struggling passenger back. Their side air bag inflated, dislodging Carter. He was thrown sideways so hard it looked as if he were being hauled by a rope. He didn't move again.

The car's metal groaned, and the car fell back, the rear tires striking the bank behind them before coming to rest.

White powder filled the cab, and she couldn't see. Carter slumped beside her.

She shook him, screaming his name, then remembered it was dangerous to shake an accident victim. Then she shook him again. He didn't rouse.

White swirling dust began to settle on them like frost. The stillness deafened.

Chapter Six

Amber had to find the handcuff key. The guys in Benson had kept theirs in their wallets.

She released her seat belt. When she rolled her shoulder, she winced. Where was Muir's pistol?

First things first. She pushed the unconscious Muir forward into the deflating air bag and groped his back pockets, finding nothing. On her second try she located his wallet, in the front pocket of his blazer. She opened the worn brown leather and saw the license which read: Warren Cushing.

"Muir," she muttered and continued her search, locating the small handcuff key that most resembled a tiny luggage key.

How long until one of them woke up? She kept the wallet and used the key, more worried when Carter's hands dropped limply to his lap.

"Wake up, Carter!"

She tried the door again to the same end and then stared at the gap between the seats. It took only a moment to vault through the opening and lunge across the driver to reach the door release. The latch clicked, and she felt like crying in relief. Instead, she continued, head first out the door, clasping the armrest in passing to keep from sprawling on her face.

Once outside the SUV she spotted the driver's gun in

a holster clipped on his belt. His face was a bloody mess as it seemed the air bag had broken his nose. She reached Leopold's gun, or whatever his name really was. His pistol went in the back of her waistband as if she were a gangster. She shut the door and hurried to the rear door where Carter slumped. Amber tugged Carter's door open and reached for him. He was heavy, and she realized she could tip him out, but then what?

She considered shooting both the unconscious impostors and dismissed the notion as she wrinkled her nose in disgust. She couldn't. She knew that much.

Her eyes caught the glint of something shiny, and she spotted the gun on the floor mat by Carter's feet. That pistol went in the front of her waistband. She could hear Warren Cushing groan as he started to regain consciousness.

She felt the pressure of time and the choice of leaving Carter or staying here with these two strangers. Well, she had the guns. What if Carter had been wrong and these men were really FBI and she and Carter had just attacked federal officers and wrecked a federal vehicle?

Amber's shoulders slumped. She wiped back tears and retrieved Carter's phone from his rear pocket. For the second time in one day she called for help, only this time she used Carter's favorites list to find and dial Jack Bear Den's cellular phone.

"Where are you?" asked Detective Bear Den.

She told him as best she could, not liking the high frantic quality of her voice. "We crashed the car. These men said they're FBI. Carter says they aren't, and one has an ID reading Warren Cushing, and he told me his name was Muir and—"

"Slow down," said Bear Den.

She grabbed a breath and swallowed, then started again. Her words came out a jumbled mess, and it took a moment for her to realize that Detective Bear Den was shouting her name. She stopped talking.

Then she noticed something, the meaning rising to fill her consciousness.

"I smell gas."

"What?" asked Bear Den. "Get him out of the vehicle!"

She thrust the phone in her pocket as the implications made her heart beat in her throat, choking out the stench. She gave Carter another sharp poke in the ribs. This time he groaned.

"Wake up, Carter," she said. "Wake up now!"

"Amber?" The voice came from the phone behind her. She ignored it to grasp Carter by the front of his soft chambray shirt.

She glanced about for cover. The closest thing was a large rock, to the left by the water, but it was too close and still half submerged in cold water. Next was a second outcropping along the bank that was maybe fifteen feet away. She glanced up the incline to the road above them, and it seemed impossibly steep.

She slung Carter's arm over her shoulders and tugged.

"Come on, Carter. Move!"

He groaned, and his arm tightened on her shoulders.

"Up, soldier! That's a direct order."

Another groan, but he swung his own legs out of the SUV and slid against her. His eyes fluttered.

"What happened?" He lifted a hand to his head.

"Later."

"Yeager. Get Yeager." Was he back in Iraq?

He slipped to a knee, and she had a sinking feeling that she'd never get him up again.

"Gas," he said.

"Yes. Let's go."

He used her as a crutch, and the weight nearly buckled her knees as they inched past the rear of the smoking Subaru and along the rocky bank of the stream. She threaded them under an overturned juniper, which had toppled from the bank above and now hung precariously before them.

They had come only twenty feet. But it would have to do because Carter dropped, carrying her to the ground with him. The juniper branches, still lush and loaded with the tight gray berries, fell like a curtain between them and the Subaru. She feared it would be little protection if the vehicle exploded. She got him to his side, and he groaned again.

"Like getting kicked by a horse," he muttered.

She picked up the sound of car doors closing and cowered. Was that help or the impostors coming after them?

Carter's ears buzzed as if he had just come from a rock concert. Dappled light filtered down on him with shards of sunlight so bright they seemed to slice the tissues of his eyes. His face hurt. His neck ached. He groaned.

"Quiet now," said a soft female voice, and a small hand pressed to his shoulder.

Who was that? He forced his eyes open. There, lying beside him, was an unfamiliar woman who seemed to be covered in baby powder. For just a moment he thought he was dreaming as he looked on the sacred deity, Changing Woman, who brought rebirth to the land.

He lifted a hand to touch her cheek and found it warm and alive. Tear stains cut tracks through the white dust, revealing the soft brown skin beneath.

He glanced at his wrist, all red and raw skin, as if he'd been tied. Carter's gaze flicked back to hers.

"Amber?" he asked.

He had never seen her like this, disheveled and lost. What had happened?

He rocked his jaw, wondering who had hit him as he moved his hand from her face to his.

Amber took hold of his hands and squeezed. The ache now moved to his chest. Only she could make his heart ache and his body come alive with longing.

He'd loved her as a girl and lost her when she became a woman. He'd tried to forget her. Carter admitted now that he never could. Not this one, because she still owned a piece of his heart. He knew this because that piece now bled with longing for her. The woman who'd left him. But worse, she'd left her family and abandoned her people.

"Amber," he whispered, reaching up and cupping her cheek.

She smiled, and the powder on her face flaked at the corners of her eyes. Her hair was also powdered like George Washington's and tucked up in a knot at the back of her head. She used to wear it down so that it brushed the waistband of her jeans and his thighs when she sat astride him as they made love.

Why? Why had she thrown it all away? Their future—a life together here where they both belonged? Why was she ashamed of who and what she was?

Now her bun had shifted. Tendrils had escaped and hung about her powdered face. Her Anglo blazer was streaked with grime and sand, and she'd lost the top two buttons of her blouse. He reached up and cupped her chin, his thumb brushing that tiny crescent scar at her mouth.

"What happened?" he asked.

"Hush. Someone is here."

"Who?" he whispered and craned his neck in the direction she faced. That's when he realized he was lying against a wall of dirt behind a fast-running stream. The sun that hit them full in the face did not touch the opposite bank. Afternoon then or morning. He tried to make sense of his surroundings.

It all came back to him, up to and including the air bag punching him like a prizefighter.

"Where are we?"

"About ten miles outside Pinyon Forks," she whispered. Then Amber cocked her head. Now he heard the voices.

"Down here," said a male voice. The way he spoke made Carter think he was Anglo, Southern.

Who? he mouthed. She shrugged. Then she moved up close to his ear and whispered.

"I called your brother. He's coming. But the Subaru was leaking gas, and he told me to get you out."

And she had. How the devil had this little woman moved him?

Her lips brushed his ear as she spoke again. "I have their guns. Those guys. But someone else is here now."

"Jack?" he whispered.

"I don't think so."

From the top of the bank, seemingly right above them, came the voice again.

"Where is she?"

That one sounded Anglo, he thought.

Next came another voice, deeper, with a speaking pattern that lacked the Texas twang.

"They got away."

"They can't have gone far," came the reply.

Amber flattened into the warm earth beside him, covering her mouth with one hand and retrieving a gun from the waistband of her slacks. She looked like she knew what she was doing. She rolled to her side and then reached behind and beneath her blazer, laying a second gun on his chest. He took it, and their eyes met. He saw no fear now. Only a cold determination and willingness to do what was necessary. She would have made a good soldier. His gut twisted, so damn glad she had not been there with him in the Sandbox.

"They're right on our tails," said the first voice. "We have maybe another two minutes."

"But she's right here!" said his companion.

Amber's eyes widened. She was the only "she" out here.

"No time," repeated the first man. "Get my brother. We'll have to come back for her.

"Hurry up," said the first man.

A car door opened, the metal groaning a protest.

The same voice again. "Let's go."

Carter looked at Amber. Her hand was pressed to her mouth again as if to keep from screaming. Her eyes were wide. Seconds ticked by, and then two more doors slammed and tires patched out on the gravel that lined the shoulder of the road.

Amber slid her hand away from her mouth. "Are they gone?"

Carter nodded. "I think so."

"Should I check?" she asked.

He shook his head. There was no reason for her to see this. He could protect her from that image, the kind that stuck in your mind and flashed back like a thunderstorm.

They said they had two minutes.

"We wait," said Carter.

Insects buzzed in the grass above them, and the wind brushed through the long needles of the ponderosa pines on the opposite bank. Amber returned her gun to her waistband and then gripped his arm with two of hers as she huddled close.

"How did you get me out?" he asked.

"You walked, mostly."

"Mostly?"

There was a whooshing sound, as if from a strong gust of wind. Black smoke rose up behind them, billowing in a dark column in the bright blue sky.

"Fire," said Carter.

Had the men retrieved Muir and Leopold before setting the Subaru ablaze?

Tires crunched on sand. Amber's grip tightened, and she ducked her head.

"They're back," she whispered, her voice strained.

"Carter? Amber?"

He knew that voice. It was Jack.

"Here!" he yelled. When he stood, the dizziness came with him, clawing at him and making the ground heave. Amber was there beside him, steadying him, holding him so he didn't fall.

"Slow," she said. "Go slow."

She could have run to his brother. But she didn't. She helped him walk, leaning into him as she wrapped an arm about his middle and gripped his opposite arm, now draped over her narrow shoulders. Then he scrambled up the steep bank on his hands and knees toward the road topping the rise and saw the SUV consumed in flames.

Chapter Seven

Amber felt safe again, at least for now. Detective Bear Den had transported them back to Pinyon Forks and the Turquoise Canyon police station. On the way they had told Carter's brother everything. Once they arrived, she'd had a chance to wash her face and hands, brush out the powder from her hair and drink some water with Carter standing guard outside the door.

We'll have to come back for her.

Who where they? And why did they need to come back for her? She wrapped her arms about herself and shivered. She had gotten tangled up in something, but she didn't know what.

She now sat with Carter in Tribal Police Chief Tinnin's office devouring a sandwich, chips and a cookie provided by the same woman who prepared the meals for the prisoners. Amber was so hungry she barely tasted the food. Carter's was already gone, and he sat back to finish his third bottle of water.

Some of the powder had settled in his part, clinging to his black hair. He wore a new clean T-shirt courtesy of his brother who had a locker across the hall. He also wore an unbuttoned green-and-white chambray shirt that was obviously Jack's, because, though Carter was a big man, he had to roll the sleeves.

Carter watched her eat and smiled.

"Wish we had some fry bread," he said.

Fry bread! She hadn't had any since she'd visited her sister over the holidays. It was just one of many things she missed. She returned Carter's smile.

He lifted the water bottle and drank, his Adam's apple rising and falling with the rhythm of each swallow. Her mouth went dry, and her entire body electrified. Even after all this time he still made her want him without even trying.

She cut her gaze away, refusing to torture herself with the sight of him. But she was too weak, and her eyes found him again. The bottle lay between his two broad hands, tucked between strong thighs. She exhaled.

"Amber. You okay?"

She forced her gaze away from his groin, but it was too late. Now his eyes blazed in return, the sexual awareness crackling between them like static electricity.

"Amber," he whispered, leaning forward.

She shook her head but moved closer until his fingers brushed over her cheek, leaving heat blazing in their wake.

She wished they could go back in time, back to those two kids who had fallen in love, and try again. Tell her younger self to be wise and give Carter another chance. But it was too late now, because she could never ask him to leave their tribe, and she was too ashamed to stay.

Despite her reservations, her heart hammered in giddy excitement and her skin flushed.

Focus. You're in real trouble, and this man doesn't want a woman who walked away from her family.

Carter had loved her. But he loved his people and his place among them more. He was not leaving, and she was not staying. There was no future for them. Only more pain.

"Thank you for saving us back there," she said.

"I didn't get us out. I'd have been cuffed to the handgrip in a smoldering wreck if not for you."

He'd been the reason they had a chance to get out of that SUV, and they both knew it.

Her smile drop away. "Did they find them?" she asked.

"No. Those other two got them out before torching the vehicle. No sign of them since."

"Oh, Carter. What's happening?"

He lifted his water. "I was hoping you'd know."

"I don't. I can't even imagine. It's like a nightmare."

Carter rubbed his neck. It was a gesture he used when unhappy, but she wondered now if it might stem from pain.

Carter had refused to go to the health clinic but had allowed Kurt to look him over. He declined the neck brace they recommended for the jolt he'd taken during the crash, but took the offered analgesic medication.

"Did you get through to your family?" asked Carter, changing the subject. Did he believe her? She couldn't tell.

"I did. Your brother let me use his desk phone. I called Kay. She'll get word to my mom and Ellie." But not her father. Her father had made it very clear that he wanted nothing to do with her ever again. Her stomach ached, and she felt even lower than before.

"Do you ever see them?" he asked. She could see the pain now, there in his tight expression and the watchful eyes. Did he still feel the ache that she carried like a stone in her heart?

"Sometimes. When I can. I see them at Kay's." Her younger sister had married at nineteen and moved to the smaller Rez communities of Koun'nde to the north of Pinyon Forks.

Now his eyes held accusation. "But you never came to see me again."

She hadn't. Not after that last time.

"Carter. I…" She thought of their last meeting. "I didn't think you'd want to see a *manzana*."

A *manzana* was Apache for an apple. It meant that she was red on the outside and white at the core.

She used the insult he'd thrown at her when he had

been home recovering, and Yeager had still been listed as missing.

"I shouldn't have said that."

"You told me to go away, me and my *manzana* clothing." She lifted the hem of her ruined blazer to show that she still dressed like an Anglo working in an Anglo world.

His jaw tightened. And the glimmer of desire faded from his eyes, replaced with something hard and cold.

Detective Bear Den poked his head through the open doorway.

"The FBI is here. The real FBI."

"You find them—the guys that took us or the other two?" asked Carter.

"No." Jack shifted and rested a hand on his hip. "Vanished like ghosts." He inclined his head toward the door. "They have some questions."

Carter nodded and rose.

"Ah." Jack shifted again. "They want Amber first."

Carter hesitated, and she thought he might argue.

"You gonna sit in?" asked Carter.

Jack nodded and Carter resumed his seat. Amber stood, and her lunch rolled in her belly. She reminded herself that she had done nothing wrong. But it didn't quiet her nerves as she trailed behind Detective Bear Den.

She'd had a chance to clean up in the bathroom, but the fine powder still clung to the creases of her dark slacks and jacket, resisting her efforts to beat it away. And the smell of the gasoline and the air bags clung to her like skunk spray, making her head ache.

She felt as lost as the day she left her childhood home at seventeen, and just like on that day, she didn't know what would happen next.

Her world had somehow careened off-kilter, and all she wanted was to go to her crappy rented room in the guesthouse in Lilac, shower, sleep and wake up to find this entire day was just a nightmare.

Amber followed Detective Bear Den into the interrogation room where Tribal Police Chief Tinnin introduced her to two Anglos. Field Agent Parker rose and nodded. The man was in his thirties, cleanly shaven with extremely short hair that did nothing to hide his unfortunate ears that stuck out on each side of his head like pot handles. His partner, Field Agent Seager, had an under-bite that made his jaw thrust out. He also had blue eyes and prematurely gray hair. He stared at her as if he was hungry and she was lunch. Amber took a seat between Bear Den and Tinnin and the FBI across the table.

Over the next hour she was questioned and questioned again. She worked with an FBI artist to help create an image of the man she had seen at Mr. Ibsen's home and another for the driver.

It quickly became apparent that her miraculous escape from her offices at the copper mine and then again from the home of her supervisor had set off all kinds of alarms with the FBI. The line of their questions and the repetition gradually made it apparent that they were unconvinced that she was exceedingly lucky and that Carter's arrival was a timely coincidence.

"Ms. Kitcheyan? You were saying."

"Yes. I opposed the land exchange between the Lilac Mining Company and the US Forest Service. But it's not really up to me. Is it?"

The men exchanged a look.

"Are you a member of either WOLF or BEAR?"

"Of what?"

"Ms. Kitcheyan, did you have foreknowledge of today's attack?"

"No." She sounded shocked because that's how she felt. What was happening? She knit her brow and tried to think. She glanced to Detective Jack Bear Den who watched her with interest, and she suddenly felt all alone in the room.

She glanced toward the door to the interrogation room, wondering where Carter might be.

"Did you take part in the planning of this attack?"

"No, I did not!" Did she sound defensive?

The three men stared at her as her throat began a familiar burn that told her tears were imminent.

"Why did those men take you from this station?"

"I don't know."

"But you did know them."

"No, I did not. They said they were FBI."

"Yes, that's what Chief Tinnin told us you said. But it seems more likely that you knew them."

"Well, I didn't."

"But you left the safety of the station. Why is that?"

"I wanted to smell the air."

Both men scowled at that.

"Let's go back to this morning," said Seager.

They started again, and when they got to the questions about her knowing the men who abducted her and Carter, she stopped them.

"I have helped you. But now you are just asking me the same thing over and over. So I'm not answering any more questions," she said. Now she sounded guilty as hell.

"That's certainly your right," said Parker, tugging at a pink ear. "But the man who murdered everyone in your office is still at large, and we thought you might want to help us with that."

"I do want to help you."

"We just want to be sure we understand. You left your office. You used the restroom. When you left the restroom you departed through the loading dock, breaking company procedure. There you saw the van with the driver, but you never heard a shot or saw the gunman."

"Again, yes."

"Are you sure you didn't, maybe, pass the shooter in the hallway?"

"I think I'd recall that."

The man's mouth quirked. "Do you?"

"Do I what?"

"Recall seeing the shooter?"

Chief Tinnin stood. "All right, gentlemen. You've had your interview. Detective Bear Den will walk you out. Two of my men will escort you off the tribe's land."

"We're not finished yet," said Parker.

"Oh, I'd disagree."

"We have to interview Carter Bear Den."

"Interview," said Tinnin. "Is that what you call this?"

Seager had the good manners to break eye contact. Parker just looked belligerent.

"It's federal land," said Seager.

"I'd disagree again. It is Apache land." He turned and motioned to the exit. Detective Bear Den held the door ahead of them.

Seager marched out.

Parker stopped and turned back to Tinnin before exiting. "US Marshals have been called. They're taking her into protective custody."

"She stays on tribal land," said Detective Bear Den.

His chief cast him a look of annoyance but did not oppose him before the federal agents.

Parker rubbed the bristle on his head and turned to Tinnin. "You blocking us from taking custody?"

"For now."

"There's already been two attempts on her life."

"Three," said Tinnin.

Parker stormed out after his partner.

Amber slumped in her chair, finally able to breathe again.

Chief Tinnin ambled to the door, pausing to glance back at Amber. "I can only stall them for so long. Sooner or later they'll figure it out, and then they'll take you with them."

The door clicked shut, locking her in the interrogation room alone.

Chapter Eight

Carter waited while his brother walked the two FBI agents down the hall and out of sight. He supposed that meant they were not interviewing him next.

His brother's boss appeared after that.

"They don't want to take my statement?" asked Carter.

"They sure do. Nearly pissed themselves in anticipation. I called a halt, but they'll be back tomorrow. It's past supportime and I have an agreement with the missus." Tinnin gave him a good hard look. "You have any idea what you've gotten yourself tangled up in?"

"I just know that Amber is in trouble."

Tinnin's gaze was unblinking. "You could say that." Tinnin looked at the tiled floor a moment and then lifted his gaze back to Carter. "You could also say that we have four suspects at large on our reservation, that your old girlfriend is the lone survivor in one hell of a mass slaying. That the van was recovered, but the gunman and his driver are still at large. That the man who admitted the gunman to the administration building in Lilac used the very same door as Amber and that the key card he used to gain admittance to the building came from a woman who worked in human resources until this morning when she was delayed by a bullet in her forehead. So, yes, son, I'd say Amber is in trouble."

"Why are they after her?" asked Carter.

"Don't know. But that random shooting doesn't seem random at all. Not when they took out her boss and then were here to greet Amber. Love to know how they knew where to find her. Love to know why she practically walked out there to meet them. You got any ideas about that one?"

"No, sir."

"Hmm." He pressed his free hand on his hip and shifted, resting a leg. "They called the US Marshals. I can stall but eventually she'll be transferred to the custody of them as a protected witness. They want you, too, but I can give you a choice."

"We could keep her here."

"Well, no. I don't have the manpower for protecting her. And I don't fancy a mass shooting at my police station, plus she's no longer one of your tribe."

Carter knew that Tinnin was also a Turquoise Guardian. He'd spent time in the sweat lodge with him and attended prayer circles.

"I was sent to Lilac to deliver a message to Amber from Kenshaw Little Falcon."

Tinnin slipped a hand in his front trouser pocket and thought on that a while.

"She's his sister's child, as I recall. You deliver it?"

"Not yet."

"Suppose you go in there and give it to her now."

"When the marshals come, I'm going with her."

"I'd advise against that."

Carter held his gaze.

"Why's that?"

"Might shorten your life expectancy."

Tinnin was an eagle catcher, and he was a strong man who had Carter's respect. He valued his opinion and wished like hell he could do as the older man suggested.

Tinnin's insinuation that there was real danger only made Carter more determined to stay with Amber.

"I'll go see her now."

Tinnin's mouth turned down, and he nodded as if knowing already what Carter would do.

"She's not your responsibility, son. Not anymore."

Carter paused. He knew that in his head, but his heart whispered for him to protect her, that some part of her still belonged to him.

He headed to the interview room where he found Amber sitting with her arms folded on the table and her forehead resting on her arms.

"Amber?"

She popped up, looking dusty and tired and more beautiful than he had ever remembered. Her smile returned at the sight of him, and something in his middle squeezed. His throat went dry.

"Carter!" She looked relieved to see him. "Are you okay?"

"Ears are still ringing." He gave her a half smile. "How did it go in here?"

She threw herself back in her seat. "They think I know more than I do."

"What were you delivering to your boss?"

"They asked me that." She lifted her chin toward the closed door, referring to the FBI.

Carter waited and Amber met his gaze.

"Receiving slips." she said. "On a large delivery of mining equipment. I log it in, and then Ibsen follows up with payment."

Carter wondered why someone would feel it necessary to kill everyone in the receiving department. Someone who hated open-pit mining would tend toward sabotaging the mining trucks or attacking mining equipment.

A knock sounded on the door. Amber stood and glanced

at Carter. He had time to step between her and the door before it swung open.

Carter recognized Jack, and his shoulders dropped an inch.

"I called Ray and Dylan. We're taking you to a safe place for the night," said Jack.

"Where?"

"Ray suggested the lake."

He meant the restricted area of the reservation for members of the tribe only. It was where they often set a sweat lodge with the Turquoise Guardians. After purifying their bodies with sage smoke and steam, they would swim in the lake. There was only one way in, but the drive was over rough roads, and the journey would take an hour at least. More, now that it was dark. Still, he could think of no one he would rather have watching his back than Ray, Dylan and Jack.

They had joined the US Marines together and served their first tour in the same unit. More importantly, Carter had grown up with them and loved Ray and Dylan like brothers.

"They're en route. You two are heading out in a few minutes."

"You taking us?" asked Carter.

"Yes."

So it would be all four of them, Dylan, Ray, Carter and Jack—Tribal Thunder, as they were called among the Turquoise Guardians. All ex-military and some of the best fighters in the tribe. If anyone could keep Amber Kitcheyan safe, it was these men.

"Thank you."

Carter told Jack about the receiving slips and his suspicions. Jack leaned forward braced on stiff arms and fists balled on the surface of the desk, listening. When Carter finished, his brother gave them each a long look and said he needed to speak to the chief.

He walked them to the squad room and left Carter and Amber by his desk.

"Wait here."

Jack joined Chief Tinnin in his office.

Amber's attention wandered over Jack's workstation, catching on the photos. She smiled, lifting the frame that held the photo of his marine buddies. She knew them all, of course, would have graduated with them had she not left. Jack and Carter stood with arms locked around each other's shoulders in the Sandbox with their best friends and fellow tribe members Ray Strong, Hatch Yeager and Dylan Tehauno. Amber said nothing, just pointed Carter out with an elegant index finger and smiled. Carter tried and failed to avoid glancing at Hatch. He cleared his throat, trying to force back the punch of grief. How could Jack even bear to look at it?

Amber replaced the frame to the desk and lifted the one in the metal frame, looking at a photo of his family. Carter felt the tension in his chest ease. His breathing returned to normal, but sweat still popped out on his brow.

"Is that Tommy?"

Carter stepped closer, wiping away the sheen of sweat, hoping she wouldn't notice.

"Yeah. His graduation. That's eight years ago now."

When Amber had last seen him, his younger brother had been a scrawny freshman who was tall but so thin a stiff breeze could blow him down.

"He got big."

"Even bigger now," said Carter.

She glanced toward the office where his twin was deeply engaged in conversation with the chief.

"But not as big as Jack."

Carter laughed. "No one is that big."

She returned her focus to the photo in her hands. "What's Tommy doing now?"

"Shadow Wolf," said Carter, his chest lifting at the thought that his little brother had joined the elite Native American–only branch of Immigration and Customs Enforcement.

"Wow. Working on the border tracking bad guys?"

Carter nodded, his smile full of pride.

"That's right. Traffickers mostly."

"I thought he wanted to join the military like his big brothers."

Carter's smile dropped. "I talked him out of it."

"Hmm." Amber's attention went back to the photo. "And Kurt. He pilots the air ambulance?"

"He's also a paramedic and a Hot Shot."

"Your mom looks exactly the same. And your father? How's he doing?"

"He's good. Still ranching." Carter watched her and saw her brow knit.

"He really is big, isn't he?" Her index finger fell on Jack's image.

Carter returned his attention to the photograph.

All his brothers had long hair back then. He still did, and so did Tommy. This photo showed why Jack kept his hair short. Three brothers with long, straight black hair and Jack, his hair soft brown and showing a definite wave. His gray eyes startling next to the deep brown of the rest of the brothers.

"He ate more than us," said Carter, using a family joke that didn't seem very funny just now.

"Jack doesn't look like you three."

Carter locked his jaw and made a sound that was noncommittal.

"Not just his hair, but his body type, too."

It was true.

"I always noticed it, but this photo… Wow," she said.

Amber replaced the frame to the exact place it had been on Jack's desk.

Carter wrestled with a decision and acted on impulse.

"Amber. I'd like to tell you something. But it's private."

She turned her dark eyes on him, and his gut twisted as the need roused inside him, causing his blood to race.

"I understand."

"I don't want you speaking to anyone about it, not even Jack. Especially not Jack."

"Does it have to do with the case?"

"No. It's personal."

"Then I agree."

She was cautious. He liked that. Thoughtful and observant and smart.

"My brother, he…he doesn't believe that we have the same father."

Her dark brows arched, forming an elegant curve, and her lips pursed. But she didn't seem shocked or scandalized. Of course this wasn't her mother they were talking about. It was his. His mother who taught special education for twenty-eight years at one of the tribe's elementary schools, and he was implying that she had been unfaithful to their dad. It made his stomach ache.

"I'd have to agree. He doesn't look Apache. At least not only Apache."

Carter felt a stab of grief in his heart. It was a suspicion that he had tried to allay for years.

"Parents aren't perfect," she said. "They make mistakes."

The way she said this made him wonder if she spoke from personal experience.

"You mean your parents?" he asked.

She rubbed the scar above her mouth as she met his gaze. The corners of her mouth dipped, and she turned to the windows as three vehicles pulled in before the station, their headlights flashing bright in the fading daylight.

She pointed at the vehicles. "Is that Ray and Dylan?"

She was avoiding the question.

He didn't let go. "Amber, what did they say to you to make you surrender your membership in this tribe?"

Her scowl deepened. "That was a long time ago."

"Not so long."

She turned from the window and laid the palm of her hand on his chest. His breathing caught.

"Why don't we talk about that another time?"

He wanted to press, but more than that, he wanted to press Amber against him.

Carter slipped his hands in his front pockets, and his fingers touched the folded paper.

He drew out the sealed white envelope he had been charged with delivering.

"This is for you."

She stared at the offering. "Is that the letter from my uncle?"

He nodded, extending his arm across the gap between them. She hesitated and then accepted the letter. Her fingers brushed over the top of his index finger. The tingling charge of electricity fired up his arm, sending his skin to gooseflesh. Their eyes met and held. Did she feel it, too?

Her breath caught and her mouth opened. His gaze fixed on that appealing pink mouth as her teeth clamped on her lower lip.

Carter released the envelope and stepped back, his skin flushed and his heart pounding. Whatever had been between them, it wasn't over. That much he knew.

Amber stared at the message. If not for that small white rectangle of paper, she'd be dead right now.

Amber's hands trembled as she tore the end of the envelope and removed the folded white sheet of paper, opened it and stared. Then she glanced up at Carter.

"I don't understand," she said.

"What does it say?"

Amber turned the paper so he could see the blank page.

"What does it mean?" asked Amber.

But Carter was afraid he understood. Kenshaw Little Falcon had known what was coming at the Lilac Copper Mine, and he wanted his sister's child protected.

"I have to see Jack and I need to speak to your uncle."

"You don't think…" Her words trailed away as she must have reached the same conclusion as Carter. "No. That can't be."

He did not offer reassurances.

Carter had the strong urge to drop the paper in the garbage can. Instead he brought Amber into the chief's office and shared the letter with them. Jack's breath came in a long audible exhalation of air.

"I'll go see him tonight. He must have known what we'd make of this."

"It doesn't prove anything," said Amber.

"It's not good," said Jack to the page.

The chief slipped on a glove and dropped the envelope and blank page in an evidence bag.

Chapter Nine

Carter and Amber were gathered up in an impromptu caravan. Before them rode Dylan in a white pickup truck, the man who'd earned the most honors in the service. He was always where he was supposed to be and a born leader. It was natural for him to take point.

Next came Jack's truck carrying Carter in the front passenger seat and Amber on the smaller seat behind them. Ray took the tail, watching their back as always. Ray had a well-earned reputation for causing trouble and making decisions that were questionable at best. He had served time for some of his life choices, but he was rock solid when it came to Tribal Thunder. They trusted him, and she believed that he had never let them down.

Carter glanced back at Amber, silhouetted by the lights of Ray's truck.

"You okay?" he asked.

She nodded, but she wasn't. Amber had reached the point well past exhaustion back at the station, and she was not sure how she even remained upright.

"You can stretch out on the backseat. It will take a while to get there," he said. Though, how she would sleep when they bumped and jolted over the unpaved road he wasn't sure.

"Actually," said Jack, "we're not going to the lake."

Carter frowned at the change in plan. "Why not?"

"We didn't want Tinnin to know where you are. Then he doesn't have to lie."

"The lake is a very defensible position," said Carter, his mind slipping back to his military training.

"But they don't have fry bread or a barbecue grill out there."

"So you picked food over position?"

"No, our mom is picking food over position. She found out you are back from Lilac, and no amount of talk will convince her you are all right until she sees you with her own eyes."

"Does she know about Amber?"

"Of course. You think she'd cook fry bread on a Tuesday night for us?"

"Did you tell her it was dangerous?" asked Carter.

"Yes and she threatened to have Aunt Gigi drive her out to the lake with the grill and a vat of oil in the back of the truck."

Carter accepted defeat.

Jack spoke over the seat to Amber. "We're going to your sister's."

Carter saw the smile lift her tired face.

"Your mom will be there."

Her smile dropped like a curtain. Amber groaned and sank back in her seat.

"Bad idea," said Carter.

Jack laughed. "Then you tell her." He offered his phone.

Carter relented but crossed his arms in frustration.

"Relax. I called in some favors. Nobody gets past our police unless they recognized them."

Carter lifted a brow, knowing there was no department overtime. "What did you promise them?"

"Mom's fry bread."

That would do it.

"And I'm starving," said Jack.

They arrived twenty minutes later to hugs and tears by both moms. Amber's mom, Natalie, hugged Carter. The familiar odor of whiskey and cigarette smoke clung to her, but she didn't seem so drunk that she was slurring her words. Amber's sister Kay showed them in, and Carter and Jack were seated as the guests of honor. Ray and Dylan joined Carter's aunt Gigi and uncle Paul at the table. Their father, Delane, was in the backyard with Kay's husband, Aiden, cooking steaks. Kay's children, both under two, were already in bed, but Amber and Kay crept down the hall to see them.

Amber followed Kay, but her sister stopped shy of the bedroom door and turned in the hall.

"Are you all right?" asked Kay.

"Just exhausted."

"I can't believe he has the nerve to come here after what he said to you," said Kay. Amber had told Kay exactly what Carter had called her, and Kay seemed disinclined to forget.

"His only other choice was to roll out of a moving truck."

Kay sniffed. "He still has no idea. Does he?"

Amber sighed, hoping someday Carter would listen.

"I can't believe what happened today. Those Anglos are crazy. When I think what might have happened." Kay hugged her again. Then quickly let her go and smoothed Amber's blazer. "This is filthy. You need clothes."

"I do."

Kay swiped at her tearing eyes, and her lower lip protruded in a gesture that Amber knew forecast more tears.

"Don't. I'm here now. It will be all right." Except the Feds wanted her in custody as a witness or possibly a suspect and Tinnin had warned that the tribe couldn't protect her for long. Her stomach roiled, the acid sloshing like water in the washer. Amber changed the subject. "How's

Dad?" Amber's chest hurt as she waited. Kay's eyes lifted to the ceiling before returning to meet hers.

Kay picked at her cuticle, tearing away a bit of skin. "You know. The same."

The same was bad. That meant too much booze and too much gambling. Amber recalled the last time she had seen her dad.

You are my children. I made you and I can make more just like you.

"It's stealing," she had said. "You're a thief."

His face had turned purple as he ordered her out of his house.

Kay's words broke into her musings.

"They lost the truck and horses. They don't have anything left, really. Just the house, but you know, it belongs to HUD. And Dad got arrested."

"Arrested?"

"Yeah. For writing bad checks. He's got a court date. But… Amber, I think he'll have to serve some time."

She didn't know how she felt about that. Was it long overdue or just another link in a chain of sorrow?

At least Kay and Ellie had roofs over their heads, and her sisters were free and clear of debt. That made her feel some sense of accomplishment.

"And Mom?" asked Amber, recalling trying to convince their mother to leave, too. All of them. Her mother hadn't wanted to admit there was a problem, so she had watched Amber go. According to her mom, Amber was just on some kind of extended journey to find herself, as if her father had not done a thing wrong.

"She needs some help sometimes."

Amber stiffened. "You are not giving her money."

Kay shrugged. "Food mostly. Safer that way."

Amber's lips seemed fused. It must have been hard for

Kay being here, especially when her husband, Aiden, had a good job in the tribe's highway department.

Silence yawned between them.

"I'm sorry this is all on you now," said Amber.

"And I'm sorry you had to leave. You know, if you just tell them what happened, maybe…"

"I'm not going to embarrass them. He is still my father."

Kay stared at the worn carpet runner and nodded. Then she reached for the door, and they crept into the room to admire the two sleeping boys.

When they returned from the bedrooms, Amber wore one of Kay's pretty cotton dresses in a rich coral color with a wide yoke and belt. She'd also cast off her flats for silver sandals. Amber wished she'd had time to shower.

Carter had been in conversation with Dylan, but his gaze locked on her and then dropped as his eyes swept over her. His smile was full of appreciation, and Amber felt her cheeks heat.

"That dress never looked so good," whispered Kay and left her to help Aunt Gigi set the table.

Amber's brother-in-law, Aiden, held the kitchen door open as Carter's uncle Paul and Carter's dad stepped into the kitchen, bringing with them the aroma of charred steak. Amber, Kay and their mom laid the rest of the meal upon the table as Carter's mother, Annette, forked the last of the fry bread from the bubbling pot of hot oil. Everyone dug in. The fry bread was so hot, the transfer from platter to plate had to be done with speed and dexterity. Carter had not expected to be so famished, but he ate with a good appetite. Amber ate more than he had ever seen her as her mother jabbered on about Ellie, who was away at college. Amber was happy for her youngest sister's achievements, but there was a pang of regret at never having seen the inside of a college classroom.

Her mother never mentioned her dad, and Amber did not ask about him.

Carter watched the stiffness between Amber and her mother with curiosity. He knew there was bad blood but did not know exactly what caused Amber to leave home while he was away on his first tour in the Sandbox. But he had an idea it was tied to the reason she'd given him back his ring. Now he found he wanted to fill in those blank spots.

Finally the dishes were cleared. Amber rubbed her eyes and stifled a series of yawns.

"Are we staying the night?" asked Carter, suddenly so weary he feared he wouldn't be able to stand.

Dylan answered, "My place. It's here in Koun'nde. I have two bedrooms. Ray, Jack and I will take watch, and Jack recruited some of the tribal police for surveillance."

Carter did not wait but rose to his feet and helped Amber stand. Carter's mom forced the remains of the fry bread on Ray and the uneaten dessert on Dylan. Kay gave Amber a travel bag, which he assumed held clothing and such.

Amber was asleep on his shoulder before they had left the drive. They passed two tribal vehicles on the way, which was reassuring.

When they reached their destination, Carter waited in the truck with Jack as Ray and Dylan swept the perimeter. When they returned, Carter woke Amber, who was so groggy he had to walk her up the steps.

Her scent and her warm body stirred him. She felt so right there against him, and it made him long for all that they had missed. Their host directed him. Carter was pleased but not surprised to see that Dylan's house, like his person, was neat, clean and welcoming. The guest room for Amber was functional, with a queen-size bed and side table, but looked more like a library with all the bookshelves stacked to overflowing and a sagging overstuffed reading chair beside a floor lamp.

Ray and Dylan stopped in the hall as Carter assisted Amber in, where she sank into the comfortable chair.

Ray peered around the room. "Geesh, Dylan, you actually read all these?"

"Not yet."

"Looks like a library."

"There aren't a lot of books up here."

"There are now," said Ray.

Dylan had laid a clean towel on the bed with a bag from the drugstore.

"Got you two some things. There's a toothbrush, comb and some travel-sized things in there," he said and blushed. Then he thumbed over his shoulder. "You're in my room. Clean towel. You can use my shaving kit. Take any clothing you like."

Amber thanked Ray and Dylan, who left them alone. Amber left the chair to explore Dylan's offerings, lifting the bag and passing Carter one of two new toothbrushes.

"This was sweet of Dylan," she said, her voice slurred from exhaustion.

"Razor?" she asked.

He nodded his head. "Sure."

She handed over the razor and then leaned forward and rubbed the coarse whiskers on his jaw with her palm. He struggled not to capture her hand against his cheek; it felt so damned right.

A tired smile curled her lips. "Rough."

He was dead on his feet, nearly swaying with fatigue, yet that simple touch had electrified him as if he'd stuck his finger in a light socket.

"That dress is very pretty on you."

"Kay made it. She's great at sewing."

It wasn't the sewing but the fit that was perfect, showing Amber's curves and just enough leg.

His attention flicked from her hand to her eyes. She watched him, her dark eyes hooded. He tried to remember why he shouldn't kiss her. Remember the reason it was a bad idea. They were now tied inexorably to the worst murder spree to take place in Arizona. And she was, at best, a witness and, at worst, a suspect. But that wasn't the only reason, not all of it anyway. There was the ring. The one she'd dropped in the dirt and he still had.

And yet, she captivated him. No, disturbed, that was a better word. Yes, she disturbed him. Deep down and relentlessly.

She let her fingers drag over his jaw and down his throat. He captured her hand in both of his and pressed her palm over his heart, pinning her before him as he debated his choices, let her rest or…

Amber cast him a certain look.

Decision made.

Chapter Ten

Amber didn't look away or retreat as Carter stepped closer. Instead she lifted her hand to finger the collar of his shirt, letting the back of her hand graze his neck. In her wake his skin buzzed and tingled, every nerve alive and yearning for her touch. Carter lifted his hand to cup the back of her head, and she tipped forward, lifting to her toes.

"Bad idea," he said.

"The worst," she replied.

Then she tilted her head and kissed him. Her soft full lips set off a tremor inside him. The epicenter lay south of his belt. He planted a hand at the center of her back and pulled, thrusting her forward. She fell against his chest. Her hands splayed over his shoulders and then slid up until they threaded in his hair. She seemed starved for him, and he felt like the desert in a long-awaited rain.

Her mouth opened, and her tongue darted into his mouth. Carter tipped her across one arm to give him better access to her mouth and neck and...he opened one eye to find a place where he could stretch her out. What he saw was Dylan's desk piled with books.

Carter groaned and drew her back to her feet. Then he broke the kiss and stepped away, keeping only one hand on her arm to be sure she was steady on her feet, then letting her go.

He's seen that expression before. That sort of dazed stare and crooked smile of pleasure.

"Why, Amber? Why now?" he asked.

She flushed. "I just thought…I hoped that it wasn't as good as I remembered."

"And?" he asked, then tensed waiting for her reply.

"Better. So much better," she whispered and gripped both her hands before her as if to make them behave.

"Yeah," he said and rubbed his neck. "What are we going to do about it?"

"I don't know." She glanced toward the door. "They're taking me. Maybe soon. Tinnin said so."

It added urgency to his need. The thought of losing her again hit him hard. He fought it and almost told her he wouldn't let them take her. But it was a lie. She'd know there was no way to keep her from federal custody other than running, maybe to Mexico. And then he'd lose it all, his medicine society, his friends, his family and his tribe. The thought washed him cold, and he took a step back.

Her smile was weary, as if belonging to a much older woman, one who knew the disappointments life can bring.

"We should get some sleep."

"Yes. We should."

He wanted to tell her that he still had feelings for her and that he'd never gotten past the hurt and betrayal of her leaving.

Instead he played it safe, not willing to risk her rejection again because, oh, how it hurt the last time. Still hurt like a phantom limb, gone but still aching, the nerves confused at losing something so vital.

"It was nice to see everyone together tonight," she said.

Did she miss her family as much as he missed her? He couldn't imagine it, being away from them and his home. Every tour of duty he served was endurable only because he knew he would one day come home.

"Yeah."

"Dylan looks good. But Ray seems a little sad, still."

Yeager had been his best friend, Carter knew. Amber knew that, as well.

He felt like the cacti, down there on the flat scorched earth far below the mountains just waiting for the rain. Only he had waited nine years for Amber to come back, to explain, to apologize for turning her back on him and their future together. But she never came. She was here now only because she had no other choice. It hurt knowing that.

She fidgeted with a button on the dress Kay had made.

"I'm glad to see Ray doing well. A Hot Shot, too, Kay says. She was surprised after his troubles."

Was she referring to the depression or the drinking or the car he flipped while his blood alcohol level was twice the legal limit?

"He's doing okay now."

"Do you guys ever talk about it?"

He met her cautious stare and considered kissing her in an effort to get her to stop talking, but he was too slow.

"Yeager, I mean."

He locked his jaw.

"What happened to him, Carter?"

CARTER TENSED AT Amber's question about his fallen comrade, Hatch Yeager. She leaned away to look up at him, and he grimaced at the gut-twisting reaction that always punched him low and deep when he thought of Hatch.

His face flushed as he recalled the last time Amber had asked that question. He was nineteen and home after two weeks in a field hospital in Baghdad, followed by eighteen days of rehab stateside. After they'd finished picking all the tiny metal fragments from his right arm and shoulder, they'd left him to pick at all the tiny emotional fragments of the attack. Carter had breathed in grief like air and needed psychological help. She'd visited him then, in that dark time.

They only knew Hatch was missing then. Abandoned, was there any worse fate? He looked down at Amber and some tiny bridge formed in his mind. Had she abandoned him or had he abandoned her?

Amber waited. He hedged, still trying to avoid speaking of this.

"Maybe now isn't the best time," he said. "I should let you rest."

He watched the hopeful expression crumble to disappointment.

"I mean, especially not after today." He left the rest unspoken. Not on the day when her coworkers had been murdered.

She met his gaze. "Especially today. Carter, every time I rest I think of them. Every time I close my eyes I see Nancy smiling at her desk or Frank or Trisha. And I feel so guilty that I wasn't there and so grateful, too."

Carter straightened. She understood.

"But it wasn't your fault," he said.

"Wasn't it? If what the FBI said is true, then I brought that to them because of the error I pointed out to my boss. I did that."

"But you didn't know."

Her eyes narrowed, and her lips pressed tight. "And whatever happened to Hatch wasn't your fault either, even if you feel it was."

He tore his gaze from hers. She rested a hand on his back.

"Tell me, Carter. Please."

"Okay."

It wasn't okay, of course. Never would be.

"I heard he was found," she said.

"Identified," corrected Carter. "The Marines notified

his family in July of '09. We got him back in August and buried him with full honors."

His body. A casket. A flag.

"I'm so sorry."

"Yeah. It's been hard." Because they were always together, a team. The Bear Den twins, Ray, Dylan and Hatch...and Hatch. Carter's throat closed, and so he clenched his teeth, fighting for control.

Amber began a rhythmic stroking of his back. Her small hand was warm and soothing.

She was brave to tread this ground again after what he had said the last time she asked. It showed she was willing to give him a second chance. Was he willing to do the same?

On her last visit he'd been angry at Amber and himself, and so he had barked at her like a rabid dog.

"Go away, Amber. It's what you always wanted, to be rid of this place. So go."

"I just wanted—"

"Look at you. All dressed up like an Anglo." He had swept her with a look of contempt. *"You're a* manzana.*"*

The tears had come then, and she'd turned away, dashing down the steps and out of his life.

"That's right. Run away. It's all you're good at."

Amber's hand stopped, and he opened his eyes, looking down at her lovely face. She deserved better than him.

"Is it better to pretend he does not still live in the hearts of all four of you?"

She was asking what to do—remember them? Try to forget. And she was right. Yeager wasn't dead. He was the ghost that sat among them. He thought of the tattoo he had chosen with the help of their shaman and head of their medicine society. Five feathers. One for each direction and one for the center of their circle—Yeager.

She moved to sit on the bed, folding up her legs and retrieving a pillow, which she hugged before her, chin resting on the top. He sat beside her, his feet on the floor.

He would answer her question, and the realization exhausted him before he even spoke a single word.

He started talking. "Twenty-two hundred hours. May 1. We're setting up an observation post in the death triangle. It's a spot near Al-Yusufiyah, in Iraq, a bad spot. Our first tour. We were so charged to see action." He shook his head in disgust at his naïveté. "So our SFC says he wants Bear Den and Tehauno in the first Humvee with him. We all know he means me, but Jack just winks at me and takes off for the first Humvee, and the SFC doesn't make a big deal of the joke, just lets Jack go." Now, Jack felt as if Carter's wounds were his fault, but Carter kept that to himself. "So because of Jack, SFC Mullins hesitates before choosing the third man, and Ray yells, 'And Strong.' Mullins, our sergeant says, 'Fine, Strong.' But you can hear he isn't thrilled, and we all know he likes Yeager better than Ray because Ray is a wiseass." But not anymore. Not since that night. Carter swallowed.

Amber placed her hand on his shoulder, silently encouraging him to go on.

"That leaves second in command, Sergeant Tromgartner, with me, Yeager and our interpreter, Ahmed, in the second Humvee. I'm annoyed with Jack because he's got Mullins. I'm stuck with Tromgartner who always drives, and I can drive if I'm with Mullins, so I tell Yeager to take the backseat." Such a small decision but one to change all their lives. "We roll south of Baghdad and set up the observation post with the two Humvees one hundred and fifty yards apart. facing opposite directions, trying to keep insurgents from attacking our guys on the road. Instead we're ambushed by a group with automatic weapons and explosives."

Amber set aside the pillow and took his hands. He

hadn't realized he had been pounding a fist against his knee until she held him still. He glanced at her, and she nodded for him to continue.

"They blew us to hell. That second Humvee. We were on fire, and my sergeant was bleeding."

"That's how you injured your arm?"

He glanced at the spiderweb of white scars. "Yeah. Parts of the Humvee and the IEDs. Because of the smoke, I couldn't see Yeager or Ahmed. They were just gone. Tossed from the vehicle. So I grabbed Tromgartner and ran him to the first Humvee. They shot Tromgartner as I'm running him back. Then I look back and see Ahmed running after us. I yell 'Where's Hatch?' He points down the hill, and I see the insurgents already at the second Humvee. I drop Tromgartner, and Ray and Dylan have him. I turn back for Yeager, but Jack stops me. He muscles me into the Humvee and we take off."

"You thought they killed him," whispered Amber.

"No. I *prayed* they killed him. I prayed for that every minute of every day. But they didn't." They'd tortured him for months. They'd tortured him. All because Carter had taken the front seat. Or chosen to rescue his sergeant instead of searching for his friend.

"They buried him here," said Amber. "I've visited his grave."

Amber's fingers trailed over the white puckered skin that crisscrossed over his right forearm. The tattoo on his upper arm and shoulder covered some of the damage there.

"How badly were you injured?" she asked, tracing the white scars.

He removed the chambray shirt, showing her the rest, peeling back the sleeve of his borrowed T-shirt so it ringed his shoulder.

Amber winced at the damage. But her fingers continued to dance over his skin like a blind woman reading braille.

"Would you blame him if the reverse had happened?" she asked.

"I don't know. I might."

She didn't tell him that Hatch Yeager was now at peace or that it wasn't his fault or that these things happen in war or any of the other things that people say. Instead she said the one thing no one else had thought to say.

"I'm sorry. I'm sorry for you and for Hatch. He was a wonderful friend to all of you. I know you miss him."

And when he needed Carter, he had not been there. Carter felt his throat tighten, but he held on.

"I'm sorry about your friends, too."

She gave him a tight little smile and swallowed before speaking again.

"This is new," she said stroking the skin of his upper arm and the artwork depicting a medicine shield with five dangling feathers, one for each of them, Dylan, Ray, Carter, Jack and Yeager. Each feather was adorned with a turquoise bead like the one given to them as baby boys at their birth. The stretched hide of the shield depicted the imprint of a bear paw.

"I've had it since I came back. We all have one."

"The same one?"

"No, your uncle, Kenshaw Little Falcon, helped each of us choose the design." He could say no more because being chosen as a warrior of Tribal Thunder, though a great honor, was as much a secret as was the rituals of his medicine society, the Turquoise Guardians. He could not share this business, especially with a woman.

"A bear for a Bear Den. Is Jack's shield also the track of a bear?"

Carter frowned because he did not understand his shaman's choice of symbol or placement. He and Ray and Dylan were all told to choose a medicine shield, and their spiritual leader had selected their talisman. An eagle for

Ray to help him see more clearly and make better decisions. The track of a bobcat for Dylan to help him see what is hidden. But Jack was told to depict a medicine wheel on his back to help him know which direction to go.

"Jack's is a medicine wheel," said Carter.

"Good choice."

But different than the rest of them. Yet another visible separation between them.

"I do not think he likes it."

"No?"

Carter was uncomfortable speaking of his brother's insecurities.

"He told me that he wanted an animal spirit. Ray Strong doesn't have a track. His is an eagle to help him see farther ahead. But mine is a bear track and Dylan has the track of a bobcat for stealth. Jack doesn't have an animal totem."

"A medicine wheel is a powerful symbol."

"It makes him feel different. He wanted a shield, like the rest of us."

"But he's not like the rest of you."

Carter stiffened and drew his arm from her grip. "He's my brother."

Amber dropped her gaze and nodded. "They are all your brothers—Tommy, Kurt, Jack, Dylan, Ray and Hatch."

She gave him an open look, and he wondered if he might have a second chance with her.

But first he needed to know why she had gone.

"I want to know what happened."

"When?"

"The day you left us."

"I tried to tell you."

"I remember. You were worked up about your father's truck."

"No. It wasn't about his truck. It was about you treating me as a child, instead of your future wife. You actually called me childish."

"We were seventeen. We were both childish, Amber."

"Maybe. But you worked everything out with my dad. You didn't even include me until after you gave him your signing bonus."

"It's only money."

"Not to my father. To him it's a disease."

"I solved the problem."

"You made it worse."

"Oh, come on. Can't be that bad. Certainly not bad enough for you to rescind your membership in the tribe."

Amber slipped from the bed. Slowly she drew to her feet and motioned to the door.

"I think you better go."

Chapter Eleven

Carter went out to the living room to find both Ray and Dylan in conversation. Ray had a pistol in a shoulder harness beneath his left arm and Dylan's rifle with a scope leaned against the kitchen table. Just seeing his friends there made him feel better. This was what it meant to have brothers of choice, if not of blood. He couldn't ask for better fighters or better men.

He told them about the message he had delivered, and Ray and Dylan agreed to go visit Kenshaw Little Falcon and ask him about the blank page. He thanked them formally in Apache and spent a few minutes catching them up on all that had happened during the day.

They hadn't even asked. He needed help, and that was all they had to know. They trusted him, and he trusted them with his life.

A thought struck him. They hadn't asked. If he said it was important, then it was important. If he said it was life or death, then it was just that.

But when Amber told him he was not to pay her father's debts, he had downplayed her concerns. He hadn't listened, and he hadn't trusted her. She was trying to protect her sisters and her parents. She was trying to respect her father and keep him from jail and guard her sister's future. She'd spent a decade alone, without her people.

"You two back together?" asked Jack.

Carter groaned. It didn't take long to spill his guts. Amber opened the door to her room, cast them a ferocious glare and headed to the bathroom.

Carter felt gut shot.

"You okay, man?" asked Ray. Ray would understand mistakes if anyone would. One had landed him in jail for over a year and another had cost him his best friend's life. Or that was how he saw it, and nothing he or Dylan said could change his mind.

Perceptions. Reality. Was there really a difference?

He glanced to the hall where Amber exited the bathroom, freshly showered, her wet hair leaving a stain on the back of the short sleeveless nightie that must have been Kay's. She glanced at him, scowled and then shut the bedroom door with a little too much force.

"I screwed up again," said Carter.

Ray punched his arm, redirecting his attention. "Look on the bright side. Tomorrow you get another chance to screw things up all over again."

Dylan glanced at his watch. "Already tomorrow."

"I should talk to her," he said.

"Let her rest. Want a beer?" asked Ray.

"Naw. I'm beat. I'm going to hit the sack."

His friends exchanged a look.

"What?" he asked.

"Should I set up a perimeter around Amber's room?" asked Dylan.

Carter made a face and stalked toward the bathroom. It didn't hit him until he was in the shower how bone-weary he really was. He made it to Ray's bedroom, dropped the towel and slipped into bed. Amber's sister had given her an overnight bag as if she were preparing to flee the country. Maybe she was. But the next time she agreed to speak to him, he was going to give her the respect of listening without assuming the worst. He was downright ashamed of himself for doing that before and worse still, for not even recognizing what he had done. Was that why she left? Because he would not listen or understand?

Carter tossed, punched the pillow and finally eased into a restless sleep. He woke often to stare at the glowing red numbers on Ray's bedside clock before finally waking with a start at the gentle rapping on his door. He was shocked to see that the gentle gray light of morning found him still asleep.

"Bro?" That was Jack. He sagged, knowing he was hoping it had been Amber.

"Yeah," he called.

The door creaked open, and Jack's face appeared in the gap.

"Chief Tinnin is on the phone. He says he's got an FBI agent in his office, and one of the two new Feds is Black Mountain Apache." Jack cast Carter one last look. "We have to go in."

AN HOUR LATER Carter and Amber reported to the tribal police station. Amber had been cool and polite this morning. The walls were definitely back in place, and he knew he had been the mason.

At the station, they were introduced to FBI Field Agent Luke Forrest. Jack had told them en route that Forrest was instrumental in busting the crystal meth labs operating on the White Mountain Apache Reservation, but Carter saw another *manzana*. Had to be, because a man working for the FBI could be nothing else.

Carter took Amber's elbow as they entered the squad room, intending to keep her close, but felt her body tense at his touch. Carter sized up Field Agent Luke Forrest. The man's suit fit perfectly, revealing a slim, athletic white lawman with the head of an Apache. He wore his hair short in a military style Carter himself had once favored. But not anymore. He was never going to hide who and what he was at the core.

Chief Tinnin made introductions. Carter regarded Agent Forrest. The FBI had wisely sent the only Apache agent they had to negotiate the transfer of Amber to the US Marshals' protection.

Forrest cast them a confident smile that matched his handshake. His eyes were dark and cold as flint. He nodded to Amber, but his gaze lingered—whether out of appreciation or desire to take her from Turquoise Canyon, Carter wasn't sure. Carter had to hand it to Forrest. The warmth of his smile never wavered.

Carter kept Amber slightly behind him, but Agent Forrest spoke to her first and in English.

As a full-blood Mountain Apache, Forrest had the same genetic roots, but his people and Carter's had been enemies in the Apache Wars. Some things are never forgotten. The Turquoise Canyon Apache were of the Tonto Apache. Not Mountain Apache. Tonto was a name Carter despised because it was given to them by the Spanish and meant either crazy or moron, depending on who you asked. The Tonto Apache's language was different enough that most other Apache tribes could not understand them. They called themselves Dilzhę́'é, but neither their Athabaskan neighbors of Black Mountain nor the US government paid any attention to what they called themselves. Carter shook his head in disgust at the thought of who the US government had sent in as their first choice.

"Ms. Kitcheyan," said Forrest, "Chief Tinnin has told me that you know why I'm here. You are an important witness to the mass slayings in Lilac and, as I understand it, may be able to identify our killer."

Amber nodded.

"Then both you and Mr. Bear Den are key witnesses."

"Don't you have to catch someone before you need witnesses?" asked Jack, placing a hand on his hip to reveal his gold tribal police detective's shield and the pistol holstered at his hip. Carter had questioned Jack's choice to join the tribal police as many of their people saw them as little better than the Arizona highway patrol, working for the establishment instead of the people. But right now, Carter felt lucky.

Forrest kept right on talking as if Detective Bear Den were background noise.

"I know you feel an obligation to see this man and his accomplice brought to justice. I know you lost many friends and colleagues yesterday."

AMBER LACED HER hands before her, but she said nothing. Her stomach churned.

"The attack and the subsequent attempts on your life, one right here on your tribal lands, make it clear to us that you both need protection."

"But I don't want protection," said Amber. "I want to go home."

Even as she said it, she knew her request sounded crazy. She stared at the four men. Tribal Police Chief Wallace Tinnin, Carter Bear Den, Detective Jack Bear Den and FBI Agent Forrest. Her skin went damp as she imagined being caged in a safe house. Trapped with a man she'd once loved before she discovered that he did not trust her. Back then she believed love and trust were one and the same. But they were not, and she could not live without both.

"What if I refuse?" she asked.

Agent Forrest and Chief Tinnin exchanged a look. Agent Forrest got the short stick and faced her with hands open. A trick she used herself to put people at ease. It was a gesture that was intended to speak to the primal brain. *See? I have no weapons.*

"Ms. Kitcheyan, like it or not, you are a federal witness.

You arrived only moments after the shooting at the home of Harvey Ibsen. Later you were abducted by men impersonating federal agents. This seems more than the act of a disturbed mind, Ms. Kitcheyan. We need your help to figure out what happened down there."

"I'm just a receiving clerk."

"And the only surviving member of your department and, apparently, still in danger, judging from the fact that the two men who abducted you yesterday are still at large. And that happened right here in the safety of your reservation. You need protection, Amber."

She set her jaw and tipped her chin down and looked away. Forrest sighed. Then he continued.

"What if one of these men is killed trying to protect you?"

That hit home. She couldn't bear that.

"And if you refuse to cooperate, we will take you into custody."

Carter stepped in. "You can't remove her from our tribal land."

"I can because she is no longer a member of the Turquoise Canyon Tribe. Her membership was rescinded years ago."

Carter's shoulders sank, and Amber braced. It hadn't taken them long to discover her weakness.

"You can't take my brother," said Jack Bear Den.

"True. But we are requesting he accompany us."

"I don't give a flying fart what you are requesting," said Jack.

Carter pressed a hand to his Jack's beefy forearm, and the two brothers shared a long look.

"Carter, no," said Jack.

Carter drew a long breath and let it go. "I'm not leaving her."

Jack stared up at the ceiling and then back at his brother. "She had no trouble leaving you."

Amber felt small and hollow. Brittle as burned paper in the wind. She *had* left him. Saving him from trying to protect her yet again. Perhaps she could do the same today. She believed Carter still had feelings for her and was still trying to solve all her problems. Did he see her as another friend thrown from safety into danger? She prayed she wasn't his chance for redemption. His charity would be worse than his contempt.

It had been so hard to walk away last time. But no worse than marrying a man who did not listen to or trust her. She still didn't know if she had been right to go. It seemed the only way. Maybe she should have tried harder.

She turned to face Carter.

"I don't want you to come," said Amber, her voice soft and low but somehow resonating like a gunshot in the quiet room.

"Well, too damn bad. This time *I* get to choose, and I'm not letting you go alone."

"I need time to think," she said, stalling.

Forrest's expression was sympathetic. "I've read your initial statements, but I have some questions to ask in the examination room with Chief Tinnin before we go. And you are going, Ms. Kitcheyan," said Agent Forrest. "We'll be ready in just a minute."

The men moved to the far side of the squad room. Carter hesitated, lingering a few steps from her, looking back, and then joined the others.

A minute. She pressed both hands to her ears as the screaming voice of her own protests seemed to shriek inside her head like the rushing winds of a winter storm. She was going into protective custody with Carter Bear Den. For how long?

Then she thought of the shooting at her office. Her friends and colleagues. Didn't she have an obligation to help catch this man and then help convict him so he could never do such a thing again?

Forrest said he thought this shooting was more than the act of a disturbed mind. What did that mean? The man must be crazy.

But if he were crazy, then why was he so hard to find? Crazy people were not careful or organized. They were sloppy, impulsive. She certainly knew that. Crazy people were erratic. They might throw a television from its stand for no reason and then walk over broken shards with bare feet. Might fall asleep while driving or forget to pick you up at school. They might throw things at you when angry. Amber lifted a hand to her lip and then forced it down with the memories. The pulsing in her heart ached all the way up to her throat.

Why couldn't they catch the shooter?

Because Agent Forrest was correct. This man wasn't crazy. He was sane, and he was after her. The realization made her sway. Carter left the three men in their discussion and hurried to her.

"Amber, I've got you."

"Don't do this. Let me go."

"You are not getting away from me this time. We have business to settle, and if we have to be locked in protective custody to settle it, that's what we'll do."

Chapter Twelve

A few minutes later, Amber sat facing the closed door in the windowless interrogation room. Chief Tinnin and Forrest sat across from her and had brought her a glass of water. It was the only thing on the surface except for the FBI agent's laptop and a digital tape recorder with a glowing red eye. Recording.

Amber had fought back against the fear, pushing it down deep again. After this interview, they were taking her into custody. She looked at the two armed men and recognized she was already in custody.

Should she call her mother? Her father? She winced at that thought. Her father's words came back like a promise.

Listen, you, I run this family. You do what you're told or else.

Once he had disowned her, leaving had been her only choice. She had not thought he could do anything more to her once she was gone. How wrong she had been. He had still taken one thing more. And now here she sat. Powerless because of that theft.

Forrest looked up from his laptop, fingers poised. "Ready?"

She began where he asked her, before coming to work, and ran through the entire day. Forrest did not interrupt or ask questions as the other two agents yesterday had done. He just listened until she fell silent.

"Could you give me the full names of the men who held you overnight?"

"They didn't hold me."

"Their names?"

Amber closed her mouth and looked away. She was not getting Ray or Dylan in trouble if she could help it.

"Ray Strong. Dylan Tehauno and the Bear Den twins," said Tinnin.

Amber's exhale was audible. Forrest's fingers tapped away on his laptop. Then he fixed those light brown eyes on her.

"Is there any reason that you can think of that your department might be targeted?"

That was the question Carter had asked her.

"Do crazy people need to have a reason?"

"Always."

"Maybe it was just random." Her churning stomach said otherwise.

"Doesn't appear random. Targeted and very specific."

"Targeted," said Amber. "Because he killed everyone at my office and then went after my supervisor."

"And then tried to kill you. Two attempts," said Forrest.

That assertion made her flesh crawl, and she rubbed her hands up and down her arms.

"Those guys yesterday were different men. I would have recognized the man who came after me in Lilac."

"Yes." He flipped through his notes. "But what about the driver at Lilac. The guy with the blond hair and ball cap. Could that have been a wig?"

She thought back at the straw-like hair poking out from the cap.

"I only saw him for a second."

"And the driver in the glasses. You said he looked familiar. Same guy?"

She tried to think. "I'm not sure."

"But you saw him before?"

"Somewhere. Yes, I think so."

Forrest pushed aside his laptop and leaned toward her. "Amber, what has been going on in your office? Has there been anything unusual?"

She shook her head, not wanting to take this road with him. It was too terrible.

"I don't know."

"You were there when they shot Ibsen. What did you see?"

"I didn't see anything. I was outside his house."

"Did you hear anything?"

"Shots."

"Anything else?"

The question jarred her back. She had been standing before his home, her keys in her hand. She'd heard Ibsen.

I told you everything. I reported it, for God's sake. I told you we had a problem.

"Yes," she whispered. "My boss. He was shouting. He said he reported the problem."

"What did he say exactly?" asked Forrest.

"'I reported it. Told you there was a problem,'" she said, her eyes fixed on the field agent as the room seemed to spin.

"What problem, Amber?"

"I don't know."

"Think. Some detail that might be dangerous to someone."

"Yes, I…" She needed to remember. "I found something. An error on a delivery."

Forrest's eyes glittered like a hawk sighting prey. "When?"

"Monday's delivery. I brought the packing slip to…" She pressed her hand to her mouth as she seemed to hear her boss's voice begging for his life. The problem. Was it her? She squeezed her eyes shut and then forced her hand away from her mouth and continued. "I brought it to Harvey Ibsen's attention Monday afternoon. I thought he'd want to check the shipment Tuesday, but…" She shook her head. "But he… But…" Her gaze shifted as she stretched back to Monday. He'd hurried her out of his office before she even had time to point out the error. She had considered going back in his office, but he'd been on the phone. Then Tuesday morning he'd been ill. Or said he was ill.

"But what, Amber?"

"But he was sick. Right after I told him that I noticed that the slip and the shipments didn't match. I brought it to him, and he said he'd handle it."

"When?"

"Monday." She pressed both hands to her cheeks.

"The day before the shooting," Forrest clarified. "That Monday?"

She looked at him with widening eyes. "Was it me? Did I cause this?"

Forrest's alert stare gave her no comfort.

"What happened Monday?" he asked.

"I give the packing slip to Nancy once I've checked it. But usually that's after it's already unloaded by our guys. They put the boxes away, and I count the contents. You know. That's what I do."

"How was this different?"

"I met the truck because Mr. Ibsen was unavailable."

"What was the error you spotted?"

"I just check in the shipments. That's it. Ten boxes of this. Four cartons of that. But Ibsen wasn't there to talk to the driver this time. He gave me the PO to sign. I'm not allowed to do that. So I made the driver wait and took it to Mr. Ibsen. On the way I saw that the two didn't match."

"The purchase order and the packing slip?" asked Forrest.

"That's right. I told Mr. Ibsen, and he…seemed anxious, took both the PO and packing slip before I could even explain what the problem was and told me to get back to work. So I did."

Ibsen had escorted her from his office, and she had gone. But she'd stopped before his open door, thinking she had not shown him the actual overage. She'd lingered there, trying to decide if she should go back in there, so she had heard him place a call and ask for a Mr. Theron Wrangler. He'd paused and then told someone it was urgent and to have Wrangler call him ASAP. An instant later, Ibsen had appeared at his office door, spotted her loitering and turned purple, shouting at her to get back to work.

"What was the problem?" asked Forrest. "They didn't match? Were things missing?"

"No, a surplus. More in the delivery than in the purchase order."

"What was in the order?" asked Forrest.

"Blasting material mostly. Chemicals, and I don't know exactly." Amber's throat went dry as implications she had not considered came to her like a blast in the copper mine. *Explosives.* More delivered than checked in. What was happening to the extra? She wasn't in charge of inventory. That was Ibsen's job.

Amber sat back in her chair, staring out with sightless eyes as she remembered the exchange and how Harvey had kept wiping his mouth with the palm of his hand.

"But you saw the discrepancy. How much and of what, exactly?"

She told him the chemicals and supplies that she recalled and the quantities on both slips. Agent Forrest sat back in his chair.

"Are you familiar with an organization called BEAR?"

Tinnin's glance shot from Forrest to her, and she thought that the chief had heard of BEAR. The chief shifted, and a finger went under the collar of his shirt.

"Or one named WOLF?" asked Forrest.

"The agents who questioned me yesterday mentioned them. I didn't know them. I've asked about them since."

She frowned, trying to understand what this had to do with the shooting.

"Amber, your father is a member of PAN. So is your uncle Kenshaw Little Falcon."

"Lots of people are. PAN—Protecting All Nature. They're pacifists. I even joined the rally to save Mesa Summit when I was a freshmen at Turquoise Canyon High."

"Yes, I know."

She frowned. "It's an environmental organization. Preserving wild places and protecting habitats."

Forrest looked skeptical. She was at a loss as to what he wanted from her.

"PAN has ties to both WOLF and BEAR. Those are ecoterrorist groups. Radical branches of PAN."

She met his hawkish eyes. "I don't understand. Were they protesting the mine?" It wouldn't be the first time. Her mother had told her how upset her father had been at learning the name of her latest employer.

Her skin tingled, and her ears buzzed. This didn't seem real. She shook her head in denial.

It wasn't a mistake—none of it.

The explosives, she thought. Where were they? Who had them?

Forrest's phone buzzed. He retrieved the mobile and glanced at the screen. Then he closed his laptop.

"Transport is ready," he said.

Chapter Thirteen

Amber did not get a chance to speak to Carter when she left the interrogation room. They ate lunch separately, as he was in the midst of being questioned.

Finally, as the afternoon gave way to evening and the sun cast the mountains in hard angles of blue and pink, they were transported in a van, with tribal and federal escort vehicles, off the reservation to a hotel suite where they would stay until the following morning when they would be transferred to the custody of US Marshals.

Agent Forrest introduced the FBI agents, Rose and Decker, who would be protecting them, and then left to continue the search for the shooter and accomplices. Amber shook hands with their babysitters. Both had similar suits, sidearms, precision haircuts, hawkish eyes and clean-shaven jaws. But there were differences. Rose's hair was two shades lighter brown than Decker's and, while Decker had the lean body of a runner, Rose was shorter and broader across the chest.

They were marched to the elevator and rode to the top floor, six, and then marched down a garish carpet to their suite. There was an outer door. Beyond lay an alcove and two more doors. They were admitted to the first by key card. Amber found a small kitchenette with tile floor and a table with two chairs.

The FBI agents followed, and the room became small with five of them crowded in an awkward circle.

Forrest gave final instructions and said his farewells. The door clicked shut behind them, and Amber's skin began to itch. It was as if the walls were closing in around her.

Decker took a seat on the couch and opened his laptop. Rose stepped out after Forrest, presumably to take a position in the hall.

She blinked at Carter. "Want to pick a bedroom?"

The thought of Carter and bedrooms made her insides turn to goo. Her energy, which had dwindled, made a rapid return, causing her to tingle in all the wrong places.

She swallowed in disgust and gave herself a silent talking-to. This man had come to protect her. She appreciated it but agreed with his twin. Carter should have stayed on the reservation. And nothing had changed between them. She passed him and his outstretched arm and headed out of the kitchenette and she discovered another sitting room with long red couch and recliner facing a large flat-screen television.

Carter paused behind her. "All the movies we can watch."

Sitting beside Carter on that wide couch watching movies did not sound like a very good idea. Just being alone with him made her entire body twitch. The last time they'd been in a hotel together they had not been there to watch TV. She reined herself in.

They both explored the two bedrooms on opposite sides of the sitting room finding mirror images right down to the still-life prints of Acoma pottery on the wall. She dropped the small duffel Kay had packed on the king-size bed, claiming the second bedroom.

"I'm starving. You want anything?" he asked.

Amber shook her head. How could he think of food right now?

"You have to be hungry."

She was, and that annoyed her, as well.

"We can't leave," she reminded him, as if he had not been listening. Though, if she were inclined to run, now would be the time. She weighed her need for escape against her need to stay alive.

"I'll order something. One of Forrest's guys will pick it up."

"Fine."

Carter left for the kitchen, returning with a three-ring notebook holding an assortment of take-out menus to find Amber now in the living area. Carter flipped back and forth.

While he studied the menus, she studied him. His brother Jack had advised him against leaving the reservation, but he'd ignored him.

"Why didn't you listen to Jack?" she asked.

He lowered the binder and met her gaze.

"Because I want you safe."

"Why?"

He shrugged. "They say old feelings die hard."

She thought of his feelings for her. Not respect. Certainly not trust.

"What do you think love is, Carter?" she asked.

His brows came together, forming a hard line between them.

"Caring for someone else more than for yourself," he said. "Protecting them."

"I think it is about trust. Trusting another person with your vulnerabilities and your fears. Believing that person and believing *in* that person. Listening to them."

Now his brow wrinkled, and he cocked his head.

"I listen," he said.

"Do you?"

"Yes, and I forgive you for leaving the tribe, Amber."

She stood and stepped past him. She had cleared her bedroom door and had a hand on the knob when he called to her.

"Amber, please. Come back."

Instead she closed the door between them.

Amber lay on the pristine coverlet and tried to rest, but she was so angry at Carter.

He forgave her.

She could walk right back in there and explain everything to him. But she wouldn't. She was doubly infuriated that he would forgive her for something she would never do and that he could ever believe she would give up her membership in her tribe in the first place. Did he know her so little that he would believe she would voluntarily relinquish who she was? Clearly, he did because he had accepted her father's word and believed him without even speaking about it with the woman he claimed to love. This entire thing only made it more apparent why she couldn't be with him. He didn't know her or trust her.

So why did she want him still?

There was a gentle knock on her door. She squeezed her eyes shut, then cleared her throat, but the lump remained firmly lodged in place.

"Come in."

The door eased open, and Carter peeked inside. The sky had gone dark, and she must have seemed just an outline on the wide white bedspread.

"I ordered something."

"Thank you."

"Can I come in?"

It was a bad idea. She rolled to her side and pushed the button that illuminated the bedside lamp. Then she motioned him in. He sat beside her on the bed, sagging as if exhausted.

She felt pity then. He'd left their people to help her, and she had sniped at him.

"I'm sorry, Amber. I just don't understand what I did."

And to explain it was to have to ask for what should be hers by right. If he loved her, the respect and trust were just branches of the same tree.

"I know."

"Can we talk while we're waiting for dinner?" he asked.

"Sure."

She pushed up to an elbow and rested a hand on his shoulder. Amber had meant the touch to be comforting, but even through the fabric of his soft cotton shirt the heat scorched her, and the tingling tension jolted up her nerves like a pulse of electricity. She glanced up to see Carter's complete stillness. The muscles beneath her hand bunched as he turned to look down at her. His Adam's apple bobbed, and his tongue dipped to drag back and forth along his lower lip.

The action sent a quick-fire explosion through her body. Her skin tingled, and her heart thudded. This, at least, had never changed between them. She still wanted him, and the need was growing unbearable.

He assessed her, his eyes dipping to take a leisurely perusal of her body. She felt his glance as a physical thing. Her stomach muscles tightened, and she lifted to an extended arm, drawn closer by her need and this desire.

This was bad.

Carter brushed the loose wisps of hair from her face. Then lifted her chin between his thumb and curved index finger. His hand was warm and his grip steady.

He dipped, angling his head for a kiss, and she lifted her chin to meet him. Their mouths pressed together. This was no gentle coaxing seduction. This kiss felt different in every way. It was powerful and possessive. Her mind went cloudy as her resistance dissolved like honey in hot water.

She pressed forward, falling against him, her breasts tingling with the contact of the hard muscle of his chest as strong arms enfolded her.

He broke the kiss and held her. She lifted her arms to hold him, too.

They had been through so much together in the past and in the last three days.

"You still taste like mint," he whispered and nipped her ear.

She shivered with pleasure and raked her fingers over his back. From the hall, she heard a beep, and Carter set her aside. The outer door clicked, and the two agents spoke. The Anglo agent was back.

A moment later Rose stood in her open door, holding a large paper bag as he peered into the dark room "Dinner is here. You two want to eat out here or in the kitchen?" asked Rose.

"Living room," she replied.

Amber wondered if her mouth looked as puffy as it felt. It had been a while since anyone had kissed her like that.

"You two all right?" asked Rose.

"Yeah. Coming." Carter stood and offered a hand. Amber flushed and accepted it, allowing him to guide her from the bed, but she glanced back and wondered. The object of her hunger had changed from food to the man guiding her along.

Rose left them with the two bags that contained dinner, which Carter unpacked. Amber settled in the chair, and Carter took the couch. Carter offered a prayer of thanks before they ate, and she added her own. The food was Thai and better than she expected.

"What will happen now?" she asked.

"You mean after dinner?"

She tried for a smile, but the worry ate her up. Carter gave her his best guess on what the police and FBI were doing. He could not tell her how long they would be caged up.

"Will I have to go back to Lilac?" she asked.

He pressed his enticing mouth together and shook his head.

"I doubt it."

"I'm a suspect, right?"

"Did you do anything wrong?" he asked.

"I did not. But they asked me about organizations called BEAR and WOLF."

Carter set aside his noodle dish.

"Do you know them?" she asked.

"One of them." He looked worried. "WOLF stands for the *Warriors Of Land Forever*. They'd be interested in a pit mine. That group damages property, spiking trees marked for logging. That kind of thing. Might attack anything that invades wild places."

That didn't sound good.

"What about BEAR?"

"Never heard of them." He returned his attention to his plate, but he seemed distracted now.

"They knew I'd been at a PAN protest." She ate more of the jasmine rice and mixed veggies, having already devoured all the chicken. "Should I be worried?"

He didn't say no. She set aside her plate, her appetite spoiled. He offered her some of his, and she declined.

"Should I ask for a lawyer?" she asked, already wondering where and how to locate someone.

"You haven't been arrested or charged. You're in custody as a witness. Right now you just need to rest and eat." He motioned to her half-eaten supper.

She nodded her acceptance.

Rose stepped into the doorway. "Everything come out all right?"

"Like having a butler," she murmured in Apache.

"Until you try to leave," said Carter.

"You two need anything else?" asked the agent.

"Books," said Amber.

"Music," said Carter.

Rose nodded, reversed course and disappeared through the doorway.

"Would they tell us if they caught them?" she asked.

Carter finished his meal and sat back. "Yes. I think they would."

"So they haven't even caught the shooter. It's been days."

"They will. FBI. State police, sheriffs and local police are all on it."

"What if they don't?"

He gave her a long look, and she wondered if he understood. She was the target. What if they couldn't find the men trying to kill her?

"I can't stay here forever."

"Be patient. We both need some rest. Tomorrow things will be better."

CARTER WISHED AMBER would eat a little more. He also wished there was more he could do to assure her, but honestly he could not fathom how the gunman had evaded the police this long.

He found himself staring at her mouth, recalling their kiss, and had to shake himself back to attention.

He ignored the thrumming need that she stirred inside him as he collected the leftovers. They both carried the packaging out to the kitchen and returned to the living area couch.

Sated by food, a more insistent hunger continued to gnaw at him.

"Want to watch TV?" he asked.

She shook her head. "I'm afraid of the scroll bar. I don't

want to see the body count or, worse, video footage of the Lilac Mine."

Their gazes met, and the pulsing ache that had been in his chest moved south.

"You're staring at me." She used one finger to trace the outline of the scar on her lip. "It's this, isn't it?"

"I'll admit being attracted to your mouth forever, but I was wondering about that scar. You had it when you visited me when I was recuperating. But not before that. What happened?"

She flushed, her gaze dropped to her lap, and she closed her eyes. "Finally the right question," she whispered.

"What?"

"You didn't ask me how I cut it or what I did. You asked me what happened."

"Yes."

Amber pressed her lips together, making the scar turn from pink to white.

"My dad did this the day he disowned me."

Fury surged. Her father did that? He shook his head, wanting to deny it, knowing he couldn't. It took a moment to find his voice; he was so stunned at her revelation.

"He told me you left."

"I know. What I never understood was why you believed him."

He tried to catch up.

"Why didn't you tell me?"

"I did. I went to you the minute I found out about the credit fraud, and you told me that everything I owned was his."

He had said that, hadn't he?

"Then you told me to go home and that you'd take care of everything."

"I would have," he said.

"No. Some things you can't fix. Sometimes you just

have to listen and believe that the one you love knows what she is talking about."

"But you…" He checked himself at the narrowing of her eyes. He had been about to say that she had broken the engagement and follow that by reminding her that she had left them all. But he saw something in that cold, impassive stare, some warning that he was about to make another mistake. He couldn't afford to lose her again.

"Nine years. You've been gone nine years."

"Yes."

"And I never understood why."

"So ask me."

Now his eyes narrowed. "I did ask you."

"No, you asked me why I rescinded my membership in the tribe. Why I broke our engagement and why I left you." She fingered the scar. "You asked me *why* I did things. You never asked me what happened. Not once."

"I know what happened."

"Do you? Or do you only know one side of a story?"

Her father's side. Now he understood what she meant. Her father had come to him first. Explained things, and he had accepted Manny Kitcheyan's word out of respect. Had that tainted his objectivity? For a minute it felt like his first jump from an airplane, as the world rushed closer and his stomach pressed up where his lungs should be. Had he done that to her?

He sat back on the couch, his hand pressed over his mouth as he stared. Finally he dragged his hand away and squeeze it into a fist.

"Amber, are you telling me you left because I asked the wrong question?"

"Yes."

He shifted to face her and hesitated. "What happened, Amber?"

Amber moved to sit beside Carter on the couch. He

knew that what she was about to say was important and so he struggled to listen. But inside his head a voice was screaming, *the wrong question. All this time and she left because I asked the wrong question.*

He kept his face impassive, but inside a tempest swirled. He feared the power of the storm. She folded an ankle under her thigh and turned so that she sat sideways to face him.

"My father was there before me. Wasn't he?"

Carter nodded, not trusting his voice.

"I'm sure he told you I was making a big thing out of nothing."

"It was just a truck, Amber."

"No. Not just."

His impulse was to remind her that he had offered to pay for the damned thing, but instead, he kept his mouth shut. Her father's new red truck. The one that overextended the family budget and triggered the fight between him and Amber. He recalled the day she'd come to him and said she wanted to get married right that very minute. He had laughed, not realizing how serious she had been. He'd tried to send her home to apologize, to finish high school and start community college. When he told her he'd already given her father the signing bonus she went crazy and said she was going to the police.

He recalled exactly what he had said then. *As long as we're engaged, I am a part of this family.*

She had removed his ring, held it out to him. "I won't marry you."

"Don't be silly. You're not serious."

"Will you change your mind about the signing bonus?" she asked.

He narrowed his eyes. "No."

She offered his ring.

"This is childish, Amber."

"Childish?" She offered the ring. "Take it."

"No."

Carter swallowed, met her steady gaze. "Was it because I called you childish?"

"Partly. You wouldn't listen. Had already made up your mind what to do without consulting me. I could see it then. Going from my father's control to yours. You even said to me that I would be theirs until we married, and then I'd be yours."

He blinked at her. "So what did your father do that was so terrible?"

She pressed her lips together, making the scar turn from pink to white.

"My dad did this the day I left. Threw a beer bottle at me."

A cold knife blade of dread pierced his heart. He gently held her chin, turning her head from side to side as he looked at the tiny white crescent. Now he recognized the pressure cut of her tooth where it had sliced through the soft tissue of her upper lip.

"I didn't know he hit you," said Carter.

"He never did. And this was the only time he did something like this. But what else he did was worse."

Carter released her jaw and braced for the truth that he would not even consider when he was a young man.

"Tell me," he said.

And she did. She told him about the debt her father accumulated by gambling and buying things they did not need. About how, with her parents' credit in shambles, he had turned to his daughters' and stolen their identity.

"It was nearly seventy thousand dollars when I found out."

When she had gone to him about the money for the truck, she should have made him understand. Or was it that he should have listened instead of dismissing her concerns?

"He stole from me and Kay and Ellie. Ellie was eleven years old, and he charged thirteen thousand dollars in her name."

"You should have told me."

"I told you. I said he stole from us. That he had credit cards in our names. You told me to go back home and smooth things over, apologize and let you handle it. You patted me on the head. I had to go to the tribal police. Do you know what they said?"

He shook his head.

"Two choices. Either I accepted the debt as my own, or I filed charges against my father for identity theft. Then they would press charges, and he would be arrested and serve jail time."

"Or declare bankruptcy?"

"Seventeen-year-olds can't do that. I am still angry at my father, but he is my father. I could not have him arrested, embarrassed before everyone he knows. So I shut down all lines of credit. A man in Darabee with credit counseling helped me. But I couldn't restructure the debt until I was eighteen, and no one would give me a loan."

"You took this all on yourself?" Carter's stomach ached from the thought of her carrying this burden. Her eyes showed the betrayal she felt from her father, from him.

"Yes. Eventually it went to debt collectors. That's why I don't carry a mobile phone. They call all the time, and they are so terrible. I've been settling the balances bit by bit. But when my dad learned what I did—" she tapped her upper lip "—he gave me this and threw me out."

"You should have…" He stopped. She had come to him, twice. He'd sent her back home.

"I wish you had told me what he did."

"I didn't know how bad it was yet. Then you went to basic, and I got a bill from a credit card company. This had been going on for years."

"I didn't understand."

"I don't know if this makes any sense, but I wanted to protect my father, and I wanted to protect you."

"I loved you then, Amber. I would have done anything for you."

"Except what I needed most. I wasn't a child, then, and I wasn't willing to be a wife of a man who treated me like one."

"I tried to solve it."

"I never asked you to. But I did ask you to listen. To trust me. Believe that if I said it was important, then it was important."

He met her gaze, seeing the glimmer of eyes filling with tears. They fell from her lower lids, dropping all the way to her lap.

He took her hand and squeezed. "Amber, please…I'm so sorry."

She smiled as the tears continued to fall. "I'm so glad."

He had another apology to make. Amber had come back to see him once, when he'd been home recovering from his injuries. She'd met him on his parents' porch on a sunny August day when his arm was still bandaged.

"Amber, about that day in August when you came to see me."

She drew her hand away and used it to wiped at her eyes, which filled up almost instantly.

"Yeager had been captured. They took him in May. We got notification of a proof of life video that December. It was terrible. We all felt so guilty for leaving him."

"You couldn't get to him," she said.

He made a face. "Anyway, Jack was a tribal police patrolman then. He told me you relinquished your membership, and it made me so mad. But now…" Now he wasn't certain. He no longer trusted what he had heard.

He stared at her, so familiar and yet now a stranger.

She was so beautiful, even in grief. Had he misjudged her twice? "Amber, what happened?"

"My dad again. I didn't even know until you told me. I thought it was a mistake. But when I went home, my mother admitted what he had done, withdrawn his oldest child from our tribe. He did that on the day he disowned me."

"You didn't leave?"

She shook her head. "They're my people."

Her father had stolen her identity in more ways than one.

"We have to fix this," he said.

"Why? I'm going to be in protective custody."

"That's temporary," he said.

She drew a long breath. "Maybe."

Carter stood. "I have to call Jack."

Chapter Fourteen

Carter had to speak to the FBI before using his mobile, but they allowed him to call his brother. It was a sharp reminder of what he'd be facing when he went with Amber tomorrow. He'd be cut off from his family and his tribe. But Amber's safety now seemed more important than all that.

He asked his brother to look into the tribe's policy for reestablishing membership because he thought he'd seen something on their website about minor children. His brother promised to check.

Jack relayed some news about the case. The shooter and driver were still at large, but they now knew how the inside man had gained access to the Lilac administration building.

"I want to see you tomorrow morning," said Jack.

Carter knew it might be his last contact with anyone in his family until after the killers were apprehended. He thought about his mom and dad and brothers all at that dinner the night the tribe had kept them safe. His throat constricted.

"Yeah. I'd like that."

"I'll bring you some of your stuff. See you tomorrow, brother."

Carter gave the phone to Agent Rose and returned to Amber, finding her staring blankly at the television which was still off. He had the job of telling Amber that the inside man had used a stolen security key card from one of the Lilac Mine employees to gain access to her building. She stared at him wide-eyed as he told her of the development in the case.

"But how did he get Ann-Marie's card?" Her hands went to her mouth, and she spoke from behind them. "She's not involved in this. Is she?"

"She didn't do anything wrong," he said.

Amber blew out a breath, and he hated that he had to tell her the rest.

"But whoever stole her card also killed her."

Her eyes filled with tears as she shook her head in denial. "Killed her? But…but he didn't need to kill her. He could have just tied her up or…" The sobs stopped the rest.

Carter pulled her close.

Amber met his gaze as she struggled to speak past the flood of tears. "She saw his face. Just like us."

Now her hands covered her eyes as she rocked back and forth against him.

Carter drew her into his lap, and her tears soaked the collar of his shirt.

"I'll keep you safe, Amber. I swear I will."

She clung, and he stroked her head and rubbed her back. At last, her tears stopped, and her breathing changed. He rocked her like a child as she fell asleep and then gently carried her to bed. She woke as he tucked her legs beneath the coverlet.

"What time is it?" she asked.

"After midnight."

"Tomorrow already," she muttered.

"Yes."

"Taking us tomorrow." Her words were slurred as she fought the sleep that held her.

He stood over her for a moment, wishing he could stay with her.

"Carter?"

"Yes?"

She pushed over on the mattress and lay an open hand beside her. Amber's eyes remained half closed as she cast him a sultry look. But it was exhaustion, he knew. Not flirtation, so he reined in his roaring need.

"Could you hold me for a while?"

Carter hesitated at her request. "I don't think that's such a great idea."

"Just a few minutes. Please?"

She didn't want him in the way he wanted her. But perhaps she forgave him for not understanding how to correctly honor a wife. He sat on the edge of her bed.

"I'm here," he said.

He glanced at the open door and the light spilling across the industrial carpet. Then he thought of the agents in the other room.

She slid under the covers and across to the middle of the gigantic bed. Carter eased down beside her, already regretting his decision.

Amber rolled to her side and snuggled up against him, cuddling his biceps so that his muscle rested against the soft pillow of her breasts. He exhaled through his teeth and squeezed his eyes shut, thankful for the relentless air-conditioning that cooled his fevered skin. But not the longing. That burned too hot. She was different than all women since—and not just because she was his first. She was also his only, at least in his heart. There had been others since she'd left him. He'd tried and failed to move on. But he never could. Now he understood why. None of them were Amber.

"Thank you," she whispered.

"Just until you fall asleep. Okay?" After that he would need some alone time and a shower.

"'Kay," she breathed on a sigh.

Her grip eased and her mouth parted.

Carter laced his fingers together across his stomach and concentrated on his breathing. Amber rolled to her back. He saw his chance and took it, easing off the mattress.

He stood at her bedside, thinking of all the days and nights they had missed and wanting a second chance. They were different people now. His feelings for her were strong but tangled like fishing line on a low branch. He didn't know how to untie the knots. She had wanted him to have faith in her. Instead he had diminished all her concerns. He hadn't taken them, or her, seriously. What an ass he had been. But was he willing to open himself up to that kind of hurt again?

She'd left him once. She could do it again, and just like last time he wouldn't understand, couldn't understand. If she loved him, she would have stayed.

He returned to his room. He would protect her. But he wasn't going to give her his heart—not again.

CARTER DID NOT sleep well and was on his second cup of coffee when Detective Jack Bear Den was admitted to their suite the following morning.

Jack wore his usual work attire: boots, jeans, shirt and a blazer. He removed his white cowboy hat, and the brothers exchanged a hug. When they parted, Jack handed over the document Carter had requested.

"Signed by her parents. Just as you suspected."

Carter glanced over the copy of the notarized document that Amber had not signed. Joy mingled with dismay to find exactly what Amber had told him. He should have known this without the proof. Should have believed in her.

"What a jerk," he muttered.

"Yeah, he is," agreed Jack, clearly thinking of Amber's father, Manny. Somehow what Carter had done felt worse.

Amber would no more give up her heritage than he would. Carter's head hung in shame. She'd been protecting her parents at her expense.

Carter looked at her father's signature and knew that Manny Kitcheyan had done this out of malice. To punish his daughter for thwarting him.

Jack pointed to the paper. "She was supposed to sign it because she was over fifteen. Don't know how that slipped by because her birthday is right on the form."

Carter said a silent prayer. "Does that mean she can overturn it?"

"She can, and she doesn't need to mention what her father did, though why she wouldn't, I do not know."

"How?" asked Carter.

Jack reached in his breast pocket and retrieved a folded page. Then he read the pertinent section aloud.

"'Relinquishment of a Minor Child: In the case of a minor child under the age of eighteen years, the relinquishment statement must be signed by the guardian or both parents. If an enrolled member over eighteen years of age relinquishes membership…' Hold on, not that part." Jack scanned. "Here. 'However, if the enrolled member was under eighteen years of age at the time of relinquishment, said person may reapply for enrollment upon reaching the age of eighteen.'" Jack lifted his gaze in triumph. "She's in if she wants in."

Carter hugged him. Jack thumped his back and then drew away to hand over the two pages.

Jack's smile wavered, and his jaw ticking revealed that he had something more.

He turned to Carter and motioned with his head for him to follow. Carter excused them and trailed Jack to the living area.

Jack paused just inside the doorway and faced Carter. He toyed with the turquoise ring on his middle finger, twisting it from side to side. "First, Dylan and Ray checked in. They saw our shaman. He says he sent you because he wanted you and Amber to have a chance to reconcile. Said it was your destinies."

Carter's brow furrowed. "What about the timing?"

Jack shrugged. "He's saying coincidence."

Carter made a face. "You buy that?"

Jack shook his head. "Million to one. Listen, Tinnin told me to tell you that the US Marshals are taking custody of you and Amber around nine."

Carter glanced at the clock on the DVD player. It was just past seven in the morning.

The brothers exchanged a long, silent look. Carter's breathing picked up with his heart rate. Jack's face was paler than he'd ever seen it.

"Best guess?" asked Carter.

Jack shook his head and swallowed. "When they catch him and they will, we will know better. If he's working alone, you'll be released."

"If he's not working alone?" Carter knew the drill, but still he wanted Jack to say it. To know in his heart that his world was really tipping.

"If those guys were sent here, as hit men on an assignment, it gets more complicated. They have to be sure that you are not at risk. If there is reason to think your lives are in danger, they'll offer you witness protection."

The words hit him like a blunt cleaver, making him wince. "I'd be gone for good."

Jack nodded. "If you take it. You can demand to be returned to the tribe, or I can take you out right now."

"What about Amber?"

"Once she's reinstated, she could do the same." Jack

reached into his back pocket and handed over more documents. "Here's all she needs. A petition to reinstate."

"How long does this take?"

"Council meets every week." Jack twisted the ring all the way around his finger. "But you'll be in custody then. You still going with her?"

Carter said nothing, but Jack's expression told him that his brother knew his mind. His mournful look broke Carter's control. He rested a hand on Jack's shoulder. They no longer had the time he had expected. The years and years. With Amber's life in jeopardy and his, too, as her protector, Carter recognized that he might not always be here for Jack. He'd turned Jack down flat when he had first made his appeal. But what if Carter wasn't here to help him? Jack could go to Tommy or Kurt, he supposed, but it had been hard for Jack to ask him and they were twins. To ask his kid brothers would be even tougher. Carter felt in his heart that if he didn't do this, Jack would never get his answers. Never know the truth.

Carter switched to Apache. "You remember what you asked me? About the sibling test?"

A while back, Jack had wondered if Carter would be willing to take a DNA test that would show if they shared both parents. It was a way around asking Mom flat out if Jack had a different father.

"I remember."

"I'll take the test."

Jack nodded.

"Bring it soon."

Jack glanced back at the FBI agent who now stood in the doorway watching them, perhaps curious that they spoke in the language of their birth. Then he turned back to Carter.

"I did ask Mom about…you know."

Carter's eyes widened.

"What'd she say?"

"She said that she had never been with a man other than her husband."

Carter wanted to feel reassured, but Jack's gray eyes dared him to ignore what was staring him in the face. Jack's blood type, his skin tone, his wavy hair and the sheer size of him all told a different tale. In their youth, Carter had fought anyone who said Jack wasn't his brother. But in his heart the doubt grew.

"That means Mom is either a liar or I'm crazy," said Jack.

"Yeah. You believe her?" asked Carter.

"If I did, I wouldn't have asked you to take the sibling test."

Carter heard the shower turn on and glanced toward Amber's room. Had her sleep been as fitful as his?

He faced his brother and asked him if he'd ever heard of a group called BEAR. Jack had not but promised to check into it.

Jack tugged on his hat and then aimed a finger at the agent who was tall but not a male mountain like Jack. "You take care of my brother."

Chapter Fifteen

When Amber emerged from her bedroom in Kay's nightie and the hotel's plush terry-cloth robe, she found Carter at the door holding out a ceramic mug brimming with dark black coffee. She smiled in gratitude.

She tried to ignore the V of bronze male flesh revealed by his gaping cotton shirt when he extended his arm. Their fingers brushed in the exchange. Her reaction to his touch was harder to ignore. Her stomach twitched, and her eyes flashed to his. His brow quirked, and her face went hot. Carter cleared his throat.

"You slipped out last night," she said, cradling the cup.

"I said I would."

She smiled and inhaled the aroma of coffee.

"Jack stopped in. He said the marshals will be here soon."

She sipped the coffee. "Did he ask you to go with him?"

Carter rubbed his neck, and she had her answer.

"I'm not your responsibility anymore, you know?"

"I do know that." He didn't sound happy about it. "I need to see you through this, Amber."

"For old times' sake?"

He held her gaze as he gave his head a slow shake. "For now. Protecting you, I just have to. Not because you're a child or you aren't capable, but these are bad people, Amber. Really bad. Don't ask me to go."

She shook her head. "I won't. But I don't want you hurt because of me."

"I'm staying, Amber. Maybe we can figure this out together."

Did he mean what was happening or what was happening between them? Her heart accelerated as hope crept in. She took another sip of coffee. Carter twisted his fist into the palm of his opposite hand. It was a gesture she was becoming familiar with.

"I don't know how long they'll keep me. But I do know that, except for your time in the marines, you've lived in Turquoise Canyon your entire life. Your family is here. Your friends. Medicine society and your job. Everything you know. I don't want you to lose them because of me."

"I can understand that. But it won't be forever. Just until they catch these guys."

She wasn't sure. If these men who were after her were a part of a larger organization, WOLF or BEAR, then even if the FBI caught them, she might be in danger of retaliation. Certainly the authorities would keep her until the trial. That could be a long time.

She hung her head and let her hair fall over her face. What was she doing to him? She should tell him to go. But she couldn't.

Oh, no, she thought, not again. She was not going to fall in love with him again.

He brushed her hair back and lifted her chin with an index finger.

"You're lucky, Carter, to have people to come home to."

He cast her a sad smile that twisted her heart.

"I couldn't imagine a home where a parent would act like yours."

Her face and neck went hot. "It's shameful."

Carter locked his jaw, biting down until his jaw muscles pulsed. He was so angry at her father, her charming father who had glossed over all his failings and convinced Carter that Amber was just overreacting. She'd been more generous than he would have been, working nearly a decade to pay off her father's debts. She'd dropped out of school and even lost the chance to attend college.

"He should be in jail," said Carter.

She glanced at him. "Could you have sent your father to prison?"

He gave a tight shake of his head. They understood each other again. It felt strange. He tamped down the hope building inside him. She needed his protection. Had asked for nothing more. He'd made mistakes in the past, ones she found unforgivable and that he had not even known he had made. He didn't want to disappoint her again. But more than that, he didn't want her to leave him.

Agent Decker appeared in the doorway. "US Marshals are ten minutes out. Ms. Kitcheyan, get dressed, please."

Amber nodded.

Carter stroked her cheek. "We'll talk later."

She hoped so. Amber headed to her bathroom to change. A few minutes later she emerged, wearing her sister's clothes. Kay had packed her skinny blue jeans and a gauzy white cotton blouse and a long gold-tone chain with clear crystals set every six inches or so. Kay's favorite, she knew. Her feet were clad in a stylish pair of walking shoes. She left off the denim jacket for now. Kay had remembered some bathroom items, but the only cosmetics were a pink lip gloss and citrus body spray. Amber used both. She tucked the lip gloss in a tight front pocket. Kay had included a dark blue wristlet with a gold clasp that Amber recognized had once belonged to Ellie. Amber fingered the pretty necklace and then touched the jeweled snap on the bag. Something from both of them. Amber smiled as her heart ached.

She told herself that she was not going to cry again. But when would she see her sisters again?

There was a knock at her door. She looped her hand through the wristlet, which was empty except for the body spray. Then she shouldered the small duffel.

"Coming."

She stepped from the room to find Carter waiting. He had braided his hair in one thick rope down his back. His shirt was a white oxford that was open at the collar to reveal a medicine bundle he had not been wearing earlier. Had Jack brought that in the bag he had given Carter yesterday?

His jeans included a brown leather belt with a turquoise buckle she knew Jack had been wearing yesterday. On his feet were hiking boots that looked well-worn. In his hand he held his overnight bag.

She pointed to the buckle. "Jack's?"

He nodded.

She lifted the necklace and then her wrist to show the bag. "Kay and Ellie."

"They're worried," he said.

With good reason, she thought.

He offered his arm, and she took it, glad for the warm reassurance of his body. He leaned down and sniffed.

"You smell good enough to eat."

"Uh-oh, and you're starving."

He chuckled. "Usually."

"You weren't wearing that medicine bundle before."

He glanced down at her. "You are very observant. My mother sent it. Thought I should wear it."

She knew that the contents of each man's medicine bundle was a private thing, and so she asked no more.

"I wish I had some sage and sweetgrass to burn. A prayer wouldn't hurt either."

Carter squeezed her hand, and they followed the agents

out. They were escorted down in the service elevator and met the US marshals. There were two agents, one male and one female, Agent Pedro Mora Wells and his partner, Agent Eveline Landers. He was short, dark and already had a five-o'clock shadow. She was broad at the hips and shoulders and wore her hair in dangerous-looking, short bleached spikes. Her eyes were hidden behind oversize mirrored sunglasses.

The FBI walked them out through the laundry facility and into a white van that looked like the kind that hotels use as courtesy shuttles. Inside Amber found two rows of seats behind the front bucket seats. Carter helped her inside and then sat next to her in the center of the row. The marshals closed them in and then took their places in front, with Mora driving and Landers opposite. And they were off.

They drove through Darabee past the big box stores, fast-food chains, and occasional strip malls with restaurants and some shopping. Then they came to a familiar wooded stretch and passed the turnoff to their reservation. Carter's head swiveled as they passed an SUV she suspected Jack drove for work.

Amber sat back in the seat and gazed through windows catching glimpses of the azure waters of Antelope Lake, the last in the string of four bodies of water created by the damming of the Salt River. Two dams lay upstream from her reservation, including the largest, Alchesay, which held back Goodwin Lake and produced more electricity than the other three combined. Next came Skeleton Cliff Dam, Red Rock Dam and finally Mesa Salado which she could not see from the road. But she did see an Arizona State Police SUV sitting at the turnoff to Mesa Salado Dam.

They descended the mountain in a series of switchbacks for the next forty minutes. She watched the Douglas fir trees give way to pinyon pine. The appearance of agave signaled that they had returned to the lower elevations of arid rolling rock formations and the saguaro cacti. Here the road widened, becoming two lanes on each side.

The state police SUV pulled into the passing lane beside them, and Amber wondered briefly if it was the same one from up by Mesa Salado. An escort? She turned to look at them and noticed the passenger's window was open. Next she saw the passenger's face. *That face*—the face of the man leaving Harvey Ibsen's place.

She pointed as her words came out as a stammer. "The… That's him!"

"What?" said Carter, peering in the direction she pointed. The SUV now ran parallel to them, mimicking their speed. A rifle emerged from the passenger-side window.

"Gun!" shouted Carter.

Chapter Sixteen

Carter placed a broad hand on Amber's back and forced her forward as shots ripped through the vehicle's side panel. Marshal Mora slumped behind the wheel. Carter held Amber down with one hand and wrapped his other around his knees. The van veered, and the tires bogged as the front and back windshield shattered at once.

Landers screamed as they slid along the embankment. Carter straightened as the van left the road. Landers made a grab for the wheel as the van careened down an embankment and thundered on.

Mora flopped to the side, his body held erect by his shoulder restraint, his foot still evidently on the gas as they sped through the low scrub sending rocks knocking against the undercarriage.

Landers had one hand on her side and one on the wheel as she steered them perpendicular to the highway.

"Hold on!" she shouted.

Carter saw the scrub brush vanish, and the van tipped, sliding on the loose red sand, planting nose first into the ground. The rear tires remained at ground level and the front tires now rested on the floor of the arroyo, a dry river bed some three feet down.

"Out," said Landers.

Carter unfastened his belt, and Amber did the same.

Carter reached forward, checking Mora's pulse at the neck and finding none.

Landers clutched her side, blood leaking between her fingers.

"I figure you have about a minute before they get here." The marshal spoke between clenched teeth. "Take his gun and phone."

Carter did as she suggested, finding his phone in his right pants pocket.

"Thirty seconds," she said, glancing back at him. "Run."

"What about you?" asked Amber.

"Lung shot. Can't run. Go."

Carter pulled open the van door and dragged Amber down beside him. He looked right and left down the wash. In either direction he could be out of sight in thirty seconds at a dead run.

He grabbed his duffel and pointed in the more difficult direction, the one with the denuded trees and rock.

"Run," he said.

Amber did run, and she was fast. Not as fast as he was but fast enough. In twenty seconds they were out of sight of the van. In a minute they were out of sight of the place where he had last seen the van.

They ran for another minute, and then he slowed them to a jog. They were both sweating and panting but not loud enough to miss the sound of the two gunshots.

Amber stilled, looking back. She didn't ask him, just stared in wide-eyed horror. He suspected that Agent Landers was dead.

"Who was it?" asked Carter.

"The man who killed Ibsen. The Lilac shooter." She glanced back at the way they had come. "He'll come after us. I know it."

"Maybe. Depends on how badly he wants to risk getting caught."

She stared at him, her breathing slowing rapidly back to normal. She was in good shape.

Amber glanced back over her shoulder in the way they had come.

"See anything?" she asked.

"No."

Amber grabbed the hem of her gauzy blouse and tugged the entire thing up over her head. Carter's attention snapped back to her.

"What are you doing?"

"It's white. Easy to see in this wash. We're rabbits. Brown is a much better color for hiding."

He was already unbuttoning his oxford as she stuffed her blouse in his duffel with her necklace.

He stowed his top in his green duffel, trying not to stare at her slim athletic figure and the lacy black bra that hugged her breasts.

"Come on," she said.

They ran again, a fast jog that took them over uneven ground and over rocks and tangled tree branches. He didn't stop, and she didn't ask him to. But over time her stride grew clumsy, and he slowed.

"They might follow or might go back to their vehicle to try to get ahead of us. This wash roughly parallels the road. I don't know when it might cross under the highway."

She had to pause as she spoke to catch her breath. "They might…go…the wrong way."

He nodded. Then he motioned to a section of the wash wall that had collapsed, offering some cover and also morning shade.

She followed as he tucked them in close to the earthen wall. He handed her back her blouse, and she shrugged into it. Next he offered water. She took very little.

Amber was a child of the arid Southwest who knew that

water was precious. She returned the bottle, and he drank sparingly before returning it to his gear.

"What now?" she asked.

"We wait. If they show up first, we are in serious trouble. If it's the FBI or state police, we might be okay."

Amber looked up the narrow wash, topped with leafless brush, dry, yellowed grass and an occasional cactus.

"Too dangerous to continue."

"I think it will go under the road."

She peeked up over the earthen barrier at the way they had come.

"I hate to wait here like a sitting duck."

Carter lifted the marshal's gun. "Not defenseless."

Amber chose not to remind him that their attacker had used either an automatic or semiautomatic rifle.

"How did he find us again?" she asked.

"I don't know."

"He was waiting for us. I saw them parked in that state police vehicle way back in the turnoff for Mesa Salado Dam."

"Me, too."

"How did they know that we were in that van? The windows were tinted. They couldn't see us."

"Which is why they shot for the seats behind the driver," said Carter. His expression showed worry which made her more nervous.

"How did they get a state police vehicle?"

"I don't know. A copy, maybe."

"It fooled me." She glanced around at the thirsty trees that waited patiently for the July monsoons to fill the river.

"How long until the FBI find us?"

"Maybe an hour or two."

"You have cell phone service?" she asked.

He lifted out Mora's phone, an Android, and woke it up.

"Password protected," he said. He glanced at the emergency button but hesitated. Something felt wrong. "It's on. So the FBI can track us once they realize we're missing."

"Turn it off," she said.

He did.

"What are you thinking, Amber?" He trusted her, and her opinion mattered to him. She was smart, observant and completely aware of her surroundings. Any one of those attributes was rare enough.

She scrunched her forehead, making a single line form between her brows.

"If we were on the reservation, I'd say wait for help. But that was a state police vehicle."

"Or a copy."

"But it might be the real state police. So, what if we were picked up by FBI, and they weren't really FBI? Those guys at the tribal station told me they were Feds."

He settled back against the red earth wall behind them.

"I've been wondering about your question—how does that gunman get away?"

"And?"

"I think he has help."

That seemed obvious. But he felt she had more to say, so he didn't comment. They were both thinking it, but she was the one who finally came out and said it aloud.

"I hate to say it, but what kind of person can hide suspects, get inside information on the location of witnesses and then vanish again?"

He didn't like her train of thought but could not find a better explanation for what was happening to them.

She rested a hand on his knee. "Everything points to law enforcement personnel."

He set his jaw. If she was right, then waiting for help suddenly seemed a bad idea.

"Do you think they will let your brother know if you are missing?" she asked.

"I'm not sure. It is out of his jurisdiction."

"We should try to get to the reservation or to your brother."

She was right. Getting to Turquoise Canyon might be the only way to let their people know what had really happened. He knew for certain that tribal land was the one place on earth they might just be safe.

"You're right."

"But how? The reservation is at least seventy miles away and we don't have a vehicle or even a phone."

Chapter Seventeen

"They might be back there, waiting for us," he said.

"Risky to hang around, especially in a state police car. Assuming they are not state police, another trooper will definitely stop if he sees that SUV."

"Could be a while."

"You think they are still there?" she asked.

"Not sure. But there might be something useful in the van. They had a radio."

"No radios," said Amber. "We can call your brother if we get to a landline."

They made their way back to the van over the next hour, stopping to listen and scout. Once at the van they found both agents dead.

Carter looked at the bullet holes that told him that if Amber had not spotted the gunman the instant she had, they would both be dead, as well.

"You saved our lives," he said.

"No. I just pointed. You are the one who pushed us down below the path of the bullets."

Carter took a slow walk around the van, looking at the ground. Many of the Apache people were excellent trackers, and she knew Carter had this skill.

He confirmed her suspicion a moment later.

"Two men. Both in boots. One is about one-eighty and the other slighter, maybe one-fifty. They jogged down to the van and stopped there." He pointed to the place beside Mora.

Was that where they took the shot that killed Landers? she wondered.

"The smaller one circled the van around the back. He went slow, and he stopped at the door. They followed us to the river channel but went no farther. Then they both walked back up the bank."

She held her arms folded over her body as the cold reality of this situation chilled her heart.

"Did you see if they wore police uniforms?" he asked.

"I didn't notice."

"I'm going to take her gun. Look around and see if there is anything else worth carrying."

Amber searched the van and found a half consumed bottle of green tea and took that. Carter returned Mora's phone to his pocket and took Landers's service weapon.

"I have to go back to the road," he said.

"Why?"

"I need to leave a marker for my brothers."

She didn't know if he meant his actual brothers or members of his tribe. But it didn't matter.

"It's dangerous. You will be seen by passing cars."

"I'll be careful."

She nodded, and he gave her a swift kiss before jogging away. Amber pressed her fingers to her lips. His kiss was quick and possessive. She watched him go and then saw him drop to the ground, waiting. A moment later she heard a car pass. Then he moved out of sight.

She stood trembling, waiting for him to reappear. Seconds ticked by, and finally she saw him, trotting back to her.

"They wiped away the trail of the van. You could miss it easily," he said.

"What marker did you leave?" she asked.

"Five flat stones, stacked one on the other."

"Like a trail marker?"

"Yes."

Carter led them a short distance from the van and left more marks, though these he scratched in the dirt. She recognized them as Native symbols but did not know the meaning.

He drew a crooked arrow and a bull's eye, and what looked like a butterfly and then several wagon wheels.

"What does that mean?" she asked.

He pointed at the crooked arrow first and then moved from one symbol to the next.

"This one is Lightning Snake. It means escape. It will tell them we made it out. This is Buffalo Eye and signifies the need for alertness. I hope they will read that our attackers are still out there. This is a saddlebag."

"I thought it was a butterfly."

He smiled. "Saddlebags mean a journey. It will tell them that we are traveling, and this means Hogans," he said referring to the pictorial representation of the traditional domed dwelling of their people. "To let them know that we are traveling toward a town."

"Which town? Phoenix or home?" she asked.

He drew one more symbol, a series of connected straight lines and one wavy one.

"Water," she said.

Then he made a vertical line and the water symbol. He repeated this once more.

"Water. Dam. Water. Dam," he said, pointing.

"Mesa Salado Dam, Antelope Lake, Red Rock Dam, Turquoise Lake, Hogan. Home at Turquoise Reservation."

He nodded and gave her a smile.

"You said your younger brother Tommy was a Shadow Wolf. He reads sign."

"Yes. And Jack, Ray and Dylan were marines. But more importantly we are Apache. They'll know where to find us."

She studied his work, hoping their people would find them quickly.

"Anything else?" he asked.

"Why did you kiss me?"

His smile broadened. "That answer might take longer."

He offered her the water bottle, and she took another swallow. Many rough miles lay between them and civilization. It was only February and approaching noon, and the temperature felt well into the eighties. And the dry heat of the desert was already stealing away their strength.

Carter motioned back to the dry wash. They picked their way carefully now, conserving energy and stopping at mid-afternoon when the sun had dipped enough to allow the wall of the wash to cast enough shade to sit in. They had the rest of the first bottle of water and ate the pretzels he had commandeered from the FBI's stash.

The salt tasted so good she licked her fingers, and when she finished she found him watching her again. The lowered lids and the intent stare both made her stomach flutter and her body come to tingling awareness.

"What?" she asked.

"You're beautiful," he said.

She flushed.

"And you can run like the wind."

"Same goes for you," she said, now letting her attention wander over the thirsty sand and wilted gray-green trees that hugged the banks waiting for rain.

"I hate it down here in the flats," she admitted.

He nodded, understanding that. "We belong in the mountains."

"I keep seeing their faces. All the ones I worked with."

He wrapped an arm about her.

"They'll be burying them soon," she said. "This weekend, I'll bet. And I won't be there."

"At least you won't be buried with them."

Her gaze flashed to his. Then she rested her head on his shoulder, not knowing if she should feel lucky or cursed.

"I'd do anything to catch that guy," she said. "See that he goes to prison for the rest of his life."

He gave her a squeeze. "I've been thinking about what you said back there, about him working with law enforcement. I'm afraid it makes a lot of sense."

She sighed and snuggled closer.

"And, Amber? I haven't seen anyone seriously since you left. Now I know why. I still want you."

She tensed and lifted her head. "Carter, we've been apart a long time."

"Are you seeing someone?"

"No," she admitted. "Just afraid."

He blew out a breath.

"What is it you are afraid of, Amber?"

"Besides dying?" she chuckled. "I don't want to be like my parents."

"And what do you want?"

She sighed. "What I can't have. To live near my sisters, watch my nephews grow up." Be Turquoise Mountain Apache, she thought.

He noted that none of her ambitions involved changing her identity. He also noticed she did not say she wanted him.

"I wished you had come to me. Confided what he did."

"You were in basic when I figured it all out."

He stopped walking and turned to her. "Amber, you talk about trust. But you didn't trust me to help you. You didn't come to me for help when you needed it. How do you think that makes me feel?"

"You were gone, Carter. I was there alone."

"You chose to handle it alone. I would have helped you. I'd like someone who believes in me enough to stick around, even when I don't understand."

She dragged her toe in the sand, making an arching line. "I was afraid."

"Of me?"

"Of being trapped."

"Is that how you see our marriage?"

"At the time I did. You said I was my parents' responsibility and then I would be yours. I don't want to be passed along like a child, Carter. I want a partner, not a keeper."

"I was eighteen, Amber. I was trying to be a man. Take care of things. Take care of you."

"I know."

"I can't stop thinking of it and of us. I keep wondering if it could work between us."

"Carter, we almost died again today. It's natural to want to grab a hold of someone."

"Not someone. You."

She lifted a hand in the direction they had been heading, calling an end to the rest. "We should get moving."

"Amber."

"Not now, Carter. Please."

"When? They came after us again. If you hadn't recognized that guy, we might be dead right now. So I'm wondering, Amber, when is the right time to talk about the things that really matter? Things like how you smell and how you taste. And how much I want to make love to you again."

"I don't."

"What do you want, Amber?"

She looked around with frantic eyes. "I just want to get out of this arroyo."

"Back to Turquoise Canyon," he said.

She rounded on him, fists tight at her side. "That's never

going to happen, Carter! Not for me. You can go back there and you should. But I can't."

Was she trying to protect him?

He slapped himself in the forehead as he remembered what Jack had told him and given him.

She gave him an odd look.

"You don't want me to lose the tribe, my brothers, Tribal Thunder."

"Who?"

"That's our name. Me, Ray, Dylan and Jack. Kenshaw calls us Tribal Thunder."

"Carter, what are you talking about?"

"You, protecting me. Keeping me with the tribe."

"Well, of course. You love Turquoise Canyon. It's your home. I don't want you to lose it because of me."

He explained that because she had been a minor at the time she was withdrawn from the enrollment by her parent, as an adult, she could now reapply.

Her eyes widened. "Is that possible?"

"Yes." Carter dipped to a knee and retrieved the correct papers from his duffel. Then he stood and offered them to her. "Application to reinstate."

Her face lit up, and her smile dazzled. "I could. Are you sure?"

He nodded. Instead of taking the papers, Amber threw herself into his arms, and her words were muffled against his shoulder, but he understood her.

"I could come home."

But not if the US Marshals had anything to say about it.

Chapter Eighteen

The sun's low angle painted the landscape pink as they walked wearily along.

Carter's words buzzed in her mind as they trod south. She could rejoin the tribe. She could right the wrong her father had done her. She had already filled out the application that Carter again carried in his bag. She would give it to the tribe as soon as they reached home.

If they reached home.

Their destination, the Saguaro Flats tribe, was an even smaller Native American community than Turquoise Canyon, also of the Tonto band, who lived in a reservation on the outskirts of Phoenix since winning a lawsuit against the US government in the 1970s.

Carter paused. "Listen."

Car doors slammed, and voices murmured. They crept to the edge of the wash. She peered over the lip of the bank but could see nothing past the vegetation.

Together they crawled up to ground level and peeked through the juniper brush at an isolated gas station.

"What should we do?" she asked.

There was a battered blue pickup truck at the pumps but no driver. A few minutes later two men emerged from the convenience store and strode toward the truck. One tapped a pack of cigarettes as he climbed behind the wheel and set them in motion.

"We need a ride," she said. "They left it open with the keys inside."

"You want to steal a vehicle?" he asked.

"Yes."

"Okay." Carter scouted the area. "Good cover on the west side by the dumpster. You wait here."

"The hell I will."

He scowled at her but didn't ask her to remain behind again. Instead he took both guns from the duffel.

"You know how to shoot one of these?" he asked.

She wrinkled her nose and shook her head.

He blew away a breath and shoved one gun in his front pocket and the second in the waistband of his jeans.

"Tuck in your braid," Amber said.

"What?"

"They're searching for us. Two Apache Indians."

He gave her a look as if to say this was not going to substantially change his appearance, but his braid did get tucked under the collar of his dirty oxford shirt.

They had to cross the highway to reach cover. The gas station was painted in earth tones like the red rock hills beyond. The green dumpster lay far to the left past the large red, white and blue sun shield above the four pumps. To the right lay a three-car garage with all bays shut. Two cars were parked between the dumpster and the side of the squatty building.

The entire journey was only a quarter mile but took them almost an hour because of the need to move without notice. And another twenty minutes because of one failed attempt to find a driver who left his vehicle unlocked with the keys in the ignition.

It was dusk when a spotless gray compact pulled in.

"See the white sticker with the bar code on the windshield?" he asked. "That means that is a rental."

She glanced at the decal as the driver stepped out from

behind the wheel and stretched. He fumbled around in the compartment opening the trunk lock before releasing the latch to the gas tank, then filled up. When he left the car for the convenience store, Amber followed as far as the front window. There she scouted the driver.

"Buying beer," she said.

Carter walked past the pumps, glanced inside and spotted the keys. He nodded at Amber who walked quickly to the passenger side of the car. Carter closed the trunk and slipped into the driver's seat. They were away a moment later.

"He'll call the cops and they'll notify the Feds. We might have a ten minute head start," said Carter.

"Saguaro Flats Indian Reservation is fifteen miles away."

He gripped the wheel as his foot pressed the gas. "I know."

"Are we going to stop at Saguaro?" she asked.

"I'd feel better in Turquoise Canyon."

"Long way to go in a stolen car," she said.

He nodded his agreement and gripped the wheel. "Let's get on Indian Land."

Amber glanced at the digital clock on the dash and wondered if the driver had noticed the theft yet. She looked behind them for headlights.

Carter's gaze flicked to the rearview. "See anything?" he asked.

"Not yet."

But they were coming. The bad guys and the good guys. And she knew that they would not be able to tell the difference.

"How long?" she asked.

"If they are near where we started, they'll be on us anytime."

"Do you think we should leave this car and get another?"

"Where?"

She shook her head, bewildered. There was nothing out here but the desert and the sky and the hum of the tires.

"Headlights," he said.

"What if it's the police? We can't start shooting. They might be the real police," she said.

"Closing," he said, his gaze flashing from the rearview mirror and then back to her.

They were still off the Saguaro Flats Indian Reservation property.

The lights in the grille of the car behind them flashed blue and red.

"Unmarked car," she said, glancing back. "State police?"

He pursed his lips. "Don't know."

"You stopping?"

"If I do, I might have to shoot someone."

"You can't outrun them."

"Honest cop won't shoot at us or try to run us off the road. Let's see what he does."

The answer came a moment later when the car rammed them from behind. The jolt engaged her safety belt, the nylon gripping her shoulder as they careened into the opposite side of the two-lane highway.

"We won't make it," she said.

The pursuing vehicle drew beside them and bumped Amber's door. She turned toward the new threat and got a very good look at the driver. She gave a little shout and lifted a finger to point at him. His eyes widened and the driver tugged the wheel, separating their vehicles.

"How many?" Carter asked.

"One."

"You recognize him?" Carter asked.

"Yes. The...the guy. The fake FBI guy."

"What guy?"

"Driving the Subaru. The one with the busted nose. Leopold."

Carter set his jaw. "Hold on."

Carter turned the wheel, and this time he hit the other car. The impact jarred her, and the sound of squealing metal filled the air. The two vehicles raced parallel for a moment and then drifted toward the shoulder. Carter kept turning the wheel, forcing the unmarked vehicle over. When the car's wheels left the pavement, the other vehicle jolted, swerved and they flew on.

Amber released a held breath a moment before their back windshield shattered.

"Get down," Carter said, hunching as he drove.

Amber ducked, but there was no second shot.

"This is so bad," she said.

They drove in silence, the warm dry wind swirling through the gap in the rear window.

"Do you see him?" she asked.

"No." Carter kept both hands on the wheel, but hunched now as if someone had hit him in the stomach.

"Was that a shotgun?" she asked, checking the damaged window, surveying the fist-sized hole and the rear seat glittering with cubes of glass.

"Pistol. Lucky shot."

Amber blinked at the hole, wondering where the bullet went. She had her answer a moment later when she looked at Carter and saw a dark stain welling on the white fabric at the top of his right shoulder.

"You're bleeding!"

"Yeah."

"Yeah? That's it, just yeah?" Her voice held a frightening note of panic. What would she do if he was seriously injured? How would she get them to safety?

"How bad?" she asked.

"Don't know. Burns like a mother…" His words trailed off.

She unfastened her belt and reached, then hesitated. There was a hole in the top of his shirt. She placed her right and left index finger in the gap and tugged, rending the fabric.

He sucked in a breath between his teeth, the sound a hiss.

She could see his skin now, orange in the dashboard light. The rounded muscle of his shoulder was marred by a black groove from which blood welled at an alarming rate and ran down his skin in crimson rivers.

"Aw!" Carter cried. "Right though the medicine shield."

The bullet had grazed the skin at his shoulder, cutting a channel through the top of his bear track tattoo.

"What's in that bag? Do you have a shirt or something?" she asked.

"Yes."

She scrambled to get something to stop the bleeding and came up with a soft cotton T-shirt which she folded into a pad and pressed to his shoulder. He dipped away from her touch and winced.

"Damn, that hurts."

"Seems like it grazed the skin." She continued to press down. Before them a green-and-white sign announced the Saguaro Flats Indian Reservation.

"We're on reservation land."

"Is he back there?"

"Not yet."

He pulled into the visitor's center, closed now and without anyone in the parking lot. Carter drove behind the square building that was little more than a trailer on blocks.

Here he turned off both headlights and motor.

They had a clear view of the road. It was not more than a minute later the unmarked car flew past them, with its one functioning headlight.

"We have to lose this car."

Amber insisted that they dress his wound before moving. He held the sodden T-shirt as she tore up a second one. She wrapped it around his chest and shoulder, trying not to react to the nearness of him and failing as usual.

"What?" he asked.

"I just can't seem to touch you without…"

He lifted his brow and grinned.

"You just got shot," she said, her voice disapproving.

"But I'm not dead." He laughed and kissed her hard.

For just a moment she forgot where she was and why this was such a bad idea. His tongue grazed hers, and she opened for him. He deepened the kiss, his mouth slanting across hers, their tongues lapping and sliding against one another. She lifted her hand to hold him and touched the bandage. Amber pulled back.

He smiled at her, his face now blue under the starlight.

Carter twisted the key, and the engine hummed. He left the lights off as he drove, stopping at a house that had a barn beside it and several trucks in various states of repair. Carter pulled into the grouping of vehicles and left her to investigate. All the trucks had the keys dangling from their ignitions. He took the first one that turned over, leaving the rental with the rest promising himself to get the truck back to the owner when possible. It was safer that whoever lived in that house knew nothing about them. Less than an hour later they were on the road leading to Kurt's home. Carter pulled over well before the drive because he wanted to scout the place first to be certain they were alone and he didn't want the stolen truck at Kurt's place.

"More walking," he said and reached for the door.

She followed him out, insisting on carrying his bag.

"How far to your brother's place?" she asked.

"A mile or two."

"Why Kurt's place?" she asked.

"Kurt lives at the fire station as much as home, and he lives alone. Plus, he can get a message to Jack."

"They might be watching there, too."

"I'll make sure we're alone."

She felt her insides heat at that thought and admonished herself. The man had a bullet wound. But still images of Carter running shirtless down the arroyo filled her mind and her fantasies.

They opted to walk well off the shoulder of the road and the reach of the headlights of passing cars. The road was sparsely populated with residences, including the concrete block ranch belonging to his youngest brother. The empty carport and dark windows told them Kurt was out.

"Looking for us again, I'll bet," he said.

They watched the house for some time, and Carter scouted the perimeter. She watched him, a moving shadow creeping past the basketball hoop rising from a flat concrete slab beside a small shed. He moved silently under the carport, past the barbecue grill and then disappeared.

She held her breath, released it and then held it again. On the third breath he reappeared and waved her over. She joined him in the driveway at the side entrance.

She smiled. Her feet ached and her body ached, and she had never been more thirsty in her life.

He put a hand on the knob.

"It's not locked?" she asked.

Carter glanced back over his shoulder. "Kurt has an alarm system."

That surprised her. No one she knew had an alarm system.

"Wait here a minute."

Amber held her breath. Had the men who were after them anticipated Carter's move?

She wanted to call him back, suddenly afraid they were waiting for him in there.

Then she saw something inside move past the window.

"Carter wait," she whispered.

But he was already turning the knob and stepping into the house.

Chapter Nineteen

Carter's entrance set off a wild barking from Kurt's large dog. He had been to the house when Kurt was not here, and he knew that his dog, Justice, did not like visitors when his master was away. Carter had fed him when Kurt was away at school, but he had never brought another person into the house. If he had to, he'd chain the dog outside.

He paused in the kitchen as the dog continued his frantic barking. The room was illuminated by the small hood lamp over the stove. But the living room beyond was dark.

"Justice!" he said in his sternest voice. "Quiet."

The dog went silent and approached from the darkness.

Carter knew the dog could see much better than he could in the low light. All he could make out was a moving shadow and the bulk of the huge head of the pit bull.

The dog was halfway across the kitchen before Carter saw the tail wagging. He relaxed his shoulders. The dog paused and sniffed. Carter didn't know if he picked up the scent of blood or of the other human, but his hackles lifted, and he began to growl.

Carter took a chance and flicked on the light. Then he lowered himself to one knee and held out his hand.

"Damn it, Justice. You know me."

Justice pinned his beady eyes on Carter and finally the tail twitched.

"Carter?" came the whisper from behind him. "Someone is coming. A car."

He flipped off the light and drew her inside. Justice growled again.

"Quiet," he said. The dog weighed at least seventy pounds and had all his working parts.

Carter kept Amber behind him as he pulled her through the kitchen to the window over the sink. Together they watched the car roll slowly past and out of sight.

"Do you think it was him?"

"Not the same car," he answered. But he knew there was more than one man after them. He turned to find Justice halfway across the kitchen, sniffing. "Justice, I swear I will shoot you."

"He's big," she said.

"You like dogs?"

"I like cats."

Carter spoke to the dog in Apache. He told Justice that Amber was a friend and a beautiful woman and that she was welcome in his brother's house.

"That dog speaks Tonto Apache?" she asked.

"I hope so."

Finally the tail began to move, and Carter put out his hand again. Amber slowly offered hers, and Justice poked her with his wet black nose. Then he sniffed her leg and finally stuck his nose in her crotch.

Carter pulled him off. "Enough of that."

Justice sat, and Carter fed him a bowl full of chow with water. While the dog inhaled his food, Carter went to the refrigerator and retrieved two bottles of cold water. They drank them dry and then had two more.

"How are you feeling?" he asked.

She had a dull headache, and she was tired to the bone. But she was not the one who had been shot.

"We need to get you cleaned up. Does Kurt have a first aid kit?"

"He's a paramedic, so he better."

"Should you call your brother?" she asked.

"Kurt doesn't have a landline. Just uses his cell."

"What about your phone?"

"I don't trust it."

"When will he be home?"

Carter shrugged and then winced.

"Your family will be worried," she said.

"Yours, too."

They stared in silence a moment. She thought of her application to come home. Where would she live? Her thoughts turned to Carter, and the desire sparked in her chest, flooding downward to ignite her longing, deep, low and hot.

"Let's get a bandage on that."

They headed for the bathroom in the back of the house and flicked on the light. Amber found a shoe box with some medical supplies, including large gauze pads and antiseptic cream. Amber seated Carter on the edge of the tub and helped him remove the improvised bandage and his ruined shirt. The wound had begun to clot, but the removal of the dressing caused it to bleed again, sending a scarlet trail of blood down his arm. He scowled at his shoulder as if it disappointed him.

"It doesn't look too bad," she lied, when in fact, it looked terrible. The edges of the wound were raw and angry red. The inside of the groove looked like raw meat, and the entire thing made her stomach roll.

"You ever cleaned a wound before?"

"Of course." She rubbed her mouth and recalled the lip that she had iced but not had stitched until the next day because no one had noticed it until then.

Justice entered the room and sat nearly on Amber's foot

as she washed her hands with soap, relishing the feel of clean skin. Then she filled the sink with soapy water and set to work with a washcloth, washing away the blood. She tried not to admire the firm bronze skin beneath the cloth or the feel of his muscles where she gripped his arm. But she could not ignore the tiny white scars, divots and puckers that marred the skin of his arm. The marks left by the shrapnel and the surgeries to remove the tiny bits of metal.

"Do these hurt?" she asked.

"Not too much. The scar tissue tugs, and I have some numb places."

"Here?" she asked, moving the cloth in a rhythmic motion.

"No," his voice was lower now, gruff. "I can feel all that."

She continued working from his wrist and spiraling up, pausing only to rinse off the blood. One stubborn line of blood continued to flow like a river down the bright ink of his tattoo and the wide plain of his chest muscles to settle in his ribbed stomach.

She washed his stomach and chest, feeling his gaze fixed on her and refusing to look. His nipple pebbled at the touch of the cloth, and she wondered what it would be like to stroke him again and feel his body come alive. His chest rose and fell a little too fast.

He wanted to make love to her. He had told her so.

Amber lifted her gaze and found fathomless brown eyes, parted lips and an expression that registered as a different sort of pain, one tied to the same longing that thumped in her chest.

He reached his good hand out and captured her around the neck, pulling her down to kiss him again. She sank between his splayed knees and let the sensations flow. Her body stirred, and the cloth fell from her hands.

A cold nose poked her in the center of her back.

She yelped and turned. Justice sat with tongue lolling and eyes half closed.

"Justice," growled Carter. "Lie down."

The dog whined and made a show of lying down but then decided to sit on the bath mat instead.

"Let me finish up," she said, lifting the cloth and ringing it out once more. The trail of blood was back, but this time she elected to smear a piece of gauze with antiseptic gel before placing it over the open wound. "That really needs a stitch or two."

"Not going to happen."

"It will scar."

"Make me look even tougher," he said and prodded at the gauze.

She added several more pieces until the blood no longer soaked through. Then she used a two-inch ACE bandage to hold it in place. When she finished, the bandage wove around his chest, under his armpit and back around his arm in a figure eight.

"Nice. Where'd you learn that?"

"I had a rotator cuff strain. That's how we held the ice bag in place."

He nodded. She used the washcloth once more to clean away the last trail of blood.

"Eating or washing next?" he asked.

She was too tired for either, but she suggested he take a bath so he didn't soak his wound, and she offered to find them something to eat.

"I don't know what he has. Might be slim pickings."

She left him, anxious to be away from the need he stirred and the bad ideas that kept popping up. What if they were caught and killed? Would she want to spend her last hours on this earth avoiding Carter or in his arms?

She knew the answer, and that frightened her in an

entirely different way. Under normal circumstances, she would use her head. But nothing about this was normal.

She heard the bath water running as she made it to the kitchen. She didn't dare turn on the light, so she worked in the near dark. The freezer had one bag of pinto beans, ice and frozen burritos.

But in the refrigerator, she struck gold. Onions, potatoes, eggs and a nice defrosted steak. The sound of the water stream stopped, only to be replaced by splashing and humming. She focused on the cast-iron skillet and scrambling eggs. She was not imagining Carter naked and wet in the bathtub. She was not picturing all that bronze wet skin, those long muscular legs and that tight ass.

Amber groaned as she chopped the potatoes thinly so they'd cook faster. She was hungry enough to eat them raw. She had done this job often enough to be able to do it in the dark. Her first job had been off the books in the kitchen of a diner in Darabee. Into the hot pan went grease, the onions and potatoes. She added salt, pepper, paprika and cayenne for the frying potatoes.

By the time the bathroom door opened, she had the steak seasoned.

Carter emerged, wearing clean jeans, a white T-shirt, bare feet and a devilish grin.

"Smells like heaven."

"It will be a few minutes for the potatoes," she said. "You go shower. I'll do this."

She lifted her eyebrows. A man who could cook was a thing of beauty.

"I opted to leave the overhead light off. But I kept that one on."

"Fine. Go get cleaned up." He lifted a meat fork from the container of utensils beside the stove and poked at a potato. Amber moved aside.

She hesitated because she did not have the bag Kay had packed.

"Would your brother mind if I borrowed something to wear?"

"I already put out a T-shirt and a pair of pajama bottoms I know he has never worn."

"How do you know that?"

"Because he sleeps naked, like me." His brow lifted, and she felt the flush rising up her neck and heating her face.

She nodded and backed away.

"I put them in the bathroom. See you in a few."

Amber retreated to the bathroom and closed the door behind her, leaning back against the wood and releasing a breath. That man made her hotter than those frying potatoes.

She stripped out of the dirty clothes, keeping nothing but the necklace, and the bra and panties that she rinsed out in the sink and hung to dry.

Then she started the taps and stepped into the warm stream. There were few things that could not be made better by a hot shower. Amber emerged a few minutes later and tried to ignore the sensitivity of her skin as she toweled herself dry.

She was going to eat and sleep and pray that the next time she saw any law enforcement, they would be wearing the seal of the Turquoise Canyon Tribal Police.

She wondered if Carter was now imagining her damp and naked. A smile curled her lips. Then she shook her head at her reflection. She was not going to let her lust overcome her common sense. She was tired and frightened. He was safe and familiar. That was all.

Her reflection gave her a look of skepticism, and she groaned, turning away.

He wasn't just safe and familiar. He was her first true love, and those feelings died hard.

Amber tugged on the fleece pajama bottoms and frowned. They were covered with images of playing cards, poker chips and arrowheads. Clearly they were from the tribe's casino, and she could see why a man would not want to wear them. But they were clean, and so was the soft red T-shirt.

She entered the kitchen to the sound of the steak sizzling in the pan. The aroma made her stomach rumble. She closed her eyes and inhaled.

"Wow."

He smiled at her, spatula in one hand as his gaze swept her from head to heel. "You even make that look good." He pointed the spatula at the small dinette and said, "Sit."

Justice was already sleeping under the table, so she was careful with her chair. He lifted his head and then laid it back down.

"He's not going to beg?" she asked.

"Kurt never feeds him from the table. He gets leftovers in his dish with breakfast. If there are any. I'm hungry enough to eat that dog."

Justice sighed but did not rouse again as Carter brought her a plate. He'd added toast to her original menu, and she slathered the offering with butter and dug in.

He added ketchup to his eggs, and they both finished another full glass of water. Her headache was easing, and she wondered if it had to do with dehydration, fatigue or famine.

There was no conversation as they ate, and, as Carter predicted, there was little but gristle and a small portion of eggs left for Justice.

"I wish you could get word to your brother," she said. "I'm sure he's worried sick."

"They'll be on our trail. Likely made it to the gas station by now.

"No helping it. He'll be back sometime. Tonight. To-morrow. I'll see him then."

She wondered if Kurt would take the forms to the tribal council for her. She rested her cheek on her hand and sagged. "What now?"

Her eyes blinked, and she had trouble keeping them open. Amazing what clean clothes and a full stomach could do.

"Come on, Sleeping Beauty. Let's get you to bed."

Amber suddenly did not feel sleepy anymore.

Chapter Twenty

Carter watched Amber's eyes go from that sexy heavy-lidded stare to wide-eyed. He wanted to take her to his bed, but she had looked dead on her feet. Now her stare looked hungry.

"Put you to bed," he said. "Not take you to bed."

Her shoulders sank a fraction. Was that disappointment he read in her expression? He wondered about old mistakes. His. Hers. Then he thought about new beginnings. If anyone deserved happiness, it was Amber. Could he be the one to bring her life joy and meaning?

"Kurt has two bedrooms. His and one that Thomas uses when he is back from the Shadow Wolves. But I'll bet he's tracking us right now."

"Sad. Here we are in their home, and they are out there searching for us.

"Can't be helped."

"When will Kurt be back?"

"Not sure but definitely by morning, because he didn't take Justice along. Come on." He took their dishes to the sink and dropped them. She glanced at the dirty frying pan. "Leave it. Just more tracks for them to follow."

He clasped her hand and led her to Thomas's room.

"This is it."

There was little but a full-sized bed, side table and a bench along the window.

She stood in the door peeking in. "Where will you be?"

He moved to the door, and she stepped back but not enough, and their bodies grazed as he passed by. He stilled and looked down at her.

"You want to see where I'll be sleeping?" he asked.

She nodded.

He led her across the hall to Kurt's room. The bed was larger, and the furnishing included a desk and computer setup.

"Room for two," she said.

He turned to her. "Like last night?"

She shook her head. "No. Like before I left."

He watched her expression for clues. Why now? he wondered. Was it because she had hope now, hope of return to her tribe, her family and him?

"I just need you tonight."

Now why did it bother him that she said tonight? He knew why. It implied that she wouldn't need him every night or any night or all nights from here to eternity. *Just tonight.*

He should take what she offered with both hands. Instead he hesitated because he wanted more, a promise, a commitment and second chance. What did she want?

"Need the bathroom?" he asked.

She nodded and retreated there. Carter dived over the bed and opened Kurt's side table, praying aloud. He found what he was looking for, condoms of the bare skin variety. And something else, a little red squishy packet of something unfamiliar. The packet read, *Pleasure-enhancing lubricant.*

Holy heck. Now he needed to change the sheets. Where were the clean sheets? Hall closet. Inside the bathroom the water ran. He stripped the bed and made it fresh in record time. Amber emerged to find him throwing the coverlet back in place.

"You changed the sheets?" There was joy and wonder in her voice.

He nodded.

"That's sexy as hell."

He grinned. She lifted the two foil packages and considered them as his body went hot. She lowered the lubricant to the side table.

"Won't need this," she said, her eyes flashing to him.

Was she already wet for him? His skin went hot, and then he shivered with anticipation.

She raised the condom. "Might need more of these."

"I'll be right back." He hit the bathroom, finding a bottle of ibuprofen and taking three. His shoulder throbbed dully, but he knew Amber would make him forget all about it. The throbbing moved south.

When he came back, he found her curled up under the coverlet, her eyes closed and her breathing soft and even.

He stood there staring at her as his disappointment gradually turned to a twisting feeling in his stomach. The disappointment tugged, but as he gazed down at the small bump under the coverlet he began to see how little she was and feel the need to keep her safe pulling at his heart. Carter rubbed a hand over his chest trying to ease the aching there. It didn't.

Carter wanted to protect her, of course. Not just now but always. He was falling again. He knew it, and it scared him. How had he found the courage before—to offer that ring and take her into his heart, knowing she might not stay?

AMBER ROUSED IN the stillness of the night. She lay on her side tucked up close to Carter's warm body. Her leg was bent and resting on his muscular thigh, her head nestled on his good shoulder and his arm wrapped protectively around her back. His breath was slow and easy, but something had awakened her. She lifted her head from the pillow to listen. She caught movement, thinking it looked like a man crouched at the foot of the bed.

Her heart slammed into her chest as she sat up. Carter followed, his body swayed, and he groaned.

"What?" he asked.

One furry paw lifted to the end of the mattress, followed by another. Then the massive head of the pit bull lifted in silhouette against the curtains and the moonlight beyond.

"Justice!" said Carter. "Off the bed."

Justice paused and then continued his slow crawl forward.

Carter raked a hand through his hair and turned to Amber. "Kurt lets him sleep in his bed."

He threw back the covers and sat on the edge of the mattress, pointing toward the hall as he ordered Justice from the bedroom. Then he closed the door before returning to her.

"Sorry about that."

"He scared the life out of me. For a minute I thought someone was in the room."

"He's a good dog. Friendly with kids and most other dogs. The female dogs."

She giggled. "Like Kurt."

He lay back and pulled her down beside her.

"How's the shoulder?" she asked.

"It burns."

"Will you be able to sleep again?"

He turned his head and gazed at her, his dark eyes black in the night. He lifted a finger and traced the outline of the scar at her mouth, and then he traced the outline of her lower lip. She trembled as the tingling awareness rolled through her body with the power of a flash flood. She rested a hand on his chest, feeling the rapid heartbeat that matched her own.

"You want to?" he asked.

She nodded. "But I don't want to hurt your shoulder."

"We can go slow." His smile was filled with male sensuality. Somehow he made her ache down low and deep without even touching her.

She tried to remember why this was such a bad idea. Their first time she had been young, giddy and nervous. Now she was lonely and scared. She wanted comfort more than sex, didn't she?

Nope. She wanted sex with Carter Bear Den. Throbbing and raw. She wanted to feel him sliding in and out of her body, and she wanted to press herself up close and tight. Tomorrow his brother would come, and she would be in protective custody again. Tonight she wanted only to be in Carter's custody. So she could take what he offered.

Amber raked her fingers over the hard muscle of his chest, and Carter's eyes widened, flashing with heat.

He dragged her against him, as if she weighed nothing at all. As if he had not been shot tonight. As if she were the most important thing in the world to him.

Carter was very good in bed. Too good. She remembered that as he kissed her. But in the blending of lips and the fierce thrusting of tongues, she forgot everything but him.

Chapter Twenty-One

Carter breathed in the sweet smell of her clean hair. Brushing it back, he exhaled upon her exposed neck and felt her tremble. Her long hair and onyx eyes captivated him. He stared at her beautiful face and then ran his hand from her shoulder to her hip.

He'd had women since Amber. But they'd all been a poor substitute. He admitted that now, but only to himself. He hadn't moved on. Not even close. How could he when he still loved her? Every frustrating, beautiful, intoxicating inch of her.

He measured the span of her hips with his splayed hands. She had the wide, full hips of a woman, and the narrow waist of a girl. His desire for her grew with an anticipation that he understood was more than physical. He wanted to please her, of course, but also, at some primal level, he wanted to make her his again.

Amber lifted up so that she straddled his hips.

"You want top?" he asked.

"Keep you from bleeding all over the sheets," she said, her smile sweet. "Are you sure you're—"

"I'm fine."

She lay on top of him, her knees bent at his sides and her body still. He didn't know if she was being sure he was well enough for this or reconsidering. Gradually she slid her hips over his so that he throbbed beneath her. It was hard not to move.

"Still okay?"

"Amber, you don't need to keep checking. I'll tell you if it hurts."

"Does it?"

"In all the right places." He lifted his hips, and her eyes widened as he slid against her.

A sensual smile curled her lips.

He took a long look at Amber in the near darkness, knowing he needed to keep this picture for always. Her skin glowed blue as moonlight on snow, and her smile welcomed him.

He lifted his hands to her waist and stared at that flat stomach. His thumbs rubbed back and forth over taut skin as he wondered what it would be like to make a family with Amber.

He stilled, and his hands dropped away from her.

"Carter?" She dipped down to rest on her elbows to look at him, her full bare breasts now hanging just an inch above his chest.

He dragged a hand slowly along the center of her back and then pushed her forward so she fell on to his chest. Her body trembled with awareness and need as he stroked her thigh. Amber savored the tingling sensation of his fingers gliding slowly over her.

He pressed her tight against his naked chest and kissed her deeply as he pushed inside her.

They were better than before, and she nearly cried with joy at this reunion.

When they were both sated, breathing heavily, their hearts still thudding, they came to rest.

"I missed this. Missed you," he whispered and kissed her temple.

"Me, too. That was wonderful."

He made a humming sound of agreement. Her eyes drifted closed. Her body still buzzed with pleasure. She blinked her eyes, trying to think.

"Are you all right?" she whispered.

"Never better." His words had that tired slur of a man not really awake, falling as she was, into slumber.

He brushed a stray lock of hair away from her face, his hand unusually clumsy. She pressed her lips to his neck and then closed her eyes, still draped across him like a second blanket.

She did not know how long she slept, but when she next opened her eyes it was to the barking of a large dog.

Carter was out of bed in an instant. Morning light flooded around the cracks of the curtains.

"Who is it?" she said.

"Stay here."

He tugged on a pair of athletic shorts and retrieved one of the pistols from his duffel.

She lifted the sheets to her chest and then realized how ridiculous that was as a means of protection, so she scrambled from the other side of the bed. She shimmied into the polar fleece bottoms and dived into the red T-shirt. Carter had already vanished down the hall.

Justice had stopped barking. Amber stilled. Did he know the intruder or had someone silenced the dog?

CARTER STOOD FLATTENED against the wall between the kitchen and living room listening to the car door slam. A moment later, the front door opened. Justice continued to bark, but the inflection was different.

Carter suspected it was Kurt, but he waited until he heard his brother greet his dog and then let him out in the yard.

"Kurt?" Carter called. "It's Carter."

"Carter?" came the reply, his brother's voice full of shock.

"Coming in," he said.

When Carter stepped into the kitchen a moment later it was to find his brother standing beside the sink of dirty dishes with his gun drawn. Carter held up his good hand with the pistol. The other arm just didn't cooperate, so he left it half-raised.

Kurt looked like hell. Red eyes, dust covering his jeans and jacket. But instead of yelling at Carter for worrying them, his kid brother grabbed Carter in a bear hug.

The embrace hurt Carter, and he didn't quite keep the groan from escaping.

"What happened?" asked Kurt. "You okay? Mom's worried sick and Jack…" He blew out a breath and put Carter at arm's length.

Carter glanced toward the bedroom as Kurt followed the direction of his gaze.

"Amber? It's Kurt. Come out."

She stepped from Kurt's bedroom door and into the hall on slender bare feet. The dragging hems of the fleece bottoms had been rolled, but the over large T-shirt did not hide that she wore nothing beneath. Carter looked to Kurt, whose eyes widened at the picture she made, her hair still tangled from sleep and her eyes half-lidded.

Carter tucked the pistol in the pocket of his shorts.

Kurt's eyes widened even more, and he made a humming sound before glancing away.

"We've been looking for you two."

When Kurt turned back to his brother, Carter found his cheeks a little too pink and his voice a little too breathless.

"What happened to you?" Kurt said, finally noticing the ACE bandage still holding the dressing in place.

"Got shot."

Kurt's bright smile dropped away. "Shot?"

"Last night," said Amber.

"Let me check it."

"Call Jack first," Carter said.

Kurt reached for his phone. Carter stayed his hand.

"No cell phones."

Kurt blinked at him. "That's all I have. Wait, you want me to leave?"

Carter nodded.

"After I check that."

"All right."

Carter sat on a kitchen chair as Kurt unwrapped the bandage and peered beneath the dressing.

"Needs a stitch or two."

"So, stitch it."

Kurt worked as a paramedic, mostly in the air ambulance flying folks from rural areas to the larger medical facilities in Phoenix. His brother kept his personal medical kit in his truck and a similar collection of supplies in his home.

A few minutes later Carter was regretting his words, but Kurt was quick and competent. He added antibiotics to the treatment and had Carter's throbbing, stitched, disinfected shoulder dressed and bandaged again.

FROM OUTSIDE THE DOOR, Justice scratched and whined. Amber stepped toward the door, and Carter grabbed her hand.

"Let Kurt do it."

She understood. He didn't want her seen from the drive. Kurt let his dog inside. Justice was all wiggles and whines for the three of them until Kurt gave him his breakfast, and he settled down.

"You want to fill me in or should I go first?" asked Kurt.

"You first," said Carter.

Amber sat at the kitchen table, leaving the opposite

chair vacant. Kurt drew a water bottle from the refrigerator, while Carter leaned against the counter nearby.

They looked a lot alike, she realized. Same soft brown eyes and black hair. Similar bronze skin color, though it looked like Kurt spent more time outdoors. They were close in height and body build and the wide set of their eyes. But Kurt's face was younger, less angular, and his eyes held an openness missing from Carter's. Their similar build and appearance only highlighted to her more vividly how different their brother Jack was by comparison.

"Well, I heard on the news that the mine admitted that some supplies are unaccounted for. News speculations that we're talking explosives."

"What did the authorities say?" asked Amber.

"What they always say. 'No comment.'"

Amber's stomach squeezed at this. Why hadn't she suspected wrongdoing instead of chalking up the error to an honest mistake?

"They also found the car used by the shooter's inside man. Someone torched it. They're sorting through what's left. Lost cause, though."

She thought of the shooter's driver parked at the loading dock and that strange blond hair, certain now it was a wig.

Amber wondered what would have happened if she had gone over Ibsen's head to the head of the business office upstairs, and sadness threatened to swallow her up.

Carter slid orange juice before her. "Drink that," he ordered. Then he returned his attention to Kurt. "Did they find the US marshals?" asked Carter, his face grim.

"Thanks to your marker."

"Anything on the two that impersonated the FBI?" asked Carter. "The ones who took Amber and me from the station?"

Kurt shook his head.

"Might be the same guys," offered Carter.

"That's what Jack thinks, too," said Kurt.

"How long have you been looking for us, Kurt?" asked Amber.

"I got a call from Jack yesterday about one in the afternoon saying that you two never made it to Phoenix. State Police, sheriff and police out of Darabee PD were all searching for you, but they didn't see the marker. You left that for us, right?"

Carter nodded and measured out the water, then poured it into the reservoir, then flipped on the coffeemaker. The hissing and gurgling sounded promising.

"Jack spotted that and called Tommy." Kurt flicked his attention to her. "He's a tracker with the Shadow Wolves."

Carter had told her that.

Kurt continued. "He's home on leave until the end of the month." His attention returned to Carter. "Anyway, by the time Tom got down there, the state police and FBI had ruined any tracks around the van. US Marshals had also been tromping around. Crime tape, the whole deal. They let Jack in since he found the thing, and that FBI guy, Forrest, he okayed us. He's Black Mountain, you know?"

"Met him," said Carter.

"They had seen where you went down the bank and brought the dogs who, of course, caught both trails and wanted to go in both directions at once. Tommy found your message, and we headed back toward town while the rest of them went the other way. But we lost you on the outskirts when you left the arroyo."

The coffeepot was only half full, but Carter tugged it free and half filled three mugs. He gave her one first.

"Sugar," he said, pointing to the packets in a similar mug on the table.

"Now you," said Kurt to Carter.

Carter rolled his shoulder and winced. "We were attacked by two gunmen driving an SUV with state police markings. Amber saw only one man. It was the same man from the copper mine," he said as he related the details of their experience.

After some questions, Carter continued and told how they'd returned to get the second pistol from the dead US marshal.

"Tommy said you had been back," Kurt said as his smile fell. "Is that when you got shot?"

"No. During a second attack. We stole a car. Left it behind in—"

"Found it already," said Kurt. "How'd you get here?"

Carter told him about the truck and asked if Kurt could get Jack to contact the owner and return the vehicle.

"I'm sure he can. Hey, that rental you were in was pretty banged up. Looked like you got hit from behind and sideswiped by a dark blue car."

"It hit us. Then he tried to knock us off the road, but I managed to push him off the shoulder. That's when I got shot."

"You see the driver?" he asked.

Carter shook his head and then lifted his chin toward Amber. "She did."

Kurt had set aside his coffee, and his expression was uneasy. "Same guy?"

Amber shook her head. "No. Not the shooter."

"Could you identify him?"

"Yes. He drove the Subaru the day we were kidnapped. Last night I saw him again, only his nose is all swollen, purplish." She thought of the man who had been driving the Subaru, picturing him as he stepped from the SUV and then with his nose gushing blood from the impact with the air bag. Her skin prickled. Something had been familiar about him. Was he the same one driving the van in Lilac? She briefly considered that and decided they could be one and the same.

Kurt turned back to Carter who had finished his coffee and was reaching for more.

"What kind of vehicle hit you?"

"A police cruiser, dark color. Bumped us from behind and then swiped Amber's door."

Kurt sagged back against the counter.

"What's wrong?" asked Carter.

"I saw that car."

"Where?"

"On the reservation last night. Unmarked car with the mirror hanging off. It was all scraped up on the driver's side."

"Tell Jack," said Carter.

"Yeah. I did." Kurt's hand ran absently through his thick short hair. "I forgot to tell you that the van they found at Lilac was outfitted with a police scanner."

Carter shifted from side to side as if trying to find his balance. "So they have been following all radio communication."

"That's what Jack said. He's got ears." Kurt lifted his coffee and drank the remains in one swallow. "This is why they can't find him."

Amber knew who he meant. It was impossible for the Lilac Mine shooter to still be at large and switching vehicles as if he owned a car rental company, unless he had help—the kind of help that came from law enforcement.

Chapter Twenty-Two

Carter's brother showered and changed. He didn't say anything about the bed that had obviously been slept in by two people, and when he was done, he gave Carter a container holding the rest of the antibiotic capsules.

"I'd like to bring you to the fire station," Kurt said. "Safer than here, I think."

But he wasn't sure. Amber could see that from his wrinkled brow.

He continued. "I don't want to leave you here alone." His hand went to his phone and then dropped away as he recalled it was no longer a viable option.

Carter shook his head. "Whoever is after us has information from the inside."

"Jack couldn't get that kind of detail," said Kurt.

Someone higher up than a tribal detective, thought Amber.

"What do you want me to do?" asked Kurt, reverting to little brother.

"Get to Ray, Dylan or Jack. Make sure to relay what you told me about the vehicle you spotted on our Rez. Then tell them where we are and tell them to identify themselves before they come through that door."

Kurt nodded. "I'll be as quick as I can be." He let his dog back inside and then gave him a quick pat. "Take care of my brother, Justice."

Carter stood facing the closed door with the dog standing before him, tail wagging merrily. At least one of them was happy to be here.

Amber fiddled with her empty coffee mug as silence descended on the kitchen. She felt the gnawing ache that followed a mistake of epic proportions. Carter needed this reservation like he needed air. She knew she couldn't take him from this place. To experience how hard it was on the outside. How could she protect him the way he was protecting her?

Last night had proved two things. She still loved Carter, and she would have to leave him again to keep him safe.

She rose and took her mug to the sink. Carter intercepted her before she could get past him. His fingers wrapped about her forearm, staying her. She kept her eyes down.

"Amber? You okay?"

She thought of all the times she wasn't okay, back when her dad had disowned her, when she had to leave with nothing, when she'd come back to Carter and he'd rejected her, too. But of all those miserable times, this was the worst. Because she knew now that Carter understood everything and that they might have had a chance together in any other time and place. She gave one hard swallow, and she lifted her chin to face him.

"Fine."

He assessed her, studying her expression and staring into her eyes. She managed a half smile.

"Help is on the way," she said. And with it, their imminent separation.

He nodded, but kept hold of her with his hand and the steady stare.

"You want to talk about last night?"

A pain stabbed across her stomach, and she forced herself to relax, breathe, think.

She shook her head, not trusting her voice. Her jaw clamped so tight it ached.

His eyes narrowed. "Amber?"

She tried for a smile and from his growing concern, failed miserably.

"Say something," he demanded.

"I—I think you... I need a shower."

She had changed direction mid-sentence, but he didn't press.

"All right."

He let her ease past him and watched as she disappeared into the bathroom.

Despite his denial, he recognized what this was. Nine years had taught him that he wasn't going to ever get over her. Amber was too smart, too beautiful and too brave for him to chalk her up as something ordinary. She was exceptional in every way. She had fortitude and kept her wits under fire. She'd been strong enough to survive two dysfunctional parents and protect her sisters from their immorality. And he knew that she still had feelings for him even before last night. But he also knew she was holding back, and it scared him to death that she might be preparing to leave him again. She had tried to explain that she had left to protect him from making a mistake, taking on her father's debt and so becoming a partner in the crime of hurting her sisters. She had left them all out of love. The trouble she faced now was far worse. But if she still loved him, would that make her stay or go?

Carter pressed both hands to the kitchen counter and groaned. His head sank as he accepted the truth. He still loved Amber Kitcheyan.

She was the one for him. Now he had to figure out a way to keep her alive long enough to convince her to stay.

Carter headed into his brother's room. What would Amber wear? Some searching turned up a T-shirt from high school that must have been kept for nostalgic reasons. Carter packed his bag with food and water, then put both pistols in the bag.

The shower had stopped, so he knocked. "I set out some things on Kurt's bed."

She called her thanks, and he retreated to the kitchen to make breakfast. The first omelet burned a little, so he ate that one and then made another.

She emerged shortly afterward with her hair in two neat braids, flushed cheeks and smelling like his brother's deodorant. Unfortunately, that didn't dampen his reaction to the sight of her, clean and her skin pink and dewy.

She held out her arms, showing rolled cuffs at wrist and ankle, her scuffed high boots now under the denim cuffs. The jeans needed cinching at the middle but stretched across her backside in a way that made his eyebrows lift and his throat go dry.

"That will do," he said.

"Hungry?" he asked. At her nod he used the spatula to give her the second cheese omelet with more coffee. Then he hit the shower, which he found as challenging as getting dressed, thanks to his injury.

When he returned to her she gave him an odd look.

"You okay?" she asked. "You look a little green."

"I'm fine."

"They should be here soon," she said. "You don't have a fever, do you?" She carried her plate to the sink and then used the back of her hand to feel his forehead. "You'll probably need a tetanus shot or something."

"Kurt mentioned that."

Her cool hand brushed his forehead, and she frowned. Then she lifted up on tiptoes, grabbed him behind the neck and tugged. He folded obediently at the waist, and she pressed her lips to his forehead, then dropped back to her heels.

"You feel a little hot," she said.

"Every time I get close to you," he muttered.

Her gaze flashed to his, and perhaps she could see that he was not flirting because she only stared up at him with wide almond-shaped eyes.

"Me, too" she whispered.

Bad time to take her back to bed and a really, really bad time to share his feelings for her. But what if he didn't have another chance? They might not be alone again for who knows how long.

"Amber," he said, trying not to think too hard. He was better on the fly. "About last night."

She continued to stare, her dark eyes unreadable, but the tension in her mouth was not encouraging.

"Yes?"

"Well, I'm not leaving you, and I won't let them take you from me."

"They will take me, and if there is witness protection, then they'll separate us. They told me that."

"Not if you marry me."

She gaped. It took her a full half minute to close her mouth. Was it really that preposterous?

"No," she said at last.

"Why, no?"

"Because you're not leaving the reservation."

"I am if you are."

She turned away and then rounded on him. "Carter, every time you get near me, someone tries to kill us."

"And you think that's my fault?"

"Of course not. But you took a bullet yesterday. I can't live with that."

"You know what I can't live with?"

She waited, saying nothing.

"Losing you again. I am not losing someone else I love,

and I am not leaving you behind like Hatch. That is not going to happen. Like it or not, you are stuck with me."

From beneath the table Justice growled and rose to his feet. Amber stiffened as the dog began to bark. Someone was here.

Chapter Twenty-Three

Carter reached behind his back, drawing out the pistol. He lifted his index finger to his lips and motioned Amber to move out of the kitchen, which she did as fast as her wobbly legs would carry her.

The breakfast that had tasted so good had started roiling in her stomach like a tumbleweed in high winds.

She hunched behind the wall, peeking back at Carter as he crept over to the door, and in a fast motion he glanced out before ducking behind the frame. Justice's growl grew louder, but Carter shushed him and Justice ceased his noise.

"Tribal PD," he said to her in a strained whisper.

His brother, probably. Or someone in another stolen car? she wondered, crouching lower behind the wall and knowing from the nightly news that Sheetrock made a terrible barrier against bullets.

Amber waited as the sound of doors shutting reached her. Then the murmur of voices.

A male voice called a greeting in Tonto Apache from outside. Amber knew that deep voice. It was Detective Jack Bear Den. She watched Carter's face for confirmation.

His shoulders sagged, and he lowered his weapon. He met her gaze and nodded, his mouth quirking upward.

From outside came more voices. Someone else spoke. They asked permission to enter. They told them to step away from the door. Carter issued a formal invitation to enter as he moved to the hall beside her, offering a hand as she rose to stand with him.

A moment later four men entered with weapons drawn but lowered. First came Jack Bear Den, filling the frame with his massive shoulders. He was followed by Ray Strong and Dylan Tehauno. Tribal Thunder had arrived. Finally Kurt Bear Den appeared at the rear and a surprise guest, Field Agent Luke Forrest.

Carter gave Jack a look.

"He's okay," said Jack, but Carter seemed unconvinced.

Jack holstered his pistol and came forward, resting a hand on Carter's injured shoulder. "You all right?"

"Yeah. What's going on?"

"We're bringing you to our station for now." Jack glanced at Amber and then returned his attention to Carter. "Kurt told me about the unmarked car, and he said that you've been shot."

Carter tugged at the collar of his shirt to show the bandage.

"He also said that Ms. Kitcheyan saw the man who shot you."

"I did."

"That makes you a VIP witness, Ms. Kitcheyan," said Luke Forrest. "You've seen the copper mine shooter, his driver and now a third man. You are sure he wasn't one of the other two?"

"I've been thinking about that. He might be the same man who drove the van in Lilac, and he was definitely the man driving the Subaru that took us from the tribal police station."

"The one with the busted nose?" asked Forrest.

Amber nodded. "No cap. No blond hair."

"We'll need your help for a new set of composite drawings. I have a call in to send one of our artists."

"You two ready?" asked Dylan.

Carter hoisted his bag and followed them out.

At the station, Kurt changed Carter's soggy dressing and checked the twelve stitches in his throbbing shoulder.

They were both questioned separately again. Each had some time with a technician trained to use the software program to create computer-based facial composites of both the copper mine shooter and his driver and the man who shot at them last night.

Jack had been with the FBI and Amber, but he returned to Carter with some news.

"Amber's composite of the shooter looks a lot like the man Kurt described seeing in the battered police unit, right down to the busted nose."

"Same guy?"

"Yeah. They think so. We're searching for the cruiser."

Carter mentioned the truck he had stolen again and Jack assured him it was on its way back to its owner with apologies and thanks.

"I'm taking lunch orders," said Jack. "What do you want?"

It was past three and closer to dinner than lunch.

"Jack, how long am I going to be sitting in this office?"

"We're making arrangements, Carter. But we want to be careful."

Carter raked his hands through his hair, ignoring the complaint from his healing shoulder.

"Maybe I am going crazy. But I think I'm…"

"Don't say it," said Jack, hand raised to stop him. "She's a witness."

"We're both witnesses."

"Do you get what's happening? They're not going to put you two up in some ski chalet in Vail. You two are leaving this Rez, and I might not even be able to find you."

Carter's hands dropped to his sides. "What are you talking about?"

"Protection. The kind that you don't get to opt out of."

"But we'll be together."

Jack rolled his eyes. "They'll separate you two for sure."

Carter sat back, his worst fears confirmed. "I can't let them take her again."

"Again? She left on her own the last time."

"It's complicated."

Jack sat back. "Yeah."

Carter thumped back in his seat. "I gotta think."

"I'm getting you a burger and fries. You want anything else?"

Besides Amber? "No."

Kurt delivered the meal and sat with Carter as he ate.

"Sorry about breaking into your place," said Carter to Kurt.

"I'm glad you did. Glad, you know, that you're all right."

His brother had been through a long night of worry. Carter felt badly about that, too.

"I couldn't think of a way to let you know."

"I understand. You did the right thing. Scared me, though."

"Yeah. I'm sorry."

Kurt didn't reply. Instead he pressed his lips tight and nodded, his eyes glassy. He breathed in and out and then nodded a few times, gathering himself.

"Amber gave me the papers to apply for reinstatement in the tribe."

Carter perked up. "That's good."

"Yeah," he said.

Just then the door flew open, and Dylan stood in the gap.

"They got him," he said. "The copper mine killer is in police custody."

THEY CAUGHT THE Lilac Mine Killer, as the press had dubbed him. Amber heard that he was on his way to the larger jail in Darabee. She and Carter would be making an ID there just as soon as they could arrange a lineup and safe transport.

The responsibility of that weighed on her. She knew the killer's face. She was very good with faces, though the names sometimes escaped her. And this face, the one gripping that huge rifle and looking right at her, was one she knew she would never forget.

Carter's brother returned with four officers. "You two ready?"

Amber stood stiffly, feeling awkward in the body armor they had insisted she wear. The twinge of both her shoulder and hip ached from yesterday's collision. They told her that the bruised muscles had tightened up. They complained with each stride but loosened by slow degrees until she was seated again, in the back of a tribal police cruiser.

"They got him?" asked Carter.

"Seems so," Jack said.

"Will I be behind glass when I see him?" asked Amber.

"Yes," said Detective Bear Den. "They have a one-way mirror in their station. Buckle up, Ms. Kitcheyan."

Amber repressed a groan as she twisted to retrieve the shoulder restraint and clip it into place.

The drive to Darabee, some thirty minutes east, was uneventful. She tried and failed to spot the place where Carter had left the marker and had almost given up when she saw the yellow police tape fluttering from orange traffic cones by the side of the road. She said a prayer for the two US marshals killed while trying to protect them.

When they reached the station, it was twilight, but there was a great deal of light coming from the parking area beside the station. She couldn't make out what it was at first, but then she recognized the news vans with raised satellite antennae. It was clear from the bright floodlights and the press waiting with cameras poised that someone had leaked the arrest information to the news.

"Oh, great," said Jack.

"Sit tight," said Dylan, from the front passenger seat. "They have a back entrance. Darabee police are waiting to escort us in."

He passed a blanket back to each of them. They were the kind of fleece blankets you wrap around yourself at a football game, but they were blue and said FBI on them.

"These go over your heads. We don't want any photos of either of you."

She looked at Carter for rescue, and he said nothing as he unfolded the blanket. It was in that instant that Amber realized that her life would never go back to normal. Not ever.

AMBER MANAGED TO make it inside without tripping. Two athletic lawmen had held her by each arm, and she thought that her feet had barely touched the ground between the car and the neighboring police station in Darabee. She had been aware of the bright lights of the television cameras as she was rushed inside the station.

Once inside she was escorted to an interview room. There she clutched an unwanted foam cup of strong coffee as she waited to be called to identify their suspect. Both she and Carter would be called separately to make the identification from a lineup. They were told to take their time and be certain of their choice. The longer she sat here, the more nervous she became.

There would be only one opportunity to get it right. Carter would go first.

When they came for him, she stood, realizing that she would be left alone in this tiny interrogation room in his absence, and felt a rising sense of panic.

Carter gave her a warm, reassuring smile. "Be right back."

She fidgeted in the small room, drumming her fingers on the surface of the table that was bolted to the floor. She kept her eyes pinned on the door. Amber knew she should wait, but she found herself opening the door. Posted outside was a uniformed police officer, his matching blue shirt and slacks separated by a utility belt fixed with various tools of the trade. He looked surprised at her emergence. Beyond him she saw a man with a purple bruise on his face duck out of sight. Her mind flashed to an image of Carter kicking their captor in the face with his boot and their captor slapping a hand over his left eye. She lifted a finger to ask who that was.

"Ma'am?" he said. "I have to ask you to wait inside."

Could that have been the one that identified himself as Agent Muir? She knew it unlikely that the FBI impersonator was hanging out in the Darabee police station, but still, he was about the right height…and that shiner.

She turned her attention to the officer guarding the door and was about to tell him what she saw when there was a sharp report from a pistol.

The officer pushed her across the threshold as she heard the sound of more shots fired in close succession. One, two. Amber's flesh went cold. The officer's eyes rounded, and he drew his gun, gripping it with both hands. Then he hesitated.

"Stay there." He shut the door in her face. She heard a click and watched him run down the hall and out of sight.

Amber tried the door and found it locked.

She was trapped.

CARTER WAS IN the squad room. It was his understanding that the other men who would join the lineup were ready, and he was waiting only for the suspect to arrive. He was chatting with his brother when the shots sounded. His very first thought was of Amber.

Where was she?

Both he and Jack stood and Jack drew his weapon before they charged out into the hall. Carter found a scene of chaos before him. Officers shouted and tussled. He saw raised arms and the barrel of a gun pointed at the ceiling. Another shot discharged from the weapon. A young officer rushed past him. The same one that he had seen guarding Amber.

Jack looked at him, and Carter cursed. Jack went toward the shots, and Carter headed in the opposite direction at a run.

Carter reached the interrogation room to find no guard posted. Amber pounded on the locked door and shouted to let her out. He tried the knob, releasing the button that locked the door. Amber spilled out and into his arms.

"What's happening?" she cried.

"Don't know." He wrapped an arm about her and hurried her farther into the station, heading for the small kitchenette they had passed on arrival.

She clung to him as they ran through the open door which he closed behind them. The windowless staff room contained a microwave, sink, refrigerator and three small circular tables with plastic chairs. The walls were decorated with safety awareness posters. Amber didn't step away from him but continued to grip the fabric of his shirt in her fists.

"Get behind me," he ordered.

She hesitated only a moment and then did as he asked.

"Do you still have a weapon?" she asked.

"They took it." He motioned to the counter and sink that jutted from the wall. "Back behind that."

Amber wedged herself into the gap between the white refrigerator and end of the countertop with the wood grain Formica finish. Carter flicked off the lights and watched the door.

"What should we do?" she whispered.

"Wait."

They listened in silence to the voices. There were no more shots. Carter glanced to Amber who now squatted with one hand on the refrigerator and the other gripping the edge of the counter.

She told him about the man she glimpsed, the one with the black eye.

"You think it was Muir?"

She nodded.

This didn't make any sense. They were in a police station. They were supposed to be safe.

Someone opened a door down the hall. Carter couldn't see who without revealing their position.

"She's not here," said the unfamiliar voice. Was it the officer assigned to protect her or someone else?

Carter lifted a finger to his lips, and Amber nodded.

He backed away from the door as the footsteps approached. Doors opened. The footsteps again. A heavy tread. The door burst open, and Carter sprang. The intruder flicked on the light before Carter hit him in the chest carrying them both into the hall.

AMBER CROUCHED AGAINST the wall. She could see Carter's legs but not the man in the hall.

"I'm a cop," said the downed man.

"What are you doing?" asked Carter.

Amber moved out to see Carter gripping the lapels of the man's blazer in both fists.

"Looking for the woman. The idiot plebe left her."

Amber recognized a Texas accent, and her skin prickled. She stood and peered around the refrigerator to see an Anglo man in a dress shirt, slacks and tie, now askew. A badge was clipped to his hip beside his empty holster. The man's gaze flicked to her. Carter's gaze did not waver, so he must have seen the odd look the man cast her. She couldn't define it, but thought it seemed a sort of triumph, like a boy finding the last person in a game of hide-and-seek.

His attention shifted to Carter. "I said I'm a police officer. Detective Casey, DPD."

"Get my brother," ordered Carter.

"I have to take y'all somewhere secure," he said.

Carter didn't move. Had he picked up the accent?

"We're secure. Now get my brother."

"Y'all need to give me my gun back."

Carter shook his head and aimed the gun at the detective.

"It's a crime, what you're doing."

Carter didn't move, and he didn't lower his gun.

Detective Casey pursed his lips and blasted a great exhalation of breath.

"My brother?" Carter prompted.

"Sure."

He retreated a step. Amber wanted to ask what was happening but also did not want that man to linger any longer.

Finally Casey released the door and stepped out of sight. Carter did not holster his weapon. Instead he took a position before her, pressing her body against the wall.

"Texas accent," she said.

"Yeah," he replied.

The voices outside had quieted, and so it was easy to hear the footsteps. More than one person, she judged. Amber drew a breath and held it. Who was out there now?

"Carter? Amber? It's Jack. Are you two still in there?"

Amber's shoulders sagged, and the wind left her. She wrapped her arms about Carter's middle and pressed her cheek to his broad muscular back.

"Yes," he called, making his voice vibrate against her face.

"Can we come in?"

"Who?"

"Me, Forrest, Chief Tinnin and Detective Casey from Darabee."

"Just you," replied Carter.

Amber released him, coming to stand at his side. Carter lowered his weapon.

Jack entered, and Carter holstered his gun. Jack made a face.

"I have to take that," he said, motioning to the pistol holstered at Carter's hip.

"I don't think so," said Carter.

"You almost shot one of their officers."

Carter shook his head. "Guy had a Texas accent."

Jack's brow quirked, and Amber knew he understood the implications of that.

"What happened out there?" asked Carter.

Jack rubbed his neck as he answered. "Someone shot our suspect."

"Shot?" said Carter. "In a police station. How would that happen?"

"Happened to Lee Harvey Oswald."

Carter glared.

Jack filled them in. "Just outside the station, as they were bringing him in," said Jack.

"They brought him in the front door?" asked Carter.

"We didn't. It was Darabee's bust, and they wanted to show him off."

"So they brought him past the news cameras."

Jack looked positively grim during his explanation.

"We have his killer in custody," said Jack.

"Well, hurrah," said Carter.

"What about the suspect?" asked Amber.

"Dead."

"Jack, Amber thinks she saw the guy that took us. The one I kicked in the eye."

"Where?"

Chapter Twenty-Four

Carter paced from one side of the small staff room to the other. The FBI and Darabee PD had searched the station for the man Amber said she saw but came up empty. If he had been here, he was here no longer.

Agent Forrest had joined them as well as Tribal Chief Tinnin and the Darabee chief of police, Jefferson Rowe. Amber sat at one of the lunch tables, and he stood next her. Jack flanked Amber's other side as they faced Forrest, Rowe and Tinnin.

"That's just great," said Carter. "The shooting suspect is dead, and you can't find the two men who kidnapped us yesterday."

"What about the guy, the one who came to the door? He had a Texas accent."

"Yeah," said Chief Rowe. "He's one of mine. Detective Eli Casey. He came to find you two when your guard left his post."

Carter and Jack exchanged a look. Having a Texas accent wasn't a crime, but he knew Jack was on it.

"He have a brother?" asked Jack.

Rowe's eyes narrowed. "Not sure. Why?"

Amber broke in. "But he's dead. The shooter from Lilac, I mean. So they don't need us as witnesses. Right? We can go home."

Carter glanced at Amber and saw the weariness in her posture and in the dark smudges under her eyes.

"We still need you," said Forrest. "We need a positive ID on the suspect to start."

"But he's…" Amber's eyes widened and then her gaze flashed to Carter. He made it to her in two steps and grabbed a hold of her arm as she swayed. She slipped her hands around his biceps and squeezed. He tried to ignore the aching want that she triggered. Amber was done in by a day that would bring most women to hysterics.

"We can use photos," said Forrest, talking fast, his hands raised to assuage Amber's obvious agitation.

"You don't have to view the body," added Rowe.

At the word body, Amber's strength finally went out. Carter caught her, drew her in and held on.

"We'd like to move you back to the…ah, the room you just vacated," said Forrest.

"The interrogation room? The one that locks from the outside?" asked Carter. "Nope. That won't work for us. Bring the photos here. And get Amber a water or something."

Carter helped Amber to a seat at one of the circular tables and drew up a chair next to her. She sagged against him, and he curled an arm around her waist.

"I've never seen a dead body," she whispered.

"I'll be right here."

He glanced at Rowe who shook his head. "She needs to make the ID separately from you."

Amber shuddered and buried her face in Carter's chest. He stroked her head as she struggled to bring her breathing back under control. The water arrived in a plastic bottle, and Carter coaxed her to drink. By slow degrees she pulled herself together. She sipped her water, and Carter kept an arm around her narrow shoulders and his eyes on her.

"It will be all right," he said.

She turned her dark, worried eyes on him. "Will it?"

He nodded. "I'm not letting you go, Amber. We'll get through this together."

By the time Jack returned with Tinnin, Amber was sitting erect with an expression of grim determination on her face. He'd seen that same expression on his mother's face before she went in for some outpatient surgery. It was that "let's get this over with" look.

Jack spoke in a soothing tone, or what passed for soothing. Jack's voice was too gruff to be comforting, but he managed to kick it down from threatening to neutral.

"They have the photos ready," said Jack. "Carter, you're first."

Carter stood. "I'm not leaving her alone."

"I'll…" Jack turned to the door. "I'll stay. Two of Rowe's men have the door. That work?"

"That guy Casey doesn't come in here," said Carter.

"All right," said Rowe.

"Then I'll be quick." He turned to Amber. "You be all right?"

She lifted her chin and gave a stiff little nod. He'd never met a braver woman. Damn but she was magnificent.

With that he gave Amber's hand a squeeze and followed Chief Rowe out to see if he could make an ID of the prime suspect in the Lilac Copper Mine shooting.

AMBER WAS ABSOLUTELY certain that she'd have nightmares featuring those faces for a long time to come.

Amber had been nervous about the ID. But it was simple to spot the man who she had seen outside Mr. Ibsen's home and again yesterday afternoon. The harder part was knowing that she looked at the face of a dead man. They were all dead, each photo of a man about the same age, weight and ethnicity and all a little too pale, grayish and glassy-eyed to still be breathing.

"That's just great," said Jefferson Rowe, the chief of the Darabee police force. He seemed to realize he needed a shave, because he scratched at the whiskers that were mostly black.

"Is that all?" she asked.

He gave her a long look. "All for now. I'm sure the Feds will be taking you to a safe house. We've suggested a few spots, but I think they're going back to the same hotel you were in on Tuesday night. Nice place, I hear."

She didn't like his smile, and it took a moment to realize that was because it didn't reach his eyes. They were a glacial blue and just as welcoming.

The chief glanced at Field Agent Forrest, but he neither confirmed nor denied Rowe's surmise. Now Amber did smile at Forrest's poker face.

"Can I ask you about the man who killed him?" asked Amber.

The chief's jaw pulsed as his teeth came together.

"Active investigation," he said.

Of course the shooting had happened on this man's watch, right here in front of his police station. Judging by the color of his face, he found that embarrassing, and well he should.

Forrest led her out, and a second federal officer flanked her other side as they walked down the hall.

"His name is Karl Hooke," said Forrest, answering her question. "And he's a member of the Turquoise Canyon Tribe."

"What?" She couldn't believe that. It made no sense for someone from their tribe to want to murder the man who attacked a copper mine. "Did he have family there, in Lilac?"

Forrest shook his head.

"Then why?"

Agent Forrest took her elbow and guided her along. "We aim to find out."

She stopped. "Wait. Hooke. Not Morgan Hooke's father."

Forrest narrowed his eyes on her. "He has one child. A daughter, and her name is Morgan."

Amber reeled. "I know her. Or I did know her, in high school."

Agent Forrest did not seem to like that at all.

"You know her father."

"No, not really. Just by sight."

"So he wasn't the driver or one of the men who abducted you?"

She shook her head. "Those men were Anglos."

When she returned to the kitchenette, it was to find Carter and Jack Bear Den conversing in Apache. Carter was in body armor again, which meant they were moving.

Carter broke away to greet her, taking both her icy hands in his. Just the sight of him made everything seem better.

"How did it go?"

"Good," said Forrest for her. "She ID'd the same photo. We're confirming with latents we have recovered, but we are reasonably sure he's the one."

"What about the other men?" she asked. "His driver and the man who hit us last night."

Forrest stopped talking so Jack answered. From Agent Forrest's sour look she assumed he did not approve.

"We have a suspect. Searching for him now," said Jack.

And if they found him, they could find the other man.

"That's good," she said finally allowing herself to smile. "Very good."

Jack seemed to want to say more, but Forrest stepped between them.

"For tonight we are bringing you to a safe house. It's more secure than a hotel."

"Where?" she asked.

"It's on Turquoise Canyon Rez. We need you to put on this vest."

She'd worn the same vest on the trip here from Turquoise Canyon. She accepted Carter's help suiting up in the body armor. They waited while final arrangements were made. Then they were led through the prisoner holding area and out through a side entrance to a waiting van. There Chief Rowe and several officers guarded the exit. By the vehicle waited two more unfamiliar FBI agents in blue windbreakers with bold yellow lettering announcing their affiliation. Amber gave them a good looking over, but there seemed nothing obvious out of order. Still she wouldn't relax until she was back in some kind of building, preferably one on tribal land and with a steel door.

Carter and Jack both stopped at once.

She followed the direction of their gaze. They both gaped at the vehicle. This time they were moving in a Hummer. The really big kind.

Amber glanced from one to the other. Both men had gone pale, and she recalled Carter telling her of the night they lost Hatch. They'd been in Humvees. Was that the same thing?

"Carter?" she said, taking his elbow.

He glanced at her, his face now covered with sweat.

"You okay?" she asked.

"Get in, Mr. Bear Den," said Agent Forrest, his gaze shifting from them to scan the area. Amber understood the message. They were in danger here.

"Carter, we have to go," she said.

He nodded and took a hesitant step forward.

Jack did not move. She glanced back. "I'll follow," he said.

He wasn't getting in that Hummer. She could tell by the

rounding of his eyes and his stiff frame. It was the first time she'd ever seen them afraid. Both of them.

She helped Carter up and followed. Was she sitting in the spot where Hatch Yeager had been or was Carter?

"Let's go," she said, still holding Carter's arm.

Forrest stood next to the opened side door. "What's wrong?"

"Insurgents attacked Carter and his brother in this sort of vehicle."

Forrest swore.

Once they were both inside, the chief poked his head in, his smile broad and his blue eyes cold.

"Good luck, you two, and good job today." He turned to Agent Forrest, now moving up behind him. "Sure you shouldn't go to that hotel? Seems safer to stay put."

"No changes," said Forrest and swept up into the seat behind them.

"Well, we'll bring you to the boundary. Tinnin's guys will have to take it from there."

Carter's brother nodded, shouldering the responsibility, and then hurried off, wiping the sweat from his brow.

Forrest's partner climbed into the third row and closed the door. A few minutes later they were under way.

They had not left the police lot before Agent Forrest told them to move. He wanted them in the back and both on the floor.

"Why?" asked Carter.

"Theory we are working," said his partner.

"Too many people know where you were seated."

She thought of all the police officers from the station. Did they think someone there was involved?

Carter relocated first and sat on the floor, and she moved beside him. Forrest handed over helmets.

"Really?" said Carter. But when Forrest and his partner put one on, Carter fixed one on Amber's head and then his own.

"We have an escort?" asked Carter.

"Better," said Forrest.

The Hummer made a turn and Amber cuddled close to Carter who leaned against the door. He wrapped her up in his arms and pulled her onto his lap. Somehow the beating of his heart was more comforting than the Kevlar and helmet.

"You okay?" she whispered.

He pressed his nose into her neck and inhaled. "Now I am."

"Going to be a long ride this way," she said to their escorts.

"If we're right it won't be long," said Forrest.

"You want to fill us in down here?" said Carter.

"Your brother, Jack, remembered Orson Casey because he arrested him once on tribal land. D and D. Texas boy, Bear Den said. Jack says he had priors. After the arrest, Orson's brother came for him. Name's Eli and he's a police officer in Darabee."

Amber didn't like the sound of that.

"What were the priors?" asked Carter.

"Different things. Escalating. Worst was manslaughter," said Forrest.

"So why is he walking around loose?" asked Carter.

"Witness, uh, failed to make an ID."

"You mean somebody got to the witness."

"Probably. Eli, we think."

"Who did Orson kill?" asked Carter.

"Car dealership night cleaning person. Orson Casey is alleged to have burned down the dealership."

"Why?" asked Carter.

"Member of WOLF, and they object to gas guzzling cars."

"Like this one?" asked Amber.

"Quiet now, we're almost there."

"Almost where?"

"Boundary to your reservation."

They continued to speed along the road. Amber looked up and out the window.

"Going dark," said the agent driving. The headlights flicked off with the dash lights.

"What's happening?" she asked.

Carter held her tighter.

The stars were clear through the large window, pinpoints of blue through the tinted glass. Then something large came up beside them. They swerved to make room and then bumped along the opposite shoulder, slowing, turning, leaving the road.

They came to a stop.

"We left the convoy?" she asked.

"Yes."

"Why?"

"Sending a decoy in our place," said Forrest.

"That's dangerous," said Amber.

Carter chuckled. "You weren't worried when it was us in there."

"No. I was worried."

"Sit tight," said Forrest. "We've got an army out here with us. You can't see them, but they're here. And if anything is going to happen to the convoy, it will be soon."

Amber nestled against Carter who toyed with her hair. When his fingers brushed her neck, she let the tingle of pleasure slip over her skin. Electricity, she thought, every time he touched her.

The radio in the dash crackled. "Shots fired."

Silence again.

"In pursuit."

Amber felt the helicopter that passed overhead. But

she didn't see it. The vibrations thudded through her chest nearly as hard as her own heart.

"Suspect spotted," said another voice.

"In pursuit."

"One suspect in custody," came the newest update.

"How many are there?" said Forrest under his breath.

"Second suspect is down."

The driver cursed. "They better not have killed him."

It was a long silent stretch of dead air before they heard that they had apprehended Orson Casey. His brother, Officer Eli Casey, was dead.

Chapter Twenty-Five

Amber was so tired she was weaving on her feet by the time they arrived in the Phoenix federal building where an FBI field office was located. There she identified Orson Casey from a lineup. Carter made his selection afterward, and they were told they both fingered the same person.

So Orson Casey was the driver of the van in Lilac she saw on the loading dock and the driver of the Subaru impersonating an FBI officer. She also identified Orson as the man in the unmarked car who had shot Carter.

Amber had been shown a photo of Eli Casey, and her skin when icy at the sight. It was the detective at the station in Darabee, the one who had come searching for her during the shooting and who Carter had chased off.

"He was there to kill me, wasn't he?" she asked Carter.

"I think so," said Carter.

She had asked Agent Forrest about the man at the station with the black eye.

"Got him. We'll have you try to identify him pretty quick here."

"Who is he?"

"Name is Jessie Gillroy, and he is also with Darabee PD. A detective. Works with Eli Casey. Or he did. He's now in federal custody, and Eli is dead. Jessie's a match for the inside man at Lilac. Opened the doors for Sanchez. We think he and Orson Casey might help us discover who is funding this operation and where to find those missing explosives."

"Eli Casey and Jessie Gillroy both worked in Darabee?" Was that why Gillroy had looked familiar? Had he been there with Eli Casey and the others at the Darabee police department when she had arrived from Lilac with Carter via air ambulance? She clutched her arms about herself as a cold chill took hold.

Forrest nodded. "Rowe has some crooked officers up there. They've been taking payoffs from someone for information."

"Is that how they knew where to find us?"

Forrest nodded.

Amber wondered how Darabee detectives had gotten hold of a state police vehicle and known their whereabouts when they had been in the custody of US Marshals. She wanted to ask Carter about that because she didn't think a police officer could get ahold of that kind of information, which meant that someone else was involved. Someone higher up.

Plus, the man who had tried to coax her into that Subaru was still at large, and she was growing more certain he had been at the police station tonight.

She supposed that was for the FBI to unravel, and she was too fuzzy-headed to work anything else out. Still it bothered her. Something about it just felt wrong. Why go to so much trouble to kill her? The FBI was already investigating the supply chain at Lilac. What was the point of chasing after her? She didn't know anything.

Unless she did. She rubbed her tired eyes trying to think; she reviewed the sequence of events that had transpired as she'd done repeatedly since the shooting. She had told Ibsen about the overage in the delivery. He had seemed both distracted and upset. He'd told her he would take care of it and then shown her out. That was the last she'd seen him, wasn't it? Something nagged at her; she just couldn't think.

Agent Forrest sat with her in the cubicle where she'd been told to wait. This guy had about as much to say as his desk lamp, and he made her uncomfortable. But Carter trusted him. It was enough for her.

Forrest told her that the convoy with the decoy Hummer had been attacked by riflemen who took out both windows behind which she and Carter should have been seated. They'd used a caliber of bullet that went through protective glass. But they'd revealed their location, and the FBI had caught them. If they had not made the switch, Amber and Carter would both be lying beside Eli Casey in the morgue in Darabee.

"Why did they say their names were Muir and Leopold?" she asked. "Those are the names of famous environmentalists. Aren't they?"

"Very good. Muir founded the Sierra Club and Leopold founded the Wilderness Society."

She shook her head, bewildered. Why choose names of such men?

"So, did Orson tell you who Leopold really is?"

"Not yet." Forrest went quiet again, watching her. "We believe evidence will show that the man claiming to be Muir was actually Gillroy."

"And the men who came after them. Two men, Jack told me. And I heard one say, 'get my brother.' So was that Eli Casey?"

"Yes. The other man is yet unidentified. Soon we hope."

"Who is Warren Cushing? That's what I read on the ID I found in his wallet when I was searching for the handcuff key."

"Cushing ran a tourist outfit in Sedona. Crimson Hummer Excursions. They take guests on off-road tours of the canyons and rock formations. He died two years ago. He'd just received permits for expansion and was murdered at his offices."

"How did he get Cushing's ID?"

"Trophy maybe. We are looking into that."

Then she remembered. A fire. Sedona. Off-road trips.

"I saw that on the news. It was arson. That fire, and the news said—" she reached back into her memory for the information "—some group claimed responsibility."

"WOLF," said Forrest, his whiskey eyes studying her.

Amber sat back. "The other FBI agents, the real ones who questioned me, they asked me about WOLF and BEAR."

"Yes, we thought you were affiliated."

She wasn't and had only attended the PAN rally because her uncle had invited her along.

Her uncle was the head of his medicine society, the one that Carter belonged to, and Carter had some special role there, Tribal Thunder, he said. That wasn't a part of these eco-extremists.

Amber rubbed her arms.

"Cold, Ms. Kitcheyan?"

She shook her head, her mouth now firmly sealed. What did her uncle have to do with all this?

She squeezed her eyes shut, praying that Carter was not tied up in this mess. That his interest in her was genuine and not because he was a part of some vigilante environmental army.

Amber was suddenly terrified that Forrest would mention her uncle's name as a suspect.

"Did they ever catch the arsonists?" asked Amber.

Forrest kept his gaze pinned on her as he shook his head.

She wanted to ask about her uncle, but she did not fully trust Forrest. He was Apache, but not of her tribe.

"Was it those people, the WOLF group, who attacked my office?"

"We believe it was BEAR. WOLF generally tries to avoid loss of life. BEAR makes no such allowances. They believe in the preservation of the environment at the expense of human life."

The mine shooting. She pressed both palms together and lifted them to her lips.

"They did it?"

Forrest nodded. "Yes, we do believe so. Ovidio Natal Sanchez is a known member of BEAR."

Was Carter involved? He'd been there and so fast. The coincidence seemed too unbelievable. Or was it her uncle who was involved or…or both?

"Would you like some water?" he asked.

Amber turned to him. "We aren't waiting for Carter, are we?"

He shook his head. "No."

"This is an interrogation."

"Of sorts."

"Where's Carter?" she asked.

He didn't say anything. The door opened, and Agent Rose stepped in. His expression was like a guest in the receiving line at a funeral. Amber wrapped her arms around herself and rose to her feet.

"Where's Carter?"

"Amber, I think you should sit down," said Agent Rose. What was wrong with his lip? It looked split open.

She shook her head. Whatever he was going to tell her, it was bad. Really, bad.

"Is he all right?"

"Yes. Please, sit."

She shook her head, refusing his request a second time. "What's happening?"

"We've released him," said Agent Forrest.

"Released?" Her knees went wobbly.

Agent Rose got a hold of her and guided her to the chair he had tried to get her into.

"I—I don't understand," she said. Her ears were buzzing because she did understand. "We're in danger."

Forrest shook his head.

"He identified the shooter and that man is dead," said Forrest. "He identified the driver who abducted you, and that man is also dead."

"Leopold," she said.

"Not after him."

"But the extremist groups," she said.

"He seems to know nothing about that, and at present we have no reason to detain him. Chief Tinnin was insistent. He obtained a court order, and so we were compelled to release him."

Yet here she sat. Her skin went icy cold.

Her brain was trying to tell her something, but the fear and panic kept nosing it away, and she couldn't grab hold.

"But there might be more of them. They might hurt him."

"Very likely. But Mr. Bear Den appears to be no threat to anyone."

"He needs protection," she insisted. "Do you have men guarding him?"

"Watching him. Not guarding."

Rose dabbed at his oozing lip with a clean cloth.

"They shot him," she said, not liking the hysterical note in her voice.

"We believe you were the target," said Rose.

"And that you remain a threat to BEAR," said Forrest.

"How am I a threat?"

"That is why we are sitting here. You know something or saw something."

"I didn't."

Forrest shrugged. "We'll come round to it sooner or later."

Rose smiled, and his lower lip cracked open and began to bleed again.

Had Carter given him that fat lip?

Forrest spoke again. "For now you are a protected federal witness."

She shook her head in denial because she now realized that she was the target of all this. She was the last survivor from her office. The one who had spotted the discrepancy, seen the Lilac Mine shooter and at least three of the men who had been hunting her ever since. One remained at large. The pickup man with Eli Casey. Who was he? Where was he? And how many more were out there?

Amber stared from Rose to Forrest. She had never felt more alone in all her life. Rose offered her a paper cup of water, and she gulped down a few swallows before setting aside the cup that trembled in her hands.

"And now you need to come with us," said Rose.

She didn't want to but couldn't think of anything else to do. She didn't feel safe with them. She felt safe with Carter, and he was gone. Would she see him again?

"For how long?" she asked, rising to her feet. The men exchanged looks and tight expressions.

Witness protection. She knew it because they did not know who was in the extremist group called BEAR. They didn't know if the group would retaliate because of Eli Casey's death. They'd been willing to assassinate the Lilac shooter to prevent him from talking.

Amber had been cast out of her tribe many years ago. But she had still had her family. Now she was about to lose them and everything she was. She was about to become invisible.

Amber had lost control of her life once more, and yet now, as they led her away, she did not long for her mother or sisters. She longed for Carter Bear Den. She admitted to herself that she loved him still and that he was much safer without her.

CARTER GROWLED AT KURT. He'd already socked two FBI agents in the face, and Jack said he was lucky they didn't press charges. That only made him want to punch Jack, too, especially after his brother had bum-rushed him into the waiting police unit, but no one punched Jack unless they needed the exercise.

Amber was back there in Phoenix, and when she returned from identifying the surviving Casey brother, she'd be upset, and he would not be there to comfort her. If Jack was right, the next and last time he would see Amber was at Orson Casey's trial.

"Almost home," said Jack.

Jack had navigated the switchbacks up the mountain and the long stretches beside the reservoirs until they had nearly reached the stretch of river and canyon that was theirs by federal treaty.

He was positive that the Casey boys had some serious help from someone, possibly more than one person in Darabee. Eli Casey had been a cop there, and Carter just knew there were more men involved. How else had they allowed a civilian into the station with a pistol and close enough to their shooting suspect to gun down Ovidio Natal Sanchez right there in front of the television cameras?

Sanchez's killer, their very own Karl Hutton Hooke, was an unemployed widower from Turquoise Ridge, the smallest of the Turquoise Canyon communities, and full-blood Apache. Carter felt sick over that. He wondered about the accomplice at the mine. The one who let the shooter in at the loading dock.

"Not Apache, thank the Lord," said Jack. "They found Ann-Marie Glenn's key card in Orson Casey's apartment.

But he was the driver for Sanchez. Who let Sanchez in at the loading dock?"

Jack shrugged. "Eli or Jessie Gillroy, likely."

Carter sat back in his seat. That was for the FBI to untangle. Forrest had been very clear on that.

Jack had filled him in on a few missing details about the convoy attack and apprehension of the Casey boys.

Carter stared out Jack's cruiser as the light from the rising sun crept down the canyon wall, turning the rock face orange. Saturday morning, he realized, less than a week since he'd driven down to Lilac to deliver a message.

Was his truck still down there parked beside the helicopter pad?

He thought of Kenshaw Little Falcon and Forrest's implication that Amber's uncle might be involved in more than spiritual leadership of his tribe and their medicine society. Carter rubbed the tattoo on his right arm, bandaged now and the stitches were beginning to itch.

What was the purpose of Tribal Thunder? he wondered. To protect their land, of course. But how far was Little Falcon prepared to go to do that?

Forrest had told him last night that they didn't need him until the trial. Tribal leadership had involved their attorneys, who'd gained Carter's release because of the tribe's sovereign status; the FBI had agreed to release Carter if the tribe agreed not to get into a public pissing match over their star witness, Amber Kitcheyan. Who was fighting for her? Not her parents or her tribe. Nobody, that was who.

Carter had told them she had applied for reinstatement. Kurt had delivered the paperwork, but the tribal leadership had not yet readmitted her. And now they might never do so.

"But I'll see her at the trial."

Jack startled at the break in the long stretch of silence. "I don't know."

His shoulder was throbbing, and the stitches tugged. He realized he'd forgotten to take his antibiotics. He fished in his pocket for the capsules Kurt had given him and downed one dry. It stuck in his throat.

"This is wrong."

"The FBI has this investigation. You're a tribe member so…"

Carter growled like an angry bear.

Jack blew out a breath. "Mom is worried sick. Dad said his hair is falling out because of all this. How about you let them see you in one piece? Then we can figure out what to do."

Carter folded his arms over his chest, winced in pain and lowered his elbow to the armrest.

"You don't understand. I might never see her again."

"She's safe, Carter, and she's not your responsibility anymore."

But he wanted her to be. He wanted to love her and protect her and be there.

"Listen, I know you like her, but she's a federal witness in a case that seems as though it is going to be huge. They finally have one of the eco-extremists. They hope that's just a start. You have to know that she's marked for witness protection. You can't go with her."

So why was he considering it?

Jack looked at him and then back to the road and then back to him again.

"Carter, you hear me? If you go with her, you will have to leave the tribe and your family. All of us. You won't be able to see us again, ever."

Carter swallowed at the magnitude of the decision he faced.

"Say something, brother."

He looked at Kurt. "I love her."

Jack swore.

CARTER'S MOTHER AND father met him at the door. All he saw of his mother was her arms outstretched as she threw herself at him. He hugged her and then hugged his father. His mother was not quite ready to let him go and maintained a firm grip on his hand as she drew him into his childhood home.

His mother's eyes were red, and his father's rugged face seemed older than he remembered. Thomas, Kurt and Jack entered the living room a moment later, and each received a similar hug from their parents. Jack had to stoop slightly to permit his mother to get her arms around his neck.

"So, our leadership worked it out," said his father to Jack.

"Yeah. We'll need to keep an eye on him. Chief Tinnin is worried about reprisals from the Casey family."

"But the copper mine shooter is dead, and the other two are arrested or dead," said his mother.

"There is at least one guy still out there," said Jack.

"I spoke to Kenshaw Little Falcon," said his father. "He feels that some are unhappy at recent events."

"Who?" asked Carter.

His father gave no answer.

"And the explosives are unaccounted for," said Jack. "No question. Tinnin says the Feds are scrambling to find them and keep the disappearance secret."

His parents exchanged a long look.

"He's not safe here," said his mother in a whisper.

"We'll keep him safe," promised his father. It was a promise he might have a hard time keeping.

"It's happening again," whispered his mother.

Jack and Carter exchanged a confused look as their mother turned to her husband. "Was this a mistake? Taking him out of witness protection?"

Kurt spoke now. "If he enters witness protection, he's not coming back."

His mother rounded on him, her voice raised. "I know that! Don't you think I know that?" She sagged against her husband. "Not again," she whispered. "I can't lose Carter, too."

Jack's brow quirked. Carter shook his head at Jack's silent question. He had no idea what their mom was talking about. Had she said *again*?

When had this happened before? Carter was at a loss.

All four of her sons stepped back. Carter had never seen his mother act this way. Their father pulled her in close.

"It's all right, Mother," Carter said.

"No. It's not," she pressed her face into their dad's denim shirt, and it sounded like she said, "Not again."

Jack's and Carter's gazes met as if each wanted to know if the other had heard that.

"She'll be all right in a minute." Their dad wrapped an arm around his wife and patted her back. He spoke to her in Apache, calming words, tender words.

Carter was torn between the need to comfort and reassure his mother and the need to tell them all what he had decided. He appreciated his tribe's intervention to get him released from federal protection, but he couldn't stay here. Not when Amber was there.

He cleared his throat, and all the males in the room looked to him.

"You should have asked me before you pulled me out."

"We've got your back," said Thomas. "I'm taking a leave to be with you."

He didn't want that. He didn't want his brothers to have to spend their lives guarding his.

"No. You're not. Because I'm not staying. I'm going back. It's the only way I know to keep you all safe and…"

His mother lifted her head and stared at him in absolute horror.

He faltered and then had to look away before he could

continue. "I love Amber Kitcheyan. I'm not willing to let her go."

His dad stepped toward him, but his mother held him back.

"They'll separate you," said Jack.

"Not if I marry her."

Carter clamped his teeth together as he looked from one anxious face to the next. His family whom he loved stared at him in silence.

"You aren't safe with me here," he said, his voice taking on an unwelcome quaver. "And she needs me."

"You can't jump in and out of protective custody," said Jack. "We can't just return you like a dog to the pound."

"Then you better figure it out before the US Marshals take her again."

"I don't like it," said Jack.

"Neither do I. But it's my only choice."

His mother extended a hand, grasping his. "You could stay."

"Mom." He hugged her. "I can't."

She squeezed him so tight his neck ached and his shoulder throbbed.

Carter eased away, grateful to his dad for taking charge of his wife. Carter turned to Jack.

"Make a call, Jack. Tell them whatever you have to. Tell them there's been an attack, but get me back to her."

Chapter Twenty-Six

Two months later, Amber was preparing to testify. She should have been focusing on the upcoming trial and her small but vital part in the proceedings. Instead she was anticipating her meeting with Carter today.

After she had rested and had time to think over all that had happened she had recalled the phone conversation she had heard outside Ibsen's office the day before the shooting and given Forrest the name she had overheard—Theron Wrangler. Forrest had seemed stunned.

"Who is he?" she asked Field Agent Forrest.

"A documentary filmmaker, a political insider," he had said. "Since you mentioned him, we've identified several contacts between him and Harvey Ibsen."

"Is he involved in all this?"

Forrest's expression had given away nothing. "Ongoing investigation," was all he had said.

She took that to mean that Theron Wrangler was their new prime suspect.

She had asked Agent Forrest to allow her to see Carter Bear Den, and he had refused on every occasion. But with the trial approaching she had tried again and even refused to testify if she did not see Carter. Finally, Forrest agreed and arranged a meeting. Now here, she paced the inner chamber of the federal building like a caged lioness as she waited for Carter to appear.

She knew she would have only a few minutes and wondered how much she should say? The door opened, and she tried to hide her disappointment when Agent Forrest peered inside.

"Visitor for you," he said.

The next face she saw was the one she longed for. Carter stepped in, and the door closed behind him. She rushed three steps in his direction before regaining her composure. She walked the final few steps and clasped his hands.

"I'm so glad to see you."

"I saw your sisters and mom before I came. They are all well and send their love." He retrieved his hand, and she felt a tiny sting of sorrow.

Then he reached in his coat and passed her an envelope. "Photos of everyone and a letter from Kay and one from Ellie."

"Dad?" she said.

"He's in tribal jail, Amber. Jack says he's fine. Got a ninety-day sentence from the tribal courts."

She didn't know why that made her so sad. Nothing had changed; perhaps that was it.

"And you?"

He rolled his shoulder. "All healed up."

She stared at his face, trying to memorized every small detail, already dreading the knock and their separation.

"That's good."

"I have something else." He reached again and then presented her a legal-sized envelope which bore the great seal of the Turquoise Canyon Tribe.

"What's this?" she asked.

"They reinstated your membership. You are one of the people again."

Amber's lip and chin trembled, and the burning kept her from speech.

"I'm so sorry, Amber. I should have known. Should have trusted you."

She nodded and accepted the document, pressing it to her heart.

"They petitioned to have you returned, but the FBI and US Marshals made a strong case that you will be targeted by BEAR. They said you have information linking Harvey Ibsen to an important possible BEAR conspirator."

Theron Wrangler, she realized, though she would not utter his name for fear of endangering Carter. Instead she nodded. Carter did not press for answers, just cast her a sad smile.

"The tribe is not going to fight for your release."

She lowered her head. "I understand."

"I don't." He sounded angry.

She looked at him from beneath wet spiking lashes. Carter was glancing over his shoulder at the door.

"They'll be back any minute."

"Thank you for these," she nodded at the envelopes she clutched. "And for coming to say goodbye."

"I'm not here to say goodbye."

"What?"

He squeezed her hand. "I'm not leaving you again."

"Of course you are, Carter."

He gazed at her, and her heart thrummed in her chest. How many more seconds did they have?

"I love you, Amber. Please, be my wife."

She shook her head and retreated a step. "No. Not like this."

He tugged her hand, bringing her back to within inches. "It's the only way. Amber, be my wife."

"You'll lose them all."

"For a time, maybe."

"And maybe forever."

He kissed her, and in that kiss was the promise of everything she ever wanted in this world. Her heart twisted, and she broke away, sobbing. He hugged her, drawing her up back up against him, his mouth beside her ear.

"If you are my wife, they can't separate us. They have to take me with you into witness protection."

He turned her easily in his arms and pressed his mouth to hers in a scorching hot kiss that curled her toes. When he finally broke away the tears still flowed down her cheeks and her heart still ached, but something had changed. She had to be with him. She knew it. The cost, it pained her.

One look and she saw the love in his eyes. He could no more bear to be parted from her than she could stand to be without him. She saw the truth shining there in his eyes.

"Don't try to protect me from this, Amber, because the only thing harder than losing my family would be losing you."

"Oh, Carter!" She fell against him, clinging. "Are you sure?"

He stroked her head. "So sure."

"What do we do?"

"I have a marriage license. I have your uncle here. He'll marry us right now."

He lifted the familiar diamond solitaire from his blazer pocket, and she held out her hand. A moment later he slipped the ring onto her finger.

A knock sounded at the door. Agent Forrest appeared.

"You all ready?" he asked Carter.

"Not exactly." Carter turned and drew Amber up close to his side. "You can be the first to congratulate us."

Forrest's brows dipped, and he scowled at them. "Carter. What did you do?"

Amber smiled and extended her hand.

Forrest's ears drew back as his eyes rounded.

"My uncle is downstairs in the lobby. We want him to perform the ceremony right now," said Amber.

"And bring Jack, too. He's there with Little Falcon."

"No way."

"I need a best man. You can be our witness."

"You both have to testify," said Forrest.

Carter looped an arm around Amber's shoulder and dragged her beside him as they stared down the FBI field agent.

Forrest looked to Carter. "You know what you're doing, son?"

"For the first time in so long, I do."

Forrest exhaled. "Anything else? Flowers? Cake?"

"Yes," said Carter. "One thing more."

AMBER SAT FIDGETING beside Carter as they waited.

"What?" he asked.

"I'm afraid."

"You? I've seen you face armed gunmen and police lineups and all manner of chaos. What could frighten you now?"

"What if, in time, you regret this? What if you grow to hate me because you had to give up your family to be with me?"

Carter slipped to his knees before her and gathered up both her hands in his.

"That will never happen. I love my family, Amber. I will miss them. But I can live without them. I can't live without you. You are my family now."

Tears of joy mingled with the tears of sorrow.

He brushed them away.

"Don't you dare feel sorry for me. This is a happy day, and I am the luckiest man alive."

Forrest returned with a brown paper bag, which he held out to Carter.

"As you requested," said the FBI agent.

Behind him appeared Kenshaw Little Falcon, followed by Jack.

Little Falcon was her mother's older brother, and they shared a high wide forehead and beetle bright black eyes. He kissed his niece, congratulated Carter and brought them together for the joining ceremony.

"One thing first," said Carter, reaching into the bag.

Jack did not look happy; in fact he looked fiercer than Amber had ever seen him, but when he saw what Carter held his eyes went wide and his jaw dropped. She'd never seen Jack Bear Den look so astonished.

Carter held a blue box. She stepped closer to get a look at the packaging that had a distinctively medical look about it. The yellow box had *DNA Harvesting Kit: Sibling Test* written in bold black letters and beneath it: *Safe, Accurate, Easy.* At the top, in small blue letters, was written: *Lab Processing Cost Included.* She straightened and looked from one brother to the next.

Carter opened the box and gave Jack a test tube, then recovered one of his own. Carter's gaze lifted to his twin.

"You sure?" asked Jack.

"Once I'm in witness protection, you can't see me. So it's now or never, brother. Get your answers. It's eating you up. I can see it. I hope this helps you find the truth." He turned to Agent Forrest. "You know how this works?"

"Just swab the inside of your cheek. Give the tube back to Jack and he can mail it out for processing."

Carter used the swab inside his cheek and returned the sealed tube to his brother.

Jack held the offering in one hand as if it were a bird's egg. Then hugged Carter with the other arm.

Little Falcon gathered them together. He spoke prayers in Tonto Apache and in English; the ceremony was short but rich in meaning.

Beside Carter as witness stood Jack and Agent Forrest.

Amber longed for her sisters, but photos were taken and Little Falcon promised to get them to her family.

After the service, Carter and Amber signed the marriage license. Then the small gathering shared a toast with diet ginger ale served in paper cups.

Amber looked at her husband in wonder.

"I'm so lucky," she said, her voice cracking.

Carter kissed her again, there in a secure room in a secure facility, and she knew that she was strong enough to face what came next, because she would no longer be alone. She did not know how long they would be in protective custody. She did not know where or if they would be relocated in witness protection after the trial. But she did know that whatever came next, she and Carter would face it together.

Carter believed in her and trusted her and loved her with his whole heart.

* * * * *

When ecoterrorists threaten their home, it's up to Apache Protector, Ray Strong, to defend a young mother as they decipher the clues to their identity left by her dead father. She doesn't trust a man with a history for recklessness and he doesn't trust a woman with so many secrets, but until they discover the truth, he's her Eagle Warrior.

Jenna Kernan's
APACHE PROTECTOR: TRIBAL THUNDER
series continues in February 2017
with EAGLE WARRIOR.

Her eyelids snapped open, expression foggy with sleep.

"Good morning," he said, his voice gravelly and deep.

She blinked. Her hand gripped his chest hair. She moved her leg slightly against his hip. Her eyes widened; her cheeks reddened.

The pulse at the base of her throat accelerated. Her pupils dilated.

She didn't move. She pressed closer.

His heart leaped away. The burn simmering inside his gut exploded. He shook with the effort to maintain control.

He couldn't look away. She'd captured him with her gaze. He held his breath.

"Rafe," she whispered. Her tongue dampened her lips.

"You should move." He cleared his throat. "Or I should."

She lifted her hand from the bare skin of his chest. She nodded in agreement, tossing a wave of disappointment and resignation through him.

He allowed his hands to fall back to the sheets. All for the best. But right now he had to get away from here. He needed that shower or to dunk himself into a tub of ice. "I think I'd better—"

"Don't think," Sierra whispered.

SAN ANTONIO SECRET

BY
ROBIN PERINI

First Published in Great Britain 2016
By Mills & Boon, an imprint of HarperCollins*Publishers*
1 London Bridge Street, London, SE1 9GF

© 2016 Robin L. Perini

ISBN: 978-0-263-92852-5

46-0117

Our policy is to use papers that are natural, renewable and recyclable products and made from wood grown in sustainable forests. The logging and manufacturing processes conform to the legal environmental regulations of the country of origin.

Printed and bound in Spain
by CPI, Barcelona

Award-winning author **Robin Perini**'s love of heart-stopping suspense and poignant romance, coupled with her adoration of high-tech weaponry and covert ops, encouraged her secret inner commando to take on the challenge of writing romantic suspense novels. Robin loves to interact with readers. You can catch her on her website, www.robinperini.com, and on several major social-networking sites, or write to her at PO Box 50472, Albuquerque, NM 87181-0472, USA.

For my agent, Jill Marsal, and my editor, Allison Lyons.

I'm blessed to have you in my corner during
the good times and the bad.

Thank you. For everything.

Prologue

Two months ago, Denver, Colorado

Dreary November clouds hung low and menacing, blocking out the clear blue of the Denver sky. Small pricks of ice laced the air, but Rafe Vargas didn't feel the cold, even as a puff of visible breath escaped his lips. His focus lasered on the door of the warehouse. Most of the block was deserted, but orange caution tape and cones peppered the streets. Not surprising. Rafe didn't have to walk inside the building to know dynamite and detonator cords crisscrossed the location. This entire block of downtown had been scheduled to be dust in a matter of minutes. Covert Technology Confidential's resident geek, Zane Westin, better be right about the target's coordinates.

Rafe tugged the stocking cap around his ears to camouflage his identity, bowing his head to avoid providing the surveillance camera a clear image of the patch covering his left eye. That psycho serial killer Archimedes needed to believe the man currently sneaking into the building was Rafe's best friend and fellow CTC operative, Noah Bradford, otherwise two women might die: the woman Noah guarded and had fallen in love with, and the one Rafe had flown across the country to rescue, Noah's sister, Sierra.

Archimedes was attempting to use her as leverage to stop Noah's investigation. Rafe wasn't about to let that happen, but if he had a prayer of getting her out alive, he had to locate her first.

Then again, if he found Sierra in time to save her life, he might have to kill her. Or kiss her until neither one of them could breathe—the way he'd wanted to from the day they'd met.

Either choice made his gut ache. Best friends' sisters were off-limits for one. Secondly, and more immediately, Archimedes liked to play deadly games, and he didn't give a rip about collateral damage. He might just murder Sierra for the satisfaction of proving he could.

Rafe palmed his Kimber 1911 and slipped through the warehouse door. He eyed a camera and ducked behind a large concrete support in a visual dead zone. That ominous and all-too-familiar tingle skittered down Rafe's spine. He had no doubt Archimedes was watching. The man was a sick voyeur, and the moment Rafe showed himself, the serial killer would know.

"We're clear," a worker in a yellow hard hat called across the room to the blaster.

"Then let's get out of here. This sucker's going to collapse like a pancake."

The men hurried out, slamming a metal door behind them. The clang echoed through the empty building.

Rafe checked his GPS and surveyed the open area. Yep. Drilled holes stuffed with dynamite dotted columns throughout the place. No one knew the order was on hold.

They had to keep it that way. Until he found Sierra.

He followed the trail from one of the dynamite cluster's detonation cables until a *second* set of wiring caught his attention.

Well, damn and double damn.

Archimedes had been here.

Military grade dets, not used for civilian demolition. No wonder the serial killer had oozed that smug, I-know-more-than-I'm-telling arrogance during their last communication. He'd rigged the existing wire to give him complete control. Even if the demolition expert didn't set off the charge, Archimedes could. And would.

Sierra.

Rafe's heart thudded hard against his chest. He glanced at his watch. Hell, no. Five minutes.

If he shot out the cameras, Archimedes might detonate early. Rafe tapped his earpiece. "Zane, you're sure about those coordinates?"

"Unless Archimedes spoofed them. And he could have. I'd give it fifty-fifty."

"Not good enough." CTC's surveillance expert was the best Rafe had ever worked with. There had to be a way. "If the place doesn't blow, Archimedes is going to set off the dynamite. Can you jam the detonation signal?"

"I don't have the time to crack his encryption." A curse erupted from Zane. "He's one step ahead of us. Again."

"What about the cameras?"

"If I disrupt them, he'll know." A drumming sounded through the phone. "Maybe…okay, it'll just be a minute, but I have an idea."

"You don't have a minute," Rafe snapped.

A blur of tapping sounded through the phone. "If I loop the camera feed—"

"He won't know I'm here. Very Hollywood thriller of you."

"I try. It's not going to be pretty, though. If he's watching closely enough, he'll be able to tell."

"Do it."

"I already started," Zane said. "A half minute more."

The seconds ticked by. Rafe studied the path to Sierra's coordinates, timing it in his head.

"That's as good as it'll get," Zane said. "Go."

Rafe catapulted from his hiding place and raced across the large concrete building. He skidded to a halt in front of a closed metal door and turned the knob. Locked. "Sierra. I'm coming for you," he shouted.

He backed up and slammed his foot against the barrier with all his weight behind him. The door bent, but didn't open. Another kick. A third. A fourth. It wouldn't give way.

A loud ticking echoed in his head, his internal clock counting down the seconds. This wasn't working, and Archimedes could discover the deception at any moment.

A large spread of debris littered the floor nearby. A piece of rusted rebar stuck out from one heap. Rafe clutched it in his hand and wedged the end in a small crack created by his assault. With a loud groan he pried the door open.

"Sierra?"

He peered through the opening.

Empty. A mound of wiring and debris filled the small room.

What the hell?

"She's not here, Zane. Am I even in the right warehouse?"

"According to my data, she has to be within a few feet," he said.

Ninety seconds.

Normally Rafe's body grew ultracalm the more perilous the operation, but this was Sierra. His palms grew damp, a bead of sweat trailed down his temple. Where the hell was she?

He rounded a corner and on the opposite wall facing the room he'd just entered, he found another door. The metal was bent, slightly off center.

He jammed in the rebar and pried it open. Sierra lay in the small, cramped closet, feet bound, mouth ducttaped, her shirt splayed open, and blood trickling from a carving of the infinity symbol on her upper left breast.

Her eyes widened.

"Got her," he said into his comm. He knelt beside her, tugging her shirt closed and slicing through her bindings with his Bowie. "You're one tough woman to find."

Her body trembled, and she shrank from his touch.

"Easy does it." As carefully as he could, he pulled off the tape. "Can you walk?"

"I can try," her husky voice croaked. She swiped at her eyes and fought to sit up.

"We can't wait to find out." He scooped her into his arms and pushed out of her tiny prison. He bolted toward the door. She clung to his neck. A few feet from the exit a loud explosion shuddered the building. Smoke billowed at him, rolling in the waves of a nightmare.

Visibility went nil.

Rafe felt for the handle of the door and clutched the metal. He yanked it open. The ground shook beneath him. Legs pumping hard, he carried Sierra as far as he could.

They wouldn't make it.

The building pancaked behind them, a sonic boom knocking him off his feet. The force slammed them to the ground.

He landed on top of her, and she grunted at the force of his weight. Before he could check on her injuries, a deluge of debris shot out with the force of an artillery bombardment. Rafe shielded her with his body, hoping his Kevlar was enough protection. Dirt, dust, metal and glass battered them both, pummeling them as if they'd been tossed into the heart of a tornado.

The world had turned to hell, and he had no idea if they'd survive or end up buried alive.

Archimedes might very well get exactly what he wanted.

THE MOTEL ROOM was a dump. Clean, but still a dump. Rafe lay on the rickety, regular-size bed and stared at the water-stained ceiling, his Kimber within reach on the bedside table. A glint of early-morning light peeked between the cheap blinds, providing just enough visibility for Rafe to study, yet again, the odd patterns the discolorations had created. He needed the distraction.

His body thrummed with tension, with unrelenting longing. Sometime during her sleep, Sierra Bradford had worked her way across the too-small bed and settled on top of him, her soft, toasty body pinning his legs and chest to the mattress.

Nestled against him, she was killing him with every curve, every inch of flesh. Her warm, even breath burned a hole in his chest. Her brown hair, luxurious to the touch, cascaded over his shoulder. The clean soap and hint of lilac lotion she favored danced a seduction on his senses.

Just one small movement of his hand and he could caress her silky skin. He didn't know how much longer he could take the torture.

He fisted the rough sheets and closed his eyes against the temptation. He wanted to groan aloud, wrap her in his arms and lose himself in her. He longed to touch her, hold her, kiss her, make love to her.

Plain and simple, he wanted her. Bad. Even if he tried, his body refused to hide his need. The moment she stirred, she'd feel him. And there wasn't a thing he could do about it, short of getting out of this bed.

And damned if Rafe could force himself to move. Even if he should.

He could tick off a hundred reasons he shouldn't allow himself to give in to the urge. Sierra deserved a forever kind of man, a forever kind of love. The kind Noah had found with Lyssa. The kind her brother Mitch shared with his wife, Emily.

Not a man whose scars—both inside and out—made him damaged goods.

Rafe breathed in deep and slow, taking in every scent, every touch, burning the memory of the moment into his brain for the long, lonely nights to come. He'd never imagined he'd be this close to her. But here they were. Together. In a small room, in a small bed, with nowhere to go.

Every minute for the last forty-eight hours he'd hoped Sierra would reveal a flaw, something that would drag him down to earth, prove that the dreams she'd inspired since they'd met were unrealistic and impossible fantasies.

His prayers had gone unanswered. She was everything he'd imagined. Brilliant, resourceful, courageous, and passionate in her loyalty and love for her family.

He'd only identified two imperfections. She was Noah's sister, and the woman was the most stubborn and tenacious person he'd ever met. Rafe had practically had to sit on her since they'd arrived to keep her in this room, safe and sound.

Unable to go to a hospital for fear Archimedes would discover she had survived, he'd treated her wounds and located this out-of-the-way motel that would take cash only.

Two solid days had passed since the explosion. The wait was grinding on both of them, but they were stuck here until Noah caught Archimedes. Personally, Rafe hoped his best friend killed the murdering psycho.

Until then, Rafe was trapped. With a woman who challenged and attracted and intrigued him more than anyone since… Rafe shoved aside the comparison. He couldn't dwell on what he couldn't change. Only learn from it.

Sierra shifted on top of him. His entire body turned rigid. He fought back his shuddering response. Maybe she'd move off, and he could escape into the tiny bathroom for an ice-cold shower before she realized—

A small moan escaped her, a whimper. She trembled, her nails biting into his chest.

Oh, Sierra.

He glanced down at her face, the long lashes resting against shadowed eyes, frantic movement just beneath her eyelids. He recognized the signs.

Another nightmare.

She dug her nails deeper into his skin. "Please, no. Please don't."

Rafe wrapped his arms around her. "Shh," he whispered, rubbing her back, careful not to jar her injured shoulder. "You're safe."

Sierra shook her head and with a sleep-limp fist pummeled his chest. "Rafe!" she shouted. "Help me!"

"I'm here. I'm not letting you go." He cupped her cheeks, stroking the smooth skin. "Wake up, darlin'. Let me see those baby blues."

She squeezed them shut even tighter. Obstinate even in the midst of a nightmare.

"Come on, Sierra." She was entangled fiercely in a memory, and he tried to tell her it was only a dream. "He won't hurt you. Not ever again." His thumb traced the pale translucence of her skin. She'd been through so much.

Her eyelids snapped open, expression foggy with sleep.

"Good morning," he said, his voice gravelly and deep.

She blinked. She moved her leg slightly against his hip. Her eyes widened; her cheeks reddened.

The pulse at the base of her throat accelerated. Her pupils dilated.

She didn't move away. She pressed closer instead.

His heart leaped. The burn simmering inside his gut exploded. He shook with the effort to maintain control.

He couldn't look away. She'd captured him with her gaze. He held his breath.

"Rafe," she whispered. Her tongue dampened her lips.

"You should move." He cleared his throat. "Or I should."

She lifted her hand from the bare skin of his chest. She nodded in agreement, tossing a wave of disappointment and resignation through him.

He allowed his hands to fall back to the sheets. All for the best. But right now he had to get away from here. He needed that shower or to dunk himself into a tub of ice. "I think I'd better—"

"Don't," Sierra whispered, straddling his hips. "I don't want to think. I don't want to remember. I want what you've been promising me for the last two days."

Sierra sank into him, pressing her lips to his, demanding a response.

Rafe couldn't stop himself. He didn't want to. His heart racing, he shoved aside the doubts and let his body take over. With a groan, he wrapped Sierra in his arms, giving in. The world melted away. Heat and sweat and want and need overwhelmed them both.

But lingering, in the still small place deep inside, Rafe knew he was probably making the biggest mistake of his life.

Chapter One

Present Day, San Antonio, Texas

Nightmares weren't supposed to invade twice—not in the daytime, anyway.

That way-too-familiar, incessant, head-knocking throb thudded against Sierra Bradford's temples in time with her pulse. She didn't want to open her eyes, but ignoring the truth had never worked out well for her, so she squinted and *tried* to remember.

Her cheek pressed against the cool metal of a half-rusted floor. She attempted to raise her hand to ease the pounding in her head, but she couldn't move her arms. Thick rope cut into her wrists.

Her mind whirled in confusion. No. Archimedes was dead. He had been for over two months. This must be a nightmare. It wasn't real. It couldn't be.

"What was she doing with a gun? Who the hell is she?"

The man's harsh words skewered past the pounding at the back of Sierra's head. She twisted to identify the man to match the voice. All she could make out was a utility belt against a dark blue uniform. Her gut tightened. She followed her line of sight, and there it was. A badge. Before she could see his face, he turned his back and walked away. Military cut, dark hair. About five-ten, one seventy-five.

"Please. Don't hurt us."

A voice she recognized all too easily. The past couple of days careened through her mind. Her best friend's phone call asking for help. A few computer searches yielding more questions than answers.

Neither Sierra nor Mallory had expected to be stopped by the police and ambushed, though.

The sound of a vicious smack reverberated around her. Mallory cried out in pain. Desperate, Sierra struggled against her bindings and rolled to her back. Her gaze flashed through the corroded interior of an old van, landing on Mallory's terrified gaze. The corner of her mouth bled. Even worse, five-year-old Chloe clung to her mother, terror engraved on her face.

No way was Sierra letting anyone be kidnapped—especially not her goddaughter and best friend.

Okay, Sierra. Think.

Chloe whimpered, burying her head against her mother's side. Hands and feet bound, Mallory scooted her daughter behind her as best she could, away from the man looming over them, a bandanna hiding his face.

"Please," Mallory said, begging. "Let us go. We won't say anything. Chloe's just a little girl."

"We ain't letting no one go without the boss's say-so."

Sierra shifted just slightly. If she could only get enough leverage. With a shout, she bent her knee and rammed her foot as hard as she could against the guy's side. The force carried her back. She lost the follow-through.

He grunted and leaped at her. With a loud curse, he let loose and slugged her. Hard. The blow snapped

Sierra's head against the van's metal floor. "Think you're smart, don't you?"

She blinked back the tears of pain. She wouldn't give these guys the satisfaction of knowing she could barely see after that last crack across her jaw.

He climbed on top of her. "I'll enjoy teaching you a lesson," he uttered, his fetid breath close to her ear, wrinkling her nose.

She stilled, staring into his nondescript brown eyes.

He slid the cold metal knife along her throat before tugging the weapon away. "Not so tough now, are you?" He nicked her, and warm blood trickled along her skin.

She stiffened. A wash of white noise enveloped the world, overwhelming her senses. She couldn't see. She couldn't hear. Nothing. Oh, God. Nothing.

Sierra fought to stay focused, fought the roar overwhelming her. She blinked, shaking her head against the terrifying, claustrophobic memory. The horrifyingly small closet. No escape. Trapped.

She couldn't lose herself. Mallory and Chloe needed her. She squeezed her eyes tight and silently recited a half dozen letters of the alphabet backward. The fog cleared a bit.

He checked the rope around her wrists and heaved her across the van's floor. "The boss'll want to talk to you."

"Judson, I didn't sign up for kidnapping a kid." A shaking voice filtered from the front of the van.

"Shut up, you idiot." Judson opened the back of the van. "Get comfortable, you three. We're going for a one-way ride."

He chuckled and slammed the door shut. Sierra struggled to a seated position, moving closer to Mallory.

Who are they? she mouthed to Mallory. *Buddies of your ex? Would he go this far?*

Mallory blinked back tears. "I don't know," she whispered. "I thought he was setting me up at work, but this…?"

"No talking!" Judson shouted.

A slide and click echoed behind Sierra. He had a bullet in the chamber now. She'd recognize the sound of a Glock anywhere. Her brothers' favorite gun.

"Say another word and I won't wait for the boss."

"No!" Chloe screamed.

"Shh, Button," Mallory said. "We'll be okay."

"Keep her quiet or I gag you all."

Judson turned to the driver. "Get us out of here. Slow and steady until we're outside of San Antonio. We don't own *every* cop."

The engine roared to life. Over Chloe's head, Sierra met Mallory's gaze. They had one chance. Sierra's feet were still free. They couldn't stay in this van. If they did, she had no doubt they wouldn't make it out alive.

She edged toward the rear doors.

"Call the boss. Tell him we've got an extra passenger. He don't like surprises."

The van started forward. They were out of time.

Be ready, she mouthed to Mallory.

After Mallory's quick nod Sierra pressed herself against the side of the van. She wouldn't make the same mistake again. She needed the leverage, or they were all dead. She'd only have seconds to kick open the door before Judson killed her.

Tucking her legs, she aimed for the door and hit the lock with the heel of her boot. Once. Twice. The metal snapped. The door flew open.

"Come on!" Sierra rocketed out of the moving van, taking a roll, scraping her arm on the asphalt.

She looked up. Mallory struggled to nudge Chloe out with her body, but the girl didn't move. Desperation painted her mother's face.

"You can do it, Chloe," Mallory cried, squirming to the van's edge. "Jump."

The little girl shook her head. Fear froze her.

Sierra stumbled to her feet, racing toward the van. "Come on, Chloe!"

The van screeched to a halt. Mallory and Chloe tumbled backward.

"Go, Sierra!" Mallory yelled. "Run."

Sierra kept coming. She had to help them, but the two men jumped from the van, their feet hitting the highway. They slammed the door closed. Mallory and Chloe were trapped.

If Sierra went back, they'd all be caught. A gunshot exploded into the night. A bullet struck near her feet, then a hot burn pierced her thigh. She had no choice. She zigzagged down the highway, away from her best friend, praying her movements would offer Mallory another chance to escape.

Veering to the side of the road, she dived into a patch of tall grass. Headlights flashed. A semi sounded its horn at the van blocking the road. The big truck slowed.

The van took off with a squeal of tires, its mud-covered license plate useless.

Sierra fought against the pain and stumbled back to the asphalt. She ran to the edge of the road yelling, praying the trucker would see her. He drove past. She sank to her knees, blood covering her right leg.

A hiss of brakes sounded, and the semi pulled over.

She looked up as a man ran toward her.

"Mallory. Chloe," she whispered. And passed out.

MERTZON, TEXAS, WASN'T on the way to anywhere. Just the way Rafe Vargas liked it. He pulled his truck past the town's three restaurants. Each window had gone dark, a large Closed sign blinking the news. Sunday night. He should've known better than to think he'd find a restaurant open.

Rafe's stomach rumbled. After a day of training to keep his combat moves sharp, he'd been hankering for a greasy burger with onion rings. Nothing better at a small-town diner. Oh, well. Not as if he wasn't used to disappointment. He turned off toward the Mertzon Inn, a small hole-in-the-wall motel. He appreciated the location several blocks off Highway 67. Out of the way, not obvious.

He'd situated himself a couple hours from Carder, Texas, the headquarters for CTC. He liked working for Covert Technology Confidential. He liked helping people in trouble who had nowhere else to turn. He liked using the deadly skills Uncle Sam had drilled into him for the right reasons. But he also appreciated staying far enough away from headquarters that he didn't have to socialize much. Besides, lately many of his colleagues had found their soul mates. They were too damn content and satisfied. Not that he wasn't happy for them... and envious. But he didn't need the reminder of what might have been.

Of course there happened to be another reason to locate himself a good distance from an airport, be it CTC's private strip or a commercial facility. Rafe couldn't fly to Denver on a whim.

To see *her*, the biggest mistake of his life.

Sierra was *not* someone he should be thinking about. Not now. Not ever.

Rafe parked the car across from the motel, scanning the lot's perimeter. He'd stayed alive this long by being cautious, not doing the expected. This was his last night in Mertzon. He was getting too comfortable. Too recognizable. He'd move on tomorrow. Find another town, another motel. Another temporary home.

His first stop, to verify that the small slip of paper he'd inserted into the doorjamb earlier in the day hadn't been moved.

He probably could've used some of CTC's electronic toys, but sometimes low tech did the job better. And safer. No one could jam a paper's nonexistent, electronic signal.

His gaze slid above the Do Not Disturb sign. Still there. Good. He rounded the building. The motel's small office had hung out the Closed sign and locked the door. Evening church. Being in Mertzon was like going back in time fifty years. Rafe didn't mind. Fewer people; fewer questions.

Once he'd completed his surveillance, and satisfied he hadn't been located, he unlocked his small room and snagged a can of Texas-style chili out of a paper bag sitting in the corner. His movements smooth with practice, he disengaged a can opener from his utility knife and punctured the top, then headed back outside. He rested his dinner on the truck's engine to heat up. Not exactly gourmet, but filling enough on an unusually warm January night.

Rafe pulled out a longneck bottle of beer from his ever-ready cooler and waited for his dinner to heat. He had this particular meal down to a science. At least he wasn't living on protein bars. Or worse.

The curtain fluttered in the window of the room next to his. Rafe set down the beer and tensed, his hand easing toward his weapon. He'd stayed alive by never making any assumptions.

Seconds later the door cracked open, and a small head peeked through the opening.

Rafe relaxed and settled back against the truck. "Hi, Charlie."

The seven-year-old boy looked down the row of doors one way, then the other, before tiptoeing out of the room, his eyes wide, staring at the chili bubbling on the engine.

"Whatcha doing, Mr. Vargas?"

"Fixing dinner. The diner's closed."

"Yeah, I know. Mama had to close up, then she went to clean the mayor's house. She won't be home until late." The boy's stomach growled.

"Wait here, Charlie," Rafe said. He paused, raking his gaze up and down the kid in speculation. "Don't go near the engine. It's hot."

Rafe strode back into the dingy motel room, with its Spartan furnishings. Digging into his supplies, he grabbed two spoons and a bowl.

The boy stood on his tiptoes peering at the chili, balanced precariously near the engine.

"Charlie," Rafe's voice warned, quiet so as not to startle the kid, but firm. "What did I tell you?"

He grimaced and scooted back. "I didn't know you could cook like this. When we lived in our car last summer, we ate cold stuff." He wrinkled his nose. "Cold peas don't taste good. They're mushy."

"Better than being hungry." Rafe snagged the chili with a napkin and poured half the meal into the bowl before handing it to Charlie.

"I guess," the boy said, stirring the meal. He couldn't quite take his eyes away from Rafe's face. "Why do you wear a patch?"

The words sped from his mouth as if he'd been warned not to ask the question but couldn't help himself.

Rafe blew on the chili and swallowed a bite. "Well, I got used to wearing it on the pirate ship…"

Charlie's eyes grew wide with shock. "Really?"

Rafe adjusted the eye covering. "Nah. I was in the war. I got hurt, and it messed up my eye. It's taking a long time to heal." That was the fairy-tale version, of course. Fifteen men had died during the operation that had damaged his eye. It might never heal completely, but Rafe considered himself lucky to make it out alive.

"Are you a hero?" Charlie asked.

"No."

"Oh." The boy stared down at his dinner.

Rafe had disappointed the kid, but what could he say? The truth was much too complicated, so Rafe settled for another bite of dinner. The mild heat didn't give him the kick he liked. He tapped in some Tabasco Habanero Sauce. Another bite. Now that was more like it. He glanced over at Charlie's rapt expression. "Want some?"

Charlie grinned and held out his bowl.

Rafe hesitated. "You sure?"

"Yeah."

Rafe dropped a smidgen onto the chili nestled in the boy's spoon. Charlie swallowed a big bite. Immediately he started coughing. His ears turned red; his eyes widened. Rafe bit his inner cheek to hide a rare grin. He patted Charlie on the back and handed him a cold bottle of water from the cooler.

The kid chugged it down. "I don't like that stuff," he squeaked, shoving the chili at Rafe.

"I think you got the worst of it." Rafe ignored the boy's outstretched hand. "It's safe. I promise."

With a suspicious gaze into the bowl, Charlie stuck out his tongue, swiping the meat and beans for a tentative taste. "It's okay."

"Eat up."

"Thanks, Mr. Vargas." Charlie downed half the bowl, then stared at the remainder. "I'll save the rest for Mama. Her boss wouldn't let her bring leftovers home tonight."

"Tell you what, Charlie. You finish your dinner. I've got enough for your mom."

The little boy grinned and ran back to his room. Charlie was a good kid. Rafe sighed. He just prayed the next few years gave Charlie and his mom a few breaks. Rafe knew from firsthand experience how easy it could be to go down the wrong path.

Charlie returned with a chocolate snack cake. "Today is January 31. I'm seven today, and Mama bought me a couple of cupcakes." He tore one in two and handed it to Rafe. "This is for you."

"Thank you, Charlie." Rafe didn't know if he'd be able to choke down the cake, but Charlie's proud expression decided for him. "So, do you go for the frosting or the filling first?"

"Cake first." Charlie bit at the bottom of the dessert.

"I'm a filling man," Rafe said.

A few bites later the dessert was gone. "Your birthday, huh?" Rafe turned to his SUV and reached into the glove box. He pulled out a yo-yo and turned back to Charlie. "Happy birthday."

The boy reached out his hand and touched the toy with tentative fingers. "It's mine?"

"Someone gave me one when I was a little older than you." Rafe wedged his finger into the slipknot and executed a couple of throw downs. He went into a Sleeper, then Rock the Baby. "Now you try."

Rafe coached Charlie for a half an hour. A car rattled into the motel parking lot. Charlie looked over and bit his lip. "It's Mama. I'm not s'posed to leave the room."

A tired-looking woman exited the clunker vehicle. "Charlie Ripkin, exactly what do you think you're doing?"

"Look, Mama. Mr. Vargas gave me a birthday present."

She ruffled her son's hair. "Thank Mr. Vargas. You have to go to bed. School tomorrow."

Charlie walked over. "Thank you for the yo-yo. Can we play again tomorrow?"

"I don't know if I'll be around tomorrow, but you keep practicing. Here are some extra strings." Rafe tucked a hundred-dollar bill into the packet and placed it in Charlie's hand. "You might want to change the string before you play with it again."

The boy's grin widened. "Thanks, Mr. Vargas. This is the best birthday ever." Charlie gave Rafe a huge hug and disappeared into the motel room.

"I hope he didn't bother you, Mr. Vargas," Elena Ripkin said in an exhausted voice. She pushed her ash-colored hair away from her face.

Rafe took his card and wrote a phone number on the back. "I have a friend looking for help. It pays well. Give him a call. Use my name." He handed her a CTC card with his boss's name and number.

Elena's hand trembled when she clutched the bit of card stock. "Why? You don't even know me."

"I know enough," Rafe said. And he did. The background check had revealed a woman whose husband had been killed in an oil field accident. Within months, she and Charlie had been evicted from their apartment. They'd lost everything.

A lot like Rafe's family. And their story had *not* had a happy ending.

If he could give Charlie some hope…maybe he wouldn't end up like Rafe's brother, Michael. Dead at seventeen on the streets of Houston, executed by a rival gang.

THE WIND SHOOK the rickety trailer. Mallory huddled in the corner of the small bedroom's makeshift cot, wrapping her arms around her daughter. Her heart still raced. Somehow she had to save them, but the trailer's window had been boarded up and the door locked from the outside. Mallory's fingers were bleeding from working at the thick planks of their prison. She let out a frustrated sigh. There was no escape.

At least the cowboy had untied them, even if Judson had cursed while the younger man removed the binding. It gave them a shot. She rubbed her wrists. The rope burns would heal. If they got out of here alive.

Mallory had no idea where they were. Far from San Antonio, though. They'd been locked in that van for hours, driving intermittently, occasionally stopping for Judson to make a phone call.

Whoever their kidnapper had contacted, it hadn't put him in a good mood.

"Mommy," Chloe whimpered, burrowing deeper into

her mother's arms. "I want to go home. I want my kitty. Princess Buttercup will get scared if I'm not there."

With a gentle motion, Mallory hugged Chloe closer and kissed her head. "Hush, Button. Everything will be fine."

The door opened, and Judson stepped into the bedroom cradling a sawed-off shotgun in the crook of his arm. "It's not nice to lie to children."

Mallory pressed Chloe up against her, praying she could keep her daughter safe. "She's only a little girl. Please, let her go."

"That's the boss's decision. He wants to see you. Alone."

Mallory hesitated.

The man pointed his weapon toward Chloe. "I won't ask again."

Mallory kissed Chloe's forehead, then shifted to get up, but Chloe clutched at her arm, her tiny fingers digging into Mallory's skin in panicked desperation. "Mommy. Don't leave me. I'm sorry I didn't jump."

Chloe's face was streaked with tears. Mallory's heart breaking, she stroked her daughter's cheek, wiping away the dampness. She stood and fought to smile down at her daughter. "It's okay. Be brave. No matter what happens. I love you, Button. Always remember that."

Chloe whimpered, clinging to her mother.

Prying her daughter's fingers off her arm, and with one last kiss on Chloe's cheek, Mallory straightened and stepped away from the bed. "I'm ready."

Her captor smiled, his eyes cold and dead. "I doubt that. But if you tell the boss what he wants to know, he *might* be lenient."

She took one last look at Chloe, sent up a prayer and

followed her captor through the narrow hallway into a living room. She glanced through the crack between the curtains at the front of the trailer. Night had fallen, but a bright spotlight illuminated the chaotic yard, strewed with trash and unidentifiable junk alongside several rusted-out car bodies. The place appeared abandoned, with a sea of darkness as far as the eye could see. No sign of civilization. No clue as to where they were.

A police car pulled up. The passenger-side window lowered.

"Judson. Get out here," a voice called.

"Damn," the guy muttered. He nodded at the man at her side, his weapon resting in the crook of his arm. "Watch her."

Judson walked down the stairs. With tentative steps he approached the car. What kind of monster made a man who would kidnap a child that nervous?

One second later, a bullet slammed through Judson's head and he fell backward.

Mallory froze in horror. She turned her face away from the dead body. "Why?"

The cowboy turned to Mallory, his face grim. "Judson let your friend escape."

Did that mean Sierra was alive? *Please let her be alive. Please let her find us.*

The car door opened. The man beside her clutched his weapon with shaking hands. "Lady, if you want to stay alive, do exactly what he says and tell him what he wants to hear. If you don't, you and your kid won't make it out of here in one piece."

THE LONELY WHISTLE of a locomotive chugging through town pierced the night. Rafe handed Elena the last two cans of chili and directions to CTC before the exhausted women disappeared into her room.

Rafe locked his motel-room door and flopped onto the bed, not bothering to remove his boots. He took a long swig of beer and flicked on the television.

Charlie didn't know it, but he'd given Rafe a gift. A welcome interruption. Because today would have been his fifth anniversary.

Except Gabriella had died a month before the wedding.

The mission had gone so wrong so fast. Gabriella had taken a spray of bullets. She'd had no chance. Because Rafe hadn't seen the betrayal coming. He hadn't protected her. He'd let emotions overrule his judgment.

It wouldn't happen again.

Rafe's knuckles whitened around the beer bottle. Never again.

Regret for what had happened would never leave him. He'd learned his lesson. A lesson he should've learned as a kid, but hadn't. A lesson he prayed Charlie would never have to learn. *Never let your heart rule your head. You'll get your head bashed in and your heart crushed.*

Words he lived by. Except for one night. With Sierra Bradford.

It had taken one kiss for him to forget the lessons of the past. He still couldn't believe he'd loved her, like he'd dreamed of from the moment he'd met her.

That one intimate encounter with Sierra had scared the hell out of him. He couldn't risk caring for her. Caring meant allowing his emotions to rule him once more. He couldn't do that. Sierra deserved someone who would give her everything. Heart, mind, body and soul. Not a man who not only didn't know how to be a part of a family but whose heart had been used up and destroyed.

Yeah, Sierra deserved someone whole, but that didn't stop him from dreaming about each kiss, every caress, or the way she'd held him tight against her as if she'd never let him go.

He dug into a pocket of his jeans and pulled out a small velvet pouch. He opened his hand, and a thin gold chain fell into his palm.

Sierra's. It had broken during their night together. A very passionate night he would never forget.

Don't go there. He tucked the chain back into his pocket.

He didn't need another night of dreaming about her.

He flipped channels, searching for another distraction. His cell phone rang. Blocked number. Hopefully a CTC job. No one else called him. "Vargas."

"It's Noah. I need your help."

It would have to be Noah. One of the few people he trusted. One of the few people who trusted Rafe. At least Noah would trust him until he found out Rafe had seduced his sister. And worse, run out on her. Even if it was for her own good.

Bracing himself, Rafe took a swig of beer. "What's up? I thought you hung up your spy suit."

Noah had been CTC's best of the best. Now he worked as a consultant, making cool gadgets to use in covert ops. He'd been almost as quixotic as Rafe—until he'd found someone to love him and a reason not to risk his life.

"Sierra's disappeared."

Chapter Two

Fighting the adrenaline rush, Rafe carefully set the bottle on the rickety nightstand. This wasn't happening. Not again. Right before Thanksgiving he'd searched for her. He'd barely gotten her out alive. He didn't like the twisting in his gut, the uncomfortable panic driving his heart to race.

"When did you last see her?" He fought to stay calm.

"A couple days ago. She left a cryptic message about not making it to Sunday lunch. She's been so reclusive since the attack, we gave her the space, but I went by her house to check on her. She's gone with at least one suitcase, bed unmade, dishes in the sink. That's not like her. I'm worried about her, Rafe. She hasn't been the same since—"

"Archimedes. Damn him." His teeth ground together. Good thing Archimedes was dead. Rafe would have taken great satisfaction in killing the psycho for what he'd done to Sierra. "You tracked her cell phone?"

"She knows how to block her signal. Or someone else does. That's what I get for having a sister who's better than I am at electronics. Even if she doesn't believe it."

"Zane might be able to hone in on her location."

"He's at CTC headquarters. I don't want the boss

thinking she's gone off the deep end." Noah hesitated. "I know we don't want her working for CTC, but when Ransom put her on indefinite leave after Archimedes— at our insistence, if you remember—the light went out of her eyes. We screwed up there."

Rafe adjusted the patch over his eye and rose from the bed. "No, we didn't. The job's too dangerous. She could get hurt. Or worse." He'd be damned if Sierra put her life on the line any longer. She'd almost died once. If anything happened to her…

Rafe grabbed his duffel from the top of the closet. "I'll find her, and I'll bring her home. Then it's your job to keep her there."

"Just make sure she's okay. She's not herself these days, Rafe. She can't sleep. She's got circles under her eyes. I don't want to lose my sister. You and I both know how the nightmares can take over your life."

Yeah, Rafe knew. He'd had his fair share. He also had up-close-and-personal experience with Sierra's demons. Her bad dreams had led to the best—and one of the worst—night of his life.

Spending time in Sierra's arms had made him want more. That's when he'd known he'd fallen way too deep. She'd ripped a hole in the Kevlar protecting his heart. She'd made him want forever. Except Rafe had learned all too well that love destroyed. He didn't matter, but he couldn't bear to hurt her more than he already had. So he'd walked away—for her sake—and instead had taken to watching her from afar. To make certain she was always safe.

She'd nearly caught him more than once, and he'd begged Ransom for another assignment. Something that would get her out of his constant thoughts. He'd believed he'd wanted distance, but he never should've ended his surveillance. If he hadn't, he'd know exactly where to find her. "Did you check the buses and airlines?"

"I'm working on it."

"I'll call when I find her." Rafe stuffed his 1911, a Bowie and his P-11 with its ankle holster in his bag, along with ammunition, a secure satellite phone and some of Noah's more interesting tracking devices.

Now all Rafe had to do was find her.

He tapped a few keystrokes into one device and started the search. He had a bad feeling. He didn't know if his gut was warning him of trouble or if he simply dreaded seeing Sierra again. Once he found her, could he resist her? Could he walk away again…and did he even want to try?

ILLUMINATED SIGNS DOWN the San Antonio street kept the road brightly lit even though night had fallen. The 18-wheeler's engine rumbled in idle. Sierra clutched the door handle and shoved it open.

"Thanks for the lift," she said, easing out of the truck.

"You sure you don't want me to take you to the hospital?" the driver asked.

When her foot hit the ground, a shot of pain pierced her thigh. She couldn't stop the wince.

"I'm fine." And doing a lot better than Mallory and Chloe. First she had to take care of her leg. She'd be no good finding them if she passed out and ended up in the ER. Gunshot wounds at the hospital meant cops. Cops meant trouble.

She forced a smile and turned to look up at the man who'd saved her life when he'd stopped. She dragged the bag containing her laptop, extra money and credit card from the seat. She'd stashed it in the trunk when she and Mallory had left to pick up Chloe. Even though the car keys had vanished sometime during the abduction, luckily Sierra had been able to pop the trunk release just inside the driver's side door and retrieve her belongings. "Thanks again."

The diesel revved before the truck's horn blared and the vehicle rumbled down the road. Sierra walked away from the motel, limped down several long blocks and hurried as best she could across four lanes of traffic. If anyone asked the trucker about her, they wouldn't locate her easily.

After a quick stop at a convenience store for bandages, a burner phone and a few other supplies, she trudged another mile before locating the perfect, most nondescript motor inn on the street.

The place reminded her of another motel, another time. Another place.

She'd learned a lot from Rafe Vargas that week. Most lessons she preferred to forget. But how to disappear in plain sight, that was a skill she would find useful tonight.

Ready to collapse, she pushed through the motel's office door, causing a dangling bell to chime. Within a few minutes, Sierra had laid down the last of her cash in exchange for a key. Once she'd locked herself inside the room, she sagged against the door.

She dumped the medical supplies on the rickety table and unbuttoned her jeans. She slipped them over her hips. The material stuck against her thigh. She hissed and froze. The blood had dried.

Closing her eyes, she slowly, gingerly tugged the denim away from her wound.

A sharp burn sliced up and down her leg. She whimpered. Maybe she should just rip it off, like a stuck bandage.

"One, two, three—"

A quick tug and the pants dropped to the floor. Sierra's knees gave out. She sank to the floor, biting down hard on her lip to keep from screaming.

That hurt. Bad.

Her thigh throbbed, blood dripped from the reopened wound. For a moment she simply sat on the floor, rocking back and forth. When the spots stopped spinning in front of her eyes, she stood on shaky legs and padded to the bathroom.

Propping herself against the wall, Sierra irrigated the wound with hot water, picking out denim fibers and dirt, stopping every so often to lean her head against the wall and suck in several deep breaths before starting again.

A pounding knock sounded at the door.

Sierra limped to the table, wishing the kidnappers hadn't taken her gun, and grabbed the scissors she'd purchased. As fast as she could, she crossed the room and slipped behind the door, knuckles white, her teeth biting into her lip.

"Mrs. Jones?"

The motel manager's voice called through the door. He knocked again.

She said nothing. Surely he'd go away.

Her thigh throbbed in time with her pulse. She could hear every breath. She waited. After a minute or two, her muscles relaxed.

Urgent whispers filtered through the door, but she

couldn't make out the words. The doorknob jiggled. Metal on metal scraped. Damn. No one knew she was here. Had the men who kidnapped Mallory and Chloe found her?

Sierra skirted into the bathroom, gripping the scissors even tighter. If someone came in, she wanted a good look at him before she attacked.

"Mrs. Jones?"

Silent, Sierra peeked between the crack of the bathroom door just below the hinge. She made out the manager's stout figure first.

The man frowned at the towels and trash scattered around the room. "She's not here," he said. "You'll have to come back."

The door creaked. "I'm her husband."

She clutched the doorknob with a death hold. She'd recognize that voice anywhere, the deep rumble, the smooth velvet baritone, but she couldn't believe those three words had escaped his lips.

"Rafe?" Sierra nearly rushed into the room before she stopped herself. Parading around in her underwear wasn't an option. She peeked around the door.

"Hi, honey," Rafe said, his expression grim, his voice soft and deadly. "I'm home."

Before Sierra could contemplate how he'd found her, Rafe shunted the manager out of the room with an excuse, grabbed a bloodstained towel from the floor and wrenched open the bathroom door. He shoved the cloth at her. "What the hell is this?"

She snapped a clean bath towel from a rod and wrapped it around her waist to hide her high-cut panties and naked legs. "What are you doing here?"

"That's a bullet graze," he said, ignoring the question. He tugged the terry cloth back to reveal her injury, and before she could say a word, swept her into his arms. Gently, carefully he laid her on the small bed.

He straightened and tossed his Stetson on the chair beside the table.

With his six feet four inches of pure muscle and outlawesque eye patch, he looked like a hero who'd walked straight out of a romance novel. He'd certainly featured in more than one of her own fantasies. At least until the morning after one very passionate night. She'd dropped her guard, flayed open her heart and he'd stomped all over it.

"I don't need the help. I've got the situation under control." She propped herself up on her elbows and tried to shift to the other side of the bed.

He grasped her arm and held her in place, pushing aside the towel. He didn't speak, but probed at the angry skin surrounding the wound, then arched his brow as he met her gaze.

Sierra squirmed under his lingering, enigmatic look. Rafe shook his head and rummaged through the supplies. He returned to her side with antiseptic, bandages, antibiotic ointment and tape.

He straightened her leg and held her down with a firm hand. "Let me do this. I've had a lot of practice." He tilted the antiseptic onto a large gauze square. "Brace yourself," he said, and dabbed at the flesh.

She sucked in a sharp breath. Her leg jerked.

"Easy does it." He bent over the wound and blew, easing the sharp sting.

Sierra glanced away, her cheeks burning as he poked and prodded close the top of her thigh. He was nothing but professional, even distant. In fact he'd acted as if it were nothing but business as usual.

They hadn't seen each other since a very awkward Thanksgiving dinner at her father's house the week after he'd rescued her.

One look and her heart had leaped at the memory of the way he'd touched her, the way he'd driven away her nightmares. At least for a few hours.

Until he'd vanished from their bed. And then walked away without a word after the family gathering he clearly had only attended to out the fact that she worked for CTC to her family. Noah in particular.

Sierra's dreams had returned with a vengeance. Rafe hadn't come back. A time or two she'd imagined she'd recognized him in a crowd, that he'd found her, that she'd been more than a convenient and willing night of passion, that he hadn't simply used her.

She'd been wrong. A second glance and the imaginary figure had vanished. So had the rose-colored glasses.

How had she allowed herself to be duped? That she'd trusted a man who could so easily walk away.

Well, she wouldn't allow herself to be seduced again. By his memory, by her fantasies. She couldn't trust him. Not with her heart. She'd learned her lesson. And she was an excellent student.

He pressed the final strip of tape against her skin but didn't move his tan hand from her thigh. A tingling of awareness rose across her skin, settling deep in her belly.

Now if she could just convince her body to listen to her mind.

Rafe simply looked at her, the muscle in his jaw pulsing, holding her gaze hostage.

Despite her decision and best of intentions, she couldn't control her response to his closeness. Being in her underwear on the receiving end of Rafe Vargas's hot stare was a bad place to be. The man could still make her heart flip-flop. Even when he was obviously furious, like now.

She blinked, breaking the spell, and quickly tossed the bedspread over her naked legs.

Only one way to handle him. Get on the offensive and don't back down. "In what fantasyland are you my husband?"

IF THE MOTEL owner hadn't been so damn protective of Sierra's room number, Rafe wouldn't have had to resort to the lie. He wasn't about to dwell on why the statement had crossed his lips all too easily, nor was he willing to apologize for it.

He'd dreamed of having Sierra in his bed for the past two months. His hand stroked the bandage on her thigh gently. But not like this. Never like this. When Rafe had first entered the room and had seen that bloody towel on the floor, his knees had nearly buckled.

A few inches and the bullet would've nicked her femoral artery. She'd have bled out.

She'd come too damn close to dying. Twice.

But she was alive. And mostly well. She lay propped up on the bed, shadows beneath her eyes, her cheeks pale. He cataloged the injuries he could see: the scrapes, the bruise darkening her jaw and cheekbone. She must be black-and-blue.

Someone needed to pay.

At his silence, a flash of blue fire erupted in her eyes. He'd witnessed the flame more than once: usually when someone crossed her, but also when she'd wrapped her arms and legs around him.

Her very presence drew him in. The small motel room's walls closed in on him. He had to let the past go.

Every instinct inside him fought the urge to wrap his arms around her, breathe in her scent and just hold her close. If he closed his eyes, he knew he could feel the silk of her skin beneath him, smell the clean scent of her hair, remember her generosity as he held her, giving him her heart and soul.

And he'd been stupid—or smart enough—to throw it away when all he'd wanted was to stay with her.

He'd done the right thing. He had to believe that. The alternative—well, he just wouldn't consider the alternative.

Instead of acting on his urges, he cocked his head to the side. "What am I doing here? Oh, no reason. I get a call from Noah that you'd vanished from Denver without telling your family only months after being held captive by a serial killer. And then, after you use your debit card at a convenience store, I find you a mile away in a barely up-to-code motel room, shot and obviously assaulted. I don't know, Sierra. Why don't you guess what I'm doing here? Saving you one more time."

"A mile would've been far enough if anyone but you had been searching," she muttered under her breath. Her lips flattened in a straight line. "Go home, Rafe. And tell Noah if he wants to send a babysitter, pick someone else."

The words, though expected, still hurt. No distance would ever be far enough if she was in trouble. "Tough.

You got me. And I'm not budging." He lifted his hand and hovered over the stark mottling on her face. "Honey, who did this to you?"

Her eyes glistened and she looked away. "Don't be nice. I can't take it."

"What are you involved in?" He leaned closer and with gentle fingers clasped her chin, forcing her gaze to meet his. "An op?"

"You and Noah got me suspended, remember?"

"And if I remember correctly, you seem to find ways to insert yourself into places you shouldn't be."

"The Kazakhstan situation was different. Zane needed help. He just didn't know it yet," Sierra countered. "I found the link between the terrorists and that charity, didn't I?"

"Not the point. I'm not saying you're not good at your job. Hell, you're the best. We all know that."

Her mouth dropped open, but instead of coming back at him like Rafe had expected, she gripped the sheets, twisting the fabric. "I might be good at the keyboard, but not in the field. I screwed up. I should've stopped it."

Her eyes shifted away from his gaze. She seemed to be struggling for words. Finally a sharp curse escaped her. "I want more than anything to kick you out of this room and tell you and Noah to shove your concern where the sun doesn't shine."

"Sierra—"

"But I can't." She lifted her chin and met his gaze, direct, unwavering. "I bought a burner phone to call Ransom. I need CTC's help, Rafe. Someone kidnapped my best friend and her daughter. My goddaughter." She paused, pain slicing over her features. "I let it happen, and I need you to help me save them."

MALLORY COULDN'T STOP staring at the blood seeping from the dead man's body. Her insides went cold. She glanced back at the trailer. She had to get Chloe out of here, but how?

"Get rid of the body," the voice from the passenger side of the police car snapped. "And bring the girl here."

"Yes, boss," her guard said.

"No. Please." Mallory would say anything, promise anything, to keep her daughter safe.

Two men picked up Judson and carried him to the side of the trailer. Mallory's captor disappeared inside, leaving her alone.

Every instinct screamed to run.

A tall man opened the car door and stood. He wore a cop's uniform. There was a touch of gray at his temples; his eyes were obscured by sunglasses.

"I wouldn't advise trying to escape, Mrs. Harrigan. Or your daughter will pay the price."

The aluminum door fluttered closed.

"Mommy! Don't leave me anymore. I was scared." Chloe pulled at the cowboy's arm.

"Let her go," the cop ordered.

Within seconds Chloe raced to her mother. Mallory lifted her little girl into her arms and hugged her tight. She looked over her daughter's shoulder. "Please let her go. She's only five."

"Chloe, do you want to leave?" the police officer asked.

The little girl nodded against her mother's shoulder. "Princess Buttercup needs me. She has to eat her dinner. Kitties can't miss dinner, you know. You have to take good care of them."

The man smiled, a grin that made Mallory's stomach roil.

"I'll bring your cat to you, Chloe, but only if you tell me something very important."

Chloe bit her lip. "I don't know anything 'portant."

"I imagine you do. Look at me."

Twisting in Mallory's arms, her daughter stared at the man. He stroked his chin. "What's the name of the woman who tried to help you escape from the van?"

Mallory tightened her hold on her daughter.

"You're squishing me, Mommy. Not so tight." She wiggled and stared hard at the cop's chest. "You have a shiny badge, so you're not a stranger, but why do you want to know about Sierra? I saw her fall. Is she okay?"

With a silent groan, Mallory closed her eyes.

The cop smiled. "An unusual name. Perhaps your mother would be willing to tell us her friend's last name."

Chloe nodded. "Mommy knows it. I know it too. Just like my name is Chloe Harrigan. Sierra's name is Sierra Bradford."

The man nodded at his driver. "You get that?"

"Yes, sir." Within seconds he'd placed a call.

Mallory's hope sank. Now that her daughter had inadvertently put a target on Sierra's back, how would her best friend ever be able to find them? She bit her lip, her mind whirling. She was on her own. How could she save them?

The cop crossed his arms in front of him, his smirk too satisfied. "Thank you for the information, Chloe. You've been a lot of help."

"Where's Princess Buttercup?" Chloe asked with a pout. "You promised."

"And I always keep my promises," he said. "Eventually. Right now, Glen will take you to your room. Your mother and I are going to have a little…chat."

Leaning her forehead against her daughter's hair, Mallory tried not to tremble.

Glen tugged Chloe from her mother's arms.

"Mommy!"

The cop grabbed Mallory's arm. Hard. She had no idea why they'd taken her, but she was afraid she'd soon find out.

"I have a few questions for you, Mrs. Harrigan. If I hear what I want, maybe your daughter won't have to watch her mother die."

Chapter Three

The stillness in the motel room made Sierra want to squirm. She sat perched on the edge of the bed, back stiff. She'd filled Rafe in on the van, the kidnapping, everything.

How Mallory had called her after discovering missing money at her job for the San Antonio Rodeo. How Sierra had followed the money trail by digging into a few files and discovering numbers that had been adjusted after Mallory had reconciled her books. How they'd both wondered if her ex's threats about their custody battle might be related. How that routine traffic stop on the way to pick up Chloe from school had led to the abduction and her getting shot. No point in sugarcoating the truth.

Of course, in typical Rafe fashion, he hadn't said a word. The muscle in his jaw pulsed erratically, and he just stared. Stone-faced and silent.

His unblinking gaze bored into her. Uh-oh. She recognized the expression and forced herself not to look away. Rafe might be an enigma to practically everyone, but she knew a few things about him. He maintained control 99 percent of the time. She'd only seen him lose it once: their night together. One he obviously regretted—as did she.

Sierra still couldn't believe Noah had sent Rafe, of all people, to find her. Okay, maybe she could believe it. Rafe was one of the few people Noah really trusted—outside family. Still, she would have preferred to face almost anyone else from CTC.

Her discomfort didn't matter, though. She'd had no choice but to ask for his help. Mallory and Chloe couldn't wait. They needed rescuing.

And damn him, Rafe was the very best. CTC called on him when the job was too complicated, too dangerous and required no nerves and even less fear.

And now, *she* needed him.

With a shaky hand she pushed back her hair over her ear. He was full-on quiet, which meant he didn't want to speak whatever was on his mind. A waft of the antiseptic he'd used still burned. She wrinkled her nose. She hated the odor. At twelve she'd spent every afternoon at the hospital during her mother's final illness. That scent did more than make her gut ache, it made her heart hurt. She'd been unable to do anything to prevent her mother's death. Sierra could do something now…if Mallory and Chloe were still alive.

No. She wouldn't let herself even consider they weren't okay. Maybe frightened, but they had to be okay.

"I can't believe you've been kidnapped twice in two months," Rafe finally muttered with a shake of his head.

"Old news that's irrelevant," Sierra said. "And it's *almost* kidnapped. If Chloe hadn't been so scared—"

"You'd all be dead." Rafe crossed his arms. "This is how it's going to play. First, I'm calling Noah. He'll send a plane to take you back to Denver—"

"Not happening," she interrupted. No way was he pushing her out. She had to make things right. "Not until we find Mallory and Chloe."

"Sierra—"

"I'm a witness. I know them. You need me."

"Do you know who kidnapped them?"

She frowned. "They wore masks—"

"Do you have any suspects?"

He rubbed in the obvious with each question. She didn't have much to go on. "Mallory is getting ready to file paperwork to get full custody. Her ex has been fighting her—"

"Most abductions are committed by someone who knows the victim." Rafe stroked the stubble on his chin. "He involved other people, though, and that means loose ends. What does he get out of it, unless he plans to keep them prisoner? Or worse."

An icy chill settled in Sierra's gut. "The only other lead I have is that she discovered missing money at her job at the rodeo. I looked through some files Mallory brought home with her. I found a few suspicious entries, but I don't have anything solid. To be sure, I need a look at the accounting system."

"We need a warrant to do that. CTC has a contact on the San Antonio police force—"

She shook her head. "No cops. At least one helped with the kidnapping. I can't risk word getting out."

CTC had dealt with corrupt cops before. It's one of the reasons the company existed—when law enforcement couldn't or wouldn't help. Her father hated that about her career. He'd been a cop until a gunshot wound had put him in a wheelchair, but just because he was no longer on the force didn't mean you took the cop out of the man.

Rafe shook his head. "I can't promise anything but to be discreet—"

She opened her mouth to argue, but he placed his finger against her lips. "I'll call Ransom and request getting Zane out here. He's got the computer skills. We'll find your friend, but you *are* going back to Denver. We can handle this. Let me do my job."

"And you need to let me do mine." With a jerk, Sierra flung his hand away and swiveled to the opposite side of the mattress from Rafe. She stalked around the bed and picked up her soiled jeans from the floor. She didn't look forward to putting them on, but she had nothing else to wear. "I'm staying until we find Mallory and Chloe. If all you're going to do is put roadblocks in front of me, just go home. I'll contact Ransom myself and get someone else to help me." She snatched her burner phone from the table. "Mallory and Chloe don't have any more time. We've wasted too much debating already. I don't need your protection, Rafe. I need your help."

Rafe rubbed his temple. "You are so damn stubborn. Fine. I'm in."

Without a word he stalked out of the motel room, returning in moments with a duffel. He dropped it on the bed, unzipped it and threw a pair of sweatpants and a T-shirt at her. "Put them on. At least they're clean."

Catching the clothes, she nodded. "Fine."

Okay, that had been easier than she'd expected.

Surprised he'd given in, Sierra vanished into the bathroom, secretly relieved she wouldn't have to pull her jeans up over her wound.

She stepped into the huge sweatpants and slid them over her hips. After tightening the drawstring so they wouldn't fall off, she slipped on the T-shirt that fell to her midthighs despite her five feet ten inches. Rafe's clothes dwarfed her, but they would do.

Raising her chin, she stared into the mirror. "Are you sure you're up to this? Maybe Rafe and Noah are right," she said to the stranger looking back at her, scared, uncertain, despite her bravado in the other room.

No wonder Rafe was skeptical. Look at her. Circles under her eyes. Scrapes on her forehead, bruises darkening her cheek and chin. Where was the strong woman she'd always imagined herself to be? The one who could give all three of her brothers a run.

She knew the answer even if she didn't want to admit it. Archimedes had ripped something from deep inside her soul. She pulled the neck of the T-shirt lower. The infinity symbol he'd carved into her flesh glared at her, red and angry. A sign of how helpless she'd been in that small room. Completely at his mercy.

He'd gotten the drop on her then, just like the kidnappers had today. Despite her skills at the keyboard, Sierra hadn't reacted like an agent. Then or now.

But she knew in her gut she could help. Those accounts had made the back of her neck tingle. There was *something* hidden just beneath the surface. She could feel it.

"So, why didn't you see the trouble coming? Again?"

She adjusted the soft fabric to cover the scar, bent over the sink and slapped some water on her face. Rafe had instincts. But so did she. "You've followed your gut a million times. Numbers don't lie."

Right. But this case was more personal than anything she'd ever investigated. "Get a grip, Sierra." Mallory and Chloe couldn't afford for Sierra not to be on her A game.

Neither could Rafe. He needed a partner he could count on.

She gripped the edge of the bathroom sink. "You can do this," she lectured the shadow of herself. "For them."

THE BATHROOM DOOR had remained closed for too long. What was Sierra doing in there? Rafe rubbed his hands over his face. What the hell was he going to do with her? She'd been through so much, but she'd fought like hell because her friend Mallory was in trouble. He admired the loyalty. He shouldn't have expected anything less from Noah's sister. But he could also see beneath the bravado, and the anger. Even the strongest could crack under enough pressure. Sierra loved fiercely. But that emotion could boomerang. Rafe should know.

He slipped his secure phone from his pocket and dialed a number. He needed facts, not feelings.

"I don't have another job for you, Rafe." Ransom didn't mince words when he answered. "Not yet."

Rafe grabbed his duffel and walked outside. "That's not why I'm calling. I need information from the San Antonio Police Department, and I need it hush-hush."

"What the hell's going on?"

"We may have some dirty cops. How far do you trust Cade Foster?" Rafe stuffed his belongings behind the seat in his truck.

"If I could tempt him to leave the San Antonio PD, I'd hire him in a heartbeat."

"Then I need everything you can find on Mallory Harrigan. For a new case." After a quick glance around, he filled in Ransom on what he knew of Sierra's friend, but he didn't mention Noah's sister. Not yet.

"I'll get back to you," Ransom said. "Does this have anything to do with Sierra Bradford flying down there a few days ago?"

Rafe nearly dropped the phone. "How did you know?"

"The same way I know you've been holed up in Mertzon," Ransom said. "It's my job to worry about my team." He ended the call.

Sometimes Ransom Grainger could be damned scary. It made the guy the best—and the worst—to work for.

Rafe strode back into the motel room. Sierra hadn't emerged. He paced back and forth a couple of times. He glanced at the bathroom door. No movement and no way around it. He had another call to make. He tapped in a very familiar number and let it ring.

Once, twice. His grip tightened. Maybe he'd luck out.

"Did you find her?" Noah snapped through the phone.

Or maybe not. "She's okay." Rafe winced at the half-truth.

A long silence settled through the phone until a sharp curse escaped his friend.

"What aren't you telling me?" Noah asked. "What's wrong?"

"Have you got a radar for trouble or something?" Rafe rubbed the bridge of his nose and repositioned his patch.

"When it comes to my family, you bet. Spill it, Vargas. What's going on with my sister?" Worry laced Noah's voice. "She's safe, isn't she?"

How was Rafe supposed to answer that? Noah wouldn't be put off, so Rafe relayed the situation. He kept a few details to himself. No need to tell big brother everything.

"You're taking the case," Noah said. "Good. And Sierra's coming home?"

Rafe didn't answer.

"Tell me you're putting her on the plane first thing tomorrow."

Rafe shoved his fingers through his hair. "She won't leave. Not until we find Mallory and Chloe. She blames herself."

Noah let out a sharp curse. "You can't convince her?"

"How easy is it to change a Bradford's mind about anything?" Rafe asked.

"Point."

"Besides she's got the skills. You know that." Rafe could deal with the ex, but if Mallory had been kidnapped because of the money, he could very well need Sierra's expertise to save the woman and her child.

Noah let out a long sigh. "Well, if she's going to jump into the deep end, I can't think of a better man to watch over her than you."

Rafe winced. If only Noah knew.

"Keep her safe. The family can't lose her. Dad's had enough hits the past few years."

"I'll do whatever it takes to protect her, Noah. I promise you that."

With a quick tap on the screen, Rafe ended the call. He paced the floor several times before hovering outside the small bathroom. Resigned to the reality of the situation, even if he didn't like it, he tapped gently. "You okay in there?"

A bang followed by a curse erupted from inside. "I'd be better if you weren't so big."

A corner of Rafe's mouth tilted up, but before he could respond his phone vibrated. He glanced at the screen and moved to the other side of the room. "What do you have, boss?" he asked in a low voice.

Ransom rattled off a series of facts. With each one, Rafe's frown deepened. What the hell was going on?

"You're sure about this?" Sierra wasn't going to be happy about the news. Or how he'd acquired his information.

"I'll let you know what I hear. Cade's keeping his ear to the ground," Ransom said.

Rafe pocketed his phone just as Sierra walked out of the bathroom. He bit his cheek. "The clothes look good on you even though you're swimming in them."

"I've been thinking," she said, ignoring his comment and all business. "Her ex, Bud, had access to Mallory's house. He could've seen the files she brought home. He knows where Chloe goes to school, and the route Mallory takes."

"That gives him means and opportunity. The motive still feels fuzzy. What's his endgame?"

"I don't know." She grunted in disgust. "I got nothing."

"We're just getting started." Noting her uneven gait, Rafe dug into his duffel and passed a few ibuprofen and a bottle of water to her. "You're going to need it." For more reasons than one.

Sierra took a sip and swallowed the pills. "Thanks."

Rafe sucked in a deep breath. "I just got off the phone with Ransom. He has a connection with the San Antonio police—"

"You promised." She elbowed past him and stuffed the items she'd purchased into a plastic bag. "What have you done?"

"What I had to do," Rafe said, clasping her shoulders and turning her to face him. "Ransom trusts Cade. I trust Ransom. The question is, do you trust *us*?"

For a moment she didn't speak. Her gaze lowered, and Rafe let out a long, slow breath. "I see."

"It's not about you and Ransom," she said. "The kidnapper implied there was more than one cop involved. Why did you take the risk? What if word gets back to the kidnappers?"

"I've been running ops for over a decade. Accurate and complete information is the difference between failure and success." Rafe met her gaze. "Do you *trust* me, Sierra?"

She shrugged out of his grip. "I have no reason not to. Ransom counts on you. Noah believes in you." She paused. "I trust your ability to do this job."

The job. And nothing else.

The words remained unspoken, but Rafe received the message loud and clear. He didn't blame her. "Fair enough. But you *have* to trust me. Just like I have to trust you if we're going to be partners."

"That's good for a start, but I want more," Sierra said. "Keep me in the loop. No secrets. No lies. I deserve honesty from you."

She stood only inches from him and cocked her head. She didn't back down. One of her qualities Rafe truly admired.

He stretched out his hand. "Agreed."

She shook his hand. "Partners. So, what did Ransom say? And don't give me that look. I recognize Noah's

I-don't-want-to-tell-you-what-you-don't-want-to-hear look."

"Sit down and rest your leg," Rafe said. "We have a wrinkle."

After she settled on the bed, he pulled up a chair beside her. "From what you told me, the smart move would be to keep quiet about the abduction and find and eliminate the only witness—you. But this afternoon, before she and Chloe were abducted, your friend's boss called the cops and reported missing money. Tens of thousands."

She frowned at him. "I don't understand."

"The call shined a light on Mallory. When they searched her house, the place appeared as if someone had left in a hurry. You friend looks guilty as hell. Their working theory is she embezzled the money and skipped town, leaving her car on the side of the road."

Sierra shook her head. "It doesn't make sense."

"It does if that was the plan in the first place."

Rafe let his comments sink in.

Her eyes widened. "No. No way. This isn't some elaborate setup. Mallory would never do that."

"It's smart. It gives her time to disappear."

"She'd have to know I would never stop looking for her. Unless…" Sierra's voice trailed off. "Unless I was in on it."

"If that were the case, you wouldn't have asked for my help. I trust you, Sierra, but that doesn't mean I trust Mallory."

"She wouldn't. If you can't believe in her—"

"We have to explore every possibility," he interrupted. "And you have to bury your emotions. I admire your faith, but sometimes the people closest to us aren't what they seem." He placed his hand on hers and squeezed. "If you believe in her, convince me with facts, not feelings."

Sierra took a deep breath and nodded. "Mallory and I have known each other since we were eight years old, but she fell for the wrong guy when she was eighteen and got in over her head. She learned her lesson. She turned her life around. Besides, she loves her daughter more than anything. She would never do *anything* that would put Chloe in danger."

"Love and honor don't necessarily come together in a package. That love for her daughter could be the reason she betrayed you and took the money." He ran his thumb over her palm. "Some aren't strong enough to resist temptation even when they know it's wrong."

He gave her a pointed look and could see in her eyes she knew exactly what he meant. Heat rose into her cheeks. "We were discussing Mallory, not our mistake."

"Mistake. Definitely." Rafe let her hand go and put a few feet between them. "Okay. She's misunderstood and made some bad decisions. I've made my share, so I'll buy your argument. But now she's gone through a messy divorce. Her ex wants custody. According to Ransom, her credit is shot and she just received a huge deposit—received in cash by the way—into her bank account—"

"I knew about her credit, but she wouldn't take thousands of dollars. That's not possible."

"And these are the facts. *Fifty* grand," Rafe added. "It seems you *don't* know everything."

"Neither do you. Someone's framing her. Mallory *told* me money was missing from an account at the rodeo. She knows I'm a forensic accountant. So, of

course she'd come to me. She trusted me to help her."
Sierra lifted her chin. "Take me to Mallory's house. You
want facts? I've got proof Mallory couldn't have left on
her own or planned this."

"What are you talking about?"

"Princess Buttercup."

SWEAT BEADED ON Rafe's forehead. And not just from the
unseasonably warm January. Even in the dead of night,
the interior of the vehicle had heated up.

But Sierra Bradford was the reason the man who
most of CTC knew as an unemotional iceman was
sweating.

Damn, she was something else. She did everything
with passion, and he really loved…no strike that. He
liked that about her. She'd refused to back down for
Mallory Harrigan. He respected the fight in her. Even
if he could see the inevitable problems staring him in
the face.

As to other passions…he pulled at the collar of his
T-shirt. He should just stuff those memories into a cold
shower as soon as possible.

With long-practiced discipline, he pulled himself out
of the past. "I'll admit the cop's version of your friend's
story is easy."

"Too easy," Sierra said.

"Probably." From Rafe's experience, nothing tied up
that neatly, but answers weren't always a huge conspiracy either, though CTC ops tended to be more complicated than most.

He turned the vehicle onto the street heading toward
Mallory's house. "I can't believe we're breaking and

entering into a crime scene because your friend didn't take her cat."

"What's the big deal? Like you can't pick a lock at least as fast as my brother? I've read enough of your op reports to know exactly how far you'll go to get the job done, Rafe."

"I usually make nice with local authorities even if I'm lying… I don't go antagonizing them. Makes it hard to talk our way out of jail if we get caught," he countered.

"Princess Buttercup is Chloe's cat. That little girl loves her pet. Though I gotta admit, she's a spooky thing. She listens." Sierra sent a side-glance toward Rafe. "Besides, if she's there it's a fact in my favor. If she's in that house, Mallory didn't run."

"It's just a cat."

"Didn't you ever have a pet growing up?"

He shrugged. "No. We…moved around too much." Rafe's face closed off. Not that any of the hellholes his first—and worst—foster father had dragged him to would have been a safe place for a pet. It hadn't been safe for him or his brother. "Probably gets underfoot," Rafe said.

"Just wait until you meet her. If you don't like Princess Buttercup, you don't have a heart."

"I never claimed to." A bitter smile etched on Rafe's face. "I thought you knew that."

Sierra crossed her arms. "I'm not taking the bait, Rafe. I've read your ops reports. You may walk away from everything, but you care or you wouldn't do what you do." Sierra leaned forward. "Mallory's house is just around this bend."

The neighborhood was old, but well kept, and in line

with Mallory's salary. Rafe pulled the truck to the curb a half block away from the house. Only a van sat parked in front of the house. Yellow tape barred the front entrance. "You recognize the vehicle?"

"It's not Mallory's. Or Bud's," she said, unclipping her seat belt. "I expected more people here."

"They don't believe anyone's in imminent danger," Rafe said. "They think she ran. They probably grabbed her computer equipment and left."

"They're wrong." She gripped Rafe's arm. "Can't you give us the benefit of the doubt? Just for a while."

"I am," Rafe said. "If I weren't, you'd be on your way to Denver." He paused. "You have your weapon?"

She shook her head. "The kidnappers took it."

Rafe pulled a gun from his duffel and handed it to her. "Take it. Use it if you need it. I have several."

"Always prepared?" she asked.

"I'm no Boy Scout, but I believe in the motto."

Sierra turned the gun in her palm, holding it with ease. Ransom wouldn't let anyone on the team without good firearm training. She tucked the weapon in her bag.

Rafe eased open the door of his truck. "Just wait here…and be on alert."

He exited the vehicle, his stride quiet and catlike, ultra-aware. He scouted out several hiding spots behind the shrubbery surrounding the house, constantly glancing back at the car where she waited.

Everything was quiet. Too quiet.

Rafe walked around the truck, but Sierra had slipped out before he opened the door.

"How are you feeling?" he asked, cupping her elbow. "Dizzy, headache?"

"Just worried."

Sierra didn't have a poker face. She grimaced with each step. She needed rest. They'd grab the damned cat, and he'd put her to bed. "What do you know about Mallory's ex?" he asked, trying to distract her, and himself from where his mind had wandered. Sierra…in his bed. Alone.

"Bud," Sierra grimaced again, looking over the hood of the truck. "Not my favorite person. Mallory hid the truth from me for a long time, but I should've known. She refused to let me come visit the last couple of years, instead bringing Chloe to meet me halfway in Dallas. The last time she wore heavy makeup, but I could see the bruises."

"No one wants to admit they can't handle their life. Did he hurt his daughter, too?"

"Once. Chloe got between them. It's why Mallory finally left."

He led her to the side of the house. "No reason to beg questions from the neighbors," he whispered. "We have three options with him. He created this elaborate ruse to kidnap the two of them, which seems unlikely. Mallory and Bud are working together, which also seems unlikely unless he's extorting her. Or, he's framing Mallory because a great way to get custody is to put your ex-wife in jail. Does he want his daughter that much?"

"He wants to hurt Mallory that much."

Rafe scanned the side yard carefully. No strange movements. They quickly disappeared into the back. A swing set took up most of the small, grass-covered area. A tree swing hung on a large oak that had probably been there thirty years.

"She's made a good life for her and Chloe." Sierra turned to Rafe. "We have to find them."

A slim figure moved across the kitchen window. Rafe tugged Sierra behind a large cypress, hunkering down beside her. He pulled a Glock from the back of his jeans. "Someone's inside."

Sierra gripped the bark and shifted her weight off her injured thigh. "A cop?"

"No police cars out front. I doubt it," Rafe said, with a suspicious glance at her leg. "How bad?" he asked.

"Fine."

Beads of sweat clung to her upper lip. She hurt. She couldn't hide the truth. "Stay put. I'll check it out. It could be your friend coming back to get the cat."

"It's not her," Sierra countered, slipping the gun from her bag.

"Just sit tight. Don't take any risks."

"I won't let them get away."

She'd tackle the guy if she had to. Which made it all the more important for Rafe to take care of this without getting Sierra involved.

He worked his way to the back door of the ranch-style house, each movement calculated to be silent, and sidled up to the door, his body taut, his face intense.

Behind the curtains a figure appeared. The silhouette shifted.

"Gun!" Sierra shouted from behind him.

Rafe cursed and burst through the door.

Chapter Four

Sierra raced from behind the cypress, limping as fast as her injured leg would allow. She ignored the pain radiating from her wound. Rafe had disappeared into Mallory's house without backup.

"Rafe?" she shouted.

A loud crash exploded from inside.

She stepped up on the rear porch. "I'm coming in!"

Before she could throw open the door, a figure slammed into her, knocking her onto her backside. He leaped over her and took off at a full sprint. She sat up and aimed her weapon, but she could barely make out his shadow in the moonlit night. "Stop!"

He didn't so much as pause, streaking away from her. Sierra hesitated, and he darted out of her line of sight toward the front of the house. She vaulted to her feet to chase after him, but her leg buckled and her knees hit hard, crashing into the grass.

Rafe barreled out of the house. He skidded to a halt beside her. A scowl darkened his expression.

She waved him off. "I'm fine. Get him."

Rafe cast a quick glance at her with that this-isn't-over look. He'd just rounded the house's corner when tires squealed away.

Sierra lay on her back, gazing at the star-filled sky, trying to recall the man's features, but it had happened so fast.

Leather boots plodded over. Rafe knelt beside her. "You okay?"

"I didn't get a good look at his face," Sierra said, frowning, "but Bud is a lot stockier than that guy."

"Whoever he is, he wore a mask and boots and took off in that beat-up van. License plate was splattered in mud and unreadable." Rafe held out his hand and helped her to her feet, keeping hold of her shoulders to steady her. "Why the hell didn't you follow orders?"

"You can't be in two places at once." She tested the weight on her leg. Not bad, just not normal. "I'm fine," she repeated.

He glanced down at her thigh, then shoved his hand through his hair. Not saying a word, he grunted and strode back into the house.

Sierra followed behind him and gasped when she entered her best friend's kitchen. Every cabinet had been opened, dishes broken. The place had been completely ransacked.

"I wonder how much of this the cops did when they searched the place," Sierra said, picking up a broken serving dish from the floor and setting it in the sink. "And how much that guy did."

"Hard to tell, but her ex is a bit lower on my list right now." Rafe crossed the kitchen and looked into the living room. "This room isn't much better. You said she'd taken files from work?"

Sierra stepped through the chaos. The sofa lay on its back. Photos that had decorated the entertainment center were knocked over. "I was working on the file before we left to pick up Chloe from school. I should've taken them with us." Sierra shook her head in disgust. "I left them on the coffee table."

"The cops found them. Since your friend wasn't supposed to have those records, it looks even worse."

He could've said so much more, but he didn't. She'd screwed up, and she knew it. She stared up at Rafe. "How do we find Mallory and Chloe?"

"You're the forensic accountant," Rafe said. "Go back to the beginning and follow the money."

"I need access to the rodeo's accounts." Sierra bit her lip. "I have an idea. It's a long shot, though."

She trudged up the stairs and entered Mallory's bedroom. The mattress had been upended, the drawers emptied. Rafe followed her, and she walked into the closet. More chaos, but Sierra shoved back some hangers. "When we were in college, Mallory had a jerk boyfriend who'd log on to her computer and buy stuff. She started hiding her passwords. She used it for personal stuff, but maybe—"

Sierra sank to the floor, ignoring the twinge in her leg. She tugged at the edge of the carpet in the corner of the closet and slipped out several sheets of paper.

Rafe knelt beside her. "The cops never would have found this. Neither would our burglar."

She unfolded one of the papers and scanned the document. "Account names and passwords for her personal bank account."

"Could come in handy," Rafe said.

With a glare, she snatched the paper back. He shrugged. "Just saying. We don't know what's really going on."

Her gaze narrowed at the second paper. "These are the passwords for the rodeo." Sierra's gut sank when she read one entry. "Her boss's log in information is here, too."

"I see."

Rafe's tone gave away his skepticism.

"Lots of admins and accountants keep their boss's log-in info," she said.

"At home?"

She hated those short clipped sentences coming out of his mouth, but he had a point. Whatever her standard operating procedure at work, Mallory should *never* have kept her boss's log-ins at home. It simply didn't look good.

More than that, it looked downright bad. What had Mallory been thinking? Or doing?

Don't let your mind go there, Sierra. Her friend wasn't like that, and Sierra hated that she'd even let the possibility Mallory could be involved cross her mind. It seemed so disloyal, but Rafe's doubts had chipped away at her certainty.

What kind of friend did that make her?

Sierra didn't like that his distrust had poisoned her faith.

"You're wondering, aren't you?" he asked, his breath close to her ear.

Crouched in the corner of the closet, he leaned in closer, looking over her shoulder at the list, his heated body lightly touching her back. The light pine scent of his soap encircled her senses. She had no way to escape; he'd blocked her.

His presence melted into her. She resisted shifting closer, but her belly flip-flopped at the low baritone of his voice. Her brain screamed that she shouldn't be losing herself in the blind attraction she'd experienced the moment Noah had introduced them. She remembered it so well. She'd dreamed of those few seconds night after night, despite what he'd done.

His chocolate-brown gaze had swept over her body; his full lips had curved into a half smile. When he'd shaken her hand, his thumb had ever so slightly rubbed her palm. Sierra couldn't stop the shiver at the memory. Whatever he might be, Rafe Vargas defined sexy.

She cleared her throat.

He held out his hand and helped her to her feet. His dark eyes blazed. The room closed in around them. She couldn't look away. No doubt about it, Rafe was the kind of man you fantasized about, but not the kind you fell in love with. Not if you didn't want your heart broken and stomped on.

Despite the logic she swayed closer, seduced by the unvarnished passion in him. No wonder her body didn't listen to her mind.

Rafe's head lowered, just a bit. Slowly, seductively, temptingly. Her tongue licked her lips, wetting them. A deep growl rumbled from Rafe's chest.

A loud screech erupted from behind them. Rafe whirled around, weapon drawn. A ball of fur flew at him. He shouted and fell back into a slew of hangers and clothes.

Sierra stared down at the mostly white animal clinging to him.

Rafe lay on the floor glaring at the feline still digging its claws into his chest. "Princess Buttercup, I presume?"

THE SPOTLIGHT OF the moon and a few pinpricks of stars were the only light breaking through the cloak of darkness in front of the trailer.

Mallory's captor squeezed her arm and dragged her toward a rusted tin shed. She shifted her weight against him in resistance.

"Don't bother." He dug his fingers into her arm until she cried out. "Get inside."

The man shoved her through the door of the small building. She fell to her knees in the dark. Before she could stand, he strode in behind her and shut the door.

On all fours, Mallory's throat closed in panic. She squinted through blackness, but she couldn't see anything around her. The man hit a switch and a dim light-bulb hanging from an exposed wire crackled to life. Her gaze darted around the room. A chair sat in the center, a coil of rope huddled like a rattler lying in wait. A bat, its end stained with dark splotches, had been tossed nearby. Streaks of red and rust splattered the walls, a color that made her stomach churn.

Whatever he did, whatever happened, she had to survive. She had to get Chloe away from this place.

"Get up," he said, his voice soft and menacing. "And sit in the chair. We're going to have a little chat."

She hesitated.

"You do not want to challenge me. Not when I can destroy your world with a single order."

She swallowed with an audible gulp.

"That's right. Your daughter. I won't ask twice. In the chair. Now."

Legs shaking, she had no choice but to comply.

"Where are the files?" he asked.

She blinked. "At…at my house."

"Not those. We *have* those. I'm talking about the electronic files you copied."

Her eyes widened.

"Yes, we know. You made a big mistake, Mrs. Harrigan. Let's hope your daughter doesn't pay for your bad judgment."

Mallory could feel the blood drain from her cheeks. Her head spun. Oh God, he knew. She'd thought she'd covered her tracks so well. "I… I don't know—" she lied.

He bent over her and, with two fingers on either side of her windpipe, clutched her throat, squeezing hard. The world turned gray. Stars danced in front of her gaze. Blood roared through her head.

"Don't lie to me. The records weren't on your laptop or any of the equipment at your house. So where did you hide them?"

She grabbed at his hands, trying to pry his vise-like grip. She couldn't breathe. She blinked. She'd copied some files, but she hadn't had time to review them. She'd planned to give the thumb drive to Sierra. Now, it was hidden away in place she doubted anyone would find it. Even her best friend. Would this man make a deal? To save Chloe. And maybe even herself.

"Pl…please," she choked out. "I'll tell you."

He released her and shoved her away. The chair flew backward and clattered to the floor. Mallory's skull slammed against the dirt. She lay there for a moment, stunned.

"Pick up the chair and let's try this again." His large figure loomed over her, badge gleaming in the dim light.

Head throbbing and arms shaking, Mallory struggled to her hands and knees, and rose. She righted the chair, hesitating, eyeing the distance between her and the door.

"Sit. Down."

She had no choice.

He crossed his arms, expression grim, unyielding. "Talk."

Mallory shivered under his gaze. She closed her eyes to work up her courage, finally opening them and staring him down, unblinking. For Chloe. "Let my daughter go, first."

The man's smile widened, his eyes wrinkling with satisfaction. "You think you can bargain with me? We'll see." He walked to the door. "Glen, bring the kid!" he shouted into the night.

What had she done? Mallory's entire body trembled. She'd made the wrong choice. *Please, God, don't let Chloe pay for my mistakes.*

Mallory squirmed in her seat under his stare and an enigmatic smile that caused a shiver to settle like a cold lump in her gut. After what seemed like forever, a soft knock tapped against the door. Glen's skin appeared almost green in the pale light of the shed. "Boss, are you sure—"

"Where's my mommy?" Chloe asked, her innocent voice piercing the tension. Mallory's chest tightened in fear.

Please let me do the right thing, say the right thing.

The cop threw open the door and grabbed Chloe like a sack of flour, holding her under his arm. The little girl screamed, kicking her feet.

"Shut up, kid."

Chloe went silent, and Mallory tried to smile at her daughter. She placed her finger to her lips and closed her eyes. Chloe nodded and squeezed her eyes tight, pressing her lips together. It was a game they'd played when Bud had gotten so drunk he'd been completely unpredictable.

"Get the hell out." The cop glared at Glen. "Think about what you have at stake. You know what we can do to you. And your family."

The cowboy's face went milk pale, and Glen gave the cop a quick nod. With a pitying glance at Mallory, he backed away, closing the door quietly, leaving them alone with a man who'd clearly left his oath by the wayside long ago.

The cop sat Chloe down, a harsh grip on her shoulders. "That's a good girl. Stay right there, where I can see you."

Eyes still closed, Chloe stumbled over the rope and fell to the ground. She sniffled, but didn't cry out.

"You trained her well," he said to Mallory. "Where are the files, and how many copies did you make? Tell me that, and I might let your kid leave here in one piece."

He slipped a knife from a scabbard and rested it against Mallory's neck. He nicked her throat.

Mallory froze. Chloe whimpered.

"Where?" he shouted and slapped her across the face. Mallory fell to her knees.

"No!" Chloe shouted. "You can't hurt Mommy!"

Chloe grabbed the baseball bat and swung with all her strength at the cop's legs, just like T-ball. The man's leg buckled, and he lunged at Chloe. Mallory twisted and yanked the bat from her daughter. She swung at his head. He fell to the floor.

Tears streaming down her face, Mallory grabbed Chloe into her arms and ran out of the shed. She raced toward the SUV and yanked open the door. No keys.

She spun back toward the yard. What now? Maybe the cop had them? A kickup of dust blurred the road.

She recognized the shield on the side of the car. Cops. No time to search the man she might've killed.

At that moment, Glen opened the trailer door. He stared at them, eyes wide with shock. "You can't run," he yelled.

The hell they couldn't.

"Mommy?" Chloe whimpered.

Clutching her daughter, Mallory took off toward a grove of trees. She had to get as far away from the trailer as she could.

She looked back. Glen stood staring in disbelief.

Legs pumping, she raced across the field, nearly tripping more than once. Just as she reached the trees, shouts of fury slammed into her from behind. Three men were headed her way. Glen lay on the ground, still and unmoving.

Hugging Chloe tight, she peered into the wooded area. A path veered to the right. Mallory took off running to the left.

A branch slapped her face, cutting her. She blinked back the blood. No time to rest. She had to find help. She had no doubt if the cop caught up to her, she and Chloe were both dead.

UNDER THE COVER of night, Rafe escorted Sierra from Mallory's house to the truck. He placed her luggage and computer case behind the seat while she climbed into the passenger side.

He slammed the truck door and started the vehicle. Beside him, Sierra sat with the cat in her lap. The damned thing purred in ecstasy with each stroke of Sierra's hand. Rafe glared at the animal, but he couldn't stop himself from envying the beast's location. He wouldn't have minded lying in Sierra's lap being stroked. Hell, he might purr, too.

They hadn't found any other evidence pointing to Mallory and her daughter's whereabouts. With every hour, the chances of finding them both safe and alive diminished.

He recognized the tightness around Sierra's mouth, the worry creasing her forehead. There was nothing he could say that she didn't know. She might not do field-work, but she knew the statistics.

Her face was pale. The ibuprofen had to be wearing off, so he knew she was in pain. On a normal op he'd have headed straight to the rodeo—or called up Zane or Sierra to have them hack in.

He tapped his cell phone.

"Westin." Zane's voice carried over the phone. "I hope you found our missing chickadee, Rafe. Boss man isn't a happy camper, and that means the rest of us aren't, either."

Sierra frowned. "I'm right here, Zane."

"Oops. Hi, gorgeous. You sure know how to cause chaos."

"Like you don't," she retorted.

"Could you two give it a rest?" Rafe sighed. "Zane, we need you to hack into the San Antonio Rodeo. We're looking for—"

"They're moving money around. Fifty thousand at least," Sierra offered. "Can you identify who and how much? The evidence points to Mallory Harrigan, but she's being framed."

"That's one theory," Rafe interjected.

Zane was quiet for a moment. "I've followed that trail, Sierra. You sure it's a frame, because it doesn't look like it. There are deposits into a separate account under her name. She has access, and records show *she* transferred the money."

Sierra sighed. "You don't believe me, either."

Rafe grabbed the phone. "Mallory Harrigan's house was tossed. There's a kid in the mix. It's too easy, Zane."

She stared openmouthed at him. Was she that shocked at his defense of Mallory? He might have been skeptical of Sierra's best friend, but he couldn't deny the truth. Being agile—in body and mind—had kept him alive.

"I can see the bank accounts," Zane said, "but I haven't been able to access their books or their local system."

"Firewall?" Rafe scratched his temple.

Zane snorted and Sierra chuckled.

"What's so funny?" Rafe asked.

"A firewall wouldn't stop Zane," she said. "Or me. Are you thinking it's a stand-alone box?"

"We'd do better with a hands-on look," Zane added.

"Then we're going to the rodeo." Rafe glanced at his watch. "If we don't check out that office tonight, we'll lose another dozen hours. It'll be too complicated to break in during daylight. Especially during the rodeo events."

"I'll keep working the search at this end," Zane said. "Let me know what I can do."

Rafe tapped his phone and glanced at Sierra searching for signs of pain or fatigue. Except for the faint tightness in her lips, she hid the pain well. "You up for a little nighttime surveillance?"

"If it gets us closer to finding Mallory and Chloe, do you even have to ask?"

With a quick twist in his seat, Rafe reached into his duffel and pulled out a bottle. "Take a couple more of these. You should be resting that leg."

Sierra downed the pills. "Thanks. Again."

It took about twenty minutes to reach the San Antonio Arena. The lot wasn't completely dark despite the late hour, with the minimum security lights bathing the asphalt in an eerie yellow glow.

He parked in a darkened corner and studied the layout. Leaving the truck close to the entrance might provide a quick entry, but it would attract attention.

Rafe opened the door, leaving the dang cat comfortably in the front seat. The creature circled and settled on the soft cushion, blinking her strange iridescent eyes.

With that pitiful expression, he couldn't *not* scratch Princess Buttercup's…okay, he had to stop with that name. He needed something not quite so…princess-y.

Perhaps P.B. for short. Not bad.

"I need to get to that rodeo office before they erase all traces of what happened," Sierra said, exiting the passenger side.

Rafe rounded the truck. "They know you escaped, and they know Mallory had access to the information. If she's innocent, chances are they've cleaned out the office of anything that doesn't support her guilt. The data is probably gone."

"There's a chance. Mallory could have hidden the records," Sierra said. "There are ways to recover erased files, unless they're using some very sophisticated file-wiping technology."

Rafe closed the door and locked it. "Let's get this over with. I don't like being out in the open with you on a bum leg."

She touched his arm. "Thank you, Rafe. For giving Mallory the benefit of the doubt."

"Don't thank me yet. Besides, I'm still not completely convinced your friend didn't betray you in the end. This doesn't smell right, but—"

Sierra dropped her hand. "Do you suspect everyone you meet?"

"Yes. Human beings are flawed. And no matter how good the intentions, most take the easy path."

Hadn't he done the same thing as a kid? Hadn't his brother? He never would've changed if his brother hadn't paid the ultimate price for his mistakes.

"You're wrong," she said with a sympathetic shake of her head. "Sometimes people are exactly who they appear to be."

"Like you?" Rafe quirked an eyebrow at her.

She met his gaze with a daggerlike glare.

"Just saying. You spent nearly a year hiding that you worked for CTC. You didn't come clean because it would cause conflict with your brothers and father. Easy route."

"You don't know anything about the situation," she said. "There was nothing easy about keeping the truth from my family. Don't judge what you can't understand."

Rafe shifted closer to her and tilted her chin up to his. "I know a hell of a lot about you, Sierra Bradford. More than you think." He dragged his finger down her cheek to her neck and along her collarbone.

She shivered at his touch. He should stop; he shouldn't tempt himself, or her, but he couldn't help it. Being this close to her made him want something real.

And Sierra Bradford was the real deal, even with her secrets. Maybe because of them.

He lifted his other hand to her horribly bruised cheek. "I know a few spots that turn you on at the slightest touch." He leaned in closer and nipped her ear. The hairs on her arms stood up.

"I know you're as smart as Noah, even if you don't believe that." His lips inched along her jaw. "And I know you want more than anything to prove yourself, when you don't have to."

In one desperate motion his lips covered hers, gently. She groaned and opened herself to him. The flash of lightning he'd experienced the night they were together roared back. He tasted the sweetness of her lips and knew his body and his heart owned him at this moment. His head had gone AWOL.

Sierra clutched his shirt in her hands. Rafe wrapped his arms around her and pressed her against him, but when she let out a gasp of pain, he immediately released her. "God, I'm sorry."

She pulled back, her lips swollen, her gaze foggy. She blinked away the passion, her look one of caution. "I can't seem to resist you," she said softly.

"You'd tempt a saint," Rafe said. "And I've broken too many commandments to qualify."

She bit her lip. "You hurt me when you left that morning. How can I trust you?"

"You can't."

Chapter Five

The air grew heavy with humiliation. Sierra pulled away from Rafe. "You're honest at least."

Her body thrummed with unfulfilled need, but Sierra tamped it down. Rafe had the same idea. He shifted, and her gaze fell to the front of his jeans. He couldn't hide his wants. Then again, neither could she. Her nipples had gone hard, hypersensitive against the soft T-shirt she wore.

"Let's go inside," she said softly. "The sooner we find Mallory, the sooner you can go back to wherever you live and I can return to Denver."

And not have to see you.

She left the words unspoken, but they settled between them like a concrete wall dividing them.

As they made their way toward a side door at the arena, Rafe pulled out his phone and pressed a key.

Sierra leaned toward him taking a quick look at the app. "A jammer?"

"Your brother and Zane developed it. Just in case there are cameras. We don't need anyone tying us to this place."

Forty more yards and they reached the door. Rafe tested it. Locked.

He didn't hesitate, but reached into his pocket and pulled out two picks.

Within seconds the door opened and they entered the large space, the scent of livestock and hay floating on the air. Long, broad hallways led to the eerily silent arena, but they bypassed them and headed toward the row of offices.

"I expected to see crime scene tape," Sierra said.

"Could be enough political clout buys more than just a fixed parking ticket."

Sierra rubbed her nape, the tension coiling her muscles into stiff ropes. "We *have* to find a lead here. If we don't…"

"This isn't your fault."

"If I'd taken Mallory's concerns more seriously, recognized the danger, maybe I could've protected her." The guilt clawed at Sierra's throat. She'd relived every second of the sight of Mallory's resigned look when Chloe had frozen. Both women had known the chances of survival when that van had disappeared.

Rafe turned her into his arms. "Look at me."

She met his gaze, his brown eyes dark and intent.

"I've been in a lot of ops. More than my share have gone to hell. You can't look back, you have to look forward. After it's over you can regret and rehash all you want. Until the next op. If you don't, you'll make a mistake. You understand?"

Sierra nodded. "Focus on the here and now. I can do that." Maybe.

The freight elevator rumbled to her right. Rafe shoved her behind a pillar and pressed her tight against the concrete. She held her breath.

Footsteps strode past them. Rafe eased them around

the column to keep out of the guard's sight. Finally the echo of the boots faded away.

She let out a long, slow breath.

"Let's move," he whispered. "As quietly as you can."

Without a sound they hurried to the office door. Rafe made quick work of the lock. He opened it and snuck through before shutting it behind them. He tugged the shade down, blocking the door's glass window to outside light. The room went dark.

Sierra dug into her side pocket for the small but powerful flashlight Noah had given her to carry on her key ring. She doubted he'd expected her to use it for breaking and entering.

"Nice. You're a regular Girl Scout. Keep the light pointed down so you don't attract attention," Rafe said. "Which computer?"

"There." She nodded at Mallory's nameplate on a desk facing the entrance. "I'm surprised they haven't confiscated it."

"It shouldn't be there." Rafe scowled. "This was too easy. Gives me a bad feeling."

"Maybe our luck is changing." Sierra rounded the desk. Give her a keyboard and a mouse, and she could do anything.

Rafe planted himself near the door. She fired up the machine, biting her lip at the light glowing from the monitor. At least it was facing away from the entrance. Still, she dimmed the screen. Hopefully no one would notice.

Holding the flashlight in her mouth, Sierra searched the desk and tugged a ledger from the drawer. She pulled out a receipt file and walked through the bank statements. She had to figure out why the numbers didn't match up.

With every line, her frown deepened. The longer she tracked, the more the back of her neck prickled. Sierra knew Mallory's capabilities. They'd gone to school together. Attended the same classes. There were too many mistakes. Nothing too large, but added up, over one million dollars so far.

Any first year accounting student could find the errors in these books by simply matching cash transactions with no pedigree. What was she missing? Or had Mallory left the trail on purpose?

Rafe cleared his throat and pointed at his watch. She nodded.

She snapped photos of the documents before pushing aside the ledger. With a click of the mouse, she opened the bank records directory on the computer. Something wasn't quite right. She studied the directory. Bigger than she'd expected. The individual files didn't jibe with the folder size. She quickly pulled up the command prompt window and typed in a few keystrokes. The view changed. Voilà. An invisible file. A *locked* invisible file.

Interesting.

She clicked on it. Password protected. Which wasn't a problem. Most people used simple passwords easily deciphered. Or, in Sierra's case, easily circumvented.

Her decryption tool did its work within minutes and she opened the file. She scanned a few rows. Right there, on the spreadsheet. The truth. Maybe not who or why, but how much.

Sierra quickly calculated the total in her head. She let out a low whistle.

Rafe's head snapped up and he walked to her, leaning over. His warm hand squeezed her shoulder. "What've you found?"

"Whoever kept this second set of books has laundered nearly five million dollars in the last year alone," she whispered.

"That's willing-to-kill money," he said with a frown.

Sierra met Rafe's gaze. "If Mallory discovered this file—"

"She's in bigger trouble than we thought."

"The records go back at least five years." Sierra rubbed her eyes as if refocusing them would change the facts. It didn't, of course. "If the previous years' were comparable to this last one, that's twenty-five million."

"We're talking a significant amount of money. With that much on the line, people get desperate. And deadly."

Rafe straightened, his frown deepening. The concern in his eyes sent a skitter of worry snaking up and down Sierra's back.

"You don't think they're—"

She couldn't say the word aloud. Rafe knelt in front of the chair and clasped her hands in his, meeting her gaze, his face half-covered in shadow in the dim light. "If all they'd wanted was to silence her, they could have killed her on the side of the road. They needed her. For something. There's a chance."

But not a good one. She recognized the truth in his expression.

"Give me a name, Sierra," Rafe whispered. "And I'll do whatever it takes to get them back."

"I'll find something," she promised, as much to herself as to him, hoping to God she spoke the truth. If they kept records of transactions, maybe, just maybe she'd uncover some identifying information. With a prayer on her lips, she selected another work sheet and scanned the text.

"You shouldn't be here," a male voice hissed from outside the door, only a few feet away.

Sierra's hand froze, tightening on the mouse. Oh God. Her gaze snapped to Rafe. His expression had gone cold and lethal. He rose, his movements silent, and pressed his finger to his lips.

With the precision of a jungle cat, he padded to the door without making a sound and slipped his weapon from its holster.

"We have to talk," another voice, urgent, almost desperate, whispered. "It can't wait."

Her heart thudded in her chest. How many people would be hovering right outside this particular office door? What if the two men came into the office? She swallowed hard. Her hands shook. She was so close to finding an answer.

Any moment now, the chance could be gone. She had to be quick. They needed this information. Hands shaking, she pulled out a thumb drive and quickly saved the file. Within seconds she'd closed down the computer system, leaving everything as she'd found it.

"We can't be seen together," the first man snapped. He jiggled the doorknob. "Damn. Where's that key?"

Their luck had run out. Rafe nodded toward her right. Her gaze followed his line of sight. Just a few feet from her a door was propped open. To a closet.

A small, tight space. Too much like another closet. The one where Sierra had almost died, where Archimedes had carved his symbol into her skin, leaving his mark forever. Her heart raced. A familiar vise closed off her breathing at the thought of entering the tiny room. No way could she go in there. She shook her head and pulled out her weapon.

He tapped his ear. She understood the signal. Rafe *could* take the men by surprise, but he didn't want to interrupt their conversation. Their chance to save Mallory depended on finding her quickly. They needed the intel first.

Rafe's jaw muscles pulsed. He pointed underneath the desk. Okay, it might be tight, but she could manage to fold her five-foot-ten-inch frame under the furniture to hide. If she had to.

"This is urgent," the second man said.

Sierra eased the chair back. A small squeak sounded from the wheels. She froze.

"Fine. But be quick. The guard's round takes about a half hour." The gravelly voice didn't sound familiar to her, except for the West Texas twang. "What's so damned important you had to pull me away from a good steak?"

"I'm getting pressure from one of our buyers. They want proof we have the real thing."

The first man let out a snort. "Cut 'em loose. We have other opportunities."

"Umm… It's not that easy. They've threatened to go to the cops."

A harsh curse echoed through the door.

"You came to me with this idea to expand our base, and I gave you one damned job. Vet the customers. I've been running this operation out of the rodeo for over five years, and no one has *ever* threatened me with the cops. Until you screwed it up."

"They're a high bidder." The man's voice trembled. "Double what you made on any one transaction last year."

"Really? That much?" The smoke-laced tone turned speculative. "Show them the stuff. Keep them happy."

"They could still talk."

"High bidder. They want it bad. They were willing to talk to you. That means they're willing to walk outside the law. They're bluffing. They won't turn us in. Now get out of here. And don't be seen."

One set of footsteps hurried away. The other man gave a huff. "Amateur," he muttered.

Not a word about Mallory, but she and Rafe needed an identity. They couldn't let him get away.

She rose from her hiding place and pulled out her weapon. Rafe must've been thinking the same thing. He placed his hand on the doorknob and gave her a questioning look. She nodded.

"Sir, what are you doing here? This is a closed area." A questioning voice intruded.

A gunshot rang out, followed by a loud curse. Rafe flung open the door. Sierra sprang from her position to follow. The guard lay in a pool of blood. A figure disappeared to the front of the arena.

Rafe gripped his weapon. "I'll—"

"Help me," the injured guard whispered through gurgling breath. "Please."

Tires squealed. The guy must've had a waiting vehicle. And since they'd jammed the cameras, there'd be no video to identify it.

Rafe knelt beside the man. He opened his shirt. Buttons flew everywhere, and Rafe let out a curse. "I need another set of hands," he said, tugging off his own shirt and pressing it to the bloody wound. "Put pressure on the wound."

She held the material down.

He flattened his hands over hers. "Harder. We have to stop the bleeding."

Sierra rose to her knees to get better leverage. "I've got it."

Rafe removed his hands and nodded. He wiped one hand on his shirt and palmed his phone. "Keep at it while I call for an ambulance. I don't want your voice on record. As it is, this is going to take a lot of tap-dancing."

DAWN WAS RAFE'S ENEMY. It would arrive soon, and the sky had lightened too much for his liking. Light meant clarity, and he preferred to move in the murk. Less likely to be identified.

He peered around the end trailer where he'd been observing the chaos at the arena. The ambulance screamed away from the arena. Hopefully the guard would survive.

The crime scene unit had arrived. Crime scene tape littered the area. Numerous uniforms milled about the scene. On another mission, he might have recruited them to help with their search. More manpower could mean finding Mallory Harrigan and her little girl faster—or discovering a weak link in the organization—but not this operation. He was convinced the chances of Sierra's friend and her daughter surviving depended on secrecy. They were on their own except for a few trusted allies.

His gaze shifted to a side road out of the line of sight of the arena. Sierra waited there. Once he'd made the emergency call, he'd sent her back to the truck partly to work on the files, but mainly to protect her. He had no idea if one of the cops had been on the road that night when Mallory and Chloe had been abducted, and he wasn't taking any chances. She was safe in his truck a good half mile away with a thumb drive that he hoped gave them a name, because whoever shot the security guard hadn't revealed enough information to be of any use. Rafe would recognize the boss's voice if he heard it again, though. He also had his theories. Given the talk of buyers and sellers this close to the border, they were pretty much referencing guns or drugs. Which could mean cartels. What a cluster.

Rafe studied an older man, a bit stocky, with a close haircut, wearing a Stetson, as he paced back and forth. He'd arrived in a Texas-sized Cadillac. A gold ring gleamed on his right hand. "And what the hell am I supposed to do about this?" he shouted, his voice carrying easily to Rafe. "I got a rodeo to run. You get your men to work faster, Captain. Or I'll make a phone call you won't appreciate."

A captain didn't typically work a scene in the middle of the night. Obviously the gentleman had clout. Which put him on the top of Rafe's suspect list.

A familiar detective standing at the perimeter eased away from the group, and after a quick backward glance, strode toward Rafe. The man was skilled and subtle at blending into the scenery, Rafe would give him that.

Detective Cade Foster rounded the trailer where Rafe had planted himself to observe. "Ransom is damned lucky I live fifteen minutes from this place. Another five and you'd be sitting in jail."

"Noted," Rafe said. "How's the guard?"

"Probably gonna make it. Thanks to you. Which is the reason I'm giving you the benefit of the doubt. That and I owe Ransom." Cade tilted his Stetson back, his frown deepening. "You're involved with the embezzlement case that hit yesterday? Mallory Harrigan. She shoot the guy?"

Rafe shook his head. "Pretty sure the perp was a man. I didn't get a good enough look to identify him, but he was around six feet, stocky, wore a white Stetson, a Western-style black suit and too-shiny cowboy boots. He drove off in a dark F350."

Cade flipped open a notebook and penned a few words. "Pretty specific, but not unlike a hundred thousand other men in this part of Texas."

"I know." Rafe scowled. "We're on a time crunch. You hear anything—"

"If it's pertinent, I'll contact you or Ransom. But quid pro quo. I want to be kept in the loop, or I come looking for you."

With a quick nod of agreement, Rafe shook Cade's hand. "We owe you."

"And I'll be collecting."

The detective headed back to the crime scene, and Rafe walked as quickly as he dared, not to attract attention. Early-morning shadows offered some cover, but that would end soon.

His phone vibrated, and he winced when he saw the screen identifying his boss.

"Vargas."

"What the hell is going on down there, Rafe?" Ransom didn't mince words. "Attempted murder, bringing in local law enforcement. You got me playing in the dark gray, and I don't like working there. Not on this side of the pond."

Rafe sighed. He'd thought about his choices, and they were few. And they involved CTC. "Sierra's stumbled onto something bigger than we thought." Rafe briefed his boss and winced at the man's curses.

"You believe the woman and girl are alive?" Ransom asked.

"*If* she can hold out and not give them what they want, maybe." Truth was, after the way the guard had been shot, Rafe was less certain than he had been. The bad guys may just cut their losses. If they owned a wide enough swath of law-enforcement officials, they could probably squelch most evidence. He and Ransom had seen it happen more than once.

"The guy shot a security guard, risking scrutiny just to hide a conversation," Ransom said. "That's no coincidence."

"Agreed. Since Sierra found evidence of at least twenty-five million being laundered through the rodeo, and these guys are working a deal that could bring in twice that over five years, I'd say they have a lot to lose. Sierra's working the electrons, boss, but we don't have a name. Not even close. If we're going to save Mallory and Chloe, we need information. And even if Cade were willing to risk his career, I don't know who's involved at the San Antonio PD."

"What are you proposing?"

"If we're going to follow the money, Sierra and I need an in at the San Antonio Rodeo. Can you do it?" Actually, Rafe had no doubts Ransom could pull it off. The trouble was, did he want to?

"Identities for *both* of you? Can't you just send her

home? She doesn't have the field experience for undercover."

"She's a lot like her brother once she has a mission in her head. She won't leave. Mallory and Chloe are important to her. Besides, I need her to follow the money."

Ransom let out a curse. "She's as much of a pain in the ass as Noah." The sound of drumming fingers filtered through the phone. "We might be able to switch you out for someone already entered in the rodeo. You did some bull riding when you were young, right?"

Like Ransom didn't know, or remember.

"It's been a while. I gave it up. Special Forces was less dangerous," Rafe said.

"With your pedigree, I think I know someone who can find you a spot. You *sure* Sierra won't let this alone?"

"No way. It's too personal. Which worries me, but the truth is, she knows the players better than I do. She may have heard something or seen something that will break the case. It's her best friend and five-year-old goddaughter. If it doesn't turn out well and we don't let her help…" He left the consequences unsaid. No need. Just the thought made Rafe's gut twist. "How do I argue with that?"

"Noah's going to kill us both when he learns she's gone undercover. Even if you're watching out for her." Ransom's voice sounded pained.

"He hasn't forgiven you yet, has he?" Rafe said. "For keeping Sierra's employment a secret for so long?"

"He flew down here just to slug me," Ransom admitted. "Guy has a killer left hook."

"Next time I'm in Carder, I might do the same."

"You both need to see Sierra for who she is. The best I've seen. That's why I hired her in the first place."

"At the computer," Rafe said, "I'd agree with you. But you took her off duty."

"For her. Not for you and Noah. She wanted to be more involved, to get hands-on experience. Archimedes's abduction gave her a look into what could happen. Made her skittish. She needed time to heal, to decide. From what Noah's said, she's not quite ready."

"I'm well aware. I'm keeping an eye on her."

"Anything happens to her, Noah and her other brothers won't let you forget it."

"If anything happens to her, it'll happen to me first," Rafe muttered. "I'll try to convince her to go home, but we both know the odds."

"Zero. Do you need backup for the op?"

"I need someone in that rodeo office with ready access to records and to run interference. I don't want Sierra put in that position. Three of these guys have seen her. Even with the disguise I have planned, I'm concerned."

"Zane's on his way since you've already read him in."

At the words, Rafe coughed.

Ransom let out a low chuckle. "You think I didn't know he was running a search for you? Really, Rafe? It takes a lot to surprise me." Ransom paused. "By the way, did you forget to mention a certain *package* you had delivered?"

Package? It took Rafe a moment. He hadn't called it in. He grimaced. "Elena. Yeah. I—"

"Another stray. I won't out you as a closet softy, Rafe. Besides, she deserves a break. The wife and kids have fallen in love with her and Charlie. I have a place for them. Give me a heads-up next time. Our security spooked her."

"She okay?"

"She's tough. And there's a bit more to her than you suspected, I think. I'll give you the details later. Back to our immediate problem. I'm using Zane as a go-between with Detective Foster until this op is over. Afterward, you, Noah and I are having a long conversation regarding Sierra."

Ransom ended the phone call, and Rafe picked up his pace heading to his truck. Was he making a mistake?

Normally, when the plan took shape, his entire body went calm and still. Not this morning. He vibrated with tension. Probably due to working with another woman he cared about. He couldn't deny his feelings for Sierra. And he couldn't stop the memories of the fallout of the last op with his fiancée. Her bullet-ridden body, the blood. Arriving too late.

He reached the vehicle and gripped the door handle with whitened knuckles. The bruises on Sierra's face had deepened in color. She sat hunched over the computer, lost in concentration.

He'd have to work on her spatial awareness. The angry bullet's graze on her thigh burned in his memory. She could've been killed, and everything inside Rafe shouted at him to pack her in Bubble Wrap and hide her away. Instead, he rapped on the window.

Sierra jerked her head up. Princess Buttercup leaped across the keyboard and placed her paws on the window.

The shock on Sierra's face melted into relief, and she rolled down the glass. "You're back. I was worried the cops…"

"Ransom's guy came through."

"Thank goodness." She let out a shuddering breath. "I half expected him to be on the take."

"We can trust Cade." He frowned. "But you can't let yourself get so immersed in your work that you're that easily surprised. I could have dropped you if I'd wanted to."

"I was tracking your movements," she said with a confident smile. "I saw your approach. I just didn't expect you to bang on the window. Don't do that again."

Rafe rubbed the brow bone over his uncovered eye. This op was going to test his patience in a big way.

The dang cat butted her head through the open window against Rafe's forearm. He shook his head but scratched the silly animal's ears anyway. "I'm not sure what Ransom did for the detective, but whatever it was, Cade was willing to risk lying to his superiors about finding the guard. He's covering for us. For now anyway."

"Is the guard going to make it?"

"He'll be out of it for a while, but it looks like it."

Sierra let out a sigh of relief.

"You get a name?" he asked.

"Nothing." Her brow furrowed, and her eyes flashed with fury. "Millions of dollars are moving through that rodeo. Whoever's doing this is smart, and secretive. We know the what, but the who and why are like smoke. No account numbers, no bank routing numbers, nothing to identify them. I've hit a brick wall."

Rafe leaned in. "Look, honey, this situation is getting complicated. And more dangerous. Following the ones and zeroes won't cut it. We need boots-on-the-ground intel if we're going to find Mallory and Chloe."

"The rodeo venue's owner is John Beckel. I'm running his background next."

"Good idea. See if anything pops." Rafe shifted his feet. "Sierra, why not head up to Carder? CTC headquarters has the latest equipment, everything you need to work your magic."

She froze and narrowed her gaze at him. "I need to be here. You need backup."

"Zane's coming in. I promise, I'll let you know what's happening every step of the way."

"You want to get rid of me. Why?" With a snap, she closed the laptop.

"You're good at your job. You can help us there."

"Mallory's told me about her job, about the rodeo. I can help more right here during the investigation…"

Her words tapered off, and her eyes widened. "You're going undercover. That's what you meant by boots on the ground."

He could almost see the gears churning in her mind. The eagerness in her eyes made his gut twist. He knew the adrenaline rush well, and he knew the risks. She had a personal investment in this op. It made for bad decision making. He should know.

She gripped his arm. "I can help you."

"If I said no, you'd insert yourself anyway, wouldn't you? Somehow, some way?"

"Let's put it this way. You aren't banishing me to Carder, anytime soon. Not until Mallory and Chloe are home safe and sound." She met his gaze. "I can't stop looking for them. Not when I should've been able to stop them from being taken."

He gripped the door through the open window. "Then I guess it's time for us to go undercover at the rodeo."

Chapter Six

A thin layer of pink-orange sky filtered through the trees. Hunkered in a depression in the midst of a small but thick grove of cottonwood trees, Mallory cradled Chloe, focusing on her daughter's even breathing. She'd finally fallen asleep. Even though Mallory could use the rest, she couldn't close her eyes. She peered through the web of branches encasing them, praying she saw nothing. That they were safe.

She'd had no idea how far they'd run, or how long. The only light visible had been a shard of moon hanging in the sky and a bevy of stars, which had offered little hope. She'd seen no sign of civilization anywhere. Not a road, not a light. Just darkness and trees and open stretches of land.

They'd almost been caught, but choosing the road less traveled had been their salvation. Finally, when the shouts and curses of their captors had dimmed, they'd trudged as long as Chloe's legs had held out. Mallory had carried her daughter as long as she could, until, finally, legs and arms shaking, she'd stumbled and pitched to the ground. She had no choice but to stop. Mallory had crawled underneath a mesh of leaves and branches.

She'd camouflaged their hideout to the best of her ability and settled in for the remainder of the night.

Darkness had provided camouflage, but now that dawn had peeked over the horizon, it would be more difficult than ever to escape detection. She stroked Chloe's hair. Tears pricked the corners of Mallory's eyes.

Their escape had been so panicked, the desperation to survive so paramount, she hadn't kept track of which direction they'd run.

If she left their hideout, she could very well end up going back toward that trailer—and their kidnappers.

Chloe squirmed in her lap. "Mommy," she whimpered.

"Shh, Button. You have to be very, very quiet."

"Or the bad people will find us." The little girl burrowed against her mother's breast.

"Yes." Mallory kissed the top of her daughter's head.

"The sun's up. I'm hungry."

"I know, but we can't eat right now. Maybe a little later, okay?"

"Pancakes?"

If only she possessed Chloe's optimism. "Maybe tomorrow," she said, praying she told her daughter the truth.

"That means no," Chloe said, pouting. She squirmed. "Mommy, I have to go pottie."

"Okay, sugar, but we need to stay quiet."

Chloe pursed her lips and nodded. Carefully Mallory pushed aside the leaves, and they crawled out of their hiding place. Mallory stood and took her daughter over to a stand of buffalo grass near a small grove of trees.

A shout carried through the landscape. "Find them! Ten grand to whoever brings them to me. Dead or alive."

Mallory's throat spasmed in panic. She grabbed her daughter's hand. "Run, Chloe! Run!"

SIERRA RUBBED HER EYES. She winced at the grit and stinging behind her lids. She'd been through more than her share of all-nighters during college, but she was out of practice. The morning sun had only risen a sliver, and the western sky still bore that dark purple-blue of night.

Rafe pulled into the motel parking lot. Princess Buttercup had plastered herself to his leg. If he moved an inch, the cat scooted closer.

Covering her mouth with her hand to disguise her small smile, Sierra eyed the pair. He didn't quite know what to make of the mostly white calico, but he sure couldn't shake that cat.

After Rafe turned off the engine, he twisted in his seat, once again pushing Princess Buttercup out of the way, gently but firmly. The cat lightly jumped onto the floor and curled around Rafe's boots. He shook his head, clearly befuddled. "Are cats trainable? At all?"

She bit the inside of her cheek. "About as much as you are."

A twinkle of humor shined in his unpatched eye. She couldn't ever remember witnessing that particular expression on his face. She liked the change, but it didn't last long. He stroked his chin. "You want to be part of this op, I have some ground rules, or we end this here and now. First one is, this is my operation. I say jump, you ask how high. I give an order, you don't question me because I may not have time to explain myself. Got it?"

She bristled at the order but knew he was right. He had the experience; she was a newbie. "Got it."

In truth, she couldn't believe he'd agreed to work with her. She knew from the jobs Ransom assigned to Rafe that he didn't do partners. Not if he could help it. But, she possessed a skill he didn't. She might excel at her job as a forensic accountant, but she also knew Rafe. He was a lone wolf. He preferred swooping in, getting the job done as quickly as possible—on his own—and swooping out, not getting too involved. Her brother had tried to warn her off when she'd been under the illusion that there might be something between her and Rafe. The warning had come too late. She'd already fallen for that mysterious aura he exuded.

Everything about him should have terrified her—the edge of danger lacing his eyes, the intensity, the aloofness. Perhaps because she'd worn her own mask for far too long, she'd recognized something more beneath the mask he wore. A kindred spirit.

He was also a true hero at heart. Mallory and Chloe were innocent. And Rafe would do whatever it took to find them. Even if it meant teaming with a beginner.

"First order of business is to move locations. We clean out the motel room and disappear. No trace. Eliminate any possibility of a tail."

Nodding, she slid out of the truck. Her leg had gone stiff after sitting so long, but at least it didn't hurt quite as much. She could feel his narrowed gaze watching her, studying her movement. She stiffened, sucking up the pain so her walk appeared even and natural.

His frown deepened, but he didn't comment. They walked to the motel room.

"Key?" he asked, holding out his hand.

Ignoring him, she unlocked the door. When she pushed it open, she couldn't stop her gasp. The room had been destroyed.

Rafe shoved her away from the entrance with one hand and unholstered his weapon with the other. Sierra wasn't nearly as quick, but she drew the Glock.

He quickly searched the small bathroom and closet. "Clear."

Stepping across the threshold, she surveyed the destruction. The drawers had been pulled out, the mattress tossed, nothing left untouched, though truth be told, she hadn't had much.

"How did they find me?"

"The same way I did. Which means they have resources. Not surprising, but definitely problematic."

A knock sounded on the half-open door. "Did your brother find you, Mrs. Jones?" the hotel manager asked, barging in. His eyes went wide with shock, and he gasped. "What have you done? Who's going to pay for this?"

Rafe tugged a wad of cash from his pocket and thrust several hundred-dollar bills into the manager's hands. "That should cover it. We'll be out of here in five minutes," he said, shoving the man out the door.

He grumbled, giving them both a dirty look before he walked away.

"Go out to the car," Rafe said.

"What are you going to do?"

"Make certain our friends didn't leave any unexpected presents."

"How can I help?" she asked.

"Know anything about explosive devices?"

Her cheeks heated, and she backed out of the room. "Be careful, Rafe."

He shot her a grin. "Always."

"And never," she muttered.

Sierra couldn't just sit in the truck waiting for the room to explode. She paced back and forth, her hand wrapped around her weapon. Princess Buttercup peered out from inside the truck, her white face tilted, and the rust and black decorating her ears and top of her head looking like a crown.

"You know something's not right, too, don't you, baby?" Sierra said, making her way over to the truck door.

Rafe strode outside with a bag in his hand and tossed it into the Dumpster across the parking lot, veering toward the motel office.

A few minutes later he opened the truck door. "The only description of your brother he gave me was a 'cowboy.' Narrows it down to half the city. At least they only tossed the place. We were lucky." He frowned at her. "They couldn't have taken any identifying information in the room?"

She shot him a heated glare.

"Then we're okay. For now." He paused and stared at the cat. "You think you could hold the beast while I drive. She's…distracting."

Sierra rounded the truck, opened the door and Princess Buttercup jumped into her arms. Sierra stroked her soft fur. "Sure thing."

But the moment Rafe joined her, the princess settled into her spot right next to him.

"I guess she likes you."

Rafe tossed his Stetson on the dash. "Now I know why I never had a pet."

He pulled onto the road and took off into the early-morning San Antonio traffic.

"Where are we going?"

"For now I'm making damn sure we aren't being tailed. After that…" He smiled at her.

She didn't like the look on his face.

Rafe shrugged. "We're getting married."

AN HOUR OF driving inanely around San Antonio had convinced Rafe no one was following them. Rush hour had begun, and the purr of the truck had lulled Sierra to sleep after she'd recovered from the shock of his *proposal*.

The shadows under her lashes made him frown. Was he making another huge mistake letting her be involved? He nearly laughed. Hell, he wasn't *allowing* her to do anything. Better that he work with her than have her as a loose cannon.

Still, anyone who would abduct a child would do anything.

He pulled in at an out-of-the-way motel with the truck facing so Sierra was protected from view.

"Watch out for her, P.B.," he muttered to the cat. The animal licked its paws and gave a soft meow.

Rafe scratched the beast's ears. A rumble-like purr vibrated in her chest. Stunned at the turn his life had taken—from black ops in Afghanistan to talking to a cat named Princess Buttercup in San Antonio—he strode into the motel's office.

The dated room appeared spotless. Before Rafe could sound the small bell on the reservation counter, a man with the look of an ex-boxer, his nose obviously broken more than once, appeared through a doorway to what appeared to be his apartment.

Within moments, Rafe had paid cash for a couple of nights and signed in under a false name. The guy rang up the transaction without a word.

Rafe studied the man for a moment, then slid a couple hundred dollars across the counter. "I'm not expecting any visitors unless I introduce them to you personally. You got me?"

The guy didn't touch the money. A frown cut the line down the middle of his forehead into a crater. "I run an honest place. You up to any funny business, there's a better location half a block down the road."

Rafe's gaze centered on the guy's tattoo signifying Special Forces. "I just want quiet," Rafe said. "I think I can get that here."

The guy studied Rafe for a few seconds. "Marines or Rangers?" he asked.

"Green Beret. Four tours. You?"

"Two with the Rangers. I made it back, but my brother died in Afghanistan. Near Kandahar." The man slid Rafe's money back across the counter. "Name's Calhoun. Anyone asks, you ain't here and never have been. Just keep it on the up-and-up."

"You got it." Rafe took the key and strode out the door.

He scooted into the truck and drove to the end of the motel strip. Sierra didn't budge from her sound sleep. Rafe couldn't remember the last time he'd rested so… okay, maybe he could. In her arms a couple months ago.

Leaving her inside, he surveilled the motel room and unloaded the truck before opening the passenger door. He lifted her into his arms.

"You coming, P.B.?" he asked the cat. With a flick of her tail and a disdainful look down her feline nose, she bounded out of the vehicle and followed him inside.

Rafe shut the door closed with his foot, then laid Sierra on the bed, slipped off her shoes and tossed a spare blanket over her. He should clean her wound again, but he'd do that when she woke up.

He locked the door and closed the curtains. No one had seen them enter, so when a completely different couple exited, there would be no surprises. He tapped his phone.

"Westin. How's it going, Rafe?"

"We're in place. When do you get here?"

"A few hours. I've got your supplies. Jared King is coming with your horse and a hell of a tall tale for the owner of the rodeo. Should be there by this afternoon sometime."

"Good." After ending the call, he grabbed a couple of metal bowls, doled out water and cat food, then set up a litter box.

"I can't believe I'm doing this," he muttered.

Small, cute snores escaped Sierra. Rafe settled on the bed beside her. She turned toward him and nestled against his chest, wrapping her arm around him, then heaving a slow, contented sigh. Rafe stared at the ceiling above him. That morning almost two months ago flashed through him. A lifetime ago. A world ago. He'd never thought they'd share the same bed again.

P.B. pounced onto the mattress. She circled around and settled at his feet, purring softly.

He glanced at the woman lying next to him, and the cat with its head on his leg, hemming him in.

A throbbing headache pulsed behind Rafe's eyes. He shifted his patch. Until they found Mallory and Chloe, he was in big, big trouble, and there was absolutely no way to escape.

He was well and truly caught.

ONE SHARP KNOCK followed by two quick raps snapped Rafe from sleep. His left hand automatically reached for his weapon. His right hand was busy holding Sierra next to him. She wasn't lying on top of him like she had the last time they'd slept together, but she'd thrown one leg across his body. Gently he eased from beneath her. Princess Buttercup opened one eye, stared at him, then settled back down.

"Some watch cat you are," he muttered.

One glance through the peephole and he opened the door, closing it behind him to greet Zane.

Across the parking lot, Calhoun stared intently at them from the motel's office. Rafe gave the guy a brief nod, and he disappeared into the office.

"Special Forces?" Zane asked, crossing his burly arms across his body.

"Ranger." No one looked less like a geek than Zane with his football-player frame and tats down one arm. Personally, Rafe got the impression Zane enjoyed the disconnect.

"She inside?" Zane asked, not bothering to elaborate. They both knew who they were talking about.

Rafe nodded.

"She okay?"

"It's just a graze." Rafe glanced down at two large duffels. "Is that everything?"

Zane nodded. "Jared King's towing Ironsides and the rest of the equipment. You going to be able to pull this off?"

"We'll find out. It's been a decade since I've been in the arena."

Zane grinned. "I wasn't talking about the rodeo, Rafe. I meant Sierra. And Noah when he finds out you two have a less-than-legal marriage license."

"Under the names Rafe and Sarah Vargas. It's not real."

"You keep telling yourself that. You've got it as bad as Noah."

Rafe scowled at his friend. Zane just smiled. "Jared will be here in a couple of hours. You'll need that long to get ready. I'll see you at the rodeo."

Zane pulled out of the parking lot and Rafe carried the large duffels into the room.

"Who were you talking to?" Sierra sat up in bed and rubbed her eyes. Her light brown hair flowed over her shoulders.

"Zane. He delivered our disguises. The men who kidnapped Mallory and Chloe saw you, so we need a cover."

"You've come up with something. Obviously."

"It's best to keep the story as close to real as possible. I'm Rafe Vargas, former teen bull riding champ. I joined the military, was dishonorably discharged after getting caught smuggling and was released from prison last year. I've bought my way in with some high stakes that I don't talk about. And you, my dear, are my wife."

"I thought you were joking before. Married?" Sierra's face had gone pale.

"The rodeo's like a family. There's an entire subculture. Families, groupies, wives, girlfriends. Best way to find out where the money's flowing is to cover both sides."

"How do you know so much about it?"

"I rode when I was a kid. Before I enlisted when I turned eighteen."

He unzipped the bag and showed her the marriage license.

"Sarah?" she asked, staring at the paper. She let the marriage license flutter to the bed and studied him with a quizzical look on her face. "How much of what you just told me is true?"

"Like I said. It's easier to stay as close to the truth as possible." Rafe shrugged. How was he supposed to explain that last mission, Gabriella's death, his fight for freedom, and the justice he'd exacted on the men who'd betrayed them? What was the point? Instead of answering, he bent over the duffel.

"You'll need to blend in, and not stand out." Rafe tossed an auburn wig at her, a hairnet and some clothes. Finally he pulled out a bra attached to a large silicon mound.

Sierra poked at the fake belly. "I'm pregnant?"

"My other choice was a hot girlfriend. You'd attract too much attention." He frowned as the neck of his T-shirt slipped down her right shoulder, revealing soft skin and the upper curve of her breast.

Her cheeks reddened, and she readjusted her top.

He cleared his throat. "No single guy should give a pregnant woman a second look. Most will probably avoid looking at you."

"And you think this will work?"

"The men trying to find you won't be looking for a redhead who's five months pregnant."

She picked up the device and weighed it in her hand. "I've never done anything like this before, Rafe. I don't know how to act pregnant, or pump people for information."

"You're smart and resourceful. You know what we need to find out, you know what Mallory said and what her skills are, and you know better than anyone else how people hide money. You can do this." He tilted her face so her gaze met his. "Would I rather you were home in

Denver safe and sound? Absolutely. But not because you can't do this job."

She fingered the clothes. "I've always worked behind the scenes. I thought you'd put me in that office to work the computer."

"Zane's taken that job. They might be suspicious of me, but around you...those cowboys will talk. Their wives will share. You're safe and accessible. Someone might say more than they intend. Besides, Zane doesn't exactly fit in on that family bench."

"I can't argue with that." She let out a long slow breath and stared at the disguise.

"Isn't this why you came to San Antonio without telling anyone?" Rafe prodded. "To prove yourself?"

"Yeah. And look what I did."

He turned her to face him. "Mallory had a target on her back before you ever arrived, Sierra. At least you were here. You did everything you could to save her. She has a chance, but you're the only witness, and they want you to run. And as far as they know, you have. You checked out, took a cab to the airport and the passenger list shows you're back in Denver."

"Zane?"

"Gotta appreciate what the man can do with records." Rafe picked up the wig. "So, you ready to meet Sarah Vargas, my baby mama?"

She glanced up at Rafe. Her blue eyes held an uncertainty she couldn't hide. "What if I make a mistake?"

"You'll make more than one. The trick is to keep cool and recover." He cupped her cheeks. "Without any other clues, it's the only way that we'll find Mallory and her daughter. You can do this."

Rafe handed her the clothes and pushed her toward the bathroom. "Oh, and you're Noah Bradford's sister."

He closed the door behind her, and Sierra faced the bathroom mirror. She looked like someone had run a truck over her. Dark circles, pale, tense, bruises blotching her face. How could Rafe think she could do this?

Noah had always been smarter and a way better sneak during his high-school years. He'd lied about his career for years.

Of course, so had she. Noah had done it to protect the family; Sierra had done it so her three brothers and ex-cop dad wouldn't try to stop her.

She leaned forward across the sink and gazed in the mirror. "Where did that woman go?"

With one finger, she tugged her T-shirt away from her left breast and gazed at the infinity-shaped scar. "Damn you, Archimedes," she whispered. She twisted on the faucet, and cold water poured out. She splashed her face.

No time for self-indulgence any longer. Mallory needed her.

Rafe needed her.

If she didn't pull her weight, she could get him killed. She straightened her shoulders and blinked at the woman staring back at her. The woman Sierra saw as vulnerable and weak. She might have played the role, might have challenged Rafe, but it was all an act. The bruise on her cheek and injured thigh proved it.

Not again. Never again.

She pulled off Rafe's sweatpants and T-shirt, but even raising her arms made her ache. She glanced down at her torso. Bruises covered half of her ribs on the right side, another had formed on her thigh. She looked like she'd been through an MMA fight.

With a groan, Sierra slipped into the shower, trying to scrub the aches and sleep away. The water pounded on her back and she winced, twisting, but she couldn't see anything. Finally she stepped out of the stall, dried her hair and slipped into the disguise and new clothes Rafe had provided. Not something she'd normally wear. The dress billowed around her newly round abdomen and fell just below her knees. At least it covered her bruises. The few on her shins she dabbed with makeup to conceal them.

Sierra rummaged through her makeup bag, concealed the facial bruises and finally added a touch of lipstick.

Sarah wouldn't wear a lot of makeup. She was a cowboy's wife.

Finally the hair. She tucked her light brown locks beneath the hairnet and secured the auburn wig.

She held her breath and turned toward the mirror. A stranger stood before her. A very pregnant stranger.

Sierra turned sideways and touched her belly, trapping the dress's fabric against her. It looked too real. With one hand she stroked the mound. Something odd fluttered in her stomach. Weird.

Babies hadn't even been on her radar. Not until her sister-in-law, Emily, had started showing. Mitch's wife had glowed; she'd looked so happy.

Because she was in love.

Sierra had believed herself to be in love. Her night with Rafe had been a good lesson. Lust wasn't love.

She let out a long slow breath. She had to put wishes

and dreams out of her mind. She straightened her back and opened the bathroom door.

Rafe stood there like something out of a Western movie. He'd changed into faded blue jeans, a black Western shirt and worn cowboy boots, not his normally black jeans and T-shirt ensemble. His eye patch stood out even more against the white hat. A grin tugged at the corners of his mouth. "Damn, you clean up...real nice." He cleared his throat.

"It looks...real?" she asked.

"All too real." His eyes darkened, and he reached out a tentative hand.

Sierra gave a nervous laugh. "It's just silicone."

He rested his hand on the fake belly. "Too real," he said, then turned from her and dug into his bag. He faced her, holding a small jewelry box. "Give me your left hand," he said softly.

Sierra's entire body trembled. Slowly she raised her arm and stuck out her shaking hand.

Rafe clasped her fingers in his, squeezing them in re-assurance. He removed a simple gold band from the velvet holder and slipped it on her finger over her knuckle until it settled there, as if it belonged.

Sierra couldn't breathe. She simply stared. She could barely process what had just happened.

Rafe didn't let go of her hand for a moment, and finally raised his gaze to hers. "It's official," he said, his voice clipped, letting her go and placing a similar band on his own finger. "The single men will take one look at that baby bump and ring and run the other way."

His words shook her out of her daze. The moment was gone. She worried the gold with her finger, fighting to hold back the emotion welling in her chest. She could do this. "Doesn't say much good about men if this will scare them off."

Rafe paused. "It's a dream for some, a nightmare for others."

"And for you?"

"Both," he said.

Chapter Seven

The winter sun shined with a hazy glow. It heated the interior of the truck. The large arena loomed close. Sierra studied the layout. The rodeo appeared quite different in the afternoon compared to the middle of the night.

Horse trailers and RVs filled a cordoned-off area behind the arena. Rafe pulled into the large parking lot.

"I'm surprised," Sierra said. "Beckel must have gotten his way with the police department. No cops or crime scene tape that I can see."

"Clearly, Beckel knows how to arm-twist the political machine so the rodeo goes off smoothly. It's a big event. Brings a lot of money to the city."

"And if Mallory's discovery put that in jeopardy—"

"A lot of people have a lot to lose."

Sierra's neck and back tensed, and it wasn't from the extra weight that pressed against her breasts and belly. Her nerves were strung as tight as a rubber band ready to be launched. This had to work.

"It's going to be fine," Rafe said, kneading her shoulder. "We'll get answers, and we'll find them."

"Am I that transparent?"

"Only to me." He slipped the truck into an empty space. "Let's join the rodeo."

He rounded the vehicle and held out his hand to her, threading their fingers. At his touch, electricity shot through her hand. He squeezed tight.

"Don't worry. I've got your back. I promise."

She nodded and pasted on a smile. As they drew closer to the arena's entrance, a tall, lanky man headed across the asphalt to meet them. He was the epitome of a rancher, jeans, Stetson and blue button-down shirt, but strode with purpose, and once he grew closer, Sierra recognized *the look*. He possessed that same edge to him that Rafe and her brother Noah wore.

Ex-military, maybe?

Or something.

He removed his Stetson and reached out his hand. "Rafe Vargas. I thought you'd fallen off the face of the earth. You haven't been out to train with Ironsides in too long."

"J.K. I appreciate you boarding him when I'm away from Carder."

"He's a good one. If you want to breed him, I'd set it up for a fair cut. He's got the barrel racing pedigree to bring you a lot of money."

Rafe tilted his own Stetson back. "I'll think about it."

Sierra looked back and forth between the two men, utterly confused. Was this part of the show, or did they really know each other?

"Your *wife* looks a little out of sorts, Rafe. She okay?"

"*Sarah*, meet Jared King. He's an old and *trusted* friend."

"I know your brother," the rancher said in a low, conspiratorial voice. "I look forward to witnessing his fiancée put a ring on his finger. He needs someone to keep him in line."

So, Jared knew Noah. Did that mean he knew *everything*? The tension at the base of her skull had moved over the back of her head and had settled in her temples. Sierra hoped she could keep up with the subtext of the conversation through the headache.

Jared looked her up and down. "Congratulations are in order, I see." He turned to Rafe. "Pregnancy is a mystery to most men anyway. They'll avoid close scrutiny. Which was obviously your intent."

"Everything is set?" Rafe asked. "You have any trouble?"

"Ransom's check didn't hurt, and the fact that I provide almost a quarter of the rodeo's stock sweetened the deal. But the clincher was your junior rodeo career. John Beckel witnessed a few good bull rides back in the day. He liked your style."

Stunned at this shocking information, Sierra stared at Rafe. "You really *do* ride? I don't know whether to be relieved or terrified. Why didn't you—"

"We'll talk later," Rafe interrupted, closing her open mouth with a bit of pressure from his finger.

He turned to Jared. "Where's my gear?"

"I stowed everything with Ironsides. The preliminaries start in a couple hours. You barely have enough time to get your feet wet."

Rafe stuck out his hand. "I owe you, J.K. Thanks."

"I'll add it to your tab." Jared's face went solemn. "Ransom told me what's at stake. I hope you find what you're looking for. If I can help, just ask." The rancher ambled away, hiking into an old rusted pickup before driving away.

"The guy should get rid of that walking tin bucket, but it's his favorite." Rafe faced her. "You ready to do this?"

"Are you?" Sierra asked. "How long since you've been on a bull?" She didn't know much about the sport, but from the few times she'd caught a glimpse on television, it looked too dangerous to even contemplate.

She frowned at him, but he just smiled and held out his hand to her. "Heck, honey. Bull riding's like riding a bike. The trick is not to lose your balance."

Sierra wasn't so sure.

Rafe waited for her, hand outstretched. She linked her fingers with his, but her stomach rolled. She had a bad feeling about this entire situation.

She didn't know who, but it felt like someone was about to get trampled.

A RODEO POSSESSED A strange combination of odors all its own. She supposed it might appeal to some, but for Sierra, her stomach teetered on rebellion with every step.

Taking a deep swallow and giving her belly a firm lecture, she strode up a ramp with Rafe. They entered the stands surrounding the arena. Seas of faces had pinned their focus on the bucking horse doing its level best to send a cowboy flying.

A shout of enthusiasm followed by a low groan erupted through the stadium.

"The bronc riders are just finishing up."

"I've got to be behind the chute shortly," he whispered. He pointed toward the VIP area behind the chutes. "That's where the wives and families sit. Just relax and get to know them. Trust your instincts."

"This is crazy," she muttered.

He kissed her nose. All for show, she tried to tell herself.

"You can do this. You know why we're here." Linking her hand with his, he escorted her across the arena.

When they arrived, the chattering stopped. Rafe tipped his hat. "Ladies, I wonder if you'd be so kind as to watch over my wife." He patted her belly. "It's her first time."

A few titters filtered across the crowd. Sierra could feel the heat settling in her cheeks.

"I'm Rafe Vargas. This is Sarah."

He held her face between his hands and kissed her lips, slowly, delicately. Her heart did that crazy pitter-patter flip. She was getting too used to his touch. Not a good thing.

"See you later, darlin'. Everything'll be fine."

He walked away and most of the women watched him leave.

"Whoo-wee, that man wears his jeans well," a woman in her midfifties commented. "Gives me a tingle right where it shouldn't."

"Nancy!" one of the women squealed.

Nancy shrugged. "What? Just because I'm a grandma doesn't mean I'm dead from the waist down." She patted the empty space next to her. "Have a seat, darlin'. Before the final round is done day after tomorrow, we'll know all your secrets and probably be able to tell you if that little one you're cookin' is a boy or a girl."

"Don't listen to her, Sarah," a second woman said with a smile. She held out her hand. "I'm Diane Manley. My husband, Travis, rides bulls. Yours?"

"Bulls, too," Sierra said, a tremor in her voice.

"It's where the money is," Diane said. "If he doesn't get hurt."

"And if he can stay on for eight seconds. Six seconds doesn't pay the mortgage," a woman commented, jostling her baby to keep him from crying.

"Or the doctor's bills, April," another chimed in.

"Don't you fret," Nancy said. "I recognize your husband's name. He was one of the best. My man and I have been around this world for three decades. I thought Rafe had smartened up and quit. I guess once rodeo gets in your blood, it's like an infection that keeps comin' back."

The opening was too good to pass up. Sierra ticked through Rafe's instructions. *Tell them just enough to know he has a dubious past and might be for sale.*

She cleared her throat. "Rafe joined the military just after he turned eighteen. That's why he quit."

"A real hero. Good for him." Nancy smiled.

Sierra looked away, dropping her gaze, trying to imitate shame or embarrassment.

"Nancy!" Diane hissed.

She smiled at Sierra. "You don't have to talk about it, Sarah."

With a weak smile, she nodded. "It's okay. I met Rafe after he was discharged. He didn't get retirement, but we make ends meet. He's a good man." She raised her chin in challenge.

A wave of whispering flowed through the crowd. So far so good. Just defensive enough to set up Rafe as a bad boy, but not too much. Hopefully.

"Good for him. And you," Diane said.

"And now, ladies and gentlemen. The event you've all been waiting for. Our Bull Riding Competition!"

The announcer's voice poured over the crowd of more than ten thousand. "First up, Travis Manley. Travis is currently tied for second on the leader board." The announcer paused momentarily. "Well, now, today's not this cowboy's lucky day. He's drawn Angel Maker, last year's bull of the year." The crowd gasped. "Never been ridden, folks. Let's hope Travis can break the streak."

Diane turned pale. "Oh no."

"What's wrong?" Sierra whispered to Nancy.

"That bull should be put down. Last year he stomped on one of the riders. Broke his leg, pelvis and a couple bones in his back. That cowboy will never be the same."

Sierra leaned forward, peering down into the bucking chute. A black bull stood still. A lean cowboy lowered himself over the bull and gripped a flat braided rope with a gloved hand.

He nodded once, his face lined with tension. The chute opened, and the moment the bull escaped the enclosure he bucked up, all four hooves leaving the dirt. He twisted right, then left, jerking the cowboy around like a rag doll.

"Travis!" Diane shouted.

The ride seemed to take forever. Angel Maker spun, airborne. The crowd leaped to its feet. The bull switched directions. Travis flew off the side, landing on his back.

Two rodeo clowns ran toward him, hoisting him to his feet and rushing him to the barrier. Angel Maker barreled after them and clipped one of the clowns with his horns. The man stumbled to the ground.

The bull raised up and stomped down.

The crowd shouted in horror. Two men bounded over the fence and pulled the clown to safety. Sierra recognized Rafe's black Western-style shirt.

The infuriated bull turned his attention to Rafe and charged. Sierra's breath caught in her throat. She twisted her dress in her grip. A gate opened. Rafe raced into it; the bull followed and Rafe vaulted over the fence.

A loud cheer went up.

"How about a round of applause for the latest addition to our competition, folks. Rafe Vargas. He tore up the junior circuit a decade ago, and now he's back. Looks like he's still got some moves." The announcer paused. "A big hand for Travis Manley. He clocked in at 6.8 seconds, ladies and gents. Second best time of the year on Angel Maker."

Sierra sagged in her seat, heart racing. Was Rafe crazy?

"That's some man you caught, girl," Nancy said. "Not bad."

"He's something, all right," Sierra muttered, rising, determined to stop Rafe. She slipped into the aisle. This was too dangerous. There had to be another way.

"Next up, local hero Rafe Vargas. Give it up for the newcomer, folks. He's drawn Sweet Sin."

Sierra froze, her entire body chilled with fear. Her gaze narrowed. The bull didn't look any less powerful than Angel Maker.

Rafe hovered over the bull and seated himself. He nodded. The chute flew open and the bull rushed out, with Rafe twisting on his back.

A strap encircled the bull's belly, driving the animal to try to buck it off. Time slowed for Sierra. Rafe's body twisted and turned, but his grip remained solid. The animal flailed in the air, and Rafe lost his hold. The bull catapulted him upside down. He hit the dirt hard. The crowd gasped.

A siren blared.

For a moment, Rafe simply lay still. Sierra grabbed the metal railing with a white-knuckle grip.

The beast charged. A clown distracted Sweet Sin, urging the bull out of the arena, leaving Rafe to slowly rise to his feet. He looked into the stands straight at Sierra and lifted his hand to wave to the crowd.

The audience groaned as his score was posted. Zero. "Too bad, folks. Seven seconds for Rafe Vargas. Welcome back, cowboy! Better luck next time."

He could have broken his neck. Sierra's knees shook, her stomach roiled with nausea.

"You okay, darlin'?" Nancy asked. "He done good for his first ride back, but you look green as an unripened tomato."

"I'll be fine. Maybe a bathroom."

Holding her mouth, Sierra raced up the stairs as quickly as she could.

After she threw up, she'd find Rafe, and she might very well have to kill him.

RAFE'S BOOTS KICKED up dust as he moved away from the chute. He slapped his hat against his jeans. The rodeo hadn't changed, but Rafe had put on ten years. Chasing bad guys and even terrorists didn't use the same muscles as harnessing a two-and-a-half-ton bull.

He weaved through several riders. A couple patted him on the back, and he fought not to wince. His body would be black-and-blue in a couple of days. At least the guys in the ring had kept Sweet Sin from stomping him. Their moniker might be rodeo clowns, but those bullfighters had saved his butt from getting creamed.

One of the men grabbed Rafe as he was leaving the area. "Vargas?"

Rafe stopped. "Yeah?"

"Name's Kurt Prentiss. I—"

"You saved my butt out there." Rafe shook his hand.

Kurt held out a strap. "From Sweet Sin. Thought you should know."

Rafe gave the leather a close look. "Cut?"

The man nodded.

"You know who did it?"

"No, but it's a tight championship this year, and you're changing up the pecking order. It could've been anyone. Most of these guys are too honest for their own good, but there are a few who'll do anything to win... and get their share of the money."

"I'll keep that in mind," Rafe said as Kurt walked away.

Was this about his investigation or simply a rider protecting his position? Just one more element to complicate an already problematic investigation.

Rafe passed by the on-site clinic and winced at the bullfighter who'd bailed out Travis Manley lying on a stretcher.

The bull rider hovered outside the entrance.

"How is he?" Rafe asked Travis.

"Hopefully they can pin him back together. He's one of the best." Travis scowled. "I should've moved faster. My neck's been acting up, and the blow stunned me." He studied Rafe. "You had a good ride for just getting back into it. Word's already spread about your national championship."

"A decade ago. I was a kid," Rafe said, rubbing his

own neck. "It's not the same. Hurts more this time around."

"That's for sure. Think we had rubber bones back then?"

"Or we were so jacked up on adrenaline we never felt it." Rafe paused. "Travis, what do you make of this?" He handed over the strap.

Rafe knew the cowboy was running second. He had a motive. Rafe wanted to see his reaction.

"Holy—" The expletive exploded. "Where'd you get this?"

"It's the strap from my ride," Rafe said.

Travis's face went white. "This was done on purpose. If it had snapped…"

"I know. Any idea who it might've been?"

Something in Rafe's tone must've clued Travis in. He crossed his arms. "You thought it might be me."

"You're in second place. You have something to gain."

"Not when I draw that damn Angel Maker and can't make my ride."

Rafe had survived a decade in covert and black ops by counting on his instincts. He trusted them. He had to, and he didn't believe Travis had been involved. His shock had been genuine. "I don't think you cut the strap, but I wonder if you've heard any scuttlebutt about someone—"

"So desperate to win they'd be willing to kill," Travis finished. "You just arrived. It's an awfully quick leap."

"Maybe they weren't willing to take any chances." Rafe met Travis's gaze. "If anything strange crosses your path, would you let me know? Whoever did this to me might do it to someone else."

Travis nodded, his frown deepening, his expression contemplative.

The roar of the crowd boomed even through the bowels behind the arena. Rafe rounded the corner and walked straight into a skinny figure propped up against the wall of the clinic. A tingling of awareness shot down Rafe's neck.

"Tough fall," the man said.

He had the wiry frame of a rider, but didn't appear strong enough.

"I'll survive." Rafe tilted his Stetson back to study the man who'd stopped him.

"You're gonna be hurtin' tomorrow. I might be able to help."

Now the guy had Rafe's interest. "Really? How? Magic beans?"

"Kind of. The docs here'll give you pills if you got insurance or the money to pay out of pocket. Most don't. I got the same stuff. We get it online from out of the country at a bargain."

"You trying to sell me sugar pills?" Rafe commented. "Not interested."

He edged around the man, but the guy grabbed Rafe's shirt. "It's the good stuff. I got customers who can vouch for me. My supplier's legit."

Prescription drugs. The rodeo circuit moved from town to town. Not a bad cover for dealing. Selling the drugs and laundering money through the rodeo made a lot of sense.

"Keep talking," Rafe said. "I can't afford insurance right now, and with my wife having a baby, we're strapped for cash."

"You won't make it tomorrow after that head dive."

"I don't have the money on me," Rafe lied, giving a concerned look around, as if he were nervous someone would see them. "Meet me later? After hours?"

The man studied him, then offered a brief nod. "Sure. Make yourself visible at the end of the day, and I'll find you."

Rafe leaned closer, pretended to lose his balance and jostled the dealer.

"Whoa, dude. Back off."

Rafe swayed. "Sorry. Guess that fall hit my head more than I thought." He walked away, taking care not to look back, then ducked down an aisle lined with stalls. Keeping out of sight, he surveyed the dealer and tapped his phone.

"Mom, is that you?" Zane asked.

"I take it you're not alone," Rafe commented. "I've got a target on the west side of the rodeo's medical clinic. He's dealing. I tried picking his pocket, but no wallet, only pills and cash. I need you to run his prints for an ID, but I couldn't risk lifting the drug package for testing. He'd be suspicious of me when he noticed them missing."

"I can do that, Mom. Milk and eggs. I'll have them to the house as soon as I can."

"Thanks, Zane."

Waiting for his CTC backup to take over, Rafe kept his prey under surveillance. He had half a mind to grab the guy and beat the tar out of him, but one hint of the net closing around the kidnapper's plans could cost Mallory and Chloe their lives. This operation had to be completed covertly and subtly.

He tugged out his phone, keeping the dealer in his line of sight.

You okay? he texted.

Turn around.

Sierra stood behind him, arms crossed. She stalked over to him and slugged him in the solar plexus.

He let out a loud oomph. "What was that for?"

"You scared me. You executed a swan dive headfirst into the dirt. You could've been hurt, or paralyzed or…" Sierra's jaw pulsed. "Don't do it again."

Rafe tilted his head. "I've taken more dangerous assignments."

She gnawed at her lip. "It's one thing to read the reports. It's another to…watch."

"I'm fine." With a glance around at several very interested faces, he walked her to the side, out of earshot of the cowboys and rodeo staff wandering in and out of the stalls, but keeping his target in view.

Unfortunately, he met the guy's gaze. The drug dealer smiled and tipped his hat. Damn. He'd seen Rafe with Sierra. He didn't want that scumbag to have her on his radar. It put her in danger. He'd give anything if she'd leave, but they were all in now.

At that moment Sierra swayed against him.

He wrapped his arm around her waist. "Are you okay? You look pale. Like you're going to pass out."

"I've just thrown up everything I've eaten in the last twenty-four hours," she said. "Burritos don't look nearly as appetizing going up. The good news is getting sick at watching your neck bend in ways it wasn't meant to solidified my undercover identity. Everyone believes I'm pregnant, that's for sure."

He studied her, trying to see through her lies.

"I promise. I'll get used to the odor. Eventually."

"Did you overhear anything suspicious?"

"A few wives complaining about money and mortgages, but not much else. And nothing about Mallory and Chloe." She let out a long sigh. "Is this going to work? Are we any closer to finding them, because I don't see it."

"Everything we've discovered points to the money. The cops agree. According to Cade, the San Antonio police are still looking at Mallory as an embezzlement suspect."

"Idiots. Can't they see the truth?" She pressed her lips together.

He really didn't like the look of her. "You're *sure* you're not coming down with something."

"I'm fine. Just worried."

"Well, too many are watching, so I guess we play the part of a newly married couple for a few minutes." Rafe cupped her face and lowered his lips, capturing her gasp.

She tasted of minty toothpaste, and her warm lips parted under his. She clutched at his shirt, and all he could think about was whisking her away, to someplace safe.

Behind them a horse snorted. Footsteps clomped closer. Rafe tensed and raised his head. He turned, placing himself between Sierra and the unwelcome visitor.

"Rafe Vargas." A man in his sixties tilted his hat back and raked his gaze from Rafe to Sierra. "You've stirred up quite a bit of excitement at my rodeo. You've got the bull riders talking, which doesn't happen often. So I gotta wonder, are you the kind of man who brings excitement or the wrong kind of trouble with you?"

Chapter Eight

Mallory lay flat on her belly. Tall buffalo grass surrounded her and Chloe like a thin, wispy curtain swaying in the breeze. No protection, merely concealment. Mallory's face dripped with sweat. Huddled next to her mother, Chloe sobbed quietly beside her.

"Where did she go?" The cop shouted from across the small meadow.

Mallory recognized his voice. She'd never forget it as long as she lived.

He let loose a flurry of curses. "Everyone backtrack. Try the other path. Failure isn't an option. The boss won't forgive. Or forget."

The cop wasn't the boss? Mallory's mind whirled in confusion. Then who was? How many people were involved?

Several sets of footsteps stomped away accompanied by muttering complaints. She waited until the sounds disappeared in the distance. Then waited several minutes longer.

When she was certain they'd gone, Mallory dropped her forehead against the dirt. Her lungs ached, and for the first time, she realized she'd been holding her breath. She gasped for air.

"Mommy?"

"Shh, Button."

Ever so slowly Mallory sat up. The sky had begun to darken, but it would take a couple hours for night to fall. They weren't safe here. If those men came back, it would be all too easy to stumble over their hiding place.

She squinted through the dim light. A few thousand yards away, a thick patch of forest erupted out of the prairie grass. The trees could hide them until Mallory figured out which way to go to get to civilization and find a phone for help.

She rose to her knees and turned in a circle, searching for another option, any sign of a road or trail, a house or a barn, but only a second patch of forest dotted the horizon, even farther away. And in the same direction the men had hiked.

Easy choice. Everything inside her told her to stay as far away from that cop as possible. Her mind made up, she held out her hand to Chloe. "Let's go, Button. We're making a run for those trees."

"It's too far. I'm hungry. And thirsty."

"I know, sweetie. I'll find you something. Soon."

Chloe thrust out her jaw and folded her arms across her chest. "No. I'm tired. I don't want to go. I want my house and Princess Buttercup."

Mallory sighed, sat back and pulled her daughter onto her lap. "I know you're exhausted, honey. So am I. But we have to keep going. Or we'll have to go back to the trailer."

Chloe's eyes widened with fear. "I don't want to go there. It smelled funny, and that man took you away from me."

Choking back a sob, Mallory closed her eyes and hugged her daughter close. "You ready?" she whispered. "We have to be brave like Sierra."

"She can run fast."

"That she can."

Mallory stood and clasped Chloe's hand.

They ran. Sweat dripped down Mallory's cheeks. The trees grew closer and closer. Mallory's feet pounded on the grasslands, her steps small so Chloe could keep up.

Only a few dozen feet more.

"We're almost there," she panted, speeding up as much as she could.

Mallory's foot sank down. She pitched forward. A sharp pain shot through her ankle and foot. She slammed to the ground on hands and knees.

"Mommy!" Chloe skidded to a halt and fell beside her mother.

Sucking in breath after breath, Mallory froze. Her leg throbbed. She rolled over. Agony shot from her foot to her knee. White spots danced in front of her eyes. The light dimmed.

Don't pass out. Don't pass out.

She stared up at the purple sky, a smattering of stars beginning to shine through. She tried to focus, and finally her head stopped spinning. She sat up and shifted her leg, biting her lip to keep from crying out in pain.

"Mommy?" Chloe's voice was small and scared.

Mallory folded her daughter to her chest. Off to the direction they'd come from, through the dim light, she caught a glimpse of several flashlight beams sweeping back and forth.

Her heart sank. If they saw the signs, they'd follow them here.

"It'll be fine, Button," she lied. "We're going to be just fine."

TROUBLE. MORE THAN one person had accused Rafe of being exactly that through the years. He didn't like being cornered, or attacked. He tended to fight back with lethal force.

As if she'd read his mind, Sierra squeezed Rafe's shoulder, her touch restraining him from uttering the choice phrases he would surely regret. He quelled his temper. This operation required finesse, not firepower.

No wonder he preferred attacking from stealth. Wham, bam, done was much more his style.

He forced a smile on his face. "No trouble from me, Mr. Beckel. I just appreciate the invitation to participate." Rafe tugged Sierra forward and pressed her against his side. "We appreciate the helping hand. Sarah and I aim to start a new life."

John Beckel stuffed a pinch of tobacco between his cheek and lower lip. He gave them both a hard stare. "Well, Jared King vouched for you, and that man knows his stock and his riders. Besides, everyone's entitled to a mistake," the rodeo owner said. "Lord knows I've married six of them. Much to my brother Warren's irritation. They're bleeding me dry. That's why I gotta keep this place out of trouble and profitable. You catch my drift, boy?"

Rafe nodded, making a note to have Zane run background checks on Beckel's exes. He'd known the rodeo's finances were tight, but now he understood one reason why. "From everything I've heard, sir, you run a well-oiled machine. That's why I picked this event to try for my comeback."

John frowned. "I *thought* I had everything under control. Until yesterday. Sometimes people surprise you. You think you know a person… I hired her, trusted her. I guess that's why I've got six exes."

Sierra leaned forward, pressing her hand against his arm. "I'm so sorry, Mr. Beckel."

He patted her hand, his eyes softening as his gaze scraped up and down Sierra's disguise. "Don't be sorry for me, young lady, be sorry for my bank account. Speaking of which, I've got a new office manager I'm breaking in. Jared King recommended him, too, but between you and me, I'm not sure he belongs in an office. I need to keep an eye on him."

Rafe held back a smile of satisfaction. Zane must be playing his part well.

"Good luck tomorrow, Vargas. If you ride well… we'll see what I can do for you. And your lovely wife." He stretched out his hand.

Rafe shook it. "It's been nice to meet you, sir. I'll do my best not to disappoint."

If Rafe were the suspicious type, which he was, he'd wonder exactly what hidden message John Beckel had just communicated. Zane definitely needed to do some research.

John tipped his hat. He was just turning to leave when Rafe noticed Zane's figure flashing past the entrance to the row of stalls over John's shoulder. Damn. Zane was heading to the drug dealer to get those prints. They couldn't afford for John to see Zane away from the office.

Rafe stepped forward. "Sir. Would you care to see my horse? Jared trains him. Ironsides is a barrel racer. I'll be riding him in the closing ceremony on the final day of the rodeo."

John paused. "Some other time, maybe," he said with

a quizzical look. "After my assistant's embezzlement, I don't want to leave the office for too long. Not for a while anyway."

Nothing for Rafe to do, but let him go.

Sierra leaned up against him. "Zane made it," she whispered in his ear. "He gave me a thumbs-up. He'll beat Beckel back to his office."

Dodged a bullet that time. "Good. We'll touch base at the hotel tonight. Hopefully he'll have our smoking gun after spending all day on that computer."

Rafe gripped Sierra's elbows and gave her the once-over. "Now, back to our previous conversation. Are you really okay?"

"How many times do I have to tell you? It's fine. I'm fine. Feeling better with every minute that passes, actually. Maybe my sense of smell has been deadened," she said.

"And your leg?"

"Almost as good as new. When are you going to stop asking?"

"When I'm convinced you're telling the truth," he muttered.

"Are you this much of a mother hen with all your partners?"

"The few partners I've had don't start the mission with a bullet wound."

She twisted her lip. "Point," she said, her tone frustrated.

An awkward pause settled between them. She smoothed her dress over her silicone belly. "I know you don't want me here," she started.

"It worries me. I don't want you hurt. I care…" He let his words die off.

She reached for his hand. "Can I meet Ironsides?"

The eyebrow over Rafe's good eye arched. Not since his brother and his foster dad had anyone shown a real interest in Rafe's passion for horses. "You really want to?"

"Something in your expression when you mentioned him made me curious."

"Come on, then." He guided her to the stall where Jared King had housed Ironsides. The large quarter horse whinnied softly.

The mahogany coat shined and the rabicano markings just above his hooves reminded her of white socks. "He's beautiful," Sierra said.

Rafe opened the gate. He walked inside and patted the side of the horse's neck. "Bet you never thought we'd be here, huh?" he whispered.

He led the horse closer to Sierra. "Meet Ironsides. Best barrel racer off the rodeo circuit." The horse nuzzled Rafe's pocket. "Sorry, boy. Nothing for you today."

"With a name like Ironsides, I expected him to be gray," Sierra said, stroking his nose.

"He's called Ironsides because he was about to be put out to pasture before his time, just like the ship," Rafe said. "He'd been neglected, and the local vet in Carder thought he might have to be destroyed. I asked if I could to take him and try to rehabilitate him. He still had some fight left."

Ironsides nudged Rafe forward.

"I think he's telling you that you should've brought a carrot or two."

"You know horses?"

Sierra shook her head. "I took a few lessons when I went to summer camp, but the closest I got to serious riding was attending the rodeo with M…my best friend."

"Good catch, in case someone's listening," he said softly in her ear.

The scent of her shampoo encompassed him. If he lowered his head just a bit, and she turned hers, he could kiss her again.

Instead, he straightened and rubbed her back. "I'll get Ironsides bedded down, and we'll return to the motel. Hopefully our friend has some news."

He'd have preferred to take her to *his* home and lock her up so he'd be certain she was protected. But Rafe couldn't take her to a place that didn't exist. His home was the occasional motel, and a piece of land near Carder, Texas, that he'd purchased on a whim. An empty piece of land with nothing on it but rattlesnakes, cacti and some very valuable copper and mineral rights.

Ironsides shifted back and forth. When he stepped on his right front leg, his gait looked off. "What's wrong, boy?"

Rafe knelt and ran his finger along the limb, feeling for the telltale signs of a tendon or ligament injury.

"Your horse have a problem?" a voice asked from behind.

Rafe turned his head to see a solidly built man with a crew cut leaning against the gate next to Sierra.

"I'm Harlen Anderson. The rodeo vet. Good-looking mount."

Standing, Rafe rested his hand against Ironsides's neck. "Rafe Vargas. My wife, Sarah. And this is Ironsides. He's a good one all right. But he might have a strained tendon."

"Ma'am." Harlen tipped his hat. "Want me to take a look?"

Rafe opened the gate. "I'd appreciate it."

Maybe their luck was changing. In addition to helping Ironsides, someone like Harlen would know practically everyone involved with the rodeo.

The vet moved slowly from limb to limb, taking his time. "Saw your ride, Vargas. Sweet Sin is no easy bull. You held your own."

"Seven seconds doesn't pay the bills," Rafe said with a frown. He ran his hand down Ironsides's flank. "I may have to start entering more events. Especially with the baby coming. Or get a part-time job."

"I'll keep my ears open," Harlen said. He stood. "That right front leg has a bit of edema, but it's not too bad. Cold compresses and rest should take care of it. I have one in my office that'll do the trick."

"Thanks." Rafe stroked Ironsides's flank. "Hear that boy? The doc's gonna fix you up as good as new."

"Don't mention it. I'll be back in a few minutes."

The vet strode away, and Rafe followed his exit with a speculative gaze.

"I know that look." Sierra leaned forward against the gate. "He seemed nice enough to me. What do you see?"

"Maybe nothing. But he came out of nowhere at the exact moment I noticed the injury."

"Coincidence?"

The moment the words were out, Rafe met Sierra's gaze. "There's no such thing as a coincidence," they said over each other.

"Ransom taught you well." Rafe let a small smile twist his lips. "It's the truth, though. I can count on one finger the times a coincidence was truly just chance."

"Actually it was Noah," Sierra said. "I was about thirteen, and my bicycle tire went flat. Joey Malone *happened* to be nearby to walk me home and steal my first kiss.

"That was probably my first lecture from Noah, but definitely not my last."

"I might've done the same thing." Rafe touched her cheek lightly, relishing the feel of her smooth skin. Did he imagine she leaned into his touch? Was it wishful thinking?

Sierra chewed on her lip for a moment. "If Dr. Anderson showing up wasn't a coincidence, what was it? He was watching us and decided just to say hi? Why? What's his interest?"

Rafe grabbed a brush and began to groom Ironsides. "Excellent question. I don't know, but we just added another name to our suspect list."

DARKNESS HAD LONG since settled over San Antonio when Sierra entered the motel room, her feet weary, her mind disheartened. Her shoulders had tensed up, her breasts ached and her back hurt from carrying the extra weight on her belly.

Princess Buttercup sauntered over to the door, passed by Zane without pause and stared unflinchingly at Rafe. He shook his head at the feline. "I'll do a quick perimeter sweep." He closed the door behind him with a firm click.

Princess Buttercup swished her tail at the door, but didn't move. Simply stared and sat down. Waiting.

"That cat's spooky," Zane said. "She's waiting for him."

"It took me a half dozen trips for her to warm up

to me," Sierra said. "The princess fell for Rafe in five minutes."

Not unlike Sierra.

She raised her arms and stretched. The cat wouldn't move until Rafe returned. "I don't even want to bother taking this thing off," Sierra groaned, taking a straight shot to the bed and flopping back on it.

She simply lay there staring at the ceiling.

Zane chuckled. "How does it feel to be knocked up?"

"You try it sometime." She gave him that look her brothers had nicknamed her Sierra-stink-eye. "You know what the worst part is? This stupid thing gave me sympathy symptoms. I couldn't keep breakfast or lunch down."

Zane scanned her. "Now that's spooky."

The key turned in the lock. Zane and Sierra both palmed their weapons within seconds when Rafe stepped through the door.

He arched a brow. "We're clear. The owner didn't see anyone suspicious hanging around today. We're good. For now."

He knelt down and scratched Princess Buttercup behind the ears. The cat purred, butted his hand, then returned to the towel he'd arranged for her in the corner of the motel room, circled and settled down, staring at them all.

Rafe's gaze lasered in on Sierra's reclining body. "What's wrong?"

"I'm f—"

"Don't say you're fine, when you're clearly not."

"I'm tired. Nothing a hot shower and a few acetaminophen won't cure."

Rafe leaned over the bed, practically nose to nose with her. "I don't like the look of you."

She pushed herself up. "You're not getting me to go back to Carder, Rafe. I made contacts today. Mallory and Chloe have been gone over twenty-four hours. We're running out of time. We all know that after seventy-two hours, their chances of survival decrease to practically nothing."

"Yes, but you won't help anyone if you can't focus," Rafe argued, not moving an inch, forcing himself into her space.

She refused to back down from his challenge. "If you want to help, why not hand me my computer so I don't have to get up." She gave him a sweet-as-licorice smile. "Zane and I work faster together."

Zane glanced between Sierra and Rafe with a wide grin on his face.

"What?" Rafe turned to his friend and barked. "You have information to share that will catch these kidnappers?"

The man frowned. "Someday you'll have to ask me about what I saw between the two of you, but for now, I can give you a report."

He opened up his laptop, lowered his large frame into one of the chairs and moved a nightstand to create a makeshift table. Within a few minutes, he'd pulled out a secure satellite link and his fingers flew across the keyboard.

"What's the access IP address?" Sierra asked, relieved when Rafe stood and crossed the room. The farther away from her he was, the better. He was too much of a distraction.

Zane rattled off a series of numbers, and Sierra used her secure token to log in to CTC's private network.

Sierra quickly ran a few queries against the names of the women she'd met in the VIP section.

While she and Zane worked the ones and zeroes, Rafe propped himself up against the door. "I met with our drug dealer today. His name is Curtis Lawson, and he goes by Spider. But only to his friends."

"Seriously?" Zane's fingers paused. "If I were a criminal, I wouldn't pick the name of an insect most people step on."

Rafe shrugged and pulled a packet of five pills from his pocket. "He sold me what he claims is oxycodone. I'm rendezvousing with Detective Cade Foster later tonight. He'll have it tested."

Zane tapped a couple more keys. "While you two were keeping the boss busy—thanks, by the way—I was able to offer 'Spider' a cold drink and grab his prints."

"And?"

"His name *isn't* Curtis Lawson, it's Curtis Leighton. He's got a long juvenile record starting when his mother remarried. He grew up in Houston with one stepsister. I haven't had a chance to go down that path yet, but he doesn't seem like the type who'd have a lot of sisterly love, so it's probably a dead end."

"And you'll check her out anyway." Rafe sounded so certain Sierra didn't know why he'd even mentioned it.

"Of course. Which brings us to my boss, John Beckel."

Zane relayed what he'd discovered, most of which Sierra and Rafe knew. Until Zane started in on the ex-wives.

"Here's where it gets interesting. He's been late on

his alimony payments the last couple of months. I count him as our most viable suspect at the moment. He has the means, motive and the opportunity, but he's also pretty clueless when it comes to computers and accounting." Zane sent Sierra a long, slow look. "He didn't do this alone. He needed help."

"What about his brother, the silent partner?" Rafe asked. "Could he be involved?"

"I don't see how. He doesn't have access to any of the systems. From what I can tell, he's more of the marketing and investing arm of the corporation. The last couple years, Warren gave John over a hundred grand to keep the rodeo afloat. While Warren seems to have the magic touch when it comes to business, John doesn't have that gift. He focuses on the rodeo alone, but Warren has a lot of fingers in a lot of pies."

"John doesn't sound like someone who's laundering millions if he needs his brother's help," Rafe muttered. "Can you tell who *does* have access to the computer system?"

Zane let out a long sigh. "Mallory Harrigan and John Beckel were the only ones with passwords until I came on board."

Sierra shook her head. "Mallory wouldn't do this, and she wouldn't make the mistakes I saw in that ledger. I think the mistakes were a signal to me. It *wasn't* her. I can feel it."

Zane shook his head slowly, and Sierra could see he didn't believe her. Then again why should he? She had no proof. Just her gut.

"If Mallory helped him," Zane said, "he could pin the crime on her, write off the loss and collect the insurance money." He cracked his knuckles. "Sorry, sugar, but your friend doesn't look all that innocent right now."

Sierra sagged into the pillow. She raised her gaze to Rafe. "I know it looks bad, but after everything she's been through, she would never risk Chloe this way."

Rafe sat on the bed beside Sierra. "I know you believe that, but Mallory keeps coming back into our line of investigation."

"Which is why they kidnapped her," Sierra said. "Maybe it really is her ex."

"Now there's an interesting possibility. Did you know Bud Harrigan got Mallory the job at the rodeo in the first place?" Zane asked. "He knows the Beckel brothers."

"From where? Is he on the rodeo's payroll?" Sierra couldn't imagine a toad like Bud having anything in common with the owner of the rodeo. They didn't travel in the same circles.

"Not on the legitimate books. I haven't found a second set yet."

"Bud Harrigan's getting more and more smelly. The more we learn about him, the more I want to have a serious conversation with this guy." Rafe drummed his fingers on the bed. "Find him, Zane."

Sierra wouldn't want to be on the receiving end of that interrogation. Rafe's expression had darkened as if he had prey in his sights.

Rafe's jaw throbbed. "I may have been wrong," he said. "I didn't think he had a motive to abduct his family, but if he's involved with the twenty-five million, that's a definite game changer."

Chapter Nine

Darkness surrounded Sierra. She didn't want to open her eyes. She didn't want to remember. A heavy weight pressed on her chest and stomach.

Confused, she reached down and touched the silicone disguise. Then she remembered. Mallory. Chloe. What was she doing falling asleep? They needed her.

Sierra had a bad feeling. Something ominous niggled at the back her of brain.

The soft click of a door closing caused Sierra's eyes to snap open. A rectangle of light shined through the door.

Her hand gripped the Glock.

"It's just me," Rafe said in a low voice. He flipped on one of the bedside lamps. "You're still dressed?"

She rubbed her eyes. "I fell asleep. Guess I was more tired than I thought."

In truth, she hadn't moved since Rafe left.

"How'd your meeting with Cade go?" she asked.

"I delivered the oxycodone. Their lab will do the testing, and he'll get back to me. Maybe they can tell its origins from the formulation. We'll see." Rafe scanned the room. "Where's Zane?"

"He was tired of Princess Buttercup pouting and

staring at the door, so he's holed up in his room with his computer." Sierra pushed up, fighting back a yawn "Exactly what I should be doing."

Rafe sat on the side of the bed. "You didn't sleep much last night. You need the rest." He clasped her hand in his. "Mallory and Chloe need you at your best. We won't find them by strength or force. We both know that. It's going to take a mistake on the kidnapper's part, and us being smarter than him."

Sierra wanted to argue, but with Zane working his magic, she knew Rafe was right. Her brain was foggy. She could barely put two thoughts together. "You'll wake me early?"

Rafe nodded. "Of course."

She stood and shrugged her aching shoulders before plodding to the bathroom. The lock snicked closed behind her, and she lifted the flowing dress over her head. Letting it drop to the floor, she tried to unhook the back of the prosthetic, but she couldn't reach it.

After several minutes of trying, she finally gave up. She held the dress in front of her and stuck her head out of the bathroom.

"Rafe?" she said softly.

He'd pulled out his own laptop. He shut the lid and peered at her with a quizzical look.

"I need some help."

His Adam's apple bobbed, but he stood and walked over. She backed away from the door.

"I can't get it off."

"Turn around," he said, his voice husky.

He unhooked the straps and laid the silicone contraption on the counter. She held the dress in front of her chest, not wanting him to look at Archimedes's symbol on the upper curve of her left breast. Not that Rafe hadn't seen it when he'd rescued her. And again when they'd made love. But the scar reminded her every day of her vulnerability. Her own weakness. She'd allowed the serial killer to get the drop on her.

Still, she hated that Rafe would be reminded of her failure. How could it not diminish her in his eyes?

"You don't have to hide from me, you know," he said softly, handing her the thin, silk robe she'd placed on the hook behind the door. "To me it's a badge of courage…and survival."

Rafe's heated look made her cheeks burn. Turning her back to him, she quickly wrapped the robe around her and tightened the belt.

"Come with me and lie down." He held out his hand to her. "I need to clean your wound. It's overdue," he ordered, his voice low.

She perched on the edge of the bed while he disappeared into the bathroom. He returned with a towel and the medical supplies Sierra had purchased yesterday.

"Lie down," he repeated.

With a deep breath, she reclined on the bed. The robe rode up her leg, but it didn't matter, because Rafe would've pushed the material aside anyway.

He eased the tape off and removed the bandage, but some of the gauze stuck to the wound. All that walking had caused it to bleed.

When he tugged, she winced.

"Sorry," he said, grimacing. "I know it hurts."

"Just get it done," she said, closing her eyes, looking away from him, staring at the motel's closet, trying to concentrate on anything but what he was doing.

"First time I bandaged up a leg, I worked on my first horse. A mare named Daisy."

If he'd seen her face, he would have witnessed her surprise. "You had a horse named Daisy? I never would have guessed."

"Not my choice of moniker."

Princess Buttercup pounced on the bed and watched Rafe intently. "Don't give me that look, P.B.," he said. "You have water and food and a place to sleep. Deal with it."

"P.B.?" Sierra asked.

"I'm not calling that cat Princess Buttercup. It's a bigger blow to my masculinity and reputation than Daisy, and I shortened her name to 'D' when my last foster father gave her to me. Best horse on his ranch."

She chanced a glance over her shoulder.

He soaked a pad of gauze with antiseptic and met her gaze. "Take a breath. This could sting."

Rafe bent over her thigh. The moment the liquid touched her open wound she couldn't bite back the gasp.

She shut her eyes tightly. "How long did you live on a ranch?" she squeaked, trying to distract herself.

He didn't respond immediately, but swabbed her injury instead. Would he answer? Rafe rarely spoke about his past.

He let out a long, slow breath. "I moved to the ranch when I was about thirteen. I hated that man when he took me in. Hell, I hated the world."

The burning dissipated, and Sierra opened her eyes, stunned at the revelation.

"What happened to you, Rafe?"

"Still prickling?" he asked, ignoring her question.

"I'll survive."

He dried the wound. Every touch needled her skin. The injury was only a little over a day old. "If you just quit touching me and leave me alone, you won't hurt me," she muttered.

His pointed gaze from his good eye pinned her to the pillow. "Unfortunately, there's nothing I can do about that. I'm going to hurt you."

Suddenly she got the distinct impression they were no longer speaking about the bullet graze, but of the tension that had been smoldering between them, increasing in intensity with each hour they'd spent together.

She clenched the bedspread with her hands. "Just get it over with."

Her gut tightened with anticipation. She stared at his steady hands while he proceeded to squeeze antibiotic ointment on a clean gauze. His hand hovered over her wound.

Sierra couldn't stop her leg from flinching, and he hadn't even touched her yet.

Rafe placed his warm hand on her thigh to hold her down. "I was eleven when my parents died in a car wreck." Very gently he wiped the thick gel across the injury. "My brother, Michael, was sixteen. We had no relatives. Child Protective Services couldn't find anyone who would take in a teenager and an angry eleven-year-old who acted out. We ran away. Michael tried to take care of me, but he fell into the wrong crowd to make money. He was shot selling drugs to feed us. I was shoved into the system and labeled as incorrigible. I decided to prove them right and ran away from a half dozen foster homes when they set me up with Old Man Lancaster. He was my last chance.

"Better?" he asked, avoiding her gaze.

"Yes." She didn't know what else to say. He'd given her the facts of his life in such a matter-of-fact tone, but anyone with a heart could see beyond the words. Rafe had lived a childhood of loss.

"Good."

She wanted to pull him close to her, to hug him tight, but the stiffness of his body stopped her from even reaching out a hand to him.

Rafe stood, gathered the supplies and disappeared into the bathroom.

"What did Mr. Lancaster do that convinced you to stay?"

"He treated me like he expected me to stay, to work, to be a part of his family. He treated me like a son," Rafe said, returning to her side and lowering the robe to cover her upper thigh.

"And he taught you to ride bulls," she surmised.

"First he instructed me how to ride a horse. Then barrel racing. I'm the one who picked bulls when I was sixteen. He didn't want me to go that direction, but I had a knack."

Sierra's heart ached for the young boy Rafe had been. Completely alone until he'd found his foster father, the ranch and the rodeo. He could so easily have taken another path.

"From what the rodeo wives said, you haven't lost your touch. They think you could win the whole thing if you rode full-time."

Rafe rubbed his neck and popped a couple of anti-inflammatories. "I'm way past my prime, honey."

Sierra bit her lip when he swallowed the pills. "You scared me today," she admitted. She'd been angry before, but alone, in the dim light of this room, the gut-wrenching terror that had frozen her when he'd flown through the air head over heels off that bull came back.

"We're getting closer. I may not even have to ride tomorrow. If we can find Mallory's ex and he's responsible, this could all be over."

Rafe cupped her cheeks. The long lashes of his eye blinked. Sierra's heart thudded, its pace quickening. She could barely breathe with him this close.

His thumb ran across her lower lip. He bent closer. "I want to kiss you," he said in a deep voice, low and urgent.

She licked her lips and he let out a low groan, not waiting any longer. His mouth parted hers, and Sierra wrapped her arms around him.

Sinking back against the pillow, she pulled him with her. He pressed one jean-clad leg between hers, arching his hips, giving her no doubt how much he wanted her.

They shouldn't do this, but Sierra's heart and body didn't want to listen to her mind. She wanted to feel Rafe again. She wanted him to love her.

Love her.

She froze. Her heart sank.

Rafe lifted his lips. "What's wrong? Did I hurt you?"

"Not yet, but you will." She shifted out from under him and sat up on the bed. "I want more than anything to lose myself in your arms tonight, but I can't do this again, Rafe." She lifted her chin. "I want more."

He sucked in a shuddering breath. His hands trembled when he touched her hair. "You deserve more," he said, his voice low and gravelly. "You deserve everything."

He rose from the bed. "Get some rest, Sierra. I'll be watching over you."

With those words, he flipped the lock on the motel room door and walked outside into the night.

Sierra buried her head in the pillow. Tears slid down her cheeks. Somewhere deep inside she'd hoped he'd say that he wanted more, too. That he wanted love and a family and forever.

Princess Buttercup let out a soft meow and burrowed her body next to Sierra, as if sensing her shattered heart.

"I should have known, P.B.," she whispered into the fur. "I should have known."

MALLORY SCOOTED ON her belly a few more inches. Her hands and knees stung. She didn't know how long it had taken to reach the edge of the grove of trees. Darkness had long since taken hold. She could see nothing around her but pitch-black darkness.

Her foot throbbed with each heartbeat, but she had to keep inching forward.

"Chloe?" she whispered.

Her daughter sniffled, her small fist tugging against her mother's shirt.

"Just a little farther, Button."

Only a few stars shined overhead, and the sliver of moonlight was diffused by cloud cover, making it even darker.

Good for hiding, not so good for seeing where you were going.

Mallory reached forward. Her hand banged against the trunk of a tree. She gripped the ground cover and pushed herself up until she was leaning back against the cottonwood.

"Mommy, are you okay?"

Not by a long shot.

"I'm fine. I just twisted my ankle."

An owl hooted. Chloe hunkered down next to her mother.

"I'm scared."

"Me, too, sweetie."

Mallory squinted her eyes and searched the darkness surrounding her. No sounds of men shouting or flashlights or dogs. Had they given up for the night?

Maybe.

She tried moving her leg, but her ankle screamed in pain. If she couldn't walk, how was she supposed to protect Chloe?

Mallory shifted up to her knees, holding her foot off the ground so as not to jostle it. She grabbed the trunk and leaned on it.

"Let's play hide-and-seek, Button."

"It's dark. I can't see anything," Chloe whimpered. "I'm scared."

Mallory rounded one tree and with her hands felt for another. When she encountered wood, she rose on one leg, keeping her weight off her foot and hopped toward the second tree. By the time she'd reached what she'd hoped was the middle of the dense forest, she couldn't even see the stars and moon above. This would have to do.

She stretched above her and grabbed a branch, stripping the leaves off to create a makeshift weapon. It wasn't much, but it was all she had.

Sweating and exhausted, she sank to the ground, leaned up again the tree and patted her lap.

"Lie down, Button. Try to get some sleep."

Her own stomach rumbled.

"Are you hungry, too, Mommy?" Chloe asked with a whimper.

"No, honey," she lied. "My stomach's just talking to me."

"My tummy's saying it's really, really hungry."

"I know."

"When the sun wakes up, can we leave?"

Mallory gripped the stick tight, leaned her head against the rough bark and sent up a silent prayer she'd hidden them well enough to survive another night.

"I hope so, Button. I really hope so."

MORNING LIGHT HADN'T improved Rafe's disposition after a night spent in his truck. His neck and back ached, his knees cracked, and the view of the closed and locked motel room door made him regret so many words and actions.

He stood next to Zane by the vehicle, waiting for Sierra to exit. What had he been thinking, giving into temptation? At least Sierra had been wise enough to push him away. He couldn't be angry at her, but he could wish he'd never caused her pain, that he'd never given in to his own feelings.

He would never stop wanting her, but he couldn't risk her, not for his own desires. Not when danger stalked him every hour of every day. Not when his past had proved how deadly his chosen career was, not just to himself, but to those he cared about.

The motel room opened, and Sierra stepped into the light. She'd chosen another long, flowing dress that clung to her fake belly. The cornflower blue brought out a sparkle in her eyes, and the red of her wig made her skin appear like alabaster.

She was beautiful. She closed the door behind her, avoiding his gaze. The shadows beneath her eyes made him wince with guilt.

"What the hell happened between the two of you?" Zane asked in a low breath. "She's frozen you into the arctic."

"Not her fault, Zane. It's mine. All mine."

Before Zane could respond, Sierra joined them. She shifted her bag on her shoulder. "I ran the wives' names this morning and discovered something *very* interesting in my background check. Diane Manley."

"Travis Manley's wife?" Rafe asked, reaching for her bag.

She ignored his outstretched hand and opened the passenger door of the truck, slipping her purse onto the floorboards. "Diane's father remarried when she was a teenager. The woman's last name was Leighton."

"As in Curtis Leighton?" Rafe asked, feeling the click of a few pieces falling into place.

"Your drug dealer," Sierra confirmed. "The rest of the wives and families checked out pretty clean. A few bankruptcies and brushes with the law, but nothing serious. Certainly nothing to imply they'd have anything to do with laundering twenty-five million dollars."

Zane patted Sierra on the back. "Good job, sugar. You did better than I did. I kept running down never-ending trails on my search into John Beckel. The guy smells bad. I just don't know why."

"Keep looking, and follow up on Sierra's information," Rafe said. He glanced at his watch. "We'd better get moving."

"See you over there," Zane said. "I'll keep in touch."

He waved as he pulled out of the parking lot.

Rafe faced Sierra. "Search Diane's things if you can. Maybe we'll get lucky."

"I know what to do." Sierra slid into the truck and waited for him, staring out of the side window.

Boy, this was going to be fun. Trouble was, Rafe didn't blame her one bit. He sat behind the steering wheel and buckled his seat belt, but didn't start the truck.

Finally he let out a long sigh. "We have a job to do, and we have to work together. If I could bow out, I would, but—"

"We've established our cover. I know." Sierra slipped her Glock from her bag and placed it in the side pocket. "I'm fine, Rafe. Mallory and Chloe are all that matter. They are all that's between us."

"You're still my wife," he said with a frown. "Can you act like one?"

She gave him a false smile. "I can pretend as well as you do. In fact I've learned to fake it from the best. Now let's get to the rodeo."

His conscience stinging, Rafe yanked the truck into gear. He trusted Sierra to do her part because she wanted Mallory and Chloe back. But he had destroyed their relationship, and the camaraderie and friendship they'd found over the last day.

Perhaps it was for the best, but the hole in his heart had tripled in size.

BY THE TIME they arrived at the rodeo, Sierra could barely stay still. She didn't know how much longer she could sit next to Rafe without letting her emotions take over. She couldn't figure out why her feelings were so volatile. Maybe her injury, maybe her terror for Mallory and Chloe, but it seemed as if she had no reserves, no control over her emotions.

Rafe held her hand lightly as they walked through the rear entrance of the arena. He turned her to him and lightly brushed his lips across hers. She closed her eyes and hated her heart for doing that pitter-patter of a response.

"Be careful," he said. "You find anything, you call me. No need to do this alone."

Except there was every need. She nodded and turned her back on him, heading toward the VIP section. She forced herself not to turn around. What else could be said?

She strode past a large concrete pillar. A hand curled around her arm and whirled her around.

Her eyes widened at the man who gripped her tight. Mallory's ex, Bud Harrigan.

"I *knew* it was you, Sierra Bradford," he shouted, gripping her shoulders with both hands. He shook her. "I'd recognize those interfering blue eyes anywhere. What have you done with my wife and daughter?"

Shocked, Sierra froze, but only for a moment. She let her training take over and thrust her hands between his and directly at his nose. In a quick defensive move, she extricated herself from his hold.

Bud lost his balance and fell backward, hitting his head on the pillar. His eyes narrowed. Nose bloody and face flamed red, he jumped to his feet and lunged at her.

She sidestepped him. "I didn't do anything to Mallory or Chloe. But I think you did, Bud. Where are they?"

"Just like a woman. Trying to turn the truth on its head. I know you. Think new hair and getting yourself pregnant changes you?" He raked his gaze down her rounded body in disgust. "I knew you weren't as perfect as my wife believed."

With a move quicker than she'd expected, he grabbed her arm and twisted it behind her. "Where is my wife?"

A loud shout erupted from the side. Sierra's arm wrenched back so hard she thought it might break, then suddenly she was free.

With one punch Rafe knocked Bud to the ground. Lifting him by the collar, Rafe shoved the man against a door. "You touch my wife again, and you won't live to see tomorrow."

Rafe's grip tightened; Bud's face grew purple.

Sierra tugged on Rafe's arm. "Let him go," she whispered. "You'll kill him."

"He deserves it. He touched you."

"Rafe." Zane's voice intruded. "You're attracting unwanted attention."

With a growl, Rafe eased his grip. Bud choked out a cough and wheezed in a couple of breaths.

Relieved Zane had stopped Rafe from killing Bud, Sierra glanced around. "We can't stay here."

"This way." Zane led them down a deserted hallway to the rodeo's main office. "Inside," he hissed. "You're just lucky the boss left for a meeting with his brother."

Rafe shoved Bud inside. Sierra followed.

"Who are you?" Bud panted, clutching at Rafe's grip. "Where's my wife and kid? I know she knows."

With a disgusted grunt, Rafe released his grip, and Bud crumbled to the office floor. Rafe knelt next to him.

"Call Detective Foster," Rafe ordered Zane with a smile that didn't reach his eye. "He can sort out the situation. We'll let the cops search Bud here and see what they find."

Mallory's ex went pale, and he clutched his jacket pocket. "No, no, we don't have to call the cops. We can work this out. I can pay you. Just don't get the police involved."

"Sit down, Bud." Rafe pushed him back into a chair. "You're going to answer a few questions. And then maybe, just maybe, we won't call the cops."

Okay, Sierra knew Rafe's statement was a lie. No way would he let Bud go.

She stared down at Mallory's ex. "When did you last see Mallory and Chloe?"

Bud scowled. "Two weeks ago. I confronted her after I was served the new custody agreement. Chloe is *my* kid. I have every right to see her. It's *your* fault she's ignoring my phone calls. Your fault she divorced me, you meddling bitch." He rose from the chair and charged at Sierra.

Rafe grabbed his collar, slamming him back into his seat. "You try that again, *Bud*, and I'll give you a demonstration on how Uncle Sam taught me to interrogate prisoners. You got it?"

Bud's eyes widened, and he stared at Rafe's patch. A loud gulp escaped him.

Zane stood over Bud and stretched out his hand. "Give me your phone."

Bud spit in his face.

Rafe stepped forward, looming over Bud with a scowl Sierra wouldn't want directed at her. Ever.

"Let's try this again." Zane wiped his cheek and pinned Bud with a harsh glare. "Hand over your phone, or we call the cops and you explain the plastic baggie full of pills in your pocket."

With a curse, Bud yanked his phone from his pocket and shoved it at Zane.

The computer expert tapped the screen for a few minutes. "He's telling the truth. He's been trying to call Mallory for the past four days. He didn't do it."

Sierra's knees buckled, and she clutched at the door frame.

Rafe propped her up.

"What the hell is going on here?" Bud shouted. "What are you talking about?"

"Who sold you the pills?"

"I'm not saying anything else," Bud said. "Not without a lawyer."

"That can be arranged," Rafe said with a smile. "That can be arranged."

Chapter Ten

Sierra stood at the base of the steps leading into the arena. She wrapped her arms around her body and shivered. Rafe stood by her side. The last several minutes had shifted their relationship yet again, but she doubted it would ever be the same on a personal level. However, they could find a way to work together. She believed that now.

"Bud may not know what happened to Mallory and Chloe, but he could still give away my identity if he talks to the wrong person," she said, clutching her bag, taking comfort in the Glock's presence.

"Cade confiscated the drugs on Bud, enough to suggest an intent to distribute. His blood alcohol level was twice the legal limit. It'll take him some time to sober up before they can interview him," Rafe said. "Cade will continue questioning him and let us know of any leads. Ransom's going to run interference with an attorney, but in reality, we only have until tomorrow morning to figure this out. After that, we'll have to face the cops and explain everything."

"So we have today to find Mallory and Chloe." Her gut roiled, and it had nothing to do with the smell of fresh horse manure. "The money has to come from the sale of drugs. What else is there?"

Several spectators jostled past them. Rafe placed his body between hers and the crowd.

"I agree," he said. "I'll work the brother, and—"

"I'll focus on Diane and see where that leads."

A bevy of announcements started droning from the arena.

"I'd better get you seated," he said. He frowned. "She may not be involved at all. With her brother dealing, she could simply be an innocent bystander."

"I hope so." Sierra straightened her dress. "I like her. But she sees things. I get the impression she's very sharp. She watches people. She knows where the secrets are buried. If she's not guilty, she may be able to provide us with another lead."

Rafe touched her back, and they made their way through the arena. "Zane's going to keep digging into the records. He thought he'd found some hidden files yesterday. He's going to attempt to decrypt them."

Sierra breathed in deeply. "I've been adding up the numbers in my head, Rafe. Five million dollars a year is a lot of oxycodone."

"You caught onto that, too." Rafe stroked his jaw. "We're missing something. Just keep your eyes and ears open for anything that doesn't quite fit. You'll know it when you see it. You've got good instincts."

Sierra pasted on a smile as she made her way to the VIP section of the arena. "Showtime," she whispered.

"Well, if it isn't our newest member," Nancy cooed. "You're looking mighty glowy today, Sarah."

Sierra touched her belly. "She's being active today."

"I know that feeling," Diane said, jostling her sobbing baby before slipping a bottle into the boy's mouth. He settled in her arms and sucked down the milk.

"He eats like a champ," Rafe commented.

Diane smiled. "Gets that from his daddy."

Rafe pulled Sierra into his arms. "See you later, honey. Wish me luck."

She closed her eyes and let him kiss her, trying to remind herself his embrace was just part of the job, that it didn't mean anything. But the gentleness of his lips broke her heart.

"Fan yourself, ladies," Nancy said.

Rafe's cheeks reddened at the brazen compliment. "I think I'd better get out of the line of fire." He tipped his Stetson. "Ladies."

The entire group watched Rafe walk away. "That man could be the centerfold for this year's rodeo cowboy calendar." Nancy sent Sierra a narrowed gaze. "You think he'd take his clothes off for charity?"

She nearly choked. "Umm…I don't think so."

"Don't tell me he's shy."

"No, but he's private." And Sierra realized how true her statement was. Rafe had revealed more to her the last few days about his past than he'd told anyone. Certainly Noah had shared what an enigma CTC found Rafe. How he'd seemed to have sprung full grown when he'd arrived at basic training—without a history, without connections. It was one of the main reasons Noah had warned her off the operative.

Sierra sat in front of Diane and twisted in her seat. "Rafe's pretty sore today," she offered. "How's Travis?"

Diane's expression dropped. "Hurting. More than he'll let on. He needs to manage the pain in his neck, but he refuses. Can't afford the doctor visits and meds. So he toughs it out."

"Rafe refused to see the doc yesterday, and he was up all night hurting. I don't know what to do," Sierra said with a sigh—at least some of her statement bore a resemblance to the truth.

Nancy clicked her tongue. "There are ways to get what he needs even if you're short on funds. *If* you're willing to take a chance."

Sierra blinked and shifted from facing Diane to Nancy. "I'm willing to do whatever it takes."

"See how it goes today," Nancy said with a pat. "I might have a solution for you."

Had Nancy just become their prime suspect?

"How's the nausea today, Sarah?" Diane asked, shifting the conversation. "I was lucky. Mine only lasted the first fourteen weeks or so."

"I threw up every morning until that baby came out," Nancy groaned. "And my breasts, my gosh, I don't know who started the rumor that women get all sexually hot and bothered during their pregnancy. Mine just hurt like the dickens."

Several women nodded in agreement. One, though, turned bright red.

Sierra stilled in her seat. Surreptitiously she touched the side of her left breast, where Archimedes had left his mark, then her right. Only now did she realize they'd both been feeling strangely tender for a couple of weeks. She'd blamed it on the scar.

Quickly she did a calculation. Her last period had been before Archimedes had kidnapped her.

Then there was the other important fact. A night of

passion. Two months ago. With Rafe. In a motel. And the first time. No condom.

Oh my God.

"Sarah, you're looking a little green."

Nausea.

It couldn't be.

She swallowed deeply, her mind whirling at the possibility. She touched her belly. This couldn't be happening.

"Ladies and gentlemen, our bull riders have just drawn for their rides. First up, Travis Manley will be riding Evil Genius." The announcer went through several other assignments. Sierra's nails bit into her palms as each name was read. "Rafe Vargas...oh boy, folks. Rafe drew Angel Maker. Send a prayer up for our newest cowboy."

Sierra swayed in her seat.

Nancy propped her up and fanned her with her program. "Don't you worry, gal. It'll be okay. Those bull-fighters will take care of your man."

"Turn your attention to the south chute, folks. Travis Manley is currently ranked second overall. He was scoreless in round one. Let's see if he can go over the top in the second round."

Sierra blinked and tried to focus on the chute. Travis nodded. The silver-gray bull roared into the arena. She forced herself to observe Diane. The woman's mouth had tightened into a thin line. Sierra had no idea if Diane was up to anything criminal, but she was obviously worried about her husband.

The buzzer sounded. The crowd roared. Eight seconds.

Travis should jump off the bull.

He didn't.

A loud gasp washed through the crowd.

"Help him out, fellows!" the announcer yelled.

"His hand's stuck," Nancy whispered, her own face paling.

Travis's body flailed on top of the huge animal. The bull slammed onto its side, and Travis's leg was caught beneath the beast.

A gasp went through the crowd. Diane shot to her feet. "Travis!"

The bull vaulted to its feet, but Travis lay still in the dirt. Two bullfighters herded the bull into the chute, then they motioned wildly for a stretcher.

"I have to go to him," Diane muttered.

"I'll take the baby." Nancy scooped up the boy. "You go."

One of the other women hooked her arm with Diane's to accompany her. She left as if in a daze.

The entire VIP area had gone solemn and silent. Sierra met Nancy's gaze. "Will he be okay?"

Nancy frowned. "All depends on where that bull stomped on him, but he wasn't moving, and that's never good."

Sierra's entire body had chilled. Rafe had to ride Angel Maker. She'd known bull riding was one of the most dangerous sports in the country, but she hadn't realized. Not really.

Rafe could die.

She touched her belly. She had so much to say to him. If she was right, everything between them had changed.

"Hey, little guy, you need to burp?" Nancy asked Diane's baby. "Sarah, could you get me a cloth out of his diaper bag?"

Sierra tugged the multipocketed satchel to her. She opened one compartment and saw only diapers.

"Try the front," one of the women said. "I think that's where she keeps her burp cloths."

Sierra dug into another cubby and handed the cloth to Nancy. She paused for a moment, feeling strange rifling through someone else's things. Stiffening her back, she dug into the main compartment. "Do you need a diaper, too?" she asked, to cover her search.

Her hand encountered several plastic bags in one of the main pockets. Heart pounding, Sierra pulled out a disposable diaper and stilled. Beneath a layer of diapers were what might be fifty or more bags of pills.

Bud wasn't the drug supplier. Neither was Nancy. Diane Manley was.

THE COWBOYS BEHIND the chute had gone solemn. Travis Manley hadn't regained consciousness yet. Rafe didn't have much time left before his ride. He slipped away from the noise and preparations, and dialed a number.

"King." Jared's voice snapped out a greeting.

"What do you know about Angel Maker?" Rafe asked his friend.

"You drew that spawn of the devil." Jared let out a low whistle. "Great bloodlines. No cowboy's ever lasted eight seconds. In fact, I considered adding his gene pool to my stock, but even I don't know if I'm willing to pay the going rate for his genetic material." He chuckled. "Then again, I probably will."

"That's not what I'm asking."

"I know. Look, the thing that gets the riders is they psych themselves out from the start. They believe he's unpredictable, but he isn't. If he leaves the chute to-

ward his left, he'll kick that way a few times and then
do a major spin to the right. Most bulls have a pref-
erence. Angel Maker's ambidextrous. If he leaves the
shut toward his right, he'll end up spinning left. That's
when most of his riders lose their balance. Five or six
seconds in.

"If you can stay centered during that the first spin,
you've got a fighting chance."

Rafe rubbed the sore spot at the back of his neck. He
might just survive this ride after all.

"Thanks, J.K. I owe you one."

Adjusting his patch, Rafe strode into the staging
area. "You ready to face the demon, Vargas?" Kurt
Prentiss asked.

"As ready as I'll ever be."

"We've got an extra bullfighter for Angel Maker.
We'll get you out," the cowboy said.

"Vargas," the stager announced. "You're up."

Rafe climbed up to the top of the chute and stared
down at the black devil known as Angel Maker. The
bull snorted, his hooves dancing. He was the biggest
bull Rafe had ever seen. He let out a long, slow breath
and checked the strap. No tampering. He met Kurt's
gaze. The cowboy nodded.

"Just you and me, Angel Maker," Rafe muttered.

He adjusted his grip on the rope and lowered himself on top of the bull. The moment his weight hit the
beast's back he nodded.

The chute opened.

Angel Maker took off to the right.

Time slowed. Rafe fought against his instincts and
leaned right.

Sure enough Angel Maker spun left, and Rafe's posture gave him just enough balance not to fly off the back of the animal.

Rafe knew the crowd screamed, but all he could hear was his blood rushing in his head and a slow count.

One. Two. Three. Four. Five. Six. Seven. Eight.

The siren sounded.

Rafe released the rope and jumped clear of the bull. The damned thing rushed him, head down. Rafe raced to the gate and vaulted up and over.

A roar sounded through the crowd. Rafe's gaze immediately went to the VIP stands.

Sierra had vanished.

IN THE STANDS, the crowd's roar washed over Sierra. She pressed her head lower between her knees.

Every last spectator in the arena stood cheering. "Rafe. Rafe. Rafe."

The chant didn't stop. He'd done the impossible.

Nancy bent down and rubbed her back. "Your man's looking for you," she said. "I think he's worried."

Sierra closed her eyes and sucked in a deep breath. She stood, struggling not to sway, and immediately Rafe's gaze pinned her in place.

The clamoring and boot stomping, the applause and shouts faded to nothing. Only the two of them existed for that moment. She'd always thought those fade-away shots in the movies were a trick of the director, but it was real.

As if she were in a trance, Sierra made her way down to the bottom row of seats. Rafe climbed back into the arena and raced across the dirt. He vaulted over a fence and then up to the bleachers. He wrapped his arms around her and buried his head in her shoulder.

"Told you it was like riding a bike," he whispered in her ear.

"Liar." She held him close, unable to speak around the fear still caught in her throat. "Don't do that again," she said. "I can't take it."

She placed her hand over her belly. *And neither can our baby.*

Chapter Eleven

With cheering crowds surrounding them, Sierra clung to Rafe as if her life depended on it. In many ways it did. She just wished she knew what the future would hold. How would he react to her unexpected news?

She touched his dusty face. "We need to talk."

"You got a lead?"

Rafe had just faced death, and he'd shoved it aside a lot faster than she could have. Her body stilled. How could she have forgotten the reason they were here together? Even for a moment. Telling him the news would have to wait. She relayed what she'd discovered about Diane and the drugs in her diaper bag. Then about Nancy's strange offer.

"I wish I could say I'm surprised, but not a whole lot shocks me anymore. They could be working it together. Travis, too."

"I hope he's not in on it," Sierra said. "For their son's sake."

Rafe pulled out his phone. "I'll text Zane. He can do a deep dive into her finances." Once he'd sent the message, he pocketed the device and took her hands in his. "You really came through."

"Then why does it leave such a bad taste in my

mouth?" Sierra frowned. "Undercover feels like a betrayal."

With one eye on the VIP wives, he raised her hand to his lips. "Sometimes it's hard to tell which relationships are real, and which aren't."

He turned her palm face up and caressed it with his thumb. A tingle centered in Sierra's belly. Her feelings were real, but was this all an act? How could she tell?

He slipped his hand into hers. "Let's find Mallory and Chloe."

They climbed the bleachers. When they reached the reserved section, Rafe tipped his hat once again and gifted them with a smile. "Ladies."

"You showed Angel Maker what-for, Rafe." Nancy chortled. "Congratulations."

"Thank you. I got lucky that time."

"I doubt luck had anything to do with it. I think you're just that good."

Sierra leaned over Nancy and forced her voice into a low whisper. "You said you had a suggestion for Rafe's pain? He's putting on a good front, but I can tell he's hurting, and it'll be worse tomorrow."

"Couldn't tell it by me. He must be an expert at hiding what he doesn't want known. However, I do have a solution for you." Nancy grinned and pulled out a card. "Acupuncture. Kept my man riding all these years. The doc is my son. He'll give you a discount if Rafe's willing to become a human pincushion."

Sierra's shoulders lightened with relief. She wanted to hug the woman in appreciation for not being a criminal. "Thanks, Nancy." She accepted the card. "I think we'll head over to medical. Rafe wants to check on Travis."

She made a point of thanking the women for their support and advice to distract them while Rafe grabbed the diaper bag. He climbed down a few steps, and she quickly extricated herself and followed.

When she reached his side, Sierra glanced over her shoulder. "Eventually they'll miss the baby's supplies."

"It doesn't matter. We need to talk to Diane. See what she knows and find out who's working with her, because she didn't pull off this abduction by herself."

They wove through the stands and made their way to the on-site medical clinic. Zane was waiting for them, and the frown on his face gave Sierra a chill.

They veered toward him. "What's wrong?" Rafe asked.

"I don't think she's the key to finding Mallory and Chloe."

He handed Sierra a printout. "I found a separate account under Diane's maiden name, which is why we missed it. She and her brother are clearly in this together, but look at the totals. Five years' worth of drug dealing, and it's nowhere near twenty-five million. In fact, they're barely making a profit. She's not our target."

"Are you saying she wasn't involved in the abduction?" The grim possibility that they'd been searching in the wrong direction sent her pulse racing in panic. Had they wasted the most critical time to find Mallory and Chloe assuming the wrong motive for the kidnapping? Had their entire investigation been a colossal mistake? "Then who else could it be?" Sierra stalked over to Diane. Zane tried to stop her, but she avoided his grasp.

The woman stood fearfully watching the paramedics stabilizing Travis and immobilizing his leg. Sierra clasped Diane's arm. "I need to talk to you. Right now."

Diane shook Sierra off. "What are you doing? Can't you see my husband's hurt? Leave me alone."

Rafe sidled up to Sierra and raised the diaper bag. "We need to discuss your little side business, Mrs. Manley."

Her brother rushed out of the shadows and tried to grab the bag. "Leave her alone."

"Back off, Spider," Rafe said, keeping a tight hold on the evidence. "Don't make it worse. Because you're both going to jail. For a long time."

Diane cast a worried glance at Travis. She gnawed on her lip and led them away from the entrance. "You don't understand. Can't you just forget what you saw? I'm not hurting anyone."

"You're dealing drugs." Sierra crossed her arms over her chest.

"I'm selling pain relief to men who can't afford to get what they need. I don't make any money." Diane lifted her chin. "I'm doing what has to be done so we can survive."

At the intense defense, Sierra paused. "Explain it to me."

"Most of the cowboys here can't afford insurance or prescriptions," Diane said. "Rodeo is hard on the body. Some of these guys can't go from event to event and finish in the money without some help. Especially as they get older. No money means no food on the table."

"Does your husband know?" Rafe asked.

The horrified expression on Diane's face made the truth clear. Travis had no knowledge of what his wife had done.

A wave of disappointment smothered Sierra's hope. She rubbed her temples as her mind tried to process the latest setback. "You didn't kidnap Mallory Harrigan and her daughter, did you?"

"The secretary? Why would anyone do such a thing?"

Diane couldn't have faked the shock or confusion. Sierra looked over at Rafe, who shook his head. "We're at a dead end."

RAFE PLACED A hand on Travis Manley's shoulder. The cowboy had cheated death one more time at the hands of a bull. He'd have some rehab ahead, but he'd walk again. Maybe even ride again.

His family would never be the same.

Travis held his son in his arms and watched as Detective Cade Foster Mirandized his wife and brother-in-law. Two cops led the pair away in handcuffs.

"I should've known," he muttered, patting the baby's back. "She gave me those pills, said the doc had given them to us for free. I wanted to believe her."

His son reached toward Diane. "Mama. Mama."

She turned to give them one last regretful look before disappearing around a corner, in custody.

Travis shifted his body, wincing, and lifted his gaze to Rafe. "You're not here to launch a comeback, are you? You were here to catch them."

"Sorry, Travis. Your wife ended up on our radar, but not because we were searching for a ring selling prescription drugs. I'm here to find a kidnapper."

"Diane would never kidnap…" His voice trailed off. "Of course, I didn't think it was possible she could be a drug dealer, either."

"We're pretty certain she's not involved in the abduction," Rafe said. "If it's any consolation, Diane didn't make any real money on the medication. Money was never her motive. She did it to help you and everyone here. She made just enough to cover expenses."

"The right reason doesn't make the act okay."

How well Rafe knew that. "The world can be gray sometimes. Believe me, I know more than most."

Travis didn't appear convinced. His skepticism reminded Rafe he'd asked himself more than once over the last few months if he'd lived too long in the murky space between black and white.

He might not be able to help Travis accept his wife's choice, but he could assist with a better outcome. "Look, Travis, I can hook you up with a good lawyer who won't charge you too much."

"I hadn't even thought that far." After a brief hesitation, Travis nodded. "I guess I'm a little…stunned right now. Not thinking too clearly, and I don't believe that's because a bull kicked me until he knocked me out. Thank you. I owe you one."

Rafe went silent for a moment. They needed a break, and his gut told him this bull rider was worth the risk of revealing the truth. "Travis, you might be able to help me right now. You've been with the circuit awhile. You know the players. We discovered twenty-five million dollars has been laundered through the rodeo in the last five years. Any idea who or what might be involved with that kind of money? Any rumors of guns, drugs, people being bought and sold?"

Travis stroked his son's cheek, and Rafe recognized a light of recognition filtering into the man's eyes.

"I've got a pretty good idea," Travis murmured under

his breath. "Talk to Harlen Anderson. Diane mentioned the other day the guy wore a thousand-dollar pair of shoes mucking around in the stalls. Who does that if they're not rolling in dough?"

The nondescript almost forgettable veterinarian. Interesting. He could pretty much come and go as he pleased. He'd have reason to go practically anywhere at the rodeo. That much freedom would make a good cover for a whole lot of trouble.

Rafe shook Travis's hand. "Thanks. Get better. And once again, I'm sorry."

"You didn't make the choice," Travis said with a frown. "She did."

Another family destroyed. Rafe had lost count how many times he'd been directly involved in this kind of devastation. Sometimes it was deserved. Sometimes, like today, a good man was an unwitting victim who would have to raise his son alone. At least for the foreseeable future.

If nothing else, he could inform Sierra of some not-bad news. Since they'd interviewed Diane, Rafe knew they both had begun to wonder if Mallory and Chloe Harrigan would ever be found. Especially since no ransom note had been delivered.

He left the medical clinic and joined Sierra and Zane across the corridor. "I may have a potential lead."

Sierra's eyes lit up before Rafe could finish his thought.

"It's not solid enough to go full force. We have to review every note, every statement, every search. If something gives you a niggle, set it aside."

"I've pulled everything off the rodeo books I can," Zane said. "With your cover blown, I might be better off spending time in front of the keyboard instead of continuing on."

"If you're certain you have copies of all the files you need," Rafe said, when a familiar figure caught his eye. He nodded Detective Foster over.

Cade shook Rafe's hand. "Not bad work for a couple of spies."

"We didn't exactly arrest a major drug lord," Rafe countered. "And we're light on leads to find Mallory and Chloe."

"That's why I stopped by," Cade said. "I don't know if it helps, but someone in the department ran your name through the system earlier today. They also searched for information on a woman named Sierra Bradford yesterday. *Not* Sarah Vargas."

Rafe let out a long, slow breath. Whoever the puppet master was on this operation still had strings in the police department, and in the rodeo. His lips thinned and he met Sierra's gaze, knowing she understood the potential implications.

"They might know my true identity," she said.

"But *who* knows?" Rafe faced Cade. "Who ran the searches? Do they *really* know Sierra and Sarah is the same person, or is it guesswork?"

"Sarah Vargas wasn't searched, so maybe not. As to the identity of the perp, the system indicated that a cop on traffic patrol ran the search. No way he could have worked the computer and ticketed a speeding car at the same time."

"If they ran my name yesterday, I think they traced my weapon," Sierra said. "I didn't reveal my name during the abduction, but they have my gun. It's traceable."

"Makes sense," Cade said, working the rim of his

hat. "But why would the same cop run Rafe's name today?"

"They know," Rafe said. "They have to."

Which meant they no longer had the element of surprise, and Mallory and Chloe's chances of survival just plummeted. From Sierra's alarmed expression, she had already come to the same conclusion.

He sidled up to her and rubbed her back in slow, circular motions, hoping to reassure her, or at least offer the only comfort he could.

"Get out of my way," a furious voice shouted.

Rafe whirled toward the ruckus, and he placed himself between Sierra and the disturbance, hand pausing near his weapon.

An irate John Beckel rushed into the corridor, his face red and sweaty. "What the hell is going on here? I've just tried to convince dozens of scared families that this rodeo isn't too dangerous to attend. They're walking out. I'm losing thousands of dollars every minute."

He shoved Cade backward. "I had an agreement with the cops. You broke it."

"Really, Mr. Beckel. And what arrangement might that be? For us to ignore a drug operation in your facility?"

Beckel huffed and tugged out his phone. "I'm calling your captain, Detective... Foster, is it? He'll bust you down to patrol so quick, you won't have a career left."

Before Beckel could place the call, his attention snapped to Zane. "And what are *you* doing here?" His cheeks went blotchy. "You know what. I don't like you, I don't like your tattoo. You're too big to be an accountant. You're fired!"

On a roll, Beckel pointed at Rafe. "And you. I knew

you were trouble. I don't care if you did ride Angel Maker and the whole world wants to interview you. You're no longer welcome here. I'm banning you from competition and from my rodeo."

He whirled on Sierra. "And you…" He glanced down at her belly. "I don't know *what* to tell you, but I'd get away from all of them."

Cade stepped forward and faced the irate man. "You need to calm down, sir, before you say something you'll regret."

"Get them off my property," Beckel blustered. "All of them."

"Not until we get some answers," Rafe said, his jaw tightening. Seemed like the good ol' boy John Beckel pretended to be was just an illusion.

"I don't have to speak to any of you." He started to stalk off, but Cade stopped him with a firm hand. "Mr. Beckel, I strongly suggest you reconsider. I know you'd prefer to answer questions privately instead of in front of a lot of people with cell phones. And cameras."

Beckel tapped his phone and put it to his ear. "Warren, I need our lawyer at the rodeo. Call him now."

At the mention of legal counsel, Rafe knew Cade would have to back off, but not everyone had to follow the rules. He stepped in front of Cade until he stood boots-to-boots with John Beckel. "I only have two questions. What are your dealings with Harlen Anderson, and what did you do with Mallory and Chloe Harrigan?"

FOR SOME REASON Sierra had hoped they'd return to their motel room in triumph—or maybe even having found Mallory and Chloe. Instead, she sat with Rafe in his truck, her body limp with disappointment, her heart numb with fear.

Their accomplishment today—they'd ruined several lives. The drug operation had been Diane's choice, but Travis's shocking sadness and his son's inconsolable sobs had broken her heart.

As for Mallory and Chloe, Beckel either had the talent of an Oscar-winning actor or was innocent. Sierra didn't even want to put her doubts into words. They may already be too late to save them. Just the thought made her eyes burn with despair.

"I really believed Diane or her brother or even Bud would lead us to Mallory, Rafe. What are we going to do?"

"We regroup and start from scratch," Rafe said, his tone biting and frustrated. "Figure out what we missed."

Sierra didn't take it personally. Rafe didn't like to lose, and she took comfort in the determined line of his jaw. He hadn't given up, but she couldn't deny her gut twisted with uncertainty.

He squeezed her hand. "Zane's meeting us back at the motel. Maybe he's been able to break that encrypted file from Beckel's office."

"I thought he might be guilty, but he's all show."

"And little substance," Rafe said. "I doubt he could pull this off. He might get lucky a time or two, but not for five years straight. He certainly was cagey about Harlen, though. Didn't want to give us any information."

"Do you think Harlen's involved?" Sierra asked.

"The search of his clinic at the rodeo didn't turn up anything. Ransom's checking him out. Hopefully we'll hear from the boss soon."

Which meant the only thing left to do would be wait, and search their records to find Mallory and Chloe.

Sierra clutched her purse tight, trying to center the whirlpool that had become her life. If she were honest, ever since Archimedes had taken her, nothing had been the same—and if she was right, her life had changed forever.

She just prayed Mallory and Chloe would be a part of it.

"You look pale again, honey. Are you sure it's allergies and you're not getting sick?"

Then there was the lie she'd told Rafe. That she'd needed some allergy medication from the pharmacy. Instead, she'd picked up two pregnancy kits.

She grimaced at the falsehood, but nodded. If she was wrong—and she probably was given all the stress over the last few months—she didn't want to worry Rafe.

No, that wasn't true. In reality she didn't want to face his reaction at all, because she had no idea how he would respond and, in a corner of her heart, a small hope for a future with him still burned too brightly.

He rounded the truck and helped her out of the vehicle as if she were spun of glass. If she were pregnant, she'd have to break him of the hovering, or she'd kill him before their baby arrived.

And there she went again, assuming the best. When a deep foreboding had settled at the base of her neck.

Her heart longed for a happy ending that her head recognized to be unlikely.

She glanced down at her disguise. "I'm stripping out of this outfit," she said. "My entire body aches. I'll be thrilled to say goodbye to Sarah Vargas once and for all. What a nightmare."

At her words her gaze snapped to Rafe. She hadn't meant that the way it sounded.

Rafe had stilled, frozen midmovement. His frown had deepened, but he gave her a stiff nod, opening the motel room door. "I guess we're getting an annulment."

Before she could apologize, Princess Buttercup bypassed her and streaked to Rafe, jumping into his arms.

"What's wrong, P.B.?" he asked, stroking the cat with a reassuring hand. "You're trembling."

Sierra's heart melted at the big bad spy guy cuddling the trembling cat. She never would have guessed he could be that gentle. If he chose, Rafe would make a wonderful, loving father. She was certain of that. She just didn't know if he'd want that life.

Lifting her suitcase, she set it on the bed to retrieve a change of clothes. She gripped the zipper tag and yanked it open. She'd have her answer in a few minutes. Her gut ached with tension.

A rattling sounded from the suitcase.

Sierra froze. "What the…?"

Like a scene from a horror movie, a small snake slithered from between the zipper's silver teeth. The creature hissed. The rattle at the end of the tail shook in warning.

She couldn't breathe. The snake's body coiled, its triangular-shaped head rose. Rafe dropped the cat, raced across the room and swept her back just as the snake struck. It missed her by inches. Then, to her horror, at least two dozen small rattlers poured from the bag.

"They're more dangerous than the large ones," Rafe whispered in her ear. "Concentrated venom."

They poured in a slithering mass to the floor. Rafe pulled her toward the door. "Come on!"

At their side, Princess Buttercup hissed and pounced toward the rattlers.

"No!" Sierra shouted.

"Stop, P.B." Rafe reached for the animal.

The angry feline scooted out of the way and bounded toward the snakes. A rattling symphony erupted. Princess Buttercup's back went up, but within seconds, she slunk back.

Rafe scooped her into his arms, and they all quickly backed out of the motel room, slamming the door shut.

"Did they bite her?" Sierra asked, whirling.

Rafe palpated the cat's paws. "I don't think so. She would've yelped. Snakebites hurt like hell. If she becomes at all lethargic or seems sick, we'll have to get her help quickly."

He scratched her ears. "You brave, crazy cat, what did you think you were doing?"

"Protecting us. She's an attack cat after all." Sierra shivered. "Those snakes weren't an accident."

"No, I'd call it attempted murder."

Rafe called Zane. "We're moving locations. They've obviously figured out Sarah is Sierra, and I'm not taking any chances. She's not going back to the rodeo. Too dangerous. Too many *accidents* could happen. She'll work the keyboards from now on."

Rafe ended the call and shot her a challenging glare. "I'm not arguing with you about this decision or your reassignment. I'd pull anyone off undercover once it's blown."

Sierra cradled her fake belly. "I'm not arguing."

"Okay, then." That had gone better than he'd hoped.

Strangely well, in fact. He started the car and handed Sierra the cat. "She's trembling. She could use some TLC."

"Me, too. Who would do something like that, Rafe? It's a horrible way to die."

"A malicious way to kill. I have to wonder if our perp is irrational enough to believe that murder by a bunch of snakes would look like an accident."

She gasped. "Rafe, we can't just leave those snakes there. The maid or owner could walk in."

As she spoke, Rafe called the motel's owner to warn him. "He's contacting animal control, and I'll arrange for Zane to collect our things and rendezvous at the new location."

Sierra studied her fingers drifting through Princess Buttercup's paws. "Do you think this means Mallory and Chloe are alive?"

He didn't answer her, and her heart fell.

"I see. I'd hoped—"

"I wish I knew, Sierra. I really do. All I can tell you is we're getting too close to something someone doesn't want uncovered. Something they're willing to kill for."

RAFE THOUGHT OF himself as transient most of the time, but even for him, three motels in two days was excessive. "We've been tough on accommodations," he commented to Sierra, who'd finally ditched her disguise and was planning to plant herself in front of her laptop once it arrived.

While Rafe couldn't deny her figure evoked a passionate response, her more rounded look had stirred something primal within him.

In his mind, he could picture her pregnant and happy.

He just couldn't see himself by her side. She'd be married to some banker or accountant, safe, protected.

Loved by another man.

His hand squeezed the plastic cup he held into shards. He dropped them into the trash can. Okay, so he was jealous. He'd have to get used to the idea of her future. And his. Alone.

A knock sounded at their door. Rafe peered through the peephole and opened the door.

Zane stood there, weighed down with their bags.

"Next time, carry your own luggage," he groused, dropping everything but her computer bag with attitude.

Sierra stood frozen, staring at her suitcase with suspicion.

"No snakes," she said. "I know that in my head, so why don't I want to open the bag?"

"Even Indiana Jones hates snakes," Rafe said.

She tried to smile at his lame attempt at a joke, but it didn't reach her eyes. Sierra watched him with that same fidgety gaze he'd become too accustomed to since he'd ridden Angel Maker.

He'd expected her to be jittery. Who wouldn't be after a slithering nightmare come to life, but Sierra had faced much worse with Archimedes. This time, though, she displayed a caution he hadn't perceived before. Even then.

Rafe met Zane's concerned gaze. His coworker recognized the change, too.

She ignored the bag on the floor and carried her computer bag to the table. She set it down and plugged it in, but didn't settle in the chair waiting for it to boot. Instead, she buzzed around the room like a hummingbird. She refused to light anywhere.

Because she didn't trust him to protect her? Then again, why would she? He couldn't blame her for that.

She passed by him for the fourth time, and he clasped her upper arm to stop her. "What's wrong?" he asked. "Why so nervous?"

Her gaze veered to the left. The universal avoidance pattern made him pause. What the hell was going on?

Zane cleared his throat. "While you two were playing with snakes, I came up with an interesting possibility."

"A lead?" Sierra leaned over his shoulder. "Are you sure?"

"Is anything about this case certain? It's a long shot, but right now it's all I've got." Zane opened his laptop. "Cade called me when he couldn't reach you."

Rafe glanced at his phone. Sure enough, he'd missed the call sometime around the snake attack. "What did he find out?"

"Cade broke Bud. He discovered two *very* interesting pieces of information. Bud bought his drugs from Diane Manley. Evidently he got hooked after a surgery five years ago."

"That explains a lot, but I don't see a connection to the kidnapping. We closed that loop," Sierra said with a frown. Her shoulders drooped.

"Perhaps not. But Bud's monthly income wasn't what I'd expected, either." Zane passed a printout to Sierra. "He makes too much. He finally admitted he works doing odd jobs at the rodeo. Not for John Beckel, for *Warren*."

Now that was a revelation. The invisible brother.

"The brains behind the money." Sierra's eyes sparked with interest as she scanned the document.

This was the Sierra Rafe knew and understood. He could see the wheels turning.

"On a hunch, I dug into him some more," Zane added. "He put up some barriers to my original searches with several layers of shell corporations, but I finally uncovered evidence that Warren Beckel isn't quite the angel he's painted himself to be. I found several fraud arrest records about twenty years ago. Charges were strangely dropped due to evidence tampering. My guess is he's been buying off law enforcement for a long time."

Zane shoved a file at Rafe, and he quickly scanned it. "Why didn't we see this before?"

"He's been perfecting hiding for two decades," Zane said. "I wouldn't have found it if Sierra hadn't shown me a few tricks on the Kazakhstan job a while back."

"Give me the endgame," Rafe said, handing Sierra the folder.

"Warren Beckel's fingers are knuckle-deep in a lot more pies than we thought. In addition to a slew of businesses, he owns quite a few properties. Including a parcel about a four-hour drive from here. He purchased it, but it's in John's name. Sitting empty in the middle of nowhere."

"That's strange," Sierra said.

"It gets better. The land is supposed to be deserted. However, when I pulled up recent satellite imagery—"

"And exactly how'd you access that?" Rafe asked his friend.

"Oh…" Zane hesitated. "I know a guy."

Which meant somehow he'd used his old contacts to grab Department of Defense images.

"I love you, Zane," Sierra said with feeling. She kissed his cheek. The man's ears turned red, and Rafe scowled at her. He couldn't believe she'd said those words to Zane. Or that she'd kissed him.

And he certainly didn't like admitting how that small display of friendship needled at him.

"I'm relieved you're on our team and not on the bad guys' side," she added. "So, what did the photos show? Did you see Mallory and Chloe?"

Zane shook his head. "Not enough resolution, but a couple of buildings *have* been placed on the property without permits. One's a mobile home. Not something Warren would normally purchase. He's more of a five-star-hotel kind of guy."

"But it would be a good place for the Beckel brothers to hide someone or something they didn't want found. Especially given Warren's history," Rafe surmised. "I like your thinking, Zane."

"The link to them is tenuous at best, and it may not hold up in court given what I had to do to uncover the links, but it's the best lead I've got."

"We'll worry about court once Mallory and Chloe are safe," Rafe said, "but I can see in your face that's not all."

"We have a big problem," Zane said. "I can't call the local cops there to check the place out. Too many potential leaks, and according to Cade, the drugs confiscated from Diane are an identical match to a stash of black market prescription drugs the cops confiscated last year. Someone on the police force is clearly involved."

"We have to search the land," Sierra said. "But four hours away makes it an all-day round trip."

"That's what planes are for," Rafe said. "Zane could reach the place in an hour or so."

Zane grinned. "Great minds. I also took the liberty

of calling Ransom. He's sending Léon this way to back you up."

"Excellent." Rafe liked the move. Léon's identity was a closely guarded secret, but the former heir to the small European country of Bellevaux had trained as an operative. Now living a new life, Léon had a skill set that rivaled Rafe's. If he couldn't have Noah on his six, Léon would do very nicely.

"While you're heading to the Beckels' land, Sierra and I will rework the rest of our evidence. Maybe we'll see something else we missed as we focused on the drug theory."

Zane nodded. "It's a plan." He handed Sierra a thumb drive. "I dumped the files I copied from the rodeo on it. Hopefully you'll see something I didn't."

He didn't add they were scraping the bottom of the barrel. They all knew it, so he quickly left to meet the CTC plane.

"Sounds like a good lead," Rafe said, turning to Sierra, surprised she hadn't said more.

She'd gone deathly white.

Alarmed, Rafe hurried over to her.

"Excuse me," she muttered. She covered her mouth, shoved past him and raced into the bathroom, carrying the pharmacy bag with her.

Rafe knocked softly on the door. "Sierra?"

She didn't respond.

"Sierra." He raised his voice. "Are you okay?"

He pressed his ear to the door and heard the sound of running water. He banged harder. "Answer me or I'm coming in."

"Give me a minute," she said, her voice thick with emotion. "Please."

Something was very wrong. He didn't know exactly what, but she had to be okay. He needed her.

A few minutes later Sierra exited the bathroom.

"How are you feeling? Do you need a doctor?"

She shook her head slowly. "I'm fine. For now."

The pensive look on her face made him pause. "What's wrong?"

She looked up at him with fear-laced eyes, clutching a small box.

"I'm pregnant."

Chapter Twelve

The motel room went completely silent. Sierra didn't want to look at Rafe. She should have waited to tell him, but she hadn't been able to stop herself from taking the test.

And once she'd seen the indicator…

"How long have you known?" he asked quietly.

At the strange caution, even resentment in his tone, her gaze flew to his in confusion. She saw an expression of what she first took as distrust and disbelief, but then she recognized the truth. Hurt and disappointment laced his eyes.

She thrust the pregnancy test into his hand. "I was certain thirty seconds ago, but I've only suspected a couple of hours. All those wives and their talk of babies and advice about symptoms." She grasped his arm. "I didn't keep this a secret, Rafe. I wouldn't."

He rubbed his face with his free hand. "I know you wouldn't."

She let go of him and stepped back. She'd had more than a moment to consider what to think, and she was still in a state of shock. She shouldn't be wishing that he would smile at her, take her in his arms and twirl her around in celebration.

She glanced away from his still stunned look. "I shouldn't have said anything. Not yet. We can talk about it later. For now, we have a job to do."

Struggling against the nausea that threatened to boil over, she turned her back. She'd work the computer, focus on Mallory and Chloe. She could do that.

He clasped her shoulders and gently turned her to him. "Hell, no. You should *definitely* have told me. You should have told me the moment you…" His voice trailed off. "You tried to say something. After the ride."

She nodded.

He tilted her face up to his and placed his hand on her still-flat belly. "How do you feel?"

"Nauseous. Scared. Emotional." Her eyes welled. "I've been thinking about Mallory and her Chloe. I already love our baby with everything I am, Rafe. I don't know what I'd do if something happened to her. I'd do whatever I must to protect her."

She blinked hard. "Look at me. I'm a mess."

He caught a tear with his knuckle. "I'm right there with you. And Sierra, I'd kill for her. And you. Without hesitation."

His good eye flashed with an intensity she'd never seen. "You want this baby."

She placed her hand on top of his. "I didn't plan on this, but I want it. Even though I'm terrified."

Rafe took in a shuddering breath. "Does that mean you want your baby's father, too?"

Before she could answer, a vibrating phone shattered the fragile moment. "Blocked call," he said. "I have to—"

Sierra chewed the inside of her lip to attempt a modicum of control. "Take it."

He tapped the speakerphone. "Vargas."

"I hear you're looking for me."

Sierra recognized the drawl from their first day at the rodeo.

"Harlen?"

"I also heard from a reliable source that you're looking for some very specific information," the vet said. "I'm ready to talk. Everything's imploding, and the boss is getting paranoid. He's making mistakes. But I need some guarantees."

"I'll do everything I can," Rafe said.

"No deal. You have no authority. I talk to you, I end up in jail. I can give you the identity of the kidnapper. And I didn't have *anything* to do with taking that woman and her child."

Sierra grabbed the phone from Rafe's hand. "Then who did? Where are they?" Sierra shouted.

"Sarah Vargas. Or should I say, Sierra Bradford. You've made a lot of people very angry."

Rafe pried the phone away from her hand. She paced back and forth, longing to leap through the phone at the call's other end and strangle that man until he talked.

"Turn yourself in, Harlen," Rafe said. "If you help us find Mallory and Chloe Harrigan, it'll go a long way to bettering your situation."

Harlen let out a sharp laugh. "Not hardly. I talk, I'm dead. And with a significantly more painful death than a few rattlers."

Rafe let out a curse. "That was your sick idea?"

"I didn't say that," Harlen argued. "But with a unit captain and a couple of his flunkies from the local police on the take, no way am I going anywhere near a police station until they're arrested. You want information, meet me at my office at the rodeo. And come alone. I guarantee, I'll give you want you want."

THE PROTECTIVE GROVE of trees served them well. Mallory used the trunk to stand. She searched the ground for a cane.

"Button, can you bring me that stick beneath that big tree?"

Chloe nodded. Her daughter had become more and more subdued as the night went on. Her lips were parched. Mallory knew she had to find water for them in the next few hours, or they wouldn't survive.

Her daughter returned with the stick. Mallory tested her weight against the straight piece of wood.

Ever so gingerly she set her foot on the ground and inch by inch added some weight.

When the pain didn't make her cry out, a smidgen of hope welled within her.

"Can you walk?" Chloe asked.

"Maybe, Button." Mallory moved the stick forward and took a tentative step. A sharp pain ratcheted through her ankle, but it didn't send her to her knees. She could live with it.

"Let's go find some water."

Chloe nodded listlessly. "I'm thirsty."

Slowly they made their way through the dense thicket. When they passed a large boulder, a sense of déjà vu hit Mallory. A horrifying sense of foreboding settled in her belly.

They walked a bit more until they reached another thick copse of trees. Mallory moved a limb aside. When she did, she gasped. The bumper of a red vehicle appeared.

"Look, Mommy, a car." Chloe pulled at her mother's hand.

Mallory held her daughter back. "We have to be careful and quiet and still."

"They may have something to drink. Or breakfast," she whispered. "Please."

"Maybe."

"Maybe means no," Chloe said, pouting.

"Shh, Button. Please."

Even though Chloe gave her a mutinous nod, Mallory had to take the chance. Her movements as quiet as possible given her injury, Mallory limped toward the clearing. First a red truck came into view. If only the owner had left the keys inside.

Then an all-too-familiar shack loomed off to her right. Mallory gripped the staff.

The cop's shack.

Her entire body froze with terror. They'd gone in one big circle.

Now what?

The police officer with the soulless eyes slammed out of the trailer. "That woman and kid didn't just disappear. We're three days' walk from anything. They have to be out there somewhere." He cradled a rifle in his arm. "I just received orders from the boss. If you see them, kill them. Kill them both."

Chloe let out a shrill squeal.

The cop turned toward the woods. "Glen, did you hear something?"

"N-no, sir."

Mallory stepped backward and came up against a large wall of muscle.

A hand clamped over her mouth and Chloe's.

"Be quiet, or you're dead," a voice whispered in her ear. She froze. Oh God. They were caught.

RAFE PRESSED HARDER on the accelerator and glanced at Sierra. A baby. He still couldn't quite process the information, and somehow he had to find a way to focus on his job.

If he'd believed for one moment he could convince her to return to Denver—or even head to Carder—he would. But he knew the odds. Nonexistent.

Even now she flipped through a folder of printouts, searching for anything they'd missed. Once they reached the rodeo, she'd pull out her laptop. No way were they risking leaving any evidence alone in their motel room.

P.B. snuggled up against his thigh. He grown used to the miniature hot water bottle rubbing against him. He couldn't leave the silly creature alone in the room. Not after the snake attack. The poor beast hadn't stopped trembling. He turned the vehicle onto the street housing the rodeo. "You have your weapon?" he asked Sierra.

She nodded.

"I wish you would have stayed—"

"Don't even go there, Rafe. You could need backup." She held up her hand. "Before you say it, I already agreed to stay in the truck unless you don't check in on time. I promise."

Rafe's vehicle screeched into the empty parking lot. Cade had informed them that the rodeo had closed down early and the building evacuated pending a full investigation. In fact, John and Warren Beckel had both disappeared. He parked the car near a barrier for easy access and defense.

"You'll keep on your guard?" he asked.

"Of course," she said. She touched his arm. "Be careful."

"Don't worry." He cupped her face. "I have two big reasons to come back safe and sound."

He exited the vehicle and hurried to the back of the arena. Most of the horse trailers and RVs had vanished. He entered the oddly quiet hallway and, with silent footsteps, entered the vet clinic.

Harlen Anderson was crouched across the room.

"Get down," he shouted.

A shot rang out, hitting the concrete next to Rafe's feet. He dived toward Harlen, and both men scrambled behind the vet's desk.

"What's going on?"

Harlen wiped his brow. "He found out I called you. I don't know how—"

A loud boom sounded. Harlen's eyes went wide. A stain of blood bloomed across his chest.

He sank to the floor, his breathing harsh.

Rafe ripped the man's shirt and reached out for a wad of bandages on a nearby steel cart, but all the equipment in this room wouldn't save Harlen. Rafe had seen this kind of devastating chest injury too often, but that didn't mean he wouldn't fight for the man's life.

He pressed bandages as tightly as he could. Harlen grabbed his wrists.

"Photos," he whispered. "Phone."

His eyes closed, his head fell to the side. He was dead.

Rafe crouched lower. A shot came from one side, then the other. At least two shooters. A single pair of boots clomped forward. Another moved to the side. They were closing in.

Rafe glanced around. There was no back exit.

They had him trapped. He grabbed his phone from his back pocket. The glass was crushed. Damn. He couldn't warn Sierra.

"Might as well give it up, Vargas," a voice shouted. "You aren't getting out of here alive."

THE INSIDE OF the truck had warmed up quite a bit beneath the cloudless San Antonio sky. Sierra checked her watch for the umpteenth time. Where was he? He should've checked in by now.

Princess Buttercup let out a soft meow. Sierra stroked the cat's fur. "You know something's wrong, too, don't you?"

The cat butted her hand.

Unable to stay in one spot, Sierra twisted in her seat and peered through the window. What if something had gone wrong?

Her phone vibrated in her pocket. She grabbed it. "Hello? Rafe?"

"He won't be answering. Not now. Not ever."

Sierra shook her head. No, Rafe was fine. This man was lying. He had to be.

"Listen carefully," a gravelly voice whispered. "Or you'll end up just like Rafe. With a bullet hole straight to the chest."

"Who is this?" Sierra gripped the butt of her Glock. Her eyes stung. She knew better than to trust an anonymous caller. Except Rafe hadn't contacted her, and he'd promised.

"Ms. Bradford, I understand you've been looking for something. Something you'd do almost anything for in order to get it back."

The blood in Sierra's veins chilled, but her heart thudded and her pulse pounded in her ears. After all this effort, was the kidnapper really coming to her?

"I have Mallory and Chloe Harrigan."

"Are they all right?" The words spilled from Sierra's lips. *Calm down.* Focus. Be smart.

What would Rafe do?

He'd keep them talking. He'd try to learn more. She slid her finger to view her messaging application. No text from him. Where was he?

She pressed her hand to the window and looked over at the front doors to the arena. *Where are you, Rafe? Please be okay. We need you.*

"They're safe enough. For now, I want Mallory Harrigan's thumb drive."

Mallory had a thumb drive? She had no idea what was on it, much less where it was. Zane would have told her if he'd run into one at the rodeo office.

"I…I don't know what you're talking—" Sierra bit her lip. No. Rafe would pretend he knew what the kidnapper was talking about, even if he didn't.

The game was one of perception and expectation. He'd taught her that.

"Don't lie to me, Ms. Bradford. Their lives for the thumb drive. Meet me outside Angel Maker's stall."

"You'll bring Mallory and Chloe?"

"When I receive the thumb drive and verify what's on it, you'll have them back. Agreed?"

Did she have a choice? Zane was too far. Rafe wasn't answering his phone. Maybe she could reach Ransom or Léon.

"I'll be there."

"Come alone, Ms. Bradford. If you call anyone after

we hang up, or talk to anyone, they're dead. And I'll know it."

The crack of a gunshot exploded. The window shattered. Sierra fell sideways on the seat. Her phone tumbled to the floorboard.

"Rafe, where are you?"

She glanced around and stared down at her phone. She tapped on the messaging application one last time.

Rafe didn't answer. She was on her own.

Chapter Thirteen

A smattering of gunfire ceased. Rafe had to take the chance while the guy reloaded. He had only seconds and the desk provided little cover. He sprinted to the side wall and flattened his back against a steel cabinet. The shooters kept moving in. If he didn't get a clean shot and take one out to even the odds, the entire situation could get very bad, very fast.

More often than not, this kind of danger gave Rafe a high, but the thought of Sierra and his unborn child in the parking lot gave him cold chills…and a heated fury.

No more iceman.

A grunt and thud sounded from down the hallway. A staccato of gunfire followed.

"Rafe?" a slightly accented voice shouted from the corridor. "One down, one remaining."

A man weaved into the room from the hall, panic on his face. Rafe could see his badge. He charged at Rafe, weapon drawn and aimed. Damn. Rafe had no choice. He took the shot. The man dropped.

Rafe rushed over to him and knelt beside him. "Who do you work for?"

The guy smiled. "The boss." His head lolled to the side.

"Léon?" Rafe called.

The operative strode over to him, the semiautomatic weapon at his side pointed down. He frowned at the body on the floor, then at Rafe. "Don't you ever answer a call?"

Rafe raised the broken phone. "Sorry. Let me borrow yours. I need to check in with Sierra. She's in the truck."

Léon frowned. "I saw your truck outside."

That cold chill forming over his heart froze over. "Is she okay?"

"She wasn't in the truck, Rafe. It was empty except for a calico cat."

THE STALLS BEHIND the San Antonio Arena were mostly deserted. Sierra walked to one side of a long hallway leading to the bull pens. She stepped carefully and lightly, checking her phone every few seconds, praying that the caller had lied, that Rafe was okay.

Her gun at the ready, she maneuvered behind the empty vendor booths and then ventured across a large dirt-covered training area toward a series of empty stalls.

Empty except for one. Angel Maker.

A loud snort echoed from the bull just as a familiar figure stepped in front of Angel Maker's pen.

She made her way toward him.

John Beckel stared her down. When she was standing maybe ten feet from him, he frowned and crossed his arms. "You brought a gun?"

"I thought it appropriate." She could've kicked herself for not knowing he'd been behind this all the time. Who else could have fixed the books? Who else would want Mallory gone? But she really hadn't thought he had the smarts or the courage to orchestrate this conspiracy.

The bull butted its head against the pen's steel bars. The metal shook. Beckel stepped hastily away from the pen toward her.

Angel Maker slammed into the locked gate again and again and again. Could he break down his cage?

She had no idea.

"A weapon wasn't necessary," John muttered with a scowl. "You've lost weight since I saw you. Another lie. I must say you surprised me. Your husband I could have imagined doing this, but you?" He shrugged, holding a thick envelope in his hand. "I brought your money. As demanded."

He wasn't making any sense. Sierra's brow ruffled. "You contacted me."

A chuckle sounded from behind Sierra. She whirled around.

"You're both wrong. *I* set up this little meeting." Warren Beckel strode toward them, a rifle in his hands. "Lay your weapon on the ground and join my brother, Ms. Bradford. And don't make me shoot you where you stand."

Knowing she had no choice, in slow motion, Sierra knelt down and placed her weapon in the dirt.

"Kick it away."

She followed his instructions, her eyes darting right and left, searching for a way out. If he wanted to shoot, she was an easy target.

He bent and tucked her Glock into the back of his pants.

John started toward his brother, but Warren pointed his rifle at him. "Stay there."

His brother halted. "Warren? What are you doing?"

"Just shut up, John. For once in your life. Your idiotic deal with Diane Manley and her brother cost us everything when you tried—and failed—to hide buying those drugs. You ruined a very sweet deal for me."

"B-but, I'm your brother."

"You're a fool. Always have been. And I'm not bailing you out any longer."

Warren nodded toward Angel Maker. "Walk over to Angel Maker's gate, John."

The man didn't move. He turned ghostly white. His bluster had vanished.

"Do it," Warren said.

Hesitantly, John eased toward the steel structure. He stopped several feet away.

"Unlatch the pen."

The bull eyed John. He tossed his head, snorted and danced around. His hooves spewed dirt into the air.

John backed off. "No. You're cr—"

A shot rang out. John fell to his knees.

"Oh, get up, John. I didn't hit you."

Sierra couldn't stand the taunting any longer. She hurried to the man's side and helped him to his feet. He shook all over and peered at her through sad, resigned eyes. "Warren's going to kill us," he whispered.

Warren pumped the rifle's lever. The metal click echoed like a bullet off the cages. "I won't order you again, John. Unlatch the pen."

With fumbling hands, John lifted the bolt and threw it to the side.

"Get inside. Both of you."

John gripped the top white rod of the gate. "Warren…please. We're family."

"You didn't pull your weight, John. This is how it has to be. Now open the gate and walk inside. I can't explain away a gunshot wound, but I can explain stupidity. I'll play the part well. The distraught brother whose only family, for some reason, entered the den of the beast.

"Do it," Warren ordered.

John swallowed and slowly pulled open the gate. He walked inside.

Sierra hesitated. She'd seen what Angel Maker could do.

Warren's rifle dug into her back. He shoved her forward, then slammed the gate closed behind them.

Angel Maker eyed the intruders, pacing back and forth. Sierra backed against one side of the pen and froze. She couldn't move, could barely breathe. Warren threw the latch down and secured it with a padlock.

Angel Maker snorted. His hoof dug at the dirt. He lowered his head. John panicked. He hitched himself up on the barricade, trying desperately to climb out.

"Don't move," Sierra muttered.

John ignored her. He waved his arms at the bull trying to shoo him away.

It was the wrong move. The bull charged.

Hot breath swept past her. A horn caught John Beckel in the gut. The animal tossed him through the air as if he were a rag doll. John hit the side of the pen, then the ground, his eyes wide and blank.

Sierra blinked. Angel Maker turned on her, snorting anger, his eyes red with fury.

Please don't let it end this way. Please, God, help me save my baby.

MALLORY COULDN'T ESCAPE the thick arm pinning her against a hard chest, or the extra-large hand clamped over her mouth. A football-field length away, the cop who'd threatened to kill her shouted out orders.

"Don't hurt my mommy," Chloe yelled.

The man holding her grunted.

The cop whirled toward them. "That way. Get them!" he shouted.

"Well, damn it, lady."

"You shouldn't cuss—" Chloe said.

Their attacker grabbed her daughter like a football and dragged Mallory a few steps. She cried out in pain and collapsed.

"You're hurt?" His face twisted with regret. Without hesitation, he threw her over his shoulder and ran ten feet behind a pile of construction dirt before letting her go.

"Wh-who are you?" Mallory asked.

"A friend of Sierra's. My name is Zane Westin."

"Is she safe?"

"Worried about you," Zane said, unslinging a mean-looking rifle. He looked down at Chloe with a half smile. "That's a tough little girl you got there, Mrs. Harrigan. She's got a good kick. You a soccer player?"

Chloe nodded. "And T-ball. Did I hurt you?"

The question was almost gleeful.

"Absolutely," Zane said, all the while prepping his weapon and laying out extra ammunition.

"I thought you were a bad guy. You got lots of tattoos, and you're really big and you grabbed my mommy hard like my daddy used to when he hurt us."

Mallory flushed red at the revelation, but Zane didn't look at her with judgment, only sympathy.

"Not all big guys with tattoos are bad." He met Mallory's gaze. "Stay behind me, and hide her eyes. We clear?"

"There are so many. Too many."

Zane shrugged and took aim. "Once I cut off the snake's head, the rest of those cowards will fall like dominos." He passed a gun to Mallory. "It's ready to fire. If anything happens...do what you have to do. Just point and squeeze."

Mallory nodded and pulled Chloe close, hiding the little girl's face in her shoulder.

Zane aimed his weapon. The men racing toward them began shooting. Zane held fast and still. He waited.

Mallory's body tensed. When was he going to shoot? He had plenty of bullets. What if they overran them?

"A few more feet," he muttered. "Just a couple seconds."

He breathed in, exhaled slowly and pulled the trigger. The cop went down with one shot. The men around him skidded to a halt and stared.

The cop didn't move, didn't groan. He'd gone silent.

Zane stood. "I suggest you drop your weapons, gentlemen, or I pick you off one by one."

Glen was the first to surrender. "This ain't worth it." The rest of them followed.

"Mrs. Harrigan, if you could hold this weapon on them, I'll find some cord or rope. We have some bad guys to tie up." Zane paused. "If he moves, just pull the trigger."

Mallory took a deep breath. "I can do that, but you have to get a message to Sierra for me."

Zane nodded. "I'll tell her you're safe."

Mallory shook her head. "No, let her know the thumb drive is in the mouse."

A GUNSHOT ECHOED through the empty arena. Rafe met Léon's furious gaze.

"Sierra!"

Rafe grabbed his weapon, Léon at his side. They raced toward the sound.

When they reached the back of the building, they had two choices: toward the animal pens or offices.

A loud bang decided them. When they hit the open dirt, Rafe skidded to a halt.

Sierra had plastered herself against the side rail inside the pen with Angel Maker. The bull paced opposite her, watching, staring.

"Don't move, honey," Rafe muttered, knowing she couldn't hear him.

Somehow she knew what to do. She stayed still.

A few feet from the pen's gate, Warren Beckel stood watching, a rifle cradled in his elbow.

Rafe would ask himself later how Warren figured into the story, but for now, he had only one mission: to save the mother of his unborn child.

He signaled Léon, and they ducked out of sight.

Léon lifted his sniper rifle, aimed at the pen and searched through the scope. "One body in the pen. Older guy. He's dead. The gate's padlocked."

"Your weapon won't take down that animal," Rafe said, his adrenaline rushing. The timing had to be perfect, or he'd lose Sierra and the baby. "Even if we create a distraction, she may not be able to climb that fence in time to save herself. She needs me to be her bullfighter."

"I could shoot the padlock. You move in and get her. I'll take out the perp if he makes a move."

"Let's do it."

"It's gonna be a tough shot."

"You have one chance. I trust you Léon."

Rafe circled the dirt area, keeping out of sight. Warren was so focused on the bull and Sierra, he didn't notice.

The closer Rafe moved, the more he could see the bastard's smile. He was enjoying this.

He reached one last barricade twenty feet from Sierra. He'd be out in the open with almost no chance for Warren not to see him. He raised his hand.

Léon fired. Rafe took off running, legs pumping hard.

The padlock exploded.

Rafe barreled into Warren, knocking him off balance.

The bull snorted and charged at Sierra. At the last moment, Rafe wrenched open the metal barrier, grabbed Sierra and pulled her to the side. The bull stormed out and headed straight for Warren. The man staggered up in the center of the open space.

"Run!" Rafe shouted.

The bull lowered his head. The warning came too late.

SEVERAL HOURS LATER night had fallen over San Antonio. Sierra stood inside a small police department conference room with Rafe, looking through a window at chaos. Police, media, politicians.

They were still trying to piece together what had happened. Confusion reigned.

The door opened, and Detective Cade Foster led in Jared King.

"It's a madhouse." Cade walked into the room. "Rafe, do you always cause this much trouble? I got a police captain and patrolman dead. A half dozen thugs coming in from a crime scene several hours from here. A dead veterinarian. Not to mention two deceased Beckel brothers trampled by a bull. I'm going to be doing paperwork until I retire."

Sierra rushed over to Cade. "Mallory and Chloe?"

"On their way. Hungry and thirsty, but Zane's taking good care of them."

Sierra sagged into her chair. "Thank goodness." She reached for Rafe's hand. "I still don't understand why," she said. "Warren Beckel could have taken control of the rodeo anytime he wanted."

"It wasn't about the rodeo." Rafe flashed a photo of a large steel container.

"Is that a cryostorage tank?" she asked.

Jared King nodded. "This picture from the vet explains a lot. Everything Warren did was about Angel Maker. Or more specifically, the money to be made from his genetic material."

"How?" Sierra asked.

"Angel Maker's *donations* are stored in the tank. Along with scores of other high profile stock animals'. Once he eliminated you and John, Warren planned to kill the bull and claim he did it trying to save you. That would kick the value of the semen he'd collected from Angel Maker ten-, maybe even one-hundred-fold. He already had bidders. Angel Maker was the prize, but adding that to the rest of the stock, he stood to make millions."

"Mallory found out?"

"She didn't know as much as he thought. She found the encrypted file he used to detail transaction information. She didn't know what she had."

"The thumb drive."

A loud knock sounded at the door, and before Cade could open it, Zane strode in carrying a clinging Chloe. Mallory followed on crutches. Sierra broke into a smile and raced over to her friend.

"You're okay. You're alive."

Mallory held her close. "I knew you'd find us. Did you find the thumb drive?"

"Inside Princess Buttercup's toy mouse. Just like you said."

"I wish I'd understood what I had." Mallory frowned. "I was planning to show it to you that night."

Zane lowered Chloe to the floor and sent a very admiring and tender look toward Mallory. "If you hadn't hidden it, no telling what that crazy cop would've done."

Chloe pulled on Sierra's top. "Where's Princess Buttercup?"

"I'll get her," Rafe said, and strode out of the room.

Sierra bent and gave Chloe a hug. "I missed you, Button."

"Those bad men took us away to a yucky place, Sierra."

"I know."

"Zane said you sent him to save me and Mommy." She looked up adoringly at him. "Mommy and I are going to keep him. He belongs to us now."

Mallory flushed even redder, and to Sierra's amusement so did Zane. "I see."

Rafe opened the door and crossed the room. "Is this who you're looking for, young lady?"

Chloe giggled and held out her arms. "You're a pirate."

"A pirate who saved my life." Sierra smiled at Rafe,

hoping he saw so much more than she said aloud. "In more ways than one."

Rafe squeezed her hand.

Chloe squinted at them. "You should keep him, Sierra. I think he belongs to you."

THE IMPACT OF the San Antonio Rodeo's secrets would be felt for a long time. Rafe shut the door of their motel room. It was late, but so much more needed to be said.

In the past, he would've already skipped town after a completed job, but Sierra had changed his life. She'd changed everything. Truthfully it scared the hell out of him—in a good way.

Sierra glanced over at him, and he couldn't stop staring at her. He'd almost lost her. Come so close. He opened his arms and she walked into them.

"I was so scared," she said softly. "Scared for you. For our child."

Rafe licked his lip. "About that…"

A flash of pain crossed her face, and she stiffened.

"Sierra," he said softly. "Don't look away from me."

He cupped her cheeks. "I almost lost you today. Almost lost my last chance at something special, someone special. You're the best thing that's ever happened to me. I won't take that for granted. Not ever again."

"What are you saying?" Her eyes glistened with unshed tears. "I don't want false promises, Rafe. I know this pregnancy is unexpected."

"But not unwanted," he whispered.

She blinked quickly. "Not unwanted."

"I don't know how to convince you how much I want this without telling you something I've never told anyone. Not even Noah." He took a shuddering breath.

"About five years ago, I worked with a partner on co-vert ops. Her name was Gabriella. We were engaged. She was brilliant, like you. Beautiful, like you. A be-liever in justice, like you."

Sierra shook her head. "I sit behind a computer and track people."

"Give yourself the credit you deserve. You dive into everything headfirst. That Kazakhstan job. You sur-vived Archimedes. You saved Mallory and Chloe. With-out you, they wouldn't be here." He grimaced. "Your courage is why Noah and I asked Ransom to bench you. He was afraid for the sister he loves. I was afraid…for you. And I didn't want to lose you. Not like I lost Ga-briella."

Sierra wrapped her arms around his waist and squeezed tight. "What happened?"

"Without going into classified details, Gabriella and I trusted the wrong contacts. We were betrayed. The operation caused so many deaths. Including Gabriella's. I ended up in military prison as a traitor."

Shaking her head, she pulled back and met his gaze. "You'd never betray our country. Not ever."

Rafe's throat thickened, and he could barely swallow. "Thank you for that. Until you, only Ransom and Noah truly believed me. They were able to prove reasonable doubt so I was acquitted, but my career was over."

He pulled her closer, wanting to feel her warmth against him. He looked down into her glittering blue eyes. "My missions were dangerous. I couldn't bear to risk anyone else I cared about. That's why I pushed you away." He cleared his throat. "But even then I couldn't let you go."

He pulled a gold necklace from his pocket and dropped it into her palm.

"My mother's locket," she said. "I thought I'd lost it."

"I found it on the floor of our room two months ago. The chain was broken. I fixed it, but I…couldn't seem to work up the courage to face you. I was afraid I'd never leave you if I saw you again. I couldn't admit, even to myself, that I'd fallen in love with you, Sierra."

Tears rolled down her face. "You l-love me?"

"I don't deserve you, but if you'll forgive me for leaving you, forgive me for all the mistakes I've made and the mistakes I will make, I'll do everything in my power to make you happy, to be a good father. Maybe even earn your love someday."

She set her hands on his shoulders and looked into his eyes. "I love you, Rafe Vargas. I have for a long time. For so many reasons. Because you're a man who would do anything to protect the people in your life, but mostly because of your gentle heart hidden inside the soul of a warrior."

Rafe's arms closed around her. He couldn't stop trembling. "I'm never letting you go again, Sierra. You're my family now. Always and forever."

His lips lowered to hers, and he kissed her with all the passion and love he'd never allowed himself to feel before this moment.

Her breathing grew quick and heavy. His body hardened. He swung her into his arms. "Are you ready to start our life? You and me, together?"

She grinned up at him. "So, which one of us gets to tell Noah?"

Epilogue

Noah and Lyssa's wedding reception was in full swing. Rafe stood out of sight and silently observed their first dance as husband and wife.

He was used to standing on the outside of events like this. Normally he liked to tip his hat and vanish into the night. Celebrations weren't his thing, but that was about to change.

His life was about to transform, and he couldn't be more ready. Except for one small item. His best friend.

He met Sierra's gaze across the crowded reception. She stood with her brother Chase, the only single Bradford left—not that he knew that yet—and her father. Even though Paul Bradford was wheelchair-bound, he knew how to party. He took turns giving his grandkids rides on his chair, a huge smile on his face.

Rafe tugged at the collar on his best man's tux. How could a simple shirt and tie feel like a choke hold?

The wedding waltz swelled to the final chords. Noah dipped his new bride and followed the move with a passionate kiss.

Applause filled the room, and the band started into another song. A sea of wedding guests invaded the dance floor. Rafe shifted and adjusted his patch.

A small tug pulled at his coat. He glanced down. Joshua Bradford, Mitch's four-year-old adopted son, gazed up at him.

"Are you a pirate?"

Rafe chuckled and shook his head. "Nope, but I can do magic."

He pulled a yo-yo out of his pocket. Within minutes, he'd performed Rock the Baby and Shoot the Moon to an audience of Bradford cousins with openmouthed stares.

The kids whispered to each other, and Joshua, who was obviously the leader stepped forward. "Will you teach us?"

He spent the next half hour working with the kids in the corner before they scampered off for a snack, and yes, avoiding the Bradford family. Yep, he was a coward when it came to Sierra's father and brothers.

Delaying the inevitable.

They hadn't told anyone else about the baby yet, but Rafe had to wonder if Sierra's sisters-in-law knew. They kept giving him these strange, secret looks.

With his audience vanished, he stood deserted in the corner of the room.

Sierra made her way over to him, smiling in that way that made his belly turn and his body harden. She leaned against him, her warm softness providing him a certainty and comfort he longed for. "You're hiding out," she whispered in his ear, threading her fingers through his.

He turned her to him. "Maybe."

"It'll be okay. I'll protect you." She smiled. "I can handle my family. And Noah."

"You can handle anything."

A small tap poked Rafe. He turned and faced a grinning Chloe. Mallory stood behind her daughter. Zane's arm encircled her, his posture protective and very possessive. Now why didn't that surprise him?

Rafe smiled down at the little girl. "How're you doing, short stuff? Taking good care of your mommy and P.B.?"

"I'm not short." Chloe dug her toe into the wooden floor. "I know you miss Princess Buttercup. I don't want you and Sierra to be lonely when you go home, so I got you a present."

Very slowly and deliberately Chloe handed Rafe a white box. "Be careful."

"This is for us?" Rafe asked with a smile.

"'Cause you saved my Sierra and sent Zane to rescue me and Mommy and took really good care of Princess Buttercup." She cleared her throat. "I mean, P.B."

"You didn't have to give us a present, Chloe."

"Yes, I did. It was my idea." She puffed out her chest. "Open it."

He untied the blue ribbon and pulled off the top. Inside, a small calico kitten blinked up at him.

Rafe reached inside. His throat closed up a bit. The small creature batted her paws at Rafe's fingers. He cleared his throat. "What's her name?"

Chloe gave him a wide grin. "Princess Gingersnap!"

Rafe let out a loud cough, and Chloe erupted into giggles.

"Not really," she said with a smile. "Pirates don't have princess cats. I named her Jelly. 'J' for short. 'Cause they're going to be friends."

"P.B. and J," Rafe said, and swung Chloe into his arms. "She's perfect."

Chloe hugged his neck and whispered in his ear. "Now you and Sierra can be a family, like me and Mommy and Zane."

Rafe set her down. "I'll take good care of Jelly, Chloe. I promise."

The little girl scampered away. Zane gave him a wink and led Mallory away.

Rafe stared down at the kitten in his arms. He met Sierra's gaze, and she finally broke down. Her laughter pealed across the room.

"Go ahead, laugh it up. But we both get to take care of Jelly."

Noah crossed over to them. "Seems like you've developed a soft side, good buddy."

"Can't a guy get a pet without an inquisition?" Rafe asked.

"You don't have to pretend," Noah said. His expression turned solemn. "I trust you like a brother. Always have." He met Rafe's gaze. "Always will."

Though a little concerned where the conversation might be going, Rafe nodded. "Me, too. You had my back when no one else did. I won't forget it."

Noah shook his hand. "You have a chance to make a very good thing official. Don't blow it."

Rafe stared after his best friend, stunned just as Sierra slipped her hand into Rafe's.

"See, it's going to be fine. Besides, they're going to find out sooner or later," she whispered. "About everything."

Rafe rubbed the base of his neck. "I know, but I wanted to do it right. Like you deserve," Rafe said, staring into the cobalt eyes of the woman who owned his heart.

"Do you love me?" she asked, with a tilt of her head.

His heart thudded against his chest. "You know I do."

"Then, that's all I need."

She grabbed his hand and led him to the stage. She whispered to one of the band members, and the musicians let loose a musical flourish.

Sierra took the microphone and smiled. "I know this is Noah and Lyssa's big day. I'm so happy for them, but I have a little something to say, and I wanted to share it with the people I love most in the world, who are all in this room."

Rafe could feel his face flushing. Paul Bradford rolled his chair right up to the bandstand. Noah and Lyssa, Mitch and Emily and Chase stood behind him.

Sierra knelt in front of Rafe and pulled a box out of her pocket. "Rafe Vargas. I love you. I want to spend the rest of my life with you, as my partner, my best friend, the father of my children, and the other half of my heart. Will you marry me?"

Rafe froze. A tear burned behind his eye. He glanced over at a grinning sea of faces, including Noah. His friend didn't even jump up on the stage to slug him. He simply smiled like he'd known all along.

What an irritating quality for a brother-in-law.

"Yes. Yes. Yes," the room chanted.

Rafe knew in that moment what he had to do. He faced Sierra and knelt down. He pulled a velvet box out of his pocket and flipped it open. A sapphire and diamond engagement ring the color of her eyes gleamed in the black velvet.

"You stole my line," he whispered to her, lifting her hand and slipping on the ring. "I wanted to surprise you."

A deafening wave of applause clamored through the room. Rafe didn't hear a sound. He cupped Sierra's face and lowered his lips slowly, tenderly to hers, wrapped her in his arms and kissed her with all the world watching.

"We'll tell them about the baby later," she whispered against his mouth.

"Much later," he said softly, and kissed her again.

No more secrets. No more lies.

Just love.

* * * * *